WAITING FOR ELEPHANTS

Works by Jaleta Clegg

Dark Dancer

SplinterLight

Altairan Empire series

Nexus Point

Priestess of the Eggstone

Poisoned Pawn

Kumadai Run

Cold Revenge

Jericho Falling

Obsidian Tears

Chain of Secrets

An Indecent Proposal

Phoenix in Flames

Redemption

Collections

Autumn Visions

Brain Candy

Llama Tell You a Story . . .

Soul Windows (with Frances Pauli)

Waiting for Elephants

As Editor

Wandering Weeds: Tales of Rabid Vegetation (with Frances Pauli)

LTUE Benefit Anthologies (edited with Joe Monson)

Trace the Stars

A Dragon and Her Girl

Twilight Tales

Parliament of Wizards

A Hero of a Different Stripe

Troubadours and Space Princesses (forthcoming, 2024)

Dog Save the King (forthcoming, 2025)

Legacy of the Corridor

WAITING FOR ELEPHANTS

JALETA CLEGG

EDITED BY
JOE MONSON

HEMELEIN PUBLICATIONS

Waiting for Elephants
Legacy of the Corridor, volume 9.

A Hemelein Publications Original. Copyright © 2023 by Jaleta Clegg. All rights reserved. Except for brief excerpts in the case of reviews, this book may not be reproduced in any form without prior written permission of the publisher. All stories and essays published by permission of the authors.

"Como Esperar Para Elefante" (essay) Copyright © 2023 by Joe Monson.

The works in this book are fiction. Any names, characters, people, places, entities, or events in these stories are products of the author's imagination, and any resemblance to actual people, places, entities, or events is entirely coincidental.

"Hemelein", "Hemelein Publications", the Hemelein shield logo, "Legacy of the Corridor", and "It's worth your time." are trademarks of Hemelein Publications, LLC.

Edited by Joe Monson

Cover artist: Tithi Luadthong. Used by permission of the artist.
Cover and interior layout and design: Joe Monson

Managing Editor: Joe Monson
Publisher: Heather B. Monson
Published by Hemelein Publications, LLC.
http://hemelein.com/

First Edition
First Hemelein printing, September 2023
10 9 8 7 6 5 4 3 2 1

ISBN:
978-1-64278-037-6 (trade paperback)
978-1-64278-038-3 (ebook)

Library of Congress Control Number: 2023938798

To all the strange and weird people out there
who always feel like
the square pegs in round holes.

Me, too.

TABLE OF CONTENTS

LEGACY OF THE
CORRIDOR

Way back in 1994, M. Shayne Bell put together *Washed by a Wave of Wind,* an anthology of short works by authors from "The Corridor", an area that covers Utah, most of Idaho, parts of Wyoming and Nevada, and stretches into Arizona and parts of northern Mexico. Sometimes, the area around Cardston, Alberta, Canada, is included, too. For those unfamiliar with this area, it was settled by Mormon pioneers, members of the Church of Jesus Christ of Latter-day Saints.

Shayne's anthology highlighted science fiction and fantasy works by authors from the area, as The Corridor contained an unusually high number of successful authors—for the population in the area—both genre and non-genre, both members and non-members of the predominant religion. That legacy continues today with an impressive list of authors such as:

Jennifer Adams · D. J. Butler
Orson Scott Card · Michael R. Collings
Michaelbrent Collings · Ally Condie
Larry Correia · Kristyn Crow
James Dashner · Brian Lee Durfee
Sarah M. Eden · Richard Paul Evans
David Farland · Diana Gabaldon
Jessica Day George · Shannon Hale
Mettie Ivie Harrison · Tracy Hickman

Laura Hickman · Charlie N. Holmberg
Christopher Husberg · Raymond F. Jones
Matthew J. Kirby · Gama Ray Martinez
Brian McClellan · Stephenie Meyer
L. E. Modesitt, Jr. · Brandon Mull
Jennifer A. Nielsen · Wendy Nikel
James A. Owen · Ken Rand
Brandon Sanderson · Caitlin Sangster
J. Scott Savage · D. William Shunn
Jess Smart Smiley · Eric James Stone
May Swenson · Howard Tayler
Brad R. Torgersen · Nym Wales
Dan Wells · Robison Wells
David J. West · Carol Lynch Williams
Dan Willis · Julie Wright

That's a big list of names, and it only barely scratches the surface. Hemelein Publications created this publication series to highlight authors from The Corridor, both well-known and lesser-known. We think Shayne did a wonderful job drawing attention to these amazing writers back then, and we want to continue what he started.

You can learn more about the series at:

http://hemelein.com/go/legacy-of-the-corridor/

Joe Monson
Managing Editor
Hemelein Publications

Como Esperar Para Elefante

Joe Monson

Let's deal with the elephant in the room: I've known Jaleta for a little over two decades now.

Way back in the day, we worked together on the committee that ran Life, the Universe, & Everything, the annual science fiction and fantasy symposium at Brigham Young University (it's since moved off campus). We also worked together on CONduit, the science fiction and fantasy convention in Salt Lake City, Utah, and a few other fannish events. My wife and I also occasionally got together with her family and other friends and did geeky things.

We've been co-editors on the LTUE Benefit Anthologies for over six years now, and all of those collections have been great fun to put together. *Trace the Stars* (2019), *A Dragon and Her Girl* (2020), *Twilight Tales* (2021), *Parliament of Wizards* (2022), *A Hero of a Different Stripe* (2023), *Troubadours and Space Princesses* (forthcoming, 2024), and *Dog Save the King* (forthcoming, 2025) are the titles so far, and more are planned for the future. I've also been working with her on a forthcoming collection of classic short works from A. Merritt (should be out sometime in late 2023 or 2024).

I've been a fan of her writing for at least ten years now, especially her short fiction. She has a quirky sense of humor that syncs well with mine, and she writes engaging and interesting stories. And this collection has a large sampling of her work.

There are 34 works here, including five poems and 29 short fiction pieces. I don't think I'd read any of her poetry before putting together this collection, and I now hope to read more in the future. Her way with words in the poems here reminds me a little of Michael R. Collings' poetry, which is high praise indeed. Both of them can use the imagery and structure of the poem to grab your imagination, tug at your heartstrings, and give you a glimpse into the world from an unusual perspective.

Some of these stories will make you laugh (most of them, in fact, since she inserts humor into almost everything she writes). Here, you'll find bizarre game shows, reality shows gone amok, magical weight loss clinics, secret yoga centers, tasty recipes with secret ingredients, ancient forces of nature *cum futurum,* and how one of the best-kept secrets of housekeeping could just save the universe.

Some will make you cry. A woman fighting to prevent an ancient Irish spirit from taking her husband on a distant planet. On another, fighting to stay away from the angels is more difficult than first thought. And you may question whether traveling to that new planet is such a good idea. Maybe let the experts explore a little before emigrating. I'm sure they'll figure it all out. How dangerous could it be, really?

Regardless of how you first experienced Jaleta's stories, these will keep your attention and make you think and chuckle. She's a really good writer, and I hope you enjoy these tales and verses. I know I did.

Joe Monson
Managing Editor
Hemelein Publications

A Journey
into a Wondrous Land
of Imagination

Welcome to the strange worlds of my imagination! From the farthest reaches of outer space to the depths of caves, from times long ago to times in the far future, from magic to tech, and everything in between, these are my playgrounds.

I suffer from an overactive imagination. Always have. Hopefully, I always will. Many of my stories begin with a simple, "What if?" What if old Aunt Ruby finally shares the secret to her special jam cake? What if cats are guardians against the fae? What if high fantasy quests aren't quite what we think? What is lurking in the wilds of unexplored planets?

The stories that grow from these questions range from the very silly to extremely serious, from light-hearted adventures to heavy explorations of darkness. I use short stories like these to try new genres or experimental ideas. Sometimes it works, sometimes it flops, but either way, I enjoyed the journey.

This selection of stories were mostly written between 2015 and 2023. Many of them are published elsewhere. It is my pleasure to share them with you and I hope you enjoy reading them as much as I enjoyed writing them.

Cheers!
Jaleta Clegg

WORDS

Words
Spin and tumble in my head,
Churning, spinning,
Building pressure like steam in a kettle,
Seeking escape.

Words
Buzzing in my brain
Like a wasp on a window,
Watching with alien malevolence
Waiting for me to approach,
To smother or smash into complacency,
Only to be stung as the words demand release.

Words
Burning like a flame,
Searing their path through my mind,
Consuming, devouring,
Building to a raging inferno,
Demanding complete submission.

Words
Erupting like lava,
Cascading in fiery torrents from my fingers,
Flowing from my brain,
Liquid stone, blazing with heat,
Destroying my peace, shattering my world,
Until the passion settles.
The words rest cold and hard,
Set in hexagonal columns
Like basalt,
Form immutable.

Words
Lie before me,
Holding all the fire
of my empty soul.

Words.
Nothing more,
Nothing less,

Only
Words.

WAITING
FOR ELEPHANTS

"The elephants will come back someday. Soon. I heard them whispering last night." Gramps chewed on a stick as he stared at the far horizon where the terraformers were hard at work replacing the reddish purple lumps of native vegetation with the gray-green of earthly sagebrush and bunch grass.

Momma wiped her hands on her apron as she shook her head over his nonsense. She speared me with a look. "Carla, you stay out here and keep an eye on Gramps. I've got jam on the stove."

I kicked up a fuss, just for appearances. I liked Gramps and sitting with him meant I didn't have to do the other chores on our homestead, like mucking out stalls or rounding up the pig-headed ornery beasts we called cows or helping Momma in the kitchen with dishes or scrubbing floors or even washing clothes. I'd rather sit on the porch next to Gramps' rocking chair and listen to his stories of the old days, when he left Earth to come to this planet.

The terraformers kicked up long plumes of dust as they diligently worked to change the world to a second Earth. They'd finished the land and atmosphere and oceans. We were on the fringe where the native plants grew. Within a century, the scientists said the terraformers would finally finish wiping out the bulbous growths, replacing them with Earth forests and plains. Terran animals roamed the fields. I watched a pair of bunnies fight it out over a patch of clover the other side of our front fence.

But no one had brought elephants to our world.

"I saw one once, when I was about your age," Gramps said. The rocking chair creaked. "Back on Earth. The circus came to town. They paraded an elephant down the street. Poor thing looked tired. It looked right at me. Spoke to me in my head."

I plucked a stem of grass and chewed it slowly while Gramps rambled. He was actually my mom's great-grandpa, one of the first settlers to our world. He'd had to wear breathers outside, before the atmosphere scrubbers had finished working. He was older than dirt. Everyone told me he was crazy, but I didn't believe it. I was eight and he meant the world to me.

"I saw them when they landed here, the elephants." He pointed off at the dust rising into the air. "Out there it was. They came floating down with their balloons tied around their middles, landed right out there."

"Elephants, Gramps? Ain't no elephants on this world. Never will be."

He swatted my head. "You watch your tongue, child. I saw them come over those hills, drift down to land light as a feather. Their balloons were pink and white. They were elephants, just like that circus one in the parade. I can feel them, my time is coming."

I saw something glint way off in the distance, something up the sky. Dark with pink above against the blue. I squinted to see it better.

"Didn't I tell you, girl? They've come back." Gramps cracked a smile. "The elephants are coming. Help me up, there. Give me a hand."

I glanced at the screen door to our kitchen. Momma sang as she stirred her jam. I couldn't let Gramps wander off, but she hadn't said I had to keep him on the porch. How far could he go with his cane and gimpy legs? I gave him my hand, helped pull him to his feet.

He started down the path to the gate. I trotted at his side. He didn't pause at the edge of the meadow, just kept right on going toward the elephants drifting out of the sky with balloons floating above.

I counted seven elephants before I had to hurry after Gramps. He moved fast for someone well over a hundred years old.

He stopped at the bank of the stream, shading his eyes as he looked up.

I hurried to his side and took his hand.

He squeezed mine. "The elephants came, like they promised. Help me cross the stream, now. I'm not as spry as I used to be. Back in the day, I would have jumped this little trickle. No sweat."

I stared at the beasts. They were huge, lumpy things, dark gray all over with a single light patch on their belly. They had noses that looked like stretched out hoses, waving and gesturing like boneless arms attached to their faces. Their ears flapped like wings, guiding them our way. A string rose from their back to the base of a round balloon, striped pink and white. It didn't look big enough to carry their weight, but what did I know? I was only an eight-year-old farm girl.

Gramps splashed across the stream, his hand on my shoulder to keep his balance. I didn't mind the cold water on my bare feet or the breeze that tossed my short hair around my face as the elephants landed on the hill beyond the stream.

Their feet touched lightly. The balloons dropped to float just over the broad backs of the beasts, the strings hanging slack. The nose tentacles waved and gestured, constantly moving back and forth, up and down.

Gramps clamped his hand tight, pulled me around to face him. "Go back home, young Carla. This is not for you. Not yet. They've come for me. Maybe someday, when you're old and done with life, they'll come for you. But not yet. Now, get on home. Go on, scoot." He pushed me away, back toward home.

I only took a few steps before I turned to watch him limp up the hill toward the elephants and their balloons. He stopped in front of the biggest, bowed, then reached out a hand. The elephant wrapped its nose around his hand, slid it up his arm, touched his cheek, then gently lifted him high into the air. Gramps was smiling as the elephant settled him on its wide back. The balloons rose, tugging the elephants into the air. Gramps waved as they turned to float back the way they'd come.

I searched for those elephants most of my life, combing the shrinking native areas, but never found any trace. Now it's my turn to sit in the rocking chair and whisper stories to the young ones who'll listen.

It's my turn to wait for the elephants to come, floating down gently from the sky with their pink and white balloons.

I saw elephants once, long ago, when I was young.

THE ULTIMATE
SPACE RACE

"Henry! Hurry up, it's starting." Ethel snuggled deeper into the Cuddle-Couch™ (with Soruna™ holographic projectors and Tru-Life™ surround sound speakers with ThunderRumble™ subwoofer cushions, built-in armrest controls and auto-connect, and the optional posture correcting lumbar support and SpaDee heated massage—Henry's sixty-eighth birthday present, worth every dime). She turned up the volume with a squeeze of her hand.

The announcer's handsome, chiseled face smiled from the floating projection. "Tonight, live from the Sporting Club's docks at New Vegas, it's the thrilling conclusion to the Ultimate Race. Remember, what happens in New Vegas, stays in New Vegas, the world's first and only orbiting casino. At least for another two months." He chuckled on cue. "Brought to you by our sponsors, Tummie Gummies, the fruity delicious colon cleanse. Chew two to refresh your life, inside and out."

His face switched to singing, dancing, rainbow-colored candy bears waving banners of toilet paper.

Henry plopped beside Ethel, a bag of freshly popped popcorn in his hand. "What'd I miss?"

"Nothing yet, just Calton Hooper's intro." Ethel popped a handful of the white fluff (now with 72% more fiber!) into her mouth. She grimaced. "Why can't they leave it as popcorn? What's this flavor?"

Henry looked at the bag. "Licorice root. It was on sale."

The bears concluded their animated commercial. Calton Hooper's perfect features replaced them.

Ethel tapped the massage controls as the announcer's voice filled the air.

"Four months ago, from these very docks," the camera cut to an outside shot full of space-suited figures, plastered with the blue and white Sporting Club logo, clambering over the space yachts of the rich and famous, "we launched seven crews into the black void of space. The crews were focused on one thing: Winning the Ultimate Race, brought to you tonight by Cheeritos, the world's favorite cheez snack."

The show cut to another commercial.

"I wish they hadn't disabled the commercial skip," Henry said through a mouthful of licorice popcorn.

"It would have cost us three month's rent for the premium subscription to enable that." Ethel had been sorely tempted, but sometimes the commercials were the best part of the show. She secretly hoped that the body spray man would be featured tonight. He was her favorite, his one-minute romances clever and sigh-worthy.

Henry chewed another handful of popcorn while orange puffy triangles drifted over New York's skyline. "Those things are disgusting. They did a study last month showing they caused cancer."

"Mm-hm." Ethel tuned out Henry's complaints. She'd heard them too many times over the years. She relaxed into the Cuddle-Couch™ and let the massager do its work.

Calton Hooper switched to a re-cap of the season, cutting to scenes of the crews of the yachts as they prepared to launch from the floating station of sin, as Ethel's friend Betty called it. Logos of all the sponsoring companies decorated the interiors of the ships. Their products filled the crews' lives. Their commercials punctuated the reality show's footage.

Calton walked them through the initial days of the race, when the crews fought over limited living space. It sounded so romantic, a race to Mars' moon Phobos and back. The prize money was nothing to sneeze at, but Ethel wasn't sure she would have survived being part of any of the crews. Especially not the college frat boy ship. She didn't approve of their choice of interior decorations, provided by their sponsors. Beer companies and porno sites were not appropriate for such a family-centered show as the Ultimate Race.

"What was that?" Henry spoke through his popcorn. "You said something?"

Ethel wisely didn't repeat herself. Henry thought the frat boys were hilarious. "Betty posted pictures of her dogs on the beach in Fiji. We should take a trip there someday. It looked lovely."

Henry hmphed, his answer whenever she brought up her friend's travel posts.

"Maybe we should save up for a trip to New Vegas. I'd like that."

Calton Hooper narrated the incident of the stolen chocolate stash on board the all-female ship. The women were all middle-aged hairdressers, sponsored by every beauty product known to man. They'd dropped out and had to be towed back to New Vegas after only ten days. The show cut to a live interview of the women sitting in a casino in New Vegas. They reminisced about the show, hugging and crying. Ethel rolled her eyes. The women had done nothing but fight like wet cats.

Calton broke into the canned interview. He tapped his earbud (D-Audible, only the best sound for your delicate ears), his expression serious. "We've just received word that the last two yachts have passed the Moon's orbit safely. It's neck-and-neck between the Butterfly Effect and Gone Fishin' Today. Who will win tonight? We'll keep you posted."

"Should have been the Beer Can."

"Oh, please. Those boys couldn't do anything right. I wonder if they ever got home from Mars."

"I'm sure they'll update us." Henry stirred the unpopped kernels with his finger. They rattled in the bowl. "I kind of like the licorice flavor. I'll pick up more tomorrow."

"Tasted like cough drops to me."

The show cut to Calton interviewing the crew of Lucky Lady, New Vegas' entry that had sputtered out of the competition halfway through the show. A combination of not enough food, a leaky water tank, and faulty wiring had shut down their ship three days shy of Mars. The crew looked much healthier now. They were still at Mars, all three couples told Calton they wanted to stay and file for homesteads in the Martian desert.

Ethel fidgeted despite the massaging seat. The endless stream of commercials never stopped. Scrolling texts and pictures filled the bottom of the screen, even during the interviews. Ethel wished they'd just hurry up and get to the finale. She was rooting for her favorite, the captain of the Butterfly Effect. She didn't care for his crew of engineers and scientists, they were very competent but a little too weird for her tastes. But Captain Shan Updike could give the body spray man a run for his money.

The show switched music tracks to a solemn funeral dirge while they paid homage to Homer's Revenge. Two of the crew had died in a horrible explosion. Ethel closed her eyes and fantasized about the swarthy Captain Updike and Body Spray Man instead. She hadn't liked that episode or the days of news stories afterwards. The people who signed up for the Ultimate Race knew the dangers. It was their own fault, anyway. Ethel would never trust her life to a ship built by breakfast cereal companies and office furniture retailers.

The show dragged on through more interviews and highlights. Calton Hooper updated them every few minutes on the progress of the two remaining yachts as they approached the final finish line.

Henry returned from a bathroom break, flopping onto his side of the CuddleCouch™. "I was talking to Harv the other day while he was out trimming his hedge. He said it takes at least a full day to get from the moon to New Vegas. They're lying to you when they say this is live. It's all staged and fake. Lenny at work says they film it all on a soundstage behind the casinos."

Ethel pursed her lips. "Lenny has a few screws loose. He tried to convince you that the food industry is poisoning us into becoming robot drones by putting addictive colorings in everything."

"That was Kevin. Lenny just thinks that New Vegas is a scam and the show is fake."

"It's real. Both David Lorenzo and Anita Kay had scientists on their shows talking about how it couldn't have been faked. They said this was the future of space travel—game shows and company sponsorships. They're talking about doing a reality show at the Ganymede mining base next year. Scientists vs. Miners. I think it sounds interesting. Calton Hooper is in negotiations to host the show, but they say he's asking for too much money. Twenty-seven million per episode is what I heard." Ethel secretly hoped the producers would get Body Spray Man to host it. She could watch him flex his muscles for hours.

Calton Hooper broke into a pre-recorded interview. His face was flushed with excitement. "Ladies and gentlemen, we have a sighting, live and in person here at Sporting Club's docks at New Vegas. Stay and play and make memories to last a lifetime. The winner of the Ultimate Race is about to be determined. Remember, the race isn't won—"

"Until it's won," Ethel finished the show's slogan. She chewed her fingernail as the show built the suspense. Would it be the ship of scientists and engineers captained by the handsome Shan Updike, a long-time competitor in the sailing races on Earth's oceans? Or would it be the ship of bearded outdoorsmen used to roughing it for weeks at a time as they pursued the best fishing spots in the most inaccessible corners of the continents? Stay tuned through these commercial breaks.

The cameras panned over the docks while Calton re-capped the last dozen transmissions from the two ships. The camera shifted to a shot of darkness with the Earth glimmering at one edge of the screen. The moon floated serenely in the far distance. Ethel straightened. The CuddleCouch™ adjusted the floating holographic projection to match her viewing angle.

Arrows appeared, pointing out two small dots.

Calton's voice tightened with practiced excitement. "Ladies and gentlemen, you are witnessing history today. The first-ever Ultimate Race to Mars and back is coming to an end. And it's going to be a photo-finish. Butterfly Effect and Gone Fishin' Today are closing in on New Vegas. You can see they've just come into view now. Both ships have to slow down and match orbits with the station. It's up to the captains and the skill of their crews now. Too much speed and they might miss the station. Neither has enough fuel to correct such an error. It would take three days for a rescue ship to catch up with them." He paused while the cameras switched to a shot of the waiting dock workers. "One mistake at this stage of the race could cost them more than the victory. It could cost the lives of the crew and the dedicated workers you see here. Space, ladies and gentlemen, is no place for error as we've seen tonight. Those who don't have what it takes, have failed. Those who do, will win. No matter which ship docks first, both of these crews," the screen switched to the publicity photos of the two crews taken before launch, "have proven themselves worthy of this trophy. But, there can only be one winner."

Calton's face filled the screen. "They've battled against incredible odds for four months, and it all comes down to the next few minutes. Do they have the skill and the guts for glory?"

The show cut to another montage of commercials.

Ethel flopped back into the massaging cushions with a groan. "How long are they going to drag this out?"

"The broadcast has another fifteen minutes. I need a beer. Want me to grab you something?"

Ethel shook her head.

Henry shuffled off to the kitchen.

Ethel nibbled her fingernail while the commercial messages filled her screen. A chat-box (powered by Tweeble, the new face of social networking) popped up in the corner. Betty's face grinned from the box. Ethel debated about ignoring the call, but only for a moment. Betty would make her life miserable for weeks if she didn't connect. She tapped the armrest.

"Ethel? You'll never believe what happened to me today." Betty patted her perfectly set, perfectly blond hair (brought to you by Clairvoyance, for the most natural appearance artificial hair dye can give, not tested on animals, safe for the environment). "You remember Donald, down at the megamart? Well, I was there today, just picking up a few groceries for my party tomorrow. You know how it is. You think you've got plenty of asparagus, then find out six people are coming, not the three who responded, so now you've got to pick up more. Oh, that reminds me. Are you and Henry going to make it?"

Ethel refrained from rolling her eyes, although it was sorely tempting. "We live in Albuquerque, Betty. And you live in Florida. We appreciate you inviting us, but no, we aren't coming in person."

Calton's face appeared on the screen, but the chat-box kept him muted. Ethel shifted impatiently.

"Bummer," Betty said. "Anyway, back to my story. There I was, squeezing my asparagus, when Donald shows up. He's got a cart and he bumps me with it. I made sure he would. He was so intent on the citrus that he didn't even see me. Can you believe that?" She paused to giggle. "Well, there we were. I let out a little shriek, not a loud one, just a little oh-you-bumped-me startled one, and pretended to be hurt. He started apologizing. It was so sweet of him. Have I told you how adorable he is? Not as good-looking as that guy in the commercial you're always posting, thanks for that by the way, now I'm addicted to his spots, but cute in his own rich-retired-dude-with-plenty-of-cash kind of way. He loves dogs, did I tell you that already?"

Ethel tried desperately to read Calton's lips while her friend rambled. The show cut to the shot of space again. The dots were noticeably bigger and closer. They almost looked like ships now, but they were too far away to tell which ship was which.

"Ethel, I swear you're ignoring me. Did you hear what I just said? Donald is coming to my party tomorrow and he's bringing fresh quiche. He cooks! How awesome is that?"

Ethel bit her fingernail as the tiny ships swelled on the screen. The camera zoom was fuzzy with the distance.

"I know you aren't listening, Ethel, 'cause you're chewing your nails. What are you watching?"

"Listen, Betty, I have to go. Call me later and tell me all about Donald, okay?"

Fire blossomed from one of the ships. It veered toward the other ship.

"But Ethel, I think Donald may be the one. Finally. And to think it all started over asparagus. Did I tell you he—"

"Bye, Betty."

Ethel killed the chat-box. She'd apologize later to her friend, but right now the ships on the screen had her full attention. Calton's voice came back as the call disconnected.

"—just heard. A fire has broken out on one of the ships. We've lost contact with both, but that should be restored soon."

Commercial sponsor messages flashed urgently around the edges of the screen. Calton's face appeared in a box to one side. The cameras stayed focused on the ships, still fuzzy with distance, as their paths converged. Which one was on fire? And who was hurt?

Calton frowned as he tapped his earbud. "Our team tracking the ships say they may collide. We still don't know what happened. An explosion in the fuel lines is the most likely explanation according to the engineering teams who built these ships. Our techs are working on the communication lines."

"Henry? Come quick. There's been an accident." Ethel couldn't help the shakiness of her voice.

Henry walked through the projected image of the ships and advertising sponsors.

Ethel waved him impatiently to his seat. "Something exploded on one of the yachts."

"Not the fishing boat?"

Ethel shook her head. "They don't know yet." She stared at the holograph, her stomach twisting with dread as the two ships drifted closer.

Calton's words washed over her, barely registering. "We have radio contact with Butterfly. They're leaking atmosphere. Rescue ships are on their way, but they may not arrive in time. But the crew is ready with their emergency gear. Remember, these crews have trained and drilled for emergencies. Every precaution is in place, ladies and gentlemen. We're standing by with—"

His voice died as the two ships rammed into each other. It happened slowly, like ballerinas in slow motion colliding. The cameras caught the puff of vapor as it froze in a cloud around the ship. Pieces of both ships spun loose, a cloud of debris expanding slowly into space.

Ethel bit her knuckle. This couldn't be happening, couldn't be real. Space travel was mostly safe these days. Wasn't it? The two crew members who died on the other ship were stupid and made poor choices. But these two ships, they were all smart people, trained for these things and very careful. How could this happen?

Betty's face popped up in the chat-box again. Ethel tapped ignore.

Calton's frown vanished, replaced by relief. "We have word that both crews are safe. They made it into the escape pod just before collision. We have contact with Captain Smith and Captain Updike. They report that all crew members are accounted for. There were injuries, though. We'll bring you updates as we receive them. Rescue vehicles are undocking from New Vegas as we speak."

Henry sniffed. "It's all a publicity stunt, you know. They don't want to pay out the prize money. It's rigged. Lenny says—"

Ethel removed her knuckle from her mouth long enough to tell Henry what his friend Lenny could do with his conspiracy theories.

Henry sat with his mouth hanging open at her words. He snapped it closed after a long moment. "It's just a show, sweetheart."

Ethel shook her head, her objections vague. "It's more than that, Henry."

"They'll do a season two. Ultimate Race to Venus or something." He patted her hand.

The holographic screen showed a close-up of Calton's concerned face as he reassured the audience that everything was under control. Ethel wiped a tear. She'd say a prayer for the safety of those people tonight.

And when they found out who was responsible, she vowed never to buy their products again. She had standards.

Henry patted her hand again before leaving the room.

Ethel tapped the chat-box icon, placing a call to Betty.

Betty answered immediately. "Ethel? What is going with you? You ignored me."

"Did you see what happened on Ultimate Race just now?"

"You were watching?"

Ethel shook her head. "Such a tragedy, but they say everyone survived. So, tell me about Donald squeezing your asparagus."

Betty dimpled when she smiled. "I never said he squeezed my asparagus. He bumped me with his cart. He is so gorgeous when he's apologizing."

Ethel let her friend ramble, only half-listening. Ultimate Race shifted from Calton's concerned look and shots of the doomed yachts to commercial messages. Henry was right. Commercial sponsorships would fund more shows. And people would travel farther and more dangerously. And Ethel would watch from her CuddleCouch™, safely and vicariously living their adventures. It was the way it should be.

THE QUEST

The adventurers would gather in the smoky dark of the inn, drawn by some mysterious compulsion planted in their minds by the wizard who now sat smoking his pipe, watching the flames flicker with his inscrutable gaze and stroking his long gray beard. The seven, already scarred from previous adventures, would cluster close to hear the wizard quote some scrap of prophecy, maddeningly vague. It would be desperately vital to the welfare and salvation of the throngs of innocents who went about their daily chores unaware of the evils and dangers that lurked, ready to destroy them. It should have been romantic, mysterious, something to make your heart skip a beat. It should have been a story to make a bard weep with passion.

The bard instead shot a sulking look at the wizard as he bounced along on a horse that looked like a cross between a fat pony and a cow. Spirited was the last word anyone could possibly use to describe it. Adventures like this required elegant, fiery steeds who flowed along, running like the wind. The bard's horse was a plodding brown gelding who wouldn't run even if hungry bears were trying to eat it although it looked like a noble stallion compared to the wizard's steed.

The wizard wasn't any more impressive than his horse, the bard thought sourly. He was too young, for starters. His hair was medium brown, thinning a bit on top, but still quite brown, not a hint of gray showing. He didn't have a beard, or even a drooping mustache, only a few

tufts of scraggly hair that he'd missed with his razor. His eyes, instead of
being a piercing blue or mysterious gray, were a muddy brownish hazel and
about as penetrating as rice pudding. He looked like a middle-aged, moder-
ately prosperous scribe, not a powerful wizard charged with leading an
intrepid band of adventurers on a desperate quest to save the world. Everything about him was ordinary. His clothes were what any traveler might
wear: a shirt that might have been white once but was now an uneven
yellowish color, a leather tunic worn more to protect the shirt and hide the
slight paunch than to look mean or dashing, leather pants with the seat
worn shiny from rubbing on a chair, and a dark gray cloak, now bundled
across the saddle bags. At least the boots fit the romantic wizard image in
the bard's mind. They had been military once, but only because kingdom
law required every young man to serve in the military for two years. They
showed uneven bits of polish. But the most bothersome detail about the
wizard was his name. How could any bard, even the Master Bard Thaliason,
write an epic ballad about a wizard named Pete?

The wizard Pete, unaware of the surly thoughts of the bard, turned his
horse into the yard of a ramshackle farmhouse.

"We're here," Pete announced as he scrambled ungracefully down from
his mount. The pony snuffled and chewed its bit, a string of drool dangling
from its lip and glistening in the morning sunlight.

Roland the Magnificent Minstrel dismounted, flourishing his cape
though there was no one to appreciate the way its ruby satin lining caught
the light. Good flourishes only came with practice. Appearances and
mannerisms mattered, or so Roland believed.

The door of the house opened and a prettily plump woman invited
them in, hugging Pete as he entered. Roland was treated to a warm smile.
The sounds of laughter and conversation drew them into a spacious
kitchen. Three men sat at a much abused table, eating mountains of flapjacks with homemade jam and fresh churned butter. None of them looked
like adventurers to Roland. True, one of them looked large enough crack
walnuts three at a time with his fist, but the other two looked like ordinary
farmers.

"Elsa," Pete declared as he sniffed the aromas of the kitchen, "If Shamus
hadn't married you, I would. Just for your cooking."

The men laughed, the easy sound of old friends. Elsa blushed and
planted a quick kiss on Pete's cheek before turning back to her stove and the
golden cakes there.

"Tessa said she'd be along shortly," one of the men, the nut-cracking giant, said. "She had to bribe her neighbor to take her three grandsons. Last time she left them behind, they managed to pluck the poor woman's geese half-naked, before Tessa was even out of sight."

The men roared with laughter, a shared joke that didn't include Roland. Pete pulled out a chair and sat at the table, helping himself to a pile of flapjacks.

"Join us, lad," the giant invited. "Who is he?" he asked Pete.

"Terrance thought we needed a bard along," Pete said around a mouthful of food. "His name's Roland."

Roland bristled at the casual reference. Terrance was the king's given name. It felt wrong not to preface it with at least his title.

"Sit, boy," the giant man said, waving at an empty chair. "Cakes taste better hot. We don't stand much on ceremony here. Pete never did care much for it. I'm Shamus." He extended his hand.

Roland took the proffered hand, wincing slightly at the crushing grip. Shamus released his hand and grinned.

"These two ruffians are Del and Bern, brothers by blood and mischief," he said waving at the two other men at the table. "And the last of our group is Tessa. She's the mean one with the knives."

Del and Bern nodded at Roland without stopping their eating. Both were blond and bland. Roland sat reluctantly. This was nothing like the ballads. A party should have seven adventurers, plus the wizard and the bard to make nine. Seven and nine were the defining mystical numbers. Who ever heard of just four? And what kind of mystical number could you make from six? Despite the knives, a woman didn't count, not really.

The door was opened by a stocky, grandmotherly woman. From the greetings, she was Tessa, the last member of their party. She took a seat and helped herself to Elsa's cooking. Elsa placed the last batch of cakes on the table and sat beside her husband, Shamus.

"Now that everyone's here..." Pete began.

"And you've stuffed yourself full of brambleberry jam," Del added.

"You've got some on your chin," Tessa commented.

Pete wiped his chin with his fingers and licked off the jam. "We're supposed to get Terrance's ring back from the Lady Beatrice."

Roland resigned himself to doing major revising before he made this adventure into a ballad. Fetching a ring from a lady did not make for grand adventure.

"Without anyone noticing," Shamus said.

"Which is why he hired us," Pete continued. He leaned back in his chair and loosened his belt.

"So we go ask Lady Beatrice to give us back the ring," Tessa said between bites. "Simple enough."

"Wait a minute," Roland spoke up. "Why does His Majesty, King Terrance Apponaby, need you to return a ring to him?" Maybe he could twist it into the story of a token of romantic love that should be cherished and treasured always by the forlorn lady.

"Because the ring is the royal engagement ring and Terrance isn't going to marry Beatrice." Pete turned his mild gaze on the bard.

Bern choked on a laugh. Del pounded him on the back.

"Marry Beatrice," Shamus guffawed.

Roland flushed as the adventurers burst out laughing. Even Elsa joined in with a feminine giggle.

"Buck up, boy," Shamus said, knocking Roland across the shoulder with one hand and wiping tears of laughter away with the other. "It's still an adventure."

"Let's go," Pete suggested. "If we leave now, we can be back tomorrow by supper."

They laughed at the old joke. Roland was left to wonder. No one explained it to him.

There was a general scraping and shuffling of chairs. Shamus kissed his wife goodbye. Roland followed them out the kitchen door into the farmyard. Horses waited patiently, ones that looked like what they were, farm horses tacked up for riding. There was a general bustle as the party mounted up. Roland hurried around to the front where his own horse waited. It was only a few minutes before they were sorted out and moving away down the road.

Now, Roland thought, the adventure begins. Something is bound to happen soon, just like the ballads say.

Hours of nothing happened. The horses plodded along in the dusty sunshine. Shamus and Pete traded stories for a while before lapsing into silence. Del and Bern didn't say anything. Tessa dozed in her saddle. Roland brought up the rear, waiting for something to happen and growing more desperate as the hours crept by. How could you write a grand ballad, guaranteed to make the bard famous, about a bunch of ordinary people riding along for hours with nothing, absolutely nothing, happening?

They weren't even sporting the right equipment for adventureres. Pete didn't wear a weapon, steel and magic just didn't mix, although Roland doubted Pete was much of a wizard anyway. Del and Bern wore hunting knives, long ones, but still knives. Shamus had a cudgel in his belt, a knobbed chunk of wood good for smacking stray dogs. Tessa did have a sword, a rusted ancient weapon that looked like a family heirloom that would shatter if it were actually used. Roland wondered how far he could stretch the truth and still call it a true story.

Evening came, summer twilight of gold that faded to lavender dusk. They stopped at an inn. Not a gloomy, frightening place that reeked of evil and was the haunt of thieves and worse, or a place run by a mysteriously threatening gaunt innkeeper, but a stolid common house that looked like a large house. The innkeeper was just an ordinary man, the rooms comfortable, the patrons local farmers with a few traveling merchants mixed in. None of them looked the least bit exotic or foreign. Pete announced they had a bard with them and Roland found himself singing songs and writing letters for farmers who couldn't read. It was only what was expected from a minstrel. The rest of the party paid for their rooms and dinner and left him to it.

The next day wasn't any more exciting than the first, or the three that followed. They traveled roads that wandered through farms and fields and stands of forest without a hint of brigands or a breath of danger. They slept in inns, comfortable and well-fed. The horses didn't charge gallantly down the road, they plodded. There was no sense of urgency, only the camaraderie of old friends. Roland gave up any idea of creating a legend out of this trip.

The morning of the sixth day saw them climbing into the rolling foothills of mountains. The peaks were gray above them in the distance, stark against the blue of summer sky. Roland attempted to compose rhymes about birds and mountains in his head. If he couldn't write epic ballads, he could at least write romantic love songs inspired by the beauties of nature. He looked hopefully around him. Nature wasn't cooperating, nothing looked very romantic or poetic. Nothing exciting looked like it would happen in these mountains, either. The whole adventure was a total washout.

"Cheer up," Pete said, nudging his horse alongside Roland's gelding. "You wanted to chronicle an adventure. This is what most of them are about—days of boredom interspersed with a few moments of utter terror. We haven't got to that part yet."

"So far, boredom is the best description," Roland muttered.

"The terror is up ahead," Pete answered and kicked his horse into a faster gait.

"What, is a squirrel going to menace us with wildflowers?" Roland called, his voice laced with sarcasm.

Roland watched Pete's back as his horse galloped up the line of march. No, he thought with a sigh, nothing so gallant as a gallop. It was more like a bouncy jog. Pete flopped around like a farmer on top of his mount. The horse dropped back into a shambling walk as Pete and Shamus traded bawdy limericks. Roland turned his mind back to composing sonnets and grumbling about the complete lack of adventurous spirit.

They stopped for lunch next to a stream. A tumbled fall of rocks bordered one side of the pleasant little meadow and trees provided shade near the water.

"We leave the horses here," Del informed Roland.

They left them tethered where they could reach water, grass, and shade as needed. The group then made their way over to the rocks and started climbing.

An hour later they reached a tiny meadow cupped between the rock fall and a cliff that reached into the air above them. Roland was red-faced from the heat and breathing hard. The rest weren't much better. They rested, drinking water and wiping sweat. Tessa was the only one not affected. She stood, looking over the rockfall and valley below.

"I'm getting old," Shamus complained.

"I spend too much time at my desk," Pete answered.

"Bern spends too much time mooning after his sheep," Del said slyly.

Roland waited to see what Bern would say. In the six days of traveling, Roland could count the number of words Bern used on one hand with fingers left over.

Bern said nothing. He merely poured his water skin over his brother's head. Del yelped and raised his fist.

"Stop it," Tessa said warningly.

They stopped and looked sheepish.

"Your turn to lead," Pete said to Roland. The wizard got to his feet and brushed dirt off his backside.

"I don't know where we're going," Roland protested. He saw the smug grin Shamus gave Tessa, the knowing wink. Roland yanked his tunic straight. They were laughing at him, behind his back, he was sure of it.

"See the trail?" Pete said, pointing at a faint scuffing that meandered across the meadow at the top of the rocks. It led around the side of the cliff. "We follow that."

Roland nodded and started off, stepping smartly. He heard the others fall in behind him. This wasn't the adventure he had hoped it would be, but he could still cut a dashing figure. Maybe he could show them how an adventurer should act. He lifted his chin higher, his thoughts more on how he looked than where he was going.

The trail cut around the cliff, a ledge of rock that narrowed as it climbed across the mountain flank. The clumps of grass became fewer, the trail rockier. Roland, intent on looking like a hero from a ballad, didn't notice the scorched smell that grew stronger as they climbed.

He rounded another bend and found himself in a pocket valley carved out of the mountain sometime in the distant past. A pond nestled on the far side, surrounded by a thin screen of grass and a few brave wildflowers. The trail petered out near the pond. Roland stopped, looking around.

"Where now?" he asked, turning to look at Pete, the wizard.

The five others stood back, giving him room. Roland frowned, wondering what the joke was. A shadow enveloped him, creeping from the tumbled rocks at the base of the cliff. Hot breath, laced with the smell of scorched metal, blasted over him. He shrieked as a dragon reared up from the rocks, huge and menacing. Its eyes glowed golden and angry as it glared down at him. Smoke trickled from its nostrils. Roland stood, frozen in terror, as the beast leaned close. He squeezed his eyes shut. A cloud of acrid smoke enveloped him as the dragon breathed.

"Don't they teach manners any more?" the dragon complained. Its voice reminded Roland of his music teacher, a fruity alto with overtones of chiming bells. Roland peeked out from one eye. The dragon sat back on its haunches, looking peeved.

"He's a minstrel, Beatrice," the wizard Pete said.

"Well, that explains much of it," the dragon answered. "Bothersome men writing all that drivel about dragons eating people and stealing their treasure. Just because there are a few rotten apples in the barrel, doesn't mean all of us are that way."

"Yes," Pete agreed as he walked past Roland, slapping the stunned minstrel on the shoulder. "But Terrance thought it would do the young man some good to come with us, knock some sense into him or something. How have you been?"

"It's been too many years, Pete, and you know it." The dragon settled back, blinking coquettishly. "Did you ever marry that young woman you were pining over?"

"No, she married a rich young nobleman who didn't burn holes in his robes practicing magic." Pete settled on a rock.

The rest of the group passed Roland, greeting the dragon as Lady Beatrice, then settling down for a visit. Roland watched them in growing confusion. They traded gossip about Tessa's grandchildren and Shamus's son. Beatrice giggled at one comment. Roland frowned at the sound. Dragons giggling just didn't seem right.

"Wait a minute," he finally exploded. The five adventurers and the dragon looked at him, politely waiting for him to continue. "You are the Lady Beatrice?" He pointed at the dragon.

"It is extremely rude to point," the dragon huffed. Her scales glittered green in the sunlight.

"Pardon me," Roland said and bowed, a reflex action brought on by the dragon's uncanny resemblance to his overbearing music teacher. Beatrice looked pleased by his apology. "I'm more than a little confused," he confessed.

"This is the Lady Beatrice," Pete said. "Beatrice, Roland the minstrel."

"Pleased to meet you," Beatrice said and batted her scaly eyelids at him.

"Beatrice, my darling, I'm afraid we have to discuss some business with you," Pete said turning back to the dragon. "Terrance needs his ring back."

"He gave it to me," Beatrice said and pouted.

Roland stared, he couldn't help it. A ferocious dragon, that looked just like the one in his Illustrated Encyclopedia of Magical Beasts, was pouting and flirting. It had to be the most weirdly fascinating thing he had ever seen.

"He needs it back, sweetheart," Pete said. "It's the official wedding ring of Boravia."

"Is Terrance marrying someone else? He promised to marry me."

"He has to marry a princess, so she can be queen," Pete said. "Besides, think of your children."

Beatrice giggled and blushed, her scales blooming darker green.

"He sent a very nice present to trade for it," Pete continued.

"Let me see it," Beatrice answered with a gleam of pure avarice in her eyes.

"Get the ring first and then we'll show you."

"You used to be much more fun," Beatrice muttered as she slunk back into the rocks.

Roland found enough courage to scramble up the slope to where the others sat. There was a cave behind them, tucked into a fold in the slope and invisible from below. The sound of dragonly humming came from inside.

"I think she likes you," Tessa teased Pete.

"If she weren't a dragon..." Pete mused, staring down into the cave.

"You're a wizard, you could make it work," Shamus spoke up.

Bern sighed heavily.

"Bern is sweet on her," Del spoke up, nudging his brother. "But he isn't fireproof, like Pete."

"I know a charm for that," Pete said.

Bern blushed deep crimson.

"I don't believe this," Roland muttered and sat on a rock.

Beatrice reappeared carrying a tray. "Pastries," she announced. "I get them from the baker in the village. He has the flakiest crust I have ever tasted, but he won't share his secret recipe with me. I even tried to buy it from him." She put the tray down, her claws delicately balancing it on a rock.

"Thank you, Beatrice." Pete helped himself to the sweets.

"They're lovely," Bern blurted out. "Just like you." He gazed up at the dragon, like a lovesick puppy.

"Oh, Bern," Beatrice said, and blushed, fluttering her eyelids, all six of them.

Bern settled formally onto one knee. "Your scales are like, um, grass," he said, stuttering with nerves. "Your eyes are like jewels. Your tail is, um, long. Your teeth are sharp. Your claws are, um." Nerves got the best of him and he stopped, his face burning red.

"You are too romantic," Beatrice gushed. "I never knew you had the soul of a poet." She ducked her giant, scaly head coyly. "You can pay court on me anytime."

A smile worked its way over Bern's face, spreading until Roland thought his whole head might split open.

"I hate to interrupt you young lovers," Pete spoke up, breaking the mood, "but we really do need that ring."

"You are so insensitive," Beatrice huffed. "I really don't know what I ever saw in you."

"Bern is more your type," Pete agreed. "He's a very romantic soul."

Bern blushed even more red. Beatrice smiled and batted her eyelids. Roland rolled his eyes. Maybe epic ballad was out, but romantic comedy was a possibility.

"Terrance needs his ring," Pete prodded.

"Oh, all right," Beatrice gave in with poor grace. She flounced into her cave, tail slapping the rock behind her.

Bern heaved a sigh, a silly romantic smile stretching his face. Del slapped him on the shoulder and wiped back a tear.

"You actually spoke to a female," Del said. "Ma will be so proud of you."

Bern scowled at his brother.

Pete waited, watching the entrance to the dragon cave. Sounds of rummaging filtered out. The sun slipped toward afternoon.

Beatrice reappeared. She held one claw up to the sunlight. A huge crystal set in a gold ring glittered and winked in the sun.

"That isn't it, Beatrice," Pete said blandly.

"I know, but this one is so pretty," Beatrice said, twirling the gem around her claw and sending flashes of light sparkling across the rocks. She lifted another claw and dropped a simple gold band set with a rather dull sapphire onto the pastry tray. "Tell Terrance I expect an invitation to the wedding."

"He never considered not inviting his old flame." Pete scooped up the ring then bowed to the dragon.

"My present?" Beatrice prompted.

"Ah, yes." Pete rummaged in his pocket. "One silver mirror, with gilt roses, and a packet of blackberry candies."

"Oh," Beatrice cooed as Pete handed over the mirror and a rather squashed bag. "How lovely. And he remembered my favorite flavor." She held up the tiny hand mirror, admiring the glittering decorations.

"I think Bern would like a moment alone with his lady love," Shamus said. He took Del's arm and towed him back down the trail. Tessa fell into step behind them.

"Farewell, sweet lady," Pete said to the dragon and blew her a kiss.

Bern sat on his rock and gazed lovingly at the dragon.

"Come on, minstrel," Pete said, taking Roland's arm and turning him toward the trail.

Roland looked back once just before the trail curved and hid the tiny valley. Bern was still sitting, watching Beatrice as she primped in the tiny mirror and ate blackberry candies with one delicate claw.

"So what do you think of your first adventure?" Pete asked.

"It wasn't anything like I expected," Roland admitted.

"It never is, minstrel. If it were, you'd never write another ballad, now would you?"

Roland had to nod his head in agreement.

"Perhaps next time we can arrange for some flashy spells and sword waving to happen." Pete stepped over a rock in the trail. "And you can swirl your cape. That's a very nice satin lining, by the way. Love the crimson color with that gold tunic."

"Thank you." Roland paused, pulling Pete to a halt. "Next time?"

"Oh, of course. Terrance loves to send us on errands. You will come, won't you?"

Roland studied Pete's bland face. Pete the wizard? Maybe he could change the name to something more fitting. And spice up the danger along the trail. Maybe add in a wild thunderstorm and a wizened old beggar man with a prophecy.

Pete grinned. "I can see that stories are swimming in your head. Spice it up a bit, right? That's how legends are born."

They started walking again.

"Then you're all right with it?" Roland asked.

"If you make me eight feet tall with a long white beard and piercing blue eyes? Certainly. Lady Beatrice might object if you make her the villain, though."

Roland pursed his lips. "She could be a good dragon. Maybe the ring was stolen by an evil sorcerer. Or an ogre. Or possibly a band of goblins."

"Now you've got the spirit."

Roland hiked down the mountain trail, his head spinning with ideas. Yes, this was the way to adventure. Maybe they'd stop at Elsa's kitchen on the way back and have more of her golden flapjacks and brambleberry jam. He could live with only imaginary danger. Four days of boring riding should be plenty of time for him to finish his epic saga of the Quest for the Ring. Yes, that had a good sound to it. The Quest for the Ring. Perfect.

He swirled his cape, just for practice, as he marched down the hillside to the waiting farm horses.

BAIT AND SWITCH

"Buckle up, kids, battle drill time." Lonnis flipped his station to live. The lights in the tiny room glowed red.

Tayvis fumbled with the restraint in the jump seat next to the door, excitement making his hands shake. Cadets rarely got the chance to see the weapons in action on a Patrol cruiser. Lonnis sat to his right, straddling the control console, both hands seated in the gloves that controlled the ship's weapons. Tish, his spotter, sat to his left, her face green in the glow of her targeting screens.

Lonnis rolled his shoulders, settling into his controls. "Watch closely, kid. This is more complicated than those simulators. No matter how good the programming is, it will never match the real thing. Comm, port forward is live."

"Target firing commencing in five." Hedrik, the voice of comm control, crackled from the speakers.

"Let's break our old records," Lonnis said as the screens came alive with multi-colored traces.

Tayvis tried to keep track of the screens. Each object near them appeared on Tish's screens. She marked targets with red, other objects turned gray under her rapid touches. Colored lines spread from each target, green for projected course, blue for last known heading. Lonnis twisted, firing weapons at the targets. Lights flickered and died across his screen, replaced by new targets, new tracings. Their ship position and heading, thruster settings, and other information scrolled across the bottom of his screen.

The tracings disappeared. No new ones replaced those eliminated. Lonnis' screen flashed once as the last target disappeared. He slipped his hands from the control gloves. "Targets eliminated. Port forward, locked." His hands flipped the safety switches on. The control screens faded to silver, the lights changed from red to normal. "How's my time, Hedrik?"

"You're getting slow, old man. Three point four seconds longer than your record."

Lonnis grinned. "That's because you reprogrammed the spinners again. I wasn't expecting that sharp spiral."

"Keeps you on your toes, Lonnis. You're buying the drinks next port. Comm out."

Lonnis stretched his arms over his head. "We should work on the projected courses. You were off your mark today, Tish."

"Right, blame me because you can't shoot straight." Tish unbuckled her restraint. "Not as exciting as you thought, Tayvis? Real battle is more chaotic."

"It's a game of prediction and anticipation," Lonnis said. "You figure out where the target will be and lay down a trap. Mines and missiles."

"Pulse beams are better," Tayvis answered. "Mines and missiles can be detected and detonated by counter-measures."

"True, but not if you place them right. If you fire a pulse beam inside your shields, the energy reflects back and blows your own ship to kingdom come. You have to leave the weapon port outside the field, making it vulnerable. Pulse beams are for close range combat only. Or for salvage work." Lonnis leaned on the doorframe. "Mines and missiles are more effective and safer for distance combat between ships. Of course, whether you hit them or not depends on the skill of your spotter."

Tish leaned back in her seat, crossing her long legs. "I'm the best and you know it, Lonnis."

Lonnis dropped his hand to Tayvis' shoulder. "You'll be a decent point someday, if you can get past the theory. That's what the Patrol Academy is good for, beating the nonsense out of you before you get yourself killed."

The lights blinked red, on and off before settling on a steady glow. An alarm shrilled.

"Proximity alert," Tish said, flipping her screens on. "Incoming missiles!"

"Another drill?" Lonnis reached for his controls.

The ship rocked. Smoke and explosions filled the air. The door to the gunnery pod slammed shut as more alarms sounded. Tayvis gripped the restraints as the ship's gravity field flickered off. Lonnis slammed into the doorframe.

"This isn't a drill." Tish tapped rapidly on her screen, scanning for information. "Lonnis, we're under attack. Lonnis?"

"He's out," Tayvis said, checking the older man for a pulse. Blood trickled through Lonnis' white hair.

Another round of projectiles slammed into the ship. Smoke poured through the air vents.

"Central comm!" Tish hit buttons. "Nobody's answering. Nobody's shooting back. I've got a ship out there, and more missiles incoming. Three minutes to impact, unless someone does something." She waved at the gunner's seat. "There's a comm link to the bridge. Activate it."

Tayvis rose to his feet. Half the systems in the pod were dark, unresponsive, but the gunner's seat still showed lights. Observe only, the captain had said. Was this a test?

"The red button to your left. Press it." Tish tapped her screens, then swore. "We're rotating. I lost the ship. Starboard Aft, you hear me?"

Tayvis flexed his hands. He'd never touched a live station before. Would they have staged real smoke and blood for a drill?

Tish slammed her fist into the side of the weapons screen. "Hey, stupid. Get the bridge on the line, now!"

It wasn't live weapons, it was only a comm button. Tayvis slid into the seat, straddling the controls. He tapped the red button. The control gloves hung empty, inviting. He slid his hands inside. The firing screen lit up.

Speakers crackled to life. "This is Hedrik. Port forward, what is your status?"

"Lonnis is down, but the cadet and I are fine," Tish answered. "What's going on?"

"Thank the stars someone is still down there. We got ambushed by a Fellucian marauder. The shields are holding at thirty seven percent. For now."

"The other weapons stations? I picked up another salvo headed our way before the ship drifted. I'm on the blind side now."

"No one else is responding. The marauder knew just when to hit us. End of drill and we had most of the systems resetting."

Tish frowned. "Our weapons are still live."

"We have no engines," Hedrik answered. "We have thrusters, but I don't know how much good they'll do us."

Tayvis flexed his fingers in the gloves. Anticipation and prediction, he could do this. "I can shoot."

"Cadet, you are ordered to stand down." Hedrik's voice crackled over the speakers. "You have no training or authorization to use those weapons."

"I've got enough, and you don't have anyone else. Tish, can you track those incoming missiles?"

"Cadet, stand down. That is a direct order."

Tayvis punched the button, shutting off comm control.

Tish stared at Tayvis. She licked her lip, a dart of red tongue.

"We're dead if we don't do something." Tayvis tapped the buttons at the end of the gloves, mentally reviewing what weapons each released.

"Hedrik gave you a direct order."

"The comm line must have cut out. I didn't hear anything. Give me targets, Tish."

Tish tapped her screens. "We're turning to face the ship. Targeting systems online. Incoming missiles. Impact in thirty seconds."

"Not if I can help it." Tayvis released a cloud of reflective debris on a trajectory to intercept the nearest.

"That will get the lead one, but miss the other two. Drop a few mines on a starboard curve to pick those up. And do it soon or you won't catch them in time."

Tayvis tapped the buttons in sequence, launching mines on a curving course toward the two missiles.

"Mines to port, and more missiles." Tish spoke in a clipped voice devoid of emotion. "Painted red and gold."

Colored dots sprang to life on his screens. He dropped more chaff and several mines of his own, blue dots glittering on the screen. He launched a shrapnel missile toward the enemy minefield, hoping to detonate the mines.

"Let's hope the bridge detects that one," Tish said. "And changes vectors before we blow ourselves up with our own missiles. I've got the maurader targeted."

A red dot, with a blue line tracing its last course and a green line tracing its predicted course appeared on Tayvis' screen.

"They'll use the explosions as cover and change course. It's what I would do." Tayvis flicked through his options.

"And you're an expert now?"

He fired missiles at the ship. Think of it as a game and he wouldn't panic. "They're moving into that radiation cloud so they can change vectors without us detecting it." He launched a salvo of mines to the left of the nebula cloud, scattering them across the far edge.

Tish swore as she scanned for new targets. "You're wasting mines. We have a limited supply, cadet."

"They'll come out the way they went in." Tayvis launched another round.

"Is that what you think? They're stupid if they come out the way they went in, and their attack proves they aren't stupid."

The thrusters fired, the ship veered onto a new vector. The Fellucian marauder screamed across the screen, almost close enough to touch.

"Mines!" Tish shouted as a new round of explosions rocked the Exeter. They grabbed their consoles as the ship shuddered and rolled.

The stream of damage reports across the bottom of his screen turned red. System after system failed. Smoke filled the tiny room. Lonnis coughed. Tish left her seat to check on the senior officer.

Tayvis flexed his hands, watching in disbelief as the ship faltered. The engines and thrusters were dead, shields collapsed, the missile bay destroyed; the raider had only to turn and pick them apart at leisure. He had three dozen limpet mines to fight them off, a weak weapon at best.

"Tish?"

"We have to get Lonnis to sickbay." She slapped the door controls, swearing when the lock refused to disengage.

"There won't be a sickbay if we don't find a way to destroy that ship. Help me find a way. I've got three dozen limpet mines. Everything else is gone."

"We could get in suits and shove them up his thruster ports. It might slow him a bit." Tish cradled Lonnis' head in her lap. "Limpet mines are for clearing debris."

"Is there a way to recall the mines I launched earlier?"

"If we called and surrendered, they might let us live." She brushed white hair away from the matted blood caked on Lonnis' forehead.

"Communications are dead, and wouldn't we have to do that from the bridge?" Tayvis pulled his hands from the gloves. "What kind of probes do you have on your station?"

"Scanning probes, passive and active. They won't explode. Even if they did, they're too small to do any damage."

"Can they broadcast?"

She narrowed her eyes. "What are you thinking?"

Tayvis smiled. "We launch active probes through the nebula, into the thickest part if we can. Then we broadcast call signs from other ships. We convince the marauder an entire Patrol fleet is lying in wait."

"And they run away? Are you insane? They were hiding in this nebula. They know we don't have a fleet out here."

"We launch limpet mines at the same time, then send the signal to explode. If we time it right, the shockwaves in the gases look like ships downshifting from hyperspace."

Tish's gaze traveled to her screen. She chewed her lip. "They're turning to make another pass. Dumping speed and changing vectors should take them at least twenty minutes." She shifted Lonnis back to the floor, sliding him against the wall. "We'll have to work fast."

Tayvis slid his hands into the control gloves. "This is just a simulation," he whispered as he sent the mines toward the thickest screen of interstellar gas.

"Probes are set to broadcast, but we're going to have to send the signals from here, vocal only." Her fingers drummed on the edge of her console. "I don't know if they'll buy it. They'll expect to see ships. We can't fake those signals."

"Then the Patrol is going to be testing a new cloaking field. What cruisers would be in this sector?" Tayvis launched the last set of mines.

"You're insane. We don't have cloaking fields. They don't work."

"They do now. That's why they can't see the ships, only their wake as they downshift. Launch the probes." He rattled off the location of the mines. "I'm sending the detonation codes in three minutes. Your probes need to arrive just after the explosions."

"If they don't get scared and run off, we're going to die. We've got no weapons left." Tish entered launch codes for her probes.

"We can't disable them with limpet mines and probes. We have to do something."

Tish smiled as she launched the probes. "You've got guts, kids. Crazy, but brave. I like that."

He ducked his head to hide his blush. "Detonation in two minutes."

"Marauder is turning. They'll reach us in ten minutes."

They sat in tense silence as the countdown ticked toward mine detonation. Smoke trickled through the wheezing air vents.

"Ready with the transmission?" Tayvis asked.

"Broadcast is ready when you are." She waited, her slender hands floating above her console controls.

The clock hit zero. "Detonation." Tayvis watched the ripples spread through the radiation scan on his screen.

"Time delay of forty-three seconds. The probes are in position now." Tish tapped buttons on her console. "Channel open."

Tayvis cleared his throat. "This is Admiral Green aboard the Exeter. The test of our new cloaking device has been interrupted by a Fellucian attack. All ships trace the vessel attacking us and destroy it."

Tish tapped another string of buttons. "Message broadcast to the probes, Admiral Green. They're sending back confirmation codes. Let's hope the marauder takes the bait. It's still on course for our position."

"Make the probes turn back, make it look like the fleet is closing on our position, too."

"Already done. They have limited fuel, and if they get too close, the raiders will know we're bluffing."

"I hope they intercepted the message." Tayvis chewed his thumb while they waited. He watched the red dot creep closer. The blue probes formed a half-circle, closing from the other direction. "I've got an idea."

"Another one?"

"I've got one limpet mine left, missing the blasting cap. We can track mines, can't we?"

"How do you think we keep from running over our own?"

"And they attach magnetically?"

"If the ship is close enough." She tapped her screen. The lines crisscrossed, blue and green and orange. "If they keep current course and speed, they'll pass almost on top of us. Close enough for a limpet."

Tayvis slid his hands into the control gloves. "Give me a count as they close."

"They're arming weapons. I don't think they took your bait, kid."

"Open the line again, send a string of random code. Anything to get the probes to respond."

"Yes, sir, admiral, sir." Tish typed rapidly, her fingers flying over the controls. "They're increasing speed. Are they going to ram us? You've got maybe fifteen seconds. They're firing missiles. Nice knowing you, kid."

His screen blossomed with red dots and more lines. Missiles darted past their ship, aimed at the closing probes. Tayvis punched the button, launching the last limpet mine. A bright yellow dot shot from their ship, closing on the marauder. Another barrage of missiles erupted onto the screen. Tayvis punched the button for the deflective chaff, spreading all they had left.

The Exeter rocked from the force of the missiles exploding. Shock waves rattled the ship. Debris scraped across the hull. The weapon controls shattered as pulses of raw energy passed through the ship. The lights faded to a dim emergency level. Tayvis grabbed his restraints as the ship spun.

The emergency stabilizers fired, slowing the motion of the ship. Tayvis unlatched the restraints. "Tish?"

"Crazy kid, I think they bought it." Tish slid from her chair to check on Lonnis. "Or they think the chaff exploding was us. Either way, they just made jump headed for Calvier Sector."

The speakers crackled to life. "Port forward, this is the bridge. Are you there?"

"We're here, sir," Tish answered. "Glad you're still alive up there."

"We should be able to limp back to base soon. The ship systems are a mess." Hedrik cleared his throat. "Captain Vorlais says we owe our thanks to Admiral Green and his cloaked fleet. Tell Lonnis good work."

"It wasn't him, sir." Tish grinned at Tayvis. "It was our crazy but brilliant cadet. And Hedrik, if you scan for a limpet mine signal, you should be able to track the marauder."

Hedrick laughed in answer.

MATH GAMES

So, I'm part of this reality game show, but it's kind of weird. Something tells me that these aliens, the Kroshan, don't understand how game shows work.

First, it's about math. How lame is that? We take a test once a week. If you score less than seventy percent, you're eliminated from the competition. It's like going back to school. But, whatever. I was always pretty good at math, better than I was at cheerleading.

Second, they said some weeks no one would be eliminated. But everyone could be eliminated, too.

Weirdos.

We've got this awesome mansion to hang out in, complete with a giant pool, indoor garden, maid service, and a kitchen staff. Who cares if the Kroshan are bumpy gray lizard-walruses? They cook like you wouldn't believe!

We just finished our first test. Two hours, fifty questions, no sweat. It was all elementary stuff. Addition, subtraction, multiplication, division. Yeah, we're all still here. And living it up on the Kroshan's dime.

Morty says there's a catch somewhere, that the Kroshan never mentioned a prize. I swear I heard them tell us the first day that the prize was a lifetime of comfort and ease in our very own mansion. So what if it's on their home planet, it's not like Earth is that great these days.

Week 3

Morty is an idiot. I don't care how handsome you are, you're a jerk, Morty! After promising me a romantic evening by the pool, he went and invited Julia, too! Julia with the movie star looks and seductive eyes. She doesn't even understand math. No surprise she was eliminated this week. Basic algebra. Here's x, find y. Somebody had to be first to go. I can't say I'm sad it was her. Seventeen of us left.

Week 4

The test was a little more challenging this week. Multiple variables and systems of equations, but no exponents and no factoring. Nobody went home. I wonder if they'll give all of us a mansion if we all win.

Now that I think about it, how long is the contest? How much math do they think we need to know? Morty has some ideas about that, but Morty also told me he has a PhD in math. I'll be his girlfriend if he tutors me. I don't think they'll push us too far into Calculus. I mean, how boring can it be watching people take math tests? These game shows are supposed to be about drama, like me and Julia in a cat fight. Or Jon and his gang having a food fight. The Kroshan must be wired a lot different from humans if they think math tests make great entertainment.

Week 5

Ugh! Graphing and exponents this week. Not my strong suit, but I still got an eighty-seven. Five went home. That leaves twelve. I'd give names but the head Kroshan told me not to. Some privacy or security thing.

Anyway, I can't believe they'd send five home at once. Guess they were pretty serious about that. Someone, you know who I'm talking about, whispered during our tutoring session that something funky is going on, that this isn't really a game show and the cameras are fakes. He may be cute but he's a nutjob conspiracy guy. Whatever, he still knows his math and he's my best chance at winning.

WEEK 6

Three more went home this week. Trigonometry isn't as easy as I remember. Jon decided to try sabotage. He joined our study group then started to mess with us by writing all the formulas wrong. Backfired on him, though. He's gone along with three of his buddies.

Whoops, no names. Forgot for a moment there.

Nutjob boyfriend is trying to convince me that the Kroshan aren't sending the losers home, that they're eating them or something. I think he's crazy, but cute.

WEEK 7

The Kroshan are reading our journals. Why else would they make a big deal of showing the losers flying home and being greeted by cheering crowds? Only thing is, the photoshopping software they used is crap. Totally fake video. So where are they sending the losers? Three more went home this week and it was just basic integrals. Just five left.

I think we're on the Kroshan home planet. It definitely isn't Earth. We cracked open a window last night. The air smells weird.

WEEK 8

I know you're reading this, you giant scaly walrus! Three of us left. We'll find your secrets. You can't hide from us. Gluing the windows shut won't stop us!

WEEK 9

It's a freaking zoo. The losers are living it up in the Kroshan zoo. Swimming pool, mansion, whatever they want, for life! So what if all the walls are windows and every space has a camera. It's paradise in there and so big it doesn't feel like a cage. Plus the Kroshan provide things so you can pursue your hobbies. Anything you want—painting, pottery, woodshop, even hiking and running. Yeah, they do it on a leash, but still. We got to visit one last time. Turns out the Kroshan thought getting eliminated meant winning the prize. Told you they didn't understand game shows.

Morty and me? We won, passed the last test. Now we're locked in a wire cage in a big lab. We're freaking lab rats! They keep giving us math tests. I'm worried I'll fail the next one. I'm afraid I'll be dissected when that happens. Morty's trying to tutor me, but even his PhD won't save us for long. The Kroshan are way beyond what we understand.

But they still don't get reality TV game shows.

One-Way Ticket
to Paradise

My first day on Eden wasn't the paradise I expected.

"Remember your breathing mask before stepping outside," the pilot reminded me as I stepped off the shuttle.

I snapped the mask in place without comment. I knew far more than he did about such things. I was one of four environmental systems techs assigned to the new facility. Our job on Eden was to prepare it for the first wave of colonists, due in another six months. If one breath of free air killed me, it didn't bode well for the colonists.

I jogged through Eden's dense jungle. The fresh air tasted much better than the recycled shuttle air. The world hadn't evolved animals yet, only plants and insects. I was tempted to explore but duty required me to check in first.

The research facility spread up the side of a hill, the main glass atrium reflecting the morning sun. Levels split off either side, like branches of a tree. Four greenhouses sat on the far side of the facility. Jungle foliage crowded the base of the building, deciduous forests surrounded the greenhouses and upper levels. A narrow strip of land divided the two. It looked as if someone had hacked off the jungle right at the base of the hill. I hitched my duffel higher on my shoulder as I hiked the trail to the building's main doors.

The plaza in front of the doors was new, a ragged line of bare earth along the edge. A thin film of yellow dust covered the plascrete surface.

Footprints disturbed it in a path leading straight to the door. I stooped, running my finger through the yellow particles. They were all different sizes from sand grain-size down to a fine powder. A plume of yellow floated from the nearby plants. Pollen, I didn't need a botanist to confirm it. If this was the normal level, the air filters were going to be murder to clean.

I joined the end of a line waiting to get through the airlocks into the main building. Standard protocol on a new world, keep the world out until it had been tested. The colonists would be inoculated against any ill effects of the contaminants until they could adapt to the new world. So far, only a handful of worlds had proven too dangerous to colonize.

I stepped into the airlock with the tail end of the group. Air rushed past us, blowing away any loose particulates. The inner doors whooshed open.

Sound exploded around me, people talking and arguing, equipment haulers groaning under heavy loads, footsteps echoing on the hard floor of the atrium. Outside, I'd had the wind and insect chirps. I was tempted to turn back and exit the airlock doors, but I had to report in, so I hunched my shoulders and wound through the crowd to the appropriate table.

I spread my hand on the id scanner. "Talia Korman, environmental tech."

The harried man behind the desk barely verified my credentials before shoving an id card across the table. "Women's dormitory, level three, left and all the way to the end. You're assigned to the greenhouses. They want you there as soon as possible. The filters are gummed up again."

A gangly man took my place at the table as I took my card and stepped away. I headed up the stairs in the middle of the space. The fibermat in the level three hallway showed traces of yellow powder. I made a note to recommend adding foot scrubbers to the airlocks.

I found the dormitory room and used my id card to open the door. Four sets of bunks lined the far wall with lockers and cabinets between. I picked an unoccupied bunk as far from the others as I could. The last time I'd had this many roommates, I'd ended up sleeping in a janitor's closet instead. I don't like people much, never have.

The main greenhouse lay beyond another set of airlock doors at the end of the hall. A short enclosed passage separated the two buildings with branches leading up and down the hill to connect the other greenhouses. I entered the main one. Standard procedure had two greenhouses dedicated to crops, grains that would keep the colony functioning. Botanists experimented with varieties and growing conditions to test crop viability in the new conditions. The main greenhouse was used as a garden for the preliminary crew as well as an experiment for the botanists for all the other flowers, fruits, and vegetables the colonists might want. The last greenhouse, the one most separated from the others, was where they grew native plants, testing for edibility and toxicity.

Judging by the luxuriant growth surrounding me in the main greenhouse, Eden would prove very successful as an agricultural world. I stopped to sniff some yellow flowers spilling from a hanging pot.

"The greenhouses are closed to staff, at least for the rest of the week."

I turned from the flowers to face the man who'd accosted me. "I'm Talia Korman, environmental tech assigned to the greenhouses."

The man wiped sweat from his balding head. "Good. The filters are down again. That cussed pollen gets into everything no matter what we do. Wreaks havoc on our pollination programs. We've had to dump the tomato seedlings five times now. It mutates them in the weirdest ways. Brun Heimner, chief botanist for this project."

He didn't offer his hand to shake. I didn't mind.

He walked as he talked. "Filters are on the far side. We keep scrubbing them and switching them out every twelve hours, but the fans keep clogging up. Suits are in the airlock next to them for when you go outside. We've got vines climbing up the filters. The things grow three feet an hour. If I could figure out how they do it, I'd make a breakthrough in plant genetics."

I followed at his heels. It was all standard, just like the last six assignments I'd had, except for the sheer amount of particulates. And the vines. I'd never had to hack fast growing vines off the equipment.

The fans were silent and still when we reached the far side of the greenhouse. Brun tapped the controls mounted on the wall. "We had to shut them down. Kept overheating. We've got the tightest filter they'll give us installed." He swiped his hand over the fan blade. It came away yellow. "If you can figure out how to stop it, I'll put you in for a commendation."

"I'll see what I can do."

He hurried away as I ducked under the fans to check the filter screens.

I spent an hour scrubbing the four sets of double filters then slipped them back into the vents before flipping on the fans. Warm air, rich with the smell of the jungle outside, blew across my face. I debated for a moment about suiting up to go outside before deciding to save it for later. I hated the suits. Maybe I could get away with just a mask. I headed up the hill to the grain greenhouses.

Brun stalked the aisles of the first one, three assistants scurrying at his heels. The flats of grain seedlings looked sickly, twisted and yellowed where they weren't black and rotting. Brun waved his hands over the ruined plants. "We're going to have to replant the entire crop. Try the spelt this time, and the corn hybrids." He caught sight of me near the entrance and gestured for me to join him.

A sour smell wafted from the decaying plants. I rubbed my nose, trying not to breathe it in.

"I want triple filters installed," Brun said when I reached him. "And an extra set with fans in the airlock room. The native pollen kills anything we plant in here. You'll need a laser cutter when you go outside. We've got shrubs taking over the air intakes. They don't grow as fast as the vines, but they have thorns long as your finger. Watch out for the ants, too. They're symbiotes with the bushes. As soon as you start burning, they'll swarm."

"Are they sure this world is worth colonizing?" I couldn't help asking.

Brun glared. "They're just plants and insects. Get moving. The upper greenhouse is in even worse shape. The only grain we've managed to get beyond sprouting is rye, and it's infected with some nasty fungus. This world hates grasses. We may have to use cassava or potatoes instead of grain. We're supposed to start animal trials next month, but we have nothing to feed them."

"Maybe they can eat the vines."

Brun shook his head. "Toxic sap. Wear thick gloves and disinfect when you're through. Make certain every bit of leaf or stem stays outside. These things sprout from even the smallest fragment. I don't want them inside the greenhouses."

I nodded and went to work.

The bushes outside the vents on the top two greenhouses were as bad as Brun said. Vicious insects the size of my thumb boiled out of the growth as soon as I fired up the laser cutter. Between them and the thorns on the bushes, I was very glad the suit was reinforced carbonite fabric. It was hot and the bottled air tasted stale, but I wasn't stung or scratched. I burned the bushes to the ground and spent a while zapping stray ants. Most of them scrambled into the surrounding forest, forming long snaking lines of bright red bodies and multiple legs flickering in the sunlight.

I smashed my way along a faint trail outside the greenhouses to get to the lower greenhouses. The forest ended abruptly just above the garden greenhouse. Bare earth showed in a ragged strip about five feet wide. The jungle began on the other side. It was like a neutral zone between two warring nations. I shrugged away my uneasiness over the strange situation, then checked the oxygen level of my tank. They were just plants.

The flickering force blade on the pruners made short work of the twisted growth of vines. I cut them back an extra twelve feet. I didn't want to have to suit up and prune every day if I could avoid it. The plants didn't attack me with insects like the bushes, but they left wide smears of sticky green sap across my suit. I swiped a glove over the mess. I'd have to scrub the suit before storing it. More tedious work I didn't want to do.

I walked down the faint trail to the lowest greenhouse, crushing plants underfoot as I went. The vents of the building were surprisingly clear despite only one set of filters on the fans. The yellow dust clung to the blades, but not as thickly as at the other greenhouses. I swiped a gloved hand over the filter, knocking most of the pollen off. A swarm of fluttering white-winged creatures swooped over my head, circling in front of the vents before drifting up and over the roof of the greenhouse.

I used the airlock of the lowest greenhouse, glad I didn't have to hack and burn any more plants. I stripped off the suit, careful to avoid the green smears from the vines. I hung the suit in the cleaner, sealing the door before starting the sterilization cycle.

The greenhouse was a riot of luxuriant growth. I paused near the closest flat. Squat plants with fleshy leaves sprouted curled vines like springs. I touched one. The coil flicked straight, snapping against my cheek. I wiped a smear of yellow sap from my skin.

"You want to wash that with soap."

I looked to the side where the voice came from. A young girl about ten standard years old watched me with solemn gray eyes. She kept her hands behind her back as she talked. "It's better not to touch anything in here until you know it's safe. I can tell you're new."

"Thanks." The yellow sap was starting to burn on my face and my fingers.

The girl tilted her head toward the door leading back to the main building. "There's a sink over there. Everyone's supposed to scrub before leaving this greenhouse."

She followed me through the maze of native plants to the sink. I scrubbed the burning sap away while she watched. I was torn between shooing her away or pumping her for information. The weird array of plants had me curious. I'd never seen anything like most of them. She stood in silence, waiting for me to finish. I decided as long as she didn't babble, I could stand her company, at least long enough to find out what she knew.

"How long have you been here?" I asked as I dried my hands.

She shrugged. "Since the building went up. My father is the colony governor."

I shoved the paper wipes into the trash. They'd be recycled into compost for the greenhouse.

I leaned against the sink waiting for the girl to speak. She studied me in silence, her face serious. I gave in after a long moment of listening to the plants rustle in the artificial breeze.

"What can you tell me about these plants? Besides don't touch."

A small smile twitched across her mouth. "The peonies are my favorites. They don't do anything dangerous. This way." She trotted across the greenhouse, weaving between the trays of plants. "I'm Nione. What's your name?"

"Talia."

"I saw you cleaning the filters. Is that your job?"

I nodded. "Environmental tech in charge of the greenhouse filtering systems."

"Watch out for Brun. The colony plants are dying. That makes him angry."

"I noticed."

Nione stopped at the edge of the greenhouse beside a bush covered in puffy pink flowers. "He yells a lot, but he's still nice. He gives me his dessert most of the time. I call these peonies. Listen." She stroked the petals of one flower. A low hum rose from the plant. "Try it." She reached to stroke a second flower. A different note joined the first.

I touched a flower. The petals were soft and silky under my finger. A third note joined the others. Nione giggled. We stroked more of the pink petals. The entire bush sang, the sound growing louder as we touched the soft flowers.

"I've never got it so loud," Nione said.

We both smiled as we fingered the flowers.

Something smashed into the greenhouse right above us where the roof curved down to the wall. The song died as if cut off. I ducked as more thuds sounded overhead. I glanced up. The white-winged creatures I'd noticed earlier were smeared across the glass roof, their insides leaking blue liquid. The bush rattled though the breeze barely touched it.

"That never happened before," Nione said.

"I'd better clean those off." The blue liquid etched trails over the glass panes despite the coatings meant to protect them.

Nione nodded.

"Meet me here tomorrow?" I asked. "I want to know what you know about these plants. And this world." None of the things I'd seen were mentioned in the skimpy brochure I'd been given.

"Will you get in trouble?" Nione asked.

"Will you?"

She shook her head before scampering to the airlock leading to the main building. I decided I could like Nione. She didn't talk much and wasn't as obnoxious as most children I'd encountered. I touched a pink flower with one finger before leaving to suit up again. The bush rustled. A single note floated on the air.

I'd been on Eden only a week when I was first attacked.

I was trudging up the trail to the grain warehouses, laser torch in hand. I stepped onto the bare strip of dirt between jungle and forest. Ants boiled from the shrubs on the up-hill side. I froze, one foot poised above ground that heaved and twitched as the insects plowed through the loose soil. I'd never seen so many in one place. They swarmed around my legs, climbing up to my knees. I set my foot down. Bodies popped and crunched. The swarm changed direction, circling around me and the dead ants.

They stopped moving all at once, as if someone flipped a switch. Antennae flickered. I stood in the middle of a rippling sea of red bodies. Thousands of beady little bug eyes bored into me, as if sensing me for the first time.

I swallowed a knot of sudden apprehension. I sensed a vast intelligence studying me like I'd studied these ants. I backed a step, tiny bodies crunching under my boots. My thumb rested on the trigger for the laser torch. I wondered if it had enough power to burn a path back to the airlock.

The ants tumbled forward, like a wave washing toward my feet. I hit the trigger, scrambling backward toward the dubious safety of the greenhouse. Their jaws clicked as they advanced. I burned the front ones, but the rest kept coming. The press of their bodies covered the blackened corpses with a tide of red.

Something stung my shin, right above my boot. I glanced down. A knot of red bodies clung to my suit, jaws working at a hole in the carbonite.

Their jaws snipped through the toughest fabric we had. I stomped my leg, trying to shake them off. They clung tighter, never even pausing in their chewing. One wriggled inside. I screamed as its jaws clamped onto my leg. I swept the laser torch perilously close to my foot as I burned the ants off. I slapped at the one inside, feeling it crunch under my glove.

The swarm boiled out of the forest after me. I cranked the power on the laser torch. It did little good. The things just kept coming. The laser torch sputtered, it's power drained. I threw it into the heaving mass. It disappeared under their squirming bodies and flashing jaws.

I ran for the airlock. Ants crunched under every bootstep. They climbed my back, chewing their way through the tubing. They severed the oxygen feed to my helmet. I couldn't breathe. I reached for the release catch. A knot of red ants landed on my face mask. I swiped at them with one gloved hand, crushing them into pulp. I couldn't take the helmet off, but I couldn't breathe with it on. I staggered. The mass of ants under foot made the trail slippery, treacherous. If I fell, they'd devour me.

Several ants crawled inside my suit. Their bites burned like acid. My lungs ached for air. I was too far from the airlock. Ants swarmed over my head, their feet scratching at the thin layer of protection keeping me from their snicking jaws.

I stumbled, falling to my knees. I couldn't reach the emergency com button. I was going to die under the swarm of ants on a planet supposed to be free of peril. I screamed in rage as I smashed ants with my heavy gloves.

They drew back. I stopped, hands poised over a suddenly empty patch of ground. The ants milled around the edge of the forest, a red tide shifting restlessly. I popped the latch on my helmet, drawing in deep breaths of air. Drifts of yellow powder poured from the jungle. A swarm of white flyers spiraled through it. I swear they directed the pollen onto the boiling mass of ants. I coughed on a lungful, feeling it burn in my chest.

The ants retreated into the shelter of the forest. The flyers circled. Yellow pollen fell like rain. Leaves rustled despite the lack of breeze. I crouched in the barren strip between the two forces. Sweat dripped from my nose.

The sun beat down. The flyers drifted into the jungle canopy, wings fluttering like scraps of paper. My nose itched. I lifted a glove to scratch, but stopped when I saw the smears of greenish body fluids from the smashed ants. I didn't want that on my unprotected face.

I got to my feet. Every bite burned with the ants' venom. I had to treat them soon. I limped toward the safety of the greenhouse.

I only made it two steps before the forest growth started quivering. Ants, more than before, boiled from the trees, launching themselves into the jungle. Yellow pollen erupted in clouds from the jungle plants. White flyers exploded from vines, swirling over the red mass of ants. I tucked my face into the crook of my elbow in a vain attempt to filter my breath.

I ran for the airlock. Ants smashed under my feet. Flyers tangled in my hair. Yellow pollen coated everything with a slick powder. I slid and staggered through the mess. My legs burned from bites. A flyer landed on my arm, extending a long stinger from its abdomen. I knocked it away. The ants boiled over it, burying it under a flood of red bodies and wicked pincers.

I tumbled to the ground, tripping over something. I rolled through the mass of ants, staggering to my feet as quickly as I could. Not fast enough to avoid several bites to my unprotected face.

Something pierced my neck. It felt like a lance of fire from the laser torch. I slapped a hand over the pain. Broken wings fluttered away. My hand was smeared with blue fluid.

I crunched through a tangled knot of ants and flyers. Pollen coated everything with yellow. I staggered, trying to keep to my feet despite a sudden attack of dizziness. More flyers swarmed around me. I swatted blindly, my gaze fixed on the promised safety of the airlock. Only a dozen more steps.

A wave of ants poured over my feet, surging up to my knees. I kicked and stomped. I was not going to die on Eden, killed by ants and moths. I staggered, falling to the side.

The airlock door cycled. Two figures in white suits stepped out. Fire blossomed from nozzles in their hands, sweeping the path clear of insects. The ants retreated into the undergrowth. The flyers spiraled into the air. I breathed in pollen and coughed.

The lead figure crouched beside me, flames pointed into the forest where the ants lurked. I caught sight of Brun's frown through his face mask. "Should have left your mask on."

"Couldn't. They cut the oxygen." I fumbled the words through swollen, numb lips.

"Never seen a swarm this bad." Brun clicked off the fire before slinging the flamethrower over his shoulder. The second person kept sweeping flames around us, driving the insects back.

Brun reached for my arm. He pulled me to my feet. I had to lean on him. My legs were swollen and aching with the ants' poison. The moth sting on my neck burned and throbbed. We limped to the airlock, guarded by the one thing the insects seemed to fear: Fire.

Brun paused only long enough to strip off the protective suit. I sagged against the wall. Poison slipped through my body. Strange burning triggered muscle twitches. The taste of overripe fruit filled my mouth. Halos of bluish light flickered around the wiring conduits.

"Are you listening?" Brun leaned over me. The brush of his hand on my arm sent surges of electricity sizzling over my skin. Numbness spread behind the electric shocks.

I mumbled. My tongue and lips were too swollen to form words.

"Infirmary, now."

I swayed in his hold. His assistant grabbed my other side. The ants and flyers smashed themselves against the glass walls of the greenhouse. The docile plants we'd brought with us wilted, their leaves streaked with brown. The plants outside, lush and green, whipped branches and vines though the air was still.

Brun paused at the door. The tunnel stretched to the main building, walls intact, but the floor bulged as the ground beneath heaved.

"Ants?" the assistant asked. I'd never learned his name, never bothered to care.

Brun shrugged. "It's not safe in the greenhouses. We have to chance it."

A vine slapped the roof behind us. The unbreakable glass pane shattered. Shards rained over the dying off-world plants. The jungle vines slithered inside, vines twisting as they sprouted new leaves and coiled tendrils. A swarm of white winged flyers fluttered through the hole.

"Move it!" Brun shoved me through the door into the tunnel.

Ants boiled up between the floor plates, filling the tunnel. They crawled over us, as if we didn't matter. They filled the doorway into the greenhouse. The bushes whipped their branches wildly outside, flinging thorns at the sides of the tunnel and the greenhouse. The metal frame of the building screeched as it gave way under the assault of plants and insects. I stared over my shoulder as my feet fumbled toward the main building. The greenhouse collapsed. Vines trailed every direction, burying it in moments. Ants climbed the vines, blurs of red that left dead black spots behind where they bit the fleshy stems.

"Fighting," I managed.

"The ants and moths, I know," Brun hurried us through the airlock into the main building.

I shook my head. "Plants. They know."

He stopped, staring behind at the destruction. A cloud of yellow blocked the windows. "The plants are sentient?"

I closed my itching eyes and nodded. Their poison spread through my tissues, ant bite fighting moth sting. And in my head, thoughts not my own fought for dominance. No words, plants didn't need them.

The ceiling panes of the atrium imploded with a thunderous crash. Screams filled the hallways, followed by clouds of yellow pollen.

Brun dropped my arm, running for the center. His assistant paused only a moment before abandoning me, too.

I tottered on shaky legs. The jungle fought the forest. We were caught in the middle. We were a minor nuisance. They lanced our building as if it were a boil full of pus. I heard them in my head. I choked on air full of dust and pollen. More walls collapsed. Vines twined through any opening. Moths fluttered. Ants flooded through cracked floors. I stumbled forward, not sure where I headed, only that I had to keep moving.

"Talia? What happened?" Nione appeared from a shattered doorway. She clung to my hand. Her face swelled from a sting, angry welts stretched under her skin.

"Attack." I swayed.

"Who?" She swung her head frantically searching.

"Them." I pointed at a swarm of moths fighting ants. "And them." I stomped on a plant sprouting up through the floor.

"Don't!"

Her sharp tone stopped me, foot raised over the seedling. I shuffled back a step. The seedling was a jungle tree, already knee-high and growing fast. I rubbed my swollen eyes that didn't see right. Nione's skin was turning green where the poison streaked. Tiny swirls of vines twined through her hair. Half of me rejoiced at the sight, the other half snarled in anger. No, not me, the poisons inside me. The human piece of me whimpered in terror.

White wings fluttered overhead. Nione spread her arms wide, welcoming them. I shifted back, afraid of their stings. They ignored me, moving toward the sounds of screams coming from a room ahead.

I staggered up the hall, unsure where I headed, only that I had to keep moving. Nione skipped at my heels. Moths danced behind her. Pollen filled the air with yellow. Lights exploded as power surged and pulsed. Ceilings smashed open as vines pulled them apart. Floors cracked and bulged from the ants and roots surging beneath. Bodies sprawled in the rubble, swollen and disfigured by stings and bites. I stepped over them with care. My balance was off, my head swollen and spinning.

We reached the communications room. I stopped in the entrance, swaying as I fought to stay on my feet. Roots tangled through the power conduits. A frond from a tree branch dangled from a crack in the roof. Nione's father, the governor, stood in the center surrounded by smashed and broken equipment. He looked up from the mess at his feet. His eyes were wild.

"We have to report. Someone attacked us." He spread his hands through the yellow dust that powdered every surface.

"Not someone," I said, my voice cracking and hoarse. "The plants."

"Plants don't attack. Plants can't think."

"These do." The two factions pressed on my mind, filling my thoughts with growth. The jungle was winning. The forest retreating. For now.

The governor lifted one hand in a futile gesture. Bites and stings marked his flesh. "We failed. I failed. The colonists will die." He closed his eyes.

I reached for his hand, needing the human contact to keep hold of my own humanity. The remnant of myself clung to a single thought. The colonists would arrive soon. They had to be warned away. They had to be saved.

I dug in the twisted storage cabinets, pawing through the ruined equipment despite the seeping wounds on my hands. The jungle throbbed in my head, demanding my surrender. I ignored it, like I did people most of the time. The demand faded.

The governor stood in the center of the room, face slack. His eyes were empty now. Nione danced with the moths around him, more plant than human now. The poison had changed her.

It changed me. Patches of green marked my skin. But patches of brown sprouted, too, bark from the forest where the ants had left their marks. I shifted smashed electrical boards. Something collapsed in the atrium. No one screamed, not anymore. I pulled a case from the back of the storage cubby. I flipped open the latches. The emergency beacon inside was cushioned in foam, still in one piece. I turned it on just to be sure. The colonists had to be warned. They had to be saved. I packed the beacon back in the case.

"We should go." I hefted the case. Where would be safe? Not this building. Another crash sounded from down the hall. The jungle plants tore the human construct apart, piece by piece.

The governor, I couldn't remember his name, struggled to fit words together. "Shelter. By the landing pad."

I shifted the beacon to one hand, taking his in my other. The emergency shelter would be small enough that maybe the jungle hadn't noticed. It would be stocked with food, water, the basics. We could wait there, leave the beacon listening for the colony ship.

The man stumbled beside me. Nione skipped in circles around us, singing wordless songs to the white-winged creatures dancing around her head.

"Eden control? Please answer."

I scrambled out of the hammock I'd strung between two trunks. The beacon crackled with static. Had I imagined the voices?

"Eden control, please come in."

I knelt on the earth between the massive trees. I flipped a switch on the beacon. "Hello?"

"Is this Eden? What happened? We can't get a reading on you."

I grimaced. The colony building and greenhouses were gone, utterly destroyed by the plants. The landing pad suffered the same fate. The emergency shelter stood at an angle, half buried in dirt but still accessible. Five of us survived. The governor, I'd dubbed him Sam, had completely lost his mind. He followed me like a puppy, digging in the dirt and singing nursery rhymes to himself.

Nione and two younger staff had become hands for the jungle. Their skin was green, more plant than animal. Their hair turned to coils of vine. They watched me sometimes, standing for hours, just staring. They didn't speak to me. They weren't who they had been, they'd changed too much.

I caught glimpses of others sometimes in the leaves of the canopy and between the massive trunks, but they weren't human. They'd never been human. The plants learned, copying our form and the ability to move untethered to the soil. The jungle had spread up the hill where the colony greenhouses once stood.

I'd checked there once. A few imported plants thrived, most were dead. The jungle insects fluttered over them constantly. I wouldn't be surprised if the jungle figured out how to incorporate watermelons and tomatoes into its arsenal. I didn't dare eat the fruit I found on the peach tree. It was deformed, like the tree, changed by Eden's touch.

"Are you there?"

"You have to go back. Don't land."

Static crackled between us for a long moment.

"What happened?"

"The plants, they're sentient. They attacked. Wiped out the colony."

"We'll send a shuttle to pick you up."

"No." My denial was quick and certain. I rubbed a bark patch on my arm. Eden had tainted us. And if Eden's rulers got loose among the docile plants of other worlds? Humans didn't stand a chance. "Put Eden under quarantine. Don't let anyone land here, ever. Set up warning beacons. Tell them its plague or radiation or whatever. Just don't let anyone land here. And don't ever, ever let anything leave."

"Explain it to me."

I did, all of it. I hoped they'd listen. I hoped Eden would be banned from contact. All it would take was one seed, one plant. I hoped whoever was in command of the colony ship would listen and believe.

The plants had our technology. They'd figure it out eventually. Humanity had to be prepared for when the plants moved in.

METAMORPHOSIS

"Dr. Evans, step back from the edge. Please, stay on the path."

Dr. Evans, Stephanie to her friends, moved back to the center of the path. "Why?"

Tembly, the guide, hitched his pack higher over his shoulder. "It's safe, treated to repel the native species. Keep on the path until we reach camp."

"Why is the camp so far from the landing site?" Kelly planted his fist in his back, grimacing as he stretched.

"You spend too much time at your desk. It's only a pleasant hike. Wait until we get to the field sites tomorrow." Buca pushed past Kelly, sidling next to Tembly. "I hear the river bottoms are the best place to set up camera traps."

"Depends what you want to photograph." Tembly turned his back. "We'd best move it. Don't want to be out on the trails after dark. Fairies emerge at dusk."

"Fairies?" Stephanie quickened her pace.

"Nicknamed by the first explorers. They never got close. Or they wouldn't have made it back to base to report. This world," Tembly waved his hand at the lush greenery looming over the dirt path, "is deceptive. Beautiful but deadly, especially for the unwary. And the unfit." He shot a glance at the panting Kelly.

"We were told Fistora was mostly plant life, very few animal types discovered, and those are mostly insects. How dangerous can it be?"

Stephanie frowned at the flowers lining the path, fleshy yellow blooms larger than her head.

"It's true the only large animals live in the oceans, but don't let insects fool you. I've seen some crawlers six feet long and covered in poison spines. They have a taste for meat. Watch your step and stick to the paths if you want to survive. The fairies may be only the larval stage, but they are deadly."

"And the landing site? Why on the ridge top?"

Tembly paused to let Kelly and Buca catch up. "Flat hard surface. It's easier to keep it free of tangler vines. And before you ask, the camp is located near the river because of access to running water and the grove of kisfar trees. Their sap repels most insects. Easier to keep camp safe."

Tembly set a fast pace down the hill. Buca and Stephanie stuck to his heels. Kelly fell further behind, his breath heavy and his face red as he panted.

Tembly stopped at a wide spot on the path, glaring impatiently at the struggling Kelly. "Don't touch that," he shouted as Kelly reached to brush a dangling plant from his face. The guide dropped his pack, racing back along the trail.

The warning came too late. Kelly's hand brushed the vine. It snapped into a coil, wrapping around his wrist. He screamed as the vine retracted, pulling him into the trees. Tembly leapt, grabbing the heavy man's legs. They both disappeared into the overhanging foliage. The branches thrashed. Mangled leaves drifted to the path.

"He wasn't kidding, was he?" Buca stared at the violent shrubbery.

The dense jungle lining the path shivered. Something in the bushes cheeped, waking a chorus of the sounds from all around.

"Ouch." Stephanie slapped her arm. A tiny, glowing form fluttered to the ground, wings crushed. The flicker of light flared and died along with the creature. Stephanie squatted.

"What's that?" Buca asked, bending over her.

"It bit me." She picked up the tiny carcass. "I think it's a fairy."

The trees overhead shivered. The cheeping changed to a high keening. Clouds of glowing creatures fluttered free of the bushes, glowing in all colors of the rainbow. Stephanie smiled in delight.

Until they began to feed.

She screamed, dropping the broken body to the path. She flailed her arms at the swarm of tiny creatures. Her skin was dotted with blood from bites. Her face swelled from their venom. Buca retreated, out of reach of her furiously swinging arms. The swarm showed no interest in him.

Tembly dropped from the tree overhead, landing on the path with a grunt. His clothes were streaked and stained with sticky sap the color of dried blood. Welts crossed the bare skin of his neck and arms. He took one look at the attacking swarm of fairies. "Get to camp! Run!"

He pushed Buca into motion.

Buca planted his feet. "What about Stephanie? And Kelly? Where's he?"

"Kelly's a goner. Do you want to join him? If you can't get to the kisfar trees, nothing can save you. I'll do what I can for Dr. Evans." Tembly shoved Buca into motion.

Buca didn't notice the fairy under his feet as he took off down the trail.

The fairies noticed. The swarm split, both halves keening in shrill voices that echoed through the jungle.

Tembly swore as he grabbed Stephanie's wrist. Her skin was puffy and red. Black streaks spread from multiple bite wounds. Even if they reached the safety of the camp, she would probably die. He jerked her into a run after Buca.

The fairies retreated to a cloud over Stephanie's head, their piercing shrieks blending into a deafening note.

Tembly glanced at the cloud. "Faster," he shouted to Buca. "Keep clear of the trees. Stay on the path!"

Something crashed through the bushes behind them. Buca glanced over his shoulder. He tripped and sprawled on the path.

"Get up!" Tembly slowed, reaching for the other man's hand.

Large white creatures crashed from the jungle, stamping broad feet on the path. They might have been unicorns, if unicorns were four feet high, eight-legged, built like mobile battering rams, sprouted multiple horns, and looked furious enough to destroy anything too stupid to get out of their way.

"What are those?" Buca asked.

"Fairies halfway to adult form. Get up!"

"And go where? We're surrounded." Buca rose to his feet, backing to where Tembly held Stephanie. She moaned, her face swollen almost beyond recognition. A web of black spread under her skin from the hundreds of tiny bites.

The unicorns stamped feet and tossed their spiked heads.

Tembly crossed himself. "If you have a god, you had better make peace. They've called in the next stage."

Fire exploded in the trees shading the path. Giant flowers shriveled into dried crisps. A blast of hot, dry air slammed into the three humans. The unicorns backed away, still blocking the retreat.

Buca looked up at the sound of giant wings whumping in the air. A dragon, twenty feet of claws, fire, and attitude, dropped onto the trail beside them. It opened a mouth lined with massive fangs, then roared. The dragon snapped forward. Stephanie's head and torso disappeared into its maw.

All color drained from Buca's face. "Shoot it or something," he begged.

"And bring down the wrath of the adults? She killed one of their spawn. They're very protective of their young. It may leave us alone. Don't make any sudden moves."

Flames crackled in the jungle canopy as the dragon swallowed Stephanie. It stretched its neck, lowering its head to the two men. Hot breath, stinking of charred meat, washed over them as it exhaled through wide nostrils.

Buca squeezed his eyes closed as the thing sniffed him, head to foot. It stopped near his shoe, whuffling as it drew in a deep breath. It roared in anger. Buca lifted his foot to find a tiny carcass smashed across the waffle pattern of his boots. "Oh, sh—"

The dragon's mouth snapped closed. It swallowed Buca, blood dripping from its scaled lip.

Tembly stood very still.

The dragon snorted, dismissing him. It clapped its wings, shooting into the sky. The unicorns melted back into the foliage. The cloud of fairies dispersed.

Tembly released his breath. He surveyed the blood spattered trail. They never listened to him. "Damn scientists," he muttered as he headed for the base camp. The paperwork was going to take him hours.

The Angels of
Mestora

"What's the reason for your visit to Mestora?" The custom agent gave Carver a sideways look through her thick lashes.

"Looking for work," he answered. The woman was pretty, but she was no Jenn. He'd come here to forget Jenn and her mocking laugh as she told Carver she was engaged to safe, stodgy Edmund. Mestora was the first world that popped up on the travel board, the first destination he could afford. He'd run from the safe inner worlds to the frontier to forget golden-haired Jenn. He thought she loved him.

The custom agent frowned. "You aren't an angel hunter, are you?"

"What?" He stared in confusion.

She shoved his ID chip into the reader, her face twisted into a scowl. "All the young, good-looking ones come to find the angels. None of them ever come back." She slapped Mestora's imprint on his chip with a vicious twist. "Next!" She glared past him at the next person in line.

Her face softened into a welcoming smile as he shuffled into the terminal.

He found a map near the exit. Mestora was only recently settled. The port was the only city of any size. But Carver didn't want a city. He wanted somewhere he could find a job doing hard labor, something physical, something that would leave him so exhausted at night that he would sleep without any dreams of Jenn and the future he thought was his. Jenn wanted Edmund and his predictable, and sizable, income. She didn't want

Carver and his itch to explore or his lack of marketable skills in the higher income brackets.

"You fresh in?"

He looked over at the stranger. The man looked rough around the edges, with a weather-beaten face and dusty clothes. He dressed for utility, not fashion. Refreshing change, Carver thought cynically. "Right off the ship."

"If you're looking for work, I'm hiring. You ever worked range animals?"

"No, sir, but I did do a stint at a nature park."

The man flicked a measuring glance over Carver's outfit. "What world are you coming from?"

"Dion."

"Tame and predictable, but you look young enough. I can't fault you for that. You'll toughen up fast enough or you'll go home." The man extended his hand. "Name's Zeke. I've got a spread out near Leaper's Grove. I'm looking for ranch hands. It's hard work, but the pay is decent."

Carver took the man's hand. It was calloused and rough. "I'm not afraid of work, sir."

"Good. Be at the ranch house day after tomorrow to start." Zeke turned to leave.

"Sir," Carver called him back.

"Just ask at Arlene's. She runs a hostel in Leaper's Grove. She can direct you to my place."

"It's not that," Carver answered, hesitating.

Zeke waited, tapping his finger impatiently on his belt buckle.

"What are angel hunters?" Carver blurted it out. "The custom agent said something about it, but I've never heard of angels here." He let his voice trail off.

Zeke's answer came in a tight, angry voice. "You leave them angels alone. Too many good men chasing night visions they will never catch. Too many lost. You start looking for angels, you won't be working for me."

Carver took a step back. "I'm sorry. I just didn't know."

"You leave them be. You hear me? You stay out of the desert." Zeke slapped one hand on his thigh, then blew out the rest of his anger. His next comment was milder, gentler. "You work hard and you keep your nose clean and in a few years, you might have enough saved up to get your own spread. Whatever you're running from, don't make the mistake of running to the angels. They're a lie."

"I hear you," Carver said. He'd touched a nerve in Zeke.

"Take some time to see things," Zeke continued. "I'm starting shifts in two days. Be there if you want a chance at a decent future."

This time, Carver let the man walk away. He watched the older man's straight back and slim shoulders until he disappeared into the crowded terminal. He turned to the map once again. Leaper's Grove was out on the northeast end of the settled area. Desert dunes rolled away beyond to the edge of the map. A few isolated fields showed green against the native brownish red and pink. Carver touched the marker for Leaper's Grove. New world, new job, new life. One without Jenn.

He slouched away from the terminal doors. A lonely life without her smile, but that wasn't his any more even if he'd stayed on Dion.

The door to the common house slammed open. Sunlight poured inside, outlining a wild figure standing in the opening. Carver looked up from his lunch at the sudden silence.

Arlene, the owner and manager of the common house, slapped her rag onto the counter. "You know you aren't welcome here, Matilda. Out, get out now." She bustled from behind the counter, tall and sturdy and sensible.

The wild woman in the doorway stepped inside, sniffing long and deep. "I won't take much, Arlene, just enough water to fill my bottles. Then I'll be off again." She rattled as she strode across the floor. Bags and bottles and other assorted containers dangled from her belt and a bandolier across her flat chest. Her hair twisted and rose in a crazy mass of tangles above her sharp face.

Arlene stepped in front of Matilda. "I said, 'Out.' Now." She planted meaty fists on her generous hips.

Matilda stopped abruptly. Her bottles smacked together in a dying clatter. "First law of settlement. You got to give me water."

Arlene's face twisted into a pained grimace. "Out back. You can use the tap."

Matilda waited, standing immovable as a stone until Arlene shifted toward her counter and waiting customers. Then, with wild hair waving like a flag, Matilda marched across the floor toward the back door. She stopped one step inside, turning on her heel to fix her gaze on Carver. "You're new."

Carver shifted on his chair, uncomfortable under the crazy woman's scrutiny and the sudden silence of the room. "Yes." He left it bald, unadorned with explanation.

"You'll come looking for me before the week's out, when you hear them sing." Matilda's pale eyes bored into him, steel-cold. Her voice was matter-of-fact, stating a truth that only she knew. "Don't answer the call before you talk with me." She was gone in a whirl of ragged skirts and clattering bottles before Carver could respond.

The common room came alive, as if the customers had remembered how to breathe again. Whispers circled and built among the handful of people.

"You aren't going off angel hunting, are you?" Arlene's words stung, like a slap. She towered over Carver.

"Wasn't planning on it." Carver tried to smile, to make Matilda's comment into a joke. But something lingered from her look, a cold certainty that squeezed his lungs until the room seemed small and airless. Somewhere, in his heart, the desire to hear the winds sing across moonlit dunes of red sand woke with a fierce hunger he'd never experienced in his life. Not even with Jenn.

Arlene studied him a moment longer, accusation still lurking in her piggish eyes. "I thought you said Zeke was hiring you. Tomorrow morning. Be at the depot stop by first light if you want that job. There's a truckload of workers headed out to his spread." She turned away with a judgmental sniff.

"I'll be there," Carver said.

Arlene waved one hand dismissively, as if to say Carver would be out hunting angels instead.

Morning crept slowly into Leaper's Grove. Carver waited under the bedraggled stand of trees that gave the town its name. A half-dozen others waited as well. The other workers said jobs were scarce, so when a plum as ripe as Zeke's ranch came looking for helpers, you jumped. If Zeke liked the way you handled yourself, he might even offer work for the whole season and maybe through the whole year. The others whispered of opportunity and settled life. Carver found himself staring off to the north, toward the sands.

The sky overhead was deep violet in the lingering night, punctuated by bright dots of stars in unfamiliar constellations. A soft breeze, cool in the summer dawn, rustled the leaves on the trees. The sands lay beyond the fields on the edge of the town. He only caught a glimpse from the copse of trees, a smudge of pinkish-red on the horizon. Wild hedgerows bordered the fields, a flimsy barrier against the native plants that clung tenaciously to the restless dunes.

The soft conversation of the other drifters faded as Carver focused on the sands. What were the angels? Matilda's words haunted him like the half-forgotten scent of flowers in Jenn's perfume. He closed his eyes as the memories rose unbidden.

Jenn's face, so beautiful with sculpted cheekbones, wide eyes, full lips, was twisted in an ugly mocking sneer. "You'll never amount to much, Gentry Carver, you'll never provide me the life I want. The life of luxury I deserve. It was fun, for a while, but I'm ready for better things."

A sweet melody crept across his hearing, twisting through her harsh parting words, faint and distant. He stilled, closing his heart on Jenn's betrayal. The sound teased him with its far away echo, a mere sliver of a song that shivered up and down an alien scale.

"I said, are you coming?"

A hand jostled Carver's elbow. He blinked away the last trace of music.

The foreman from Zeke's spread watched him with a sour expression. "You hear them singing? Angel touched." He spat on the ground. "You won't be worth much out on the hills, then."

"No," Carver shook his head, trying to banish the siren song. "I can work. I want this."

The man studied him with hard eyes. "Full moon is in five days. You last past that and I'll consider keeping you longer. Get in the truck with the others."

Carver scrambled into the open back and found a spot to sit. The stars faded into sunrise as they rumbled out of town. Carver craned his head for a glimpse of the alien sands as they rounded a curve beyond the trees.

"You crazy, man," one of the other drifters spoke to Carver. "You invited them angels to sing you onto the desert. You crazy as her." he stabbed a finger over the side to where Matilda stood in silhouette on a rise facing the drifting sands. Her ragged skirts swirled in the dawn breeze. A tangle of wild hair blazed with glory as the first ray of sun touched her head.

"You have to want to hear them singing," another man said. "You have to want to listen. It's just a pretty noise if you don't want them inside your head. How long you been on Mestora?"

"A couple days," Carver admitted.

"Close your ears, boy, or you're gonna end up angel bait out on the sand. Don't go looking for them. Don't go hungering after their song. It's a lie. They don't offer anything but death."

Carver nodded, pretending to accept the advice, but inside, he longed to hear that sweet sound slipping around him, soothing his hurts, opening his eyes to wonder. Banishing Jenn from his memories.

Carver rubbed sore muscles. He'd spent five solid days hauling feed for the animals, stacking bales of hay, mucking out pens, working from before sunrise until long after dark. The foreman, Travis, barked every order with a hard look and a gob of spittle. Carver stole a few moments of peace on the porch of the bunkhouse, absently rubbing his shoulder while admiring the night sky.

"Beautiful, ain't it?" Jake, another one of the hands, shuffled out of the shadows. "How many of those suns have you seen up close?"

Carver shrugged. "A few."

"Me, I'm staying here. In a few years, I'll have enough to buy my own spread. Carve my corner out of the desert." Jake leaned on the railing. "Plant good Terran stock and drive out the native stuff. It's poison to the animals."

Carver let a long moment of silence stretch between them. "What about the angels?"

"What about them? Once we plant and water the land, they stop singing."

"What are they?"

"Who knows? The government offered a bounty a few years back, but when people started disappearing into the deserts, they stopped. A handful of people go missing every year, mostly newbies. Like you."

Carver shuffled his feet. *Newbie, yes, but crazy? No.* "What about Matilda?"

"Crazy Matilda?" Jake shook his head. "She's a wild one. Claims to have seen the angels, visited a hidden oasis out in the desert. She says they're beautiful, but won't bring one in for the bounty. She keeps looking for a partner dumb enough to follow her out there. You stay away from that one. If you want a woman, I can introduce you."

"That would be nice," Carver lied. He wanted nothing to do with women, good or otherwise.

"We'll tame the angels eventually," the man said. "But for now, it's best to not listen when they sing. Just think of something else." Jake crossed the porch and entered the bunkhouse. The door slapped closed behind him.

Carver drew in a deep breath. The familiar smell of animals and hay almost buried the teasing dry scent of sand. He closed his eyes, searching for the elusive scent of the native world under the imported smells. What could be so dangerous in listening for that trace of music in the night air? Only crazy people would wander out into the desert looking for singing angels.

The angelsong was almost unnoticeable at first. Sweet and soft, high, almost like a cricket chirping but more melodic. It weaseled into his head, growing more clear as he concentrated. A shiver of tiny bells sounded. A deep humming, like an organ, joined. The rich song rose around him in a glorious harmony.

"Hey, Carver!"

Someone jerked his arm. His eyes snapped open.

Travis held his arm in a tight grip. The foreman's face furrowed. "Angel touched. Stupid idiot. Get yourself in the bunkhouse before you disappear out there." His other arm swept toward the rolling dunes beyond the horse pasture.

"Yes, sir," Carver whispered. The foreman's voice grated on his ears after the sweet glory of the angelsong. He yearned to walk into the moonlit sands, to hear the full sweep of notes echoing in his bones. A small part of him cowered in fear at the thought, but the rest knew he'd be strong enough to walk back to civilization, away from the angels. He marched across the porch to the door of the bunkhouse.

Travis shadowed his steps. "You'd best head back to the port," he spoke as Carver's hand rested on the doorknob. "You're one of the susceptible ones. Best you leave Mestora's angels alone. You aren't suited for this world."

Carver glanced back. The desert responded to the sweet golden light of Mestora's moon. Beams shivered across the sand that drifted into the compound despite every effort to hold it back, to bury it under human soil and plants. Travis was a dull lump in that glorious brilliance.

Carver looked beyond him, where the sands lifted in veils of light along the dune crests, out where the breezes pulled the angels into song. The deep notes hummed along his bones. The melody soared beyond reach of a human throat. Other notes rang out, completing chords of intricate harmony. Carver wondered how his clumsy human skin could hold the aching beauty of the song.

"First light," Travis said, his harsh words shattering the weave of music, "first light you go back to the port. I won't have another loss on my conscience. I won't let the angels take you." He reached again for Carver's arm.

Carver jerked away from his touch. "You can't force me to go."

"I can save you from your own stupidity! Man, you are angel touched if I ever saw it. Save yourself. Go inside and shut the door. I've got sleeping pills that will drown out their song."

"You can't hear them singing, can you?" Enlightenment dawned as the angelsong rang in his mind, along his whole soul.

"I hear them, but I choose not to listen. So would you, if you don't want to die on the dunes." Travis reached again, but gently. "They're only this strong at full moon. Get past tonight and you'll be all right."

Carver closed his eyes, drinking in the song. One more moment of rapture, then he would close his ears and his mind. His heart broke at the thought of never again hearing that wondrous music. He opened his eyes then deliberately turned his back on the honeyed moonlight and the dunes. "I'm okay now," he said to Travis.

"You sure? You want the pills?"

Carver shook his head.

Travis clapped him on the shoulder. "For your own sake, Carver, get yourself off this world as fast as you can."

Carver nodded. His steps were heavy and slow as he entered the bunkhouse. All the while, the angels begged him to sing with them, to join their chorus. He shut the door on Travis' concerned face.

He moved like a sleepwalker through the room, past the group of men playing a quiet game of cards, past the one snoring softly in his bunk, past the two busily shaving. He found his bunk and dropped onto it, like a puppet whose strings have been abruptly severed. Tears gathered in his eyes. The angelsong faded, drifting away. He was unworthy, unfit to listen. Too cloddish, too lumpy. Too human.

He lay back on his bed, squeezing his eyes tight shut in a vain effort to close out the hurt and rejection.

"Carver." A thin whisper, in his mind as much as his ears. "Carver, come out. Come sing with us. Carver?"

Matilda's voice. Matilda the crazy woman. Angel touched, but not dead. Not gone. Not disappeared into the dunes although she walked out there where no other human dared.

He stirred.

The room was dark, the men asleep. How had time passed so swiftly without him noticing? Golden moonlight reached through the crack in the curtains, stained the floor, painted a road for him to follow. The angelsong whispered faintly, oh so faintly, a thin thread of melody.

Carver rose from his bed, tiptoed across the floor, eased the door open.

The summer breeze toyed with his hair as he stepped onto the porch. He drifted across the compound. A horse snorted as he passed. Grass ruffled in the breeze, dark and lifeless under the moon's touch. Earth grass, humans driving the angels out, refusing to hear their song, closing their minds against the mesmerizing beauty.

Carver reached the far edge of the pasture, hesitated beside the fence. He glanced back once, at the dark humps of human occupation.

Come. The song chimed in his head. *Leave that dullness. Experience real beauty.*

His heart raced as he ducked through the wire strands of the fence. His boots crunched onto the wild desert. He stopped, looking down at his feet. This was wrong. He would crush the life from the song, stomp it into submission. No, he did not want to destroy the glorious harmony, the delicate rhythms. He bent, yanking his boots off and freeing his feet. He left boots and socks lying on the ground just beyond the fence.

The sand was soft, smooth as silk under his bare feet. He wriggled his toes. The angelsong burst through him, an explosion of sound unlike any he had ever experienced. Tears streamed unheeded down his cheeks as he danced across the dunes and into the golden bliss of moonlight and melody.

Dust. Everything tastes of dust.

The sun beat down from a cloudless greenish-blue sky. Carver licked dry, cracked lips as he stared up at the merciless eye of flame. Where was the angelsong? Where were the soft breezes and gentle enticings? He groaned as he pushed up to sit on the shifting, restless sands. Every muscle ached, as if he had run miles in the starlit night.

He was in the bottom of a flat bowl. Dunes rose on every side, restless sand trailing from their crests. Carver stood swaying. *Which way was the ranch?* The hot sands burned his bare feet. *Where were the angels, the ones that lured me out onto the sands? Have they left me to die?*

He scrambled up the side of a dune. Wind tousled his hair, threading it through with grit. He pivoted as he searched the horizon. Nothing but pinkish sand and sky in every direction. *Which way did the wind blow?* Travis had mentioned something about prevailing winds but Carver had been too busy bucking hay to really listen. With the sun high overhead, he had no direction, no compass.

"No wonder they hate the angel hunters," he said in a parched whisper. "Stupid fools like me. Angel touched. I bet their bones are out here buried in the sands."

He stumbled down the far side of the dune, feet burning in the baked sands, body aching for water, head spinning from exhaustion, heart yearning for angels. He fell into a staggered walk, moving by instinct as the wind scoured his skin. His bare feet blistered. Pain dogged his ragged trail. He blinked as his vision blurred. His eyes were gritty, raw with sunburn and dust.

He lost his balance on the crest of a dune, tumbling down the far side in a whirl of arms and legs. He sprawled at the bottom, face down in the sand, sobbing dry tears of frustration.

"Where are you?" His shout echoed like the harsh cry of a dying animal. No, it *was* the cry of a dying animal. He dropped his head to the burning sand. He had nothing left. The sand and the sun had stolen whatever gifts the elusive angels might have given him. He would die out here, like all the other foolish humans who thought themselves worthy to sing with the angels.

Something skittered on the sands. He squinted in a vain attempt to clear his sight. Legs, multi-jointed and red like blood, twitched just beyond his hand. Four claws waved above the legs, claws that glowed like rubies. Above those, a curled tail with a barbed point. A drop glistened on the tip, yellowish and thick.

He blinked his crusted eyes. He should move, run away from the danger. This was no angel, but a devil come to torment him. The claws paused in their restless movements. They pivoted toward Carver's face, like antennae homing in on a target. The legs skittered closer. He blinked again as a round, bloated body emerged from the sand. Dark red with pink, pulsing bladders along the sides, the thin insect legs dragged it closer. The tail danced high above.

The tip of a leg touched his hand. His skin crawled at the tentative contact. He jerked his hand away, rolling back and up. The stinger lashed out and down, barely missing. He backed away as the thing crept closer.

The tail whipped out and down again. Carver shouted hoarsely as he scrambled away.

Something chittered behind him. He darted a glance behind only to see two more alien scorpions emerge.

He threw himself to the side, twisting to all fours to scramble up the dune and away from the horrors. More claws emerged from the sand in front of him, red as blood. He swerved. The scorpions hissed like boiling kettles set to explode. And over the eerie whistling he heard the faint strains of angel music.

He froze. *These horrors were angels?*

"Run, you fool!" Matilda's voice echoed from the dune to his right.

Now he was hallucinating. He had to be. Angelsong mixed with the devilish hissing and the shouting of the mad woman. He closed his eyes, wavering on his feet as the music wove its hypnotic spell.

Something slammed into him, knocking him to the side and disrupting his rapture. He spit sand from his mouth as that something clamped a hand in his shirt and hauled him up the dune. The singing changed to a frenzied squealing. Overwhelming loss filled him with despair. He'd lost the angels again.

The hand let go. Carver tumbled to the loose sand on the top of the dune. He stared below at the things skittering over the sands. At least a dozen of them fought each other, tails lashing and claws snapping at the stick-thin legs of the others. Matilda stood beside him on the dune, throwing rocks at the things. She scored a hit on a bladder. It burst, spraying yellow ichor over the ground. The other things pounced on the wounded one. Claws clacked as they snipped gobbets from its body to feed the writhing mouth tentacles.

"Move, while they're distracted," Matilda said. She grabbed his arm, dragging him with more strength than he would have guessed she had in her wiry body.

He stumbled beside her across another dune, her grip on his arm dragging him along. His chest ached with dry sobs. His ears rang with the susurrus of the ever-shifting sands.

A long shape hunched amid the dunes, rising like a whale breaching from an ocean of sand. But it wasn't moving. He blinked rapidly. His eyes weren't focusing right. It was deep red, streaked with darker markings. Stone, not sand. It was no living creature, no angel. He stumbled on loose rocks as they neared the ridge. Matilda pulled him across the sand toward a dark mouth in the side. They passed from sunlight to shade. Carver sighed in relief as his feet met the cool, stone floor of the cave.

Reflected sunlight gave them plenty of light. Rounded boulders formed a wall of sorts halfway across the space. He glimpsed the corner of a cot and a tangle of blankets behind the wall.

Matilda let go of his arm. "You'll be wanting a drink of water about now," she said as she busied herself near the wall.

His legs gave out abruptly as the floor rushed to meet him. The stone soothed his sunburned and sand-scoured cheek. But nothing would ease the ache of loss inside. He wanted the angelsong in his head, filling his soul.

"Here." Matilda's voice was harsh, rough and crude beside the remembered glory.

Her hands were gentle as they lifted his head and dribbled water in his parched mouth. He came back to himself more with each swallow. Nerves steadied. Memories receded. His hands still shook when she finished, but he was sitting on his own.

"Better?" She shifted back onto her heels. The empty cup dangled in one of her thin hands.

"Yes." His voice cracked on the simple word.

Matilda bobbed her head. The wide sun hat she wore slipped to one side. She should have been comical but something in the set of her pointed face was too serious, too knowing.

"What," he started, then cleared his throat. "What were those things?"

Matilda stood, shaking out her skirts. She was missing her clattering belt of bottles. "Angels. I thought I told you to come talk with me before you answered their call. I could have warned you."

"Those—" He searched for words, his face twisted with disgust. "Those *things* are the angels?"

"Far as I can tell." She crossed to the far side of the cave, her back to him. "Dangerous critters. They lure you in and devour you. Don't leave anything except a blood smear and even that gets licked up by the smaller ones."

"Why didn't anyone tell me? They said no one knew what the angels were, only that people disappeared. And only stupid people tried to hunt them. Why haven't you told them what the angels are?" He squeezed hands into fists. The grief of Jenn's betrayal blended with the silence from the angel voices. He wanted to scream in rage, sob until he bled out his hurt on the uncaring stone. He stared at his knuckles instead.

"I have. No one listened. I'm crazy, remember? Sun-fevered, angel-touched, crazy Matilda." She dropped his boots on the stone in front of him. "Travis brought me those, asked me to find you. Said if anyone could, it was me. He saw the angels in your eyes, said he tried to stop you."

"He tried."

Matilda's lips quirked in a surprisingly pretty smile. "He doesn't understand. He can't hear them, not like you and me. We hear with our whole heart, he only hears with his ears. It's beautiful when they sing."

"Beautiful but deadly. They would have eaten me." His eyes made it a question for her.

"They don't like stone. Or the night. They like it hot. But their song is strongest at night, under a full moon."

Carver frowned. "Why? Something doesn't make sense."

"Why does it have to make sense?" Matilda's voice was sharp. "Can't you just accept the beauty?"

The sadness in her eyes didn't match the anger in her voice. She searched his face, looking for something. He had no idea what.

"When they sang to me out there, just now, it wasn't the same. It was weak, thin. Why, when they're about to pounce, would it be softer?"

Matilda shrugged. "We're human, not native. Maybe whatever they hunt hears it the other way around."

"Or maybe the night song is their mating song." Carver stood, stepping over his boots, his bare feet whispering on the cool stone as he headed for her water cache. "Or maybe they aren't the only ones singing." His angels couldn't be hideous bladder bug beasts only out to poison and eat what they coaxed onto the dunes. They weren't sirens from the old legends, luring sailors to watery graves with their unearthly songs. They were aliens. He reached for the water. She caught his hands in hers.

"You felt it, too?" Matilda spoke low, her whole body expressing her yearning. "Something deeper, more beautiful?" Her eyes shone with excitement. She squeezed his hands until he ached to pull them free. But her elfin smile held him still. She was beautiful, in a strange alien way, a match to the angelsong's glory.

"Out there," she whispered, "in the heart of the desert. The real angels. I've been to the hidden oasis where they live. I've heard them sing."

"Why didn't you stay?" He heard his own heartbreak in his harsh cry.

Tears clung to the edges of her eyes, threatening to spill onto her cheeks. "I tried, but it wasn't just for me. I had to find the others who heard it. They weren't strong enough for the angelsong. You are. I can feel it. This time it will be different. You'll see. You can hear the angel's heart singing. You will come with me to the oasis."

He deliberately dropped her hands, put a step between them. "I should go back to Zeke's, get my gear, leave Mestora."

She snapped up to her full height, her tangle of curls framing her stern face. "But you won't. They're in your heart. You'll always long for the angels. You try to fight it and you'll die."

"I stay out here with you and I will die. I almost died today!" He stabbed his finger toward the opening of the cave.

"I'll keep you alive. I'll take you there. I'll guide you." She wrapped her fingers around his, threading them between and through. "Come with me. I can't go alone."

Her hands were warm, gentle.

"Please." Her breath brushed across his cheek. "You've never heard beauty until you hear them singing. The real angels, in the oasis. They'll sing again tonight. Come with me then."

He stared into her eyes for a long moment. The angelsong teased the edge of his hearing, a promise. He nodded once, a sharp jerk of his head. He might regret it, but Matilda's pinched face and blunt honesty were more attractive than any of Jenn's wiles. He'd follow her into hell, if it meant he could hear them sing again.

She could deliver him to the angels.

The angelsong rose in glorious choirs as they ran across the glittering sands. Matilda's silvery laugh echoed, twining and mixing with the angelsong until Carver felt his heart would burst with the beauty of it all. He followed her over the dunes, through the hollows, onward to the north through the endless shifting desert. The clinking of her bottles lent a musical note to their journey.

He paused on the crest of a tall dune, spreading his arms to the wind and moonlight, drinking in the wondrous music until it filled his whole being. Harmonies sang along his nerves. Rhythms marked time with his heartbeat. His whole body vibrated to the angelsong.

Matilda's ragged skirts swirled around her slender legs as she ran, light and swift as a gazelle. She pulled ahead, out of sight over a dune. Was she leaving him behind? The music faltered as he panicked. He threw himself down the hill and up the next one, legs stretching as he fought to keep his balance in the sands.

She waited for him. "The heart," she sang. "The angel's heart. Listen to it beat. Can you hear it, Carver?"

He reached for her hand, too overcome by the thundering notes to speak.

"Quickly!" She pulled him into a dancing run over a shivering ridge of stones. "There!" She pointed to a dune more massive than any they'd crossed, a monstrous hump of wind-teased sand. "We go inside and down, down into the angel's heart."

She laughed as they ran hand in hand across the sands. Carver felt his heart bursting with joy. How could he have ever loved Jenn? She was lumpy, cloddish in her humanity. Grasping in her neediness. Jenn was nothing next to the beautiful sprite who drew him over the sands and into the sublime strains of music.

The base of the dune was stone, cool and smooth, dark under the moon's touch. Matilda led him around the side, through the drifting sand to a wide mouth. He balked at the darkness inside.

She pulled on his hand. "We're almost there. Listen to them sing!"

The voices swelled, higher and more pure than he could believe possible. He closed his eyes to drink in the ecstasy of song.

Matilda drew him into the cave, down a sloping passage. All the while, the music built. Just when he thought it could not be more glorious, the angelsong expanded to yet more depths and heights. Tears poured from his eyes at the beauty.

Golden light glowed from a cavern ahead. Matilda's steps pattered lightly over the stone. "We're almost there! Can you feel it, Carver?"

Joy washed over and through his soul. His eyes closed as he crossed the threshold. Intricate harmonies twined around and through the melodies in an overwhelming wave. Carver dropped to his knees, basking in song.

"I brought him, another one for you." Matilda's voice slid into the music like an irritant.

Something scritched over the stone, something like multiple legs with clawed hooks instead of feet.

"Please, let me see it again." Matilda's voice dropped to a whining whisper. "Just once more. I brought him for you. Take him and give me what I need."

The angelsong faded to a cacophony of noise. The harmonies slid away. The melody was only piping whistles. Carver opened his eyes.

The tunnel opened into a large cavern. Moonbeams spilled through cracks and crevices, creating a jumble of light and shadows. Matilda stood with her back to him, facing something in a darkened corner. She pled with it in a hopeless monotone.

Long sticks shifted and clicked in the shadows. No, not sticks, legs. Impossibly long insect legs. Above those, high above, a curved tail waved a dripping stinger in hypnotic circles. Carver's gaze dropped to the stone floor as it emerged from the corner. The thing's body was wider than he was tall. Pink bladders pulsed along its side. The angelsong glimmered in his mind but his ears heard only the whistling breath of the monstrous creature.

"Devil," he whispered. Not an angel, never an angel.

"Please, just one more time. Let me see it again." Matilda shuffled forward a slow step. Her hand reached through a shaft of light. "He's there, waiting for you. Just please—"

The tail whipped forward, slashing through the shadows.

Carver lunged. His shoulder rammed into Matilda's knees, knocking her clear of the poisoned stinger. They slammed to the stone, skidding to the side.

"No!" Matilda fought him, flailing with both fists.

"It's going to eat you," he shouted as he tried to pin her down.

"It's an angel, it's going to let me in this time. I know it!" Tears streamed through the dust on her face. "The oasis is just beyond that door, the one it guards. Let me go!"

Carver squirmed around, keeping the struggling woman pinned in his arms. She was all bones and sharp elbows. He tightened his grip as he scanned the shadowed end of the cavern. He saw no door, no cavern, no gleaming oasis in the darkness.

The monster scorpion's legs probed the floor around it with delicate precision. The wide mouth on top of its body puckered and stretched while the feeder tentacles writhed around it. The bladders pulsed again.

Angelsong exploded in exultant chorus. He shivered as it sang through his body and into his soul. Matilda collapsed into a sobbing heap in his hold.

"It's a lie," he whispered as the scritch of giant legs on stone warped the glorious song into nightmare.

Carver let Matilda slide free to the stone.

His hands felt along the smoothed stone of the cavern searching for a weapon. A rock, a stick, anything that he could use to fend off the beast.

Pink bladders swelled along its side. Angelsong burst forth again in a triumphant choir. But the music was not pure, not joyous. A sickening horror crept into every chord.

"No!" His hand closed over a round object. He lifted it. A human skull grinned at him. Shreds of hair still clung to it. He shouted in disgust as he flung the thing at the monster.

He glanced down to see his feet surrounded by more bones. Several skulls mocked him. *How many had died in this beast's lair?* He bent down to reach for a femur. The long bone might prove a weapon. It was all he had.

Matilda's hands shoved him over, tumbling him toward the creature. "I brought another. Let me in. That was our bargain." Her words rang off the stone.

Carver sprawled on his back as the thing's legs rose over him. The tail shot forward.

Matilda didn't even scream as the stinger plunged into her chest. She spread her arms and welcomed it with a rapturous smile. The tail whipped back. Matilda sank to her knees, still smiling.

Carver shouted wordlessly. He swung the leg bone at the thing's legs, sweeping them to the side. The massive body crashed to the stones. The bladders bleated out air in a screaming chord. Carver covered his ears to try to block out the horrendous noise. His improvised weapon clattered to the ground.

The tail swept toward him but struck stone instead. Carver shouted and stomped his boot down on the poisoned tail. The creature screeched. Carver twisted his boot, tearing off the stinger. Yellow ooze smeared the stone.

"So beautiful," Matilda murmured as she slid to the ground.

Carver grabbed the largest bones he could find, then jumped onto the thing's body. It squealed as his weight slammed it down. Its body was spongy yet firm, like stretched rubber. An unpleasant film of mucus leaked from pores across the back. The legs scrabbled on the stone as it strove to rise. The tail whipped over his head, spraying yellow ichor everywhere. A glob landed on Carver's cheek. It burned but it also brought back the angel-song. He swayed and dropped to his knees as it swept through his mind. Golden chords and harmonies exploded in paroxysms of bliss. Tears poured across his face as a vision opened to his mind. Green trees, blue waters, fragrant blossoms, a paradise spread before him. And in the center, her hair burning golden in the sunlight, was Jenn. A smiling, welcoming Jenn. But the sky was too blue, the plants too green, and Jenn had never really loved him.

"It's a lie," Carver shouted as he plunged the bones into the gaping mouth of the giant creature. He shoved them hard, then yanked them free and smashed them again into the thing. Over and over, until the legs sprawled motionless on the stone floor and the glorious, beautiful vision faded.

His breath wheezed in and out in the silence. No, not complete silence. The wind whispered through the holes in the cavern roof, a lost and lonely sound.

Carver got slowly to his feet. He was splattered with yellow ichor. The angel lay on the stone, a lifeless hulk already collapsing into slime.

He stumbled across the cave to where Matilda curled on the ground. He knew before he touched her that she was dead, her gaze fixed on a vision only she could see, her mouth twisted in a hopeless smile.

He slid his hand over her face, closing her eyes. He squatted on his heels, surveying the cave. Tatters of clothing rested among the scattered bones, a collection of victims led here by the insidious promise of the angel-song, guided by Matilda's madness. He shook his head over the waste of it all, reaching down to unfasten the water bottles from Matilda's belt. He'd need all the water he could find if he wanted to survive.

Arlene paused while shaking out a rug as Carver appeared in the morning light. He was ragged, filthy with dust and sand. His eyes were hard, his mouth set in a grim line. He marched to the front yard of the common house then stopped, eyeing the crowd that gathered.

A long moment passed in silence broken only by the distant barking of a dog.

Carver grunted, then swung a sack from his shoulder. He untied the neck and turned it upside-down, shaking out the contents. Five of the scorpion angels slithered out to lie on the beaten dirt track. They were small, barely larger than his outstretched hand, legs curled up to their bellies in death.

The waiting crowd gasped in horror.

"What are those abominations?" Arlene finally spoke.

"Those," Carver answered, "are Mestora's angels. Those are what sing your children out of their beds. Those are what lure you into the desert. To die."

He smashed his boot onto the angels, grinding them into the dirt.

Arlene watched his act of destruction with a grim face. She raised her eyes to meet his hard gaze with her own. "You want a hot meal, a room, supplies? You just ask."

Carver followed her inside.

But he knew he wouldn't stay long. The sands and the angels already called to his soul. He longed for the clean moonlight and the glorious music. He craved their poison, craved their song echoing in his bones more than he'd ever wanted anything. Even Jenn. And he'd keep hunting the demons that posed as angels until he drew his last breath.

SMOTHERED

You are like the scent of marigolds,
chrysanthemums,
hyacinths,
You hang heavy in the air, cloying,
drowning other scents.
I am like the scent of clover,
violets,
columbine,
Subtle, complex, a scent that takes time and effort
to unfold.
You bury me under your sharp pungence.

You hate silences.
You fill them all with words,
with ramblings on anything and everything.
My words die stillborn on my tongue.
I need silence to let my thoughts unfurl,
to find my voice and speak my truths.
Your voice intrudes,
killing my thoughts under a wave of noise.
You steal my silence.

You fill every space with yourself.
Like tomato vines, like pumpkins,
like kudzu.
You spread quickly, grow lush and green,
as I wither in the shade of your presence.
I need space to slowly uncurl a single leaf.
But you grow too swiftly,
and take it all before I've even had a chance.
You smother the space I hold for myself.

I curl back into my shell,
protected in my tiny thoughts,
forever small,
forever a seed who will never germinate,
never find my space and silence.
Because you have taken it all
and left
no room
for
me.

2AM ALLERGIES

How many pills will it take?

Clarice eyed the bottle in her paw. Just an allergy pill, readily available over the counter.

But how many make a fatal dose?

She glanced at herself in the bathroom mirror. *Lumpy, bottom-heavy, definitely middle-age sag.* She was a bunny and she and Phil had done what bunnies do. All those little ones had taken a toll on her figure.

Bunnies were supposed to have big hips and heavy thighs, but not as heavy as she'd gotten. They were supposed to have lots of kids. Somebody had to stay home and raise them. Clarice was a good mom, but she also tended to eat when stressed. Which was all the time lately. Teenage rabbits, clutter everywhere, and a husband who seemed to work every chance he got. Was he avoiding her?

The pill bottle rattled in her hand.

Who will miss me?

Not Phil. He'd made it clear she wasn't good for much besides wiping sticky fingerprints off furniture, chasing little ones around, and producing more little ones. Her body was too old for the last two and the sticky fingerprints had diminished as their children grew older. Now it was clothing and books and the detritus of teenagers scattered across her furniture and floors. Which Phil expected to be kept spotless.

She was so tired of arguing with her kids and disappointing her husband.

I could divorce him.

The thought slipped in, quiet and stealthy, like the pounds on her butt and belly. Phil could deal with the bills and the laundry and the phone calls and cooking and dishes and shopping and everything else. Phil could handle the frantic phone calls from their adult children when they panicked over stupid things. Phil could make his own bed. Wash his own underwear. Clean his own dishes.

Hadn't he said Clarice was next to useless just last night? Fat old nag, that's what he called her. Three years of therapy blew up in a single minute of rage. The therapist glossed over her pain, told her she was better, convinced her she loved Phil. She loved what he'd been all those years ago. They'd both been different people then. She didn't love him now and sometimes wondered if she'd ever really loved him at all.

She'd given him everything, her whole life. What did she have left?

Who would want a fat, worn-out, useless rabbit? My ears won't even stand up straight any more. And my tail droops no matter how much I exercise.

She dropped her gaze to the pill bottle.

So easy. Just swallow a handful, fall asleep, and the pain will end. Forever.

It would be easiest for everyone if she just dropped dead. Phil could move on to someone with more energy. Someone with fewer fat rolls. Someone who laughed at his stupid jokes.

Someone who actually loves him.

Her kids would be hurt. They'd wonder if it was their fault. She didn't regret those years of endless diapers and peanut butter sandwiches. She could have done without the years of tantrums, both toddler and teenage. She did love her children, but not with the ferocity of Lydia, the tiger mom who ran the local PTA.

Dealing with them now just made her head ache. She was so tired of them, of Phil, of the clutter. Of everything.

Lydia would never push her children aside, tell them she didn't want to deal with their problems. Lydia would never shout at her children and tell them to just go away. Clarice seemed to do nothing else these days. Lydia had enough energy and enthusiasm to love everyone else's children, too. Clarice would start screaming if she was asked to read one more story to the little ones.

All I want is a day to myself, no one else to worry about. I could eat on my own schedule. And eat what I want. I could sleep when I want. And I wouldn't have to worry about snoring or disturbing anyone else. Just one day alone would be heaven.

Is there something wrong with me? I'm supposed to love them all.

Clarice squeezed her eyes shut. They burned from unwept tears and lack of sleep. Two in the morning wasn't a good time for introspection.

A curtain fluttered in the breeze from the open window. The fridge clicked on downstairs. Normal night noises.

That was part of her problem. Comfortable home, comfortable cars, comfortable lives. Where was the thrill of discovery? Where were the adventures she'd dreamed of all those long years ago? When had life turned into an endless cycle of cleaning and cooking? When had her conversations with Phil become the same wooden words spoken over forgettable dinners, inane talk about bills and when to trim the roses and what kind of carrots made the best salads?

When did I stop shivering when he kissed me?

Her marriage was habit, routine. Her life amounted to nothing much. *She* amounted to nothing much. She was defined by her roles. Mom. Wife. Nothing more. No marketable skills, nothing that said, *I'm more than these. I have hobbies and interests that have nothing to do with raising children or keeping house.* She should have taken those art classes when she had the chance. But the kids needed diapers. The dishwasher needed fixed. Her husband needed a new shirt. The list went on. They never had the money. She never had free time.

Now it looked like she never would.

Who would miss a fat old house-rabbit?

She shook pills out into her hand. Bright pink against the white and tan of her fur.

How many will it take to end the pain?

Her paw shook.

So easy.

Her gaze rose from the pills to the tired brown eyes in the mirror. Nothing there but pain. She'd had dreams once, before drudgery had murdered them. Those eyes had been bright, full of life. Now they only looked sad, dead, dull as the dust of her existence.

The bed creaked.

Her hands jerked. Pink pills spilled over the counter.

Phil shuffled into the bathroom, yawning and scratching his belly fur. "Hey, hon. You okay?" He blinked sleepy eyes.

"Just fine," she said, forcing a smile. It's what she said to everyone. "Just my allergies acting up."

Look at the Bunwells, everyone would say. *Phil and Clarice are such lucky bunnies. So happy together. So in love. Such a good marriage.*

Stupid animals had no idea what really happened in her life.

She watched Phil stumble back to the bed. He didn't know, either. She loved being a mom, didn't she? She was happy being his wife. If she said it enough, maybe she'd actually believe it.

She didn't dare tell him the truth.

I want adventure. I want to feel alive. I want to wake up with something other than a sick feeling of dread in my belly that today will be just like yesterday and the day before that and the weeks and months and years before that.

I want someone to tell me I'm beautiful.

I want to believe I'm beautiful.

I want Phil to look at me the way he looks at carrot cake.

When was the last time his eyes lit up when she walked in? When was the last time he'd held her hand just because? When was the last time he said he loved her and she felt it in her heart?

When did love die?

She picked pills off the counter. They ticked into the bottle.

How many?

She sighed as she snapped the cap in place.

One pill, for my allergies.

She stared at the single tablet in her paw. Pink against tan.

Her gaze rose once again to her mirrored image.

One pill.

And tomorrow will be another day. Followed by another day, and week, and month, and year of the same. Her ears drooped down her back.

Fat, useless, aging rabbit. Not good for anything these days. Except feeling sorry for herself.

Tears blurred her vision. She clutched the edge of the sink as the sobs rose in her throat. She tried to stifle them. Phil hated it when she cried. She had stopped trying to share her feelings with him. He wanted her to be happy and when she wasn't he went into a frenzy of irritating projects and annoying, cloying behaviors. He kept trying to fix her problems for her. She wanted to scream. But then he'd be hurt and he'd pout for days until the guilt overwhelmed her and she started apologizing.

So she tried to paste a smile over whatever pain she felt. She nodded as he talked, locking her own opinions deep inside. And slowly suffocated any emotion she might have felt. Numb was better.

But what if she said what she thought? What if she spoke her mind instead of smiling her flat plastic smile? What if she opened her heart and let all those bottled emotions flow out?

No one listens to me. I quit speaking up a long time ago. Why start now? Why not start now?

Her hand clenched around the pink pill.

What would happen? She was safe here. Phil was a good provider. She had shelter, food, comfort. She had everything with him. Didn't she?

What if she spoke her mind? What would Phil do? What if she told him she hated getting out of bed at five am to stir oatmeal in a pot for him? What if she said she wanted to sleep in and eat French pastries and fried apples for breakfast? What if she started wearing the dresses she'd always admired, the ones with all the ruffles and beads and flowing skirts? What if she started speaking in an exotic accent just because she could? What if she told her neighbor Francine that she found her collection of lawn statues an affront to nature? What if she finally told Phil and her mother that she detested blue and preferred bright yellow?

What if she took that art class and learned to paint? What if she made ugly ceramic pots and left them all over the house? What if she expressed who she really, truly was?

What if she finally allowed herself to be more than Wife and Mother, to be more than just what she did every day?

No. What if I finally allowed myself to BE Clarice? Just myself. Not someone's mother or wife or daughter or PTA volunteer or anything else. What if I were to just be me, the me I've always wanted to be?

A tiny tingle of excitement tickled her belly, the first in a long time.

I don't know who I am. Who is Clarice? It's been so long I don't know if I can remember.

She could rediscover herself. She'd explore whatever caught her fancy. She'd wear outrageous outfits until she found the ones that said, *This is me. Clarice.*

What would Phil say?

A tiny smile twitched her mouth. He'd probably wrinkle his snout, twitch his nose a couple of times, and give her a confused look.

He might laugh, his buck teeth poking through a delighted smile.

It's been a long time since we laughed together.

Her smile died abruptly. How would it feel to be silly together? They used to laugh, to tell each other stupid jokes. What would it take to fan that flame back into life?

She still loved him, somewhere under the buried emotions of years of rushing to and fro, years of barely seeing each other for weeks on end.

"Honey? You coming back to bed?" Phil's voice was gentle, thick with sleep.

"Just a minute." She sniffed. She ran a glass of water, then swallowed the pink pill.

Just one. And tomorrow, I'll start living my life as Clarice.

Maybe the young Phil she fell in love with was still in there somewhere, too. Maybe he'd look past the sagging tail and droopy ears, and tell her how lovely she looked. It would be nice to hear it again.

She could start by speaking up. Tell him what she needed to hear, tell him what she dreamed, what she wanted. Their kids were old enough to fend for themselves sometimes. Maybe she'd start tomorrow by taking a day to just do whatever she wanted. No kids. No husband. No strings.

She closed her eyes as she swallowed the pill. The heavy weight of frustration and anger slid off her shoulders.

Tomorrow was suddenly full of promises and possibilities.

How many pills will it take? I hope to never find out.

TRAINED MONKEYS

Shannon gritted her teeth, hoping her smile didn't look as forced as it felt. She held the product box next to her face. "For those rumbly tummy days, just pop a few of these and those nasty and embarrassing moments will be only a memory." She tried to freeze her pose, but drifted in the null-G.

Mark shook his head as he thumbed the camera. "Cut. Let's do that again and this time, don't sound like you're in pain. And smile, Shannon. The viewers can tell you hate this. Try to fake them out, sound like you're thrilled with the product."

"Laxative gummy bears? Seriously? What's next, the foot fungus product again? Or maybe I get to sell that horrid body spray that smells like dead lizards while floating around in my underwear, spraying it in all sorts of private places for millions of viewers to watch."

"Don't flatter yourself. The viewers don't want to see you in your underwear. They'd rather watch Olivia and Brad do that one." Mark flicked buttons on the tiny camera. "Ready, again?"

"No. I'm not doing it again. That last time was close enough and you know it. The viewers hate me. I'm only on this ship because the SA knew that their celebrity-wannabes are too stupid to know which end of a wrench to use and we're too far out for SA to hold their hands through any repairs."

"And you're an over-priced, over-educated plumber with three PhD.s. Who also has a real attitude problem and a contract to fulfill. Ready for Tummie Gummies take seven."

Shannon chucked the box at him. It spun through the air on a collision course with Mark's head. She checked her own movement by grasping the handhold on the bulkhead. "You've got six takes. I'm not doing another one. If the viewers don't like it, tough. They can vote me a different product. And if the sponsors aren't happy, I'd like to see them try to get a lawyer out here to serve me any kind of paper."

Mark batted the box of medicated gummy bears away from his face. They tumbled toward the wall. "They have laws that say they can do it virtually for anyone beyond the Moon's orbit. One more time, Shannon. Voting happens tomorrow and next week's line-up includes toilet paper and feminine products. You do this right and I'll make sure you have a good excuse not to do those two."

Shannon glared across the round pod. "Come off it, Mark. You and I are the only real astronauts on this trip. Why do we have to participate in this stupid reality show? You've got seven people who want to do it. Let them push the products."

"Because the companies paying for our trip to Ganymede won't pay if we don't play, too. The public wants the scientist and engineer to compete for the prize along with the pretty faces. The viewers may hate you, but you get lots of views."

"And I'm sure in about ten minutes they'll be enjoying this conversation and purchasing boxes of Tummie Gummies. And voting for me to showcase our lovely compostable, recyclable toilet paper next week, including demonstrations on how to properly apply it."

"We're currently on a thirty minute delay after transmission time so it will be closer to an hour from now. Gives the studio goons a chance to edit your speeches to make them even more pithy and entertaining. Did you know they've dubbed you Oscar the Grouch? Someone started a petition to have you dye your hair green." Mark grinned. "If we had hair dye on this ship, you'd be doing it. The studio owns you."

"Only until we reach Ganymede." She caught the bright pink box of laxative candy.

"Then the mining company owns you."

Shannon shrugged. "Once the drill is set up and working, I can do my research in peace. Jovian Metals doesn't care what I do as long as their drill is doing what it should be doing. Unlike the media stations and advertisement companies."

"One more take, Shannon. Ready?"

She plastered her smile across her face. "Tummie Gummies. The sweet treat for those days when tummy trouble just won't quit. They'll give you dirty squirts and make you want to wear brown pants."

"Shannon."

"Eat these tasty treats any time you're plugged up worse than—"

"Cut!"

"You're seriously not going to eat that." Linzee's voice dripped with disgust as she eyed Brad's meal packet. "Those things will kill you. Fresh is the way to go every time."

"Where are you going to get fresh on this ship?" Brad zipped open the pouch and sniffed the contents. "These are better than the backpacker's survival meals I usually get. I've been eating those for years and look at this." He thumped his chest muscles. His suit was half unfastened to allow a better view. Shannon wondered how much of their conversation was posturing for the cameras placed strategically through the living area of the ship.

"You should eat wheat grass instead. It's got every nutrient you need plus all the micronutrients. And it's tasty. It grows fast. I've got five trays of it ready to harvest and it's only been three weeks."

"I'm not a cow. I don't eat grass. I eat cows."

Shannon turned her back. Neither understood the reality of what they'd agreed to do. Despite the speed they'd picked up from the rocket boosters, it would take two months to reach Mars. But no one was getting off there. They couldn't afford to drop speed. The plan was to slingshot past the planet and pick up more speed. Ganymede was another three months past Mars. Someone was sure to go psycho long before then. Their ship was going to arrive with nothing on board but bloody corpses and a raving lunatic survivor. It would be worse than the Donner party. She tore open her own packet meal. This wasn't just a game show where they could abandon it when the going got too tough. They were going to be stuck together for a minimum of a year. Five months travel, two months to set up the base, then five months to return, at least for them. Shannon was staying at Ganymede with the drilling crew. But five months was a very long time. Linzee's wheat grass might even look tasty by the time they reached Ganymede.

The ship would have been spacious if they'd kept the crew to four, but then the company got the brilliant idea to turn it into a reality show with a big prize at the end. Instead of two trained crew and two drilling engineers, it was Mark and Shannon and seven bumbling idiots with no idea what they were doing. Shannon had read their bios just before launch, when the studio officially released them. Linzee was a stick-thin vegetarian eco-freak nutjob with the conviction that she could grow her own fresh food on the trip. She had a company backing her idea with several million dollars of equipment and support. Not that Shannon objected to fresh food; that was going to become a necessity on the long trip. She objected to Linzee. Privileged tree-huggers didn't belong on a mining expedition. Besides that, Linzee was abrasive at the best of times.

Brad was a surfer who had competed professionally until an accident tore something somewhere. Shannon hadn't cared enough to remember. Olivia was a hairdresser's model, all hair and not much else. She had the IQ of a bag of potatoes. Tina and Trish were twins, one with a degree in business administration, the other a preschool teacher. Both had major sweet cravings. They'd already eaten the candy stashed in their supplies. Kenneth was the rich son of somebody famous. He was also a jerk, but very easy on the eyes. If he took the chip off his shoulder, she might actually like him. Greg was nice, but vague and uncoordinated. He tended to break equipment just by looking at it. Trained monkeys could have replaced all of them. Gerbils would have been cuter, much better company, easier to feed, and just as effective as crew.

Shannon took her meal to the window to eat. The cabin had pseudo-gravity created by rotational inertia. Or some such thing. Shannon was a geologist specializing in water ice bodies, not a physicist. By locating the living quarters at the end of a long arm and rotating it around the main bulk of the ship, they had a semblance of gravity that helped keep down and up relative to each other. They still had to exercise, something the blond twins tended to skimp on. Linzee and Olivia went overboard trying to keep up with Brad. And they talked incessantly about it. Shannon was the one who would probably go psycho on the others long before they passed Mars. Irritating, all of them. The constant surveillance didn't help, either. At least they hadn't installed cameras in the bathroom. Turning the space program into entertainment fodder was bad enough without the entire world viewing her bodily excretions.

"Hey, Shannon?"

Not Brad and Linzee, but soft and squishy Greg. She swallowed her bite before turning to him. "Yeah?"

His face pinched with worry. "Have you seen Mark? Something's fishy in the control room."

"Did you touch anything?" She bit back her frustration. The idiots thought it was funny to mess with things. Someone probably touched something they shouldn't have, despite the warnings to leave the control room alone.

Greg shook his head. A drip of perspiration trickled along his hairline. "I heard something beeping so I stuck my head in to look. The docking hatch had red lights flashing."

She shoved what was left of her meal into the disposal, knowing that she'd be eating it again in a few weeks. Everything got recycled as much as possible. Linzee's plant gardens weren't just for show.

Greg led the way to the control room, a bubble halfway up the rotating arm. He pointed at the control panel. "See? I swear I didn't touch anything. I just looked."

Shannon slipped through the door. She had training in operations. Mark had to have a competent backup on the ship. She flipped through the status checks. Everything was operational, but the docking hatch door wasn't sealed properly. Someone had opened it fifteen minutes earlier.

Shannon resisted the impulse to hit something. "Don't those idiots take anything seriously? I told them to stay out of the docking chamber." She turned to Greg. "Someone opened the door. That's all. I just need to re-set the seal on it. Tell the others we have to have another mandatory safety instruction meeting."

"They'll hate me for it."

"Then tell them to follow the rules and I'll quit making them repeat the training." She shoved her way past Greg to the ladder that ran the length of the arm. "Mark needs to know what happened. You look in the living arm, I'll check out the airlock and storage area."

She scrambled up the ladder into the null-G central hub where they recorded the company sponsorship statements. Stupid name for a commercial, but the producers insisted. She launched herself across the space with practiced ease, catching the grab bars on the other side. A box thumped into her head. She grabbed the box of Tummie Gummies and shoved it into her pocket. Leaving things floating loose was asking for trouble.

"Mark?" Her voice echoed down the shaft that led to the docking bay and deep storage. The living quarters she'd left were flanked by Linzee's hydroponics and a science complex which included the astronomy bubble. The weight of the crew arm was counterbalanced by another arm with the docking bay and storage pods at the end. The central core of the ship was mostly empty framework with building materials for the Ganymede drilling base secured to the struts.

She swung onto the ladder. The centrifugal force increased as she climbed toward the end of the arm. This one was shorter than the living arm, providing less of a pull. No one should have been messing with the docking hatch. They had no reason to go out and only a few suits if they did.

The lights were off in the pod. A single figure was silhouetted by the flashing red lights of the docking hatch controls, unfamiliar in the bulk of a spacesuit.

"Mark?"

The figure turned toward her. "The door's jammed." Mark's voice was flat, emotionless. Shannon couldn't help the shudder that ran up her spine. "I have to clear it from outside. Help me with the helmet."

She stepped forward, reaching for the clasps. "Why are the lights out?"

His voice was muffled in the helmet. "Probably a blown fuse. The switches aren't working. I'll fix that after I get the dock working."

Shannon engaged the clasps then checked the seal. She tapped the helmet. "You're good, Mark. How's the airflow?"

"I'm in the green. Radio check." He flipped the switch with his chin. "We good?"

His voice came from the speaker on the wall, tinny and crackling with static.

"Good as ever," Shannon answered. "You're clear for the emergency hatch."

Mark stepped into the tiny alcove, thumbing the switch to close the door.

Shannon gave him a thumbs up through the small window. The lights flashed red as the emergency hatch depressurized.

"Moving outside now."

She shifted to the main docking bay window. Stars burned, bright and unwinking in the blackness beyond the open hatch. Something twisted in the open door, caught in the hinges. Shannon squinted, trying to see in the emergency light's red glow.

Mark's footsteps clanked on the hull over her head as he made his way to the hatch. The beam of his flashlight caught the object, bathing it in white light.

Shannon swallowed bile. Was that an arm stuck in the hatch? Mark tugged it free, tossing it out to float away into space.

"All clear."

She hit the button on the com. "What was it?"

He stood in the docking bay, the light from his flashlight flickering over the floor and walls. Red liquid spattered everything. He turned away to shut the outer hatch before answering. "The whole hatch needs cleaned."

"Mark, answer me. What was that?"

He turned back to her. His face blank and cold in the blue light of his helmet. His voice was flat, emotionless. "Trish."

Shannon cupped her hand over her mouth. Trish, the preschool teacher.

The inner hatch door slid open. Shannon gagged as the coppery smell of blood flowed into air system from the re-pressurized airlock.

"She got tangled in the cables. The door tore her in half."

Shannon turned her back on Mark. "I didn't need to know that. I'll get the lights working while you clean up the mess. What do we tell the others?"

"It was an accident."

Shannon stole a glance over her shoulder at Mark as he pulled off his helmet. An accident like that wasn't possible, not with the safety mechanisms and redundancy built into everything. Someone had deliberately killed Trish.

"It was an accident," Mark repeated in a cold whisper.

Linzee's screams echoed through the living quarters, yanking Shannon from sleep. She sat up, narrowly avoiding whacking her head on the bottom of the bunk over her. Half the beds were empty, but that wasn't unusual. She mumbled curses as she stumbled from the room.

The lights in the galley were on, but the rest of the living pod was dark. Another round of shrieks led her to the hydroponics pod. Linzee stood in the middle of her trays of wheat grass and sprouts. Uprooted plants lay on the floor around her feet. She stood with her hands clenched into fists at her side, her eyes squeezed shut while she screamed.

"What, Linzee?" Shannon stepped carefully over the wilting mess on the floor.

Linzee shrieked again.

Shannon slapped her.

The scream cut off. Linzee's eyes popped open. "You hit me. Why'd you hit me?"

"You were screaming. What's wrong?" Shannon tried to keep her temper in check. Linzee had taken Trish's death harder than the rest of them, including Trish's twin, Tina. But it had only been three days since the accident. They needed time for reality to sink in. They knew the risks before they signed up, at least in theory. If any of them had paid attention. At least they had started taking Shannon's safety lectures more seriously.

Mark tried to keep the accidental death off the show, but the producers insisted on including it. Ratings skyrocketed, or so they reported to the crew. At least Trish's death had upstaged the toilet paper commercial.

Linzee's lip trembled as she sucked in a breath.

Shannon raised a warning hand. "No screaming, just tell me what happened."

Linzee pointed at a mass floating in the tank of nutrient water.

Shannon squinted through the blue water. She moved a floating patch of plants to the side. Olivia's naked corpse floated face down in the tank, dark hair spread around her in a tangled mass.

"She's dead, isn't she?"

Shannon prodded Olivia's shoulder. Flaccid and cold. "What happened?"

"I don't know. I came in here and found my plants all over the floor. I got mad—"

"And pushed her into the tank?"

Linzee shook her head, her bleached hair flying around her face. "I found her like that. I swear. She was just floating in there."

"Who else was here?" Shannon reached gingerly into the tank, lifting Olivia's face from the water. A large gash across her neck gaped like a second mouth.

"Nobody was in here, except me. Maybe she slipped and fell."

Shannon let the dead girl's head slip back into the tank. "Help me push her into the composter."

Linzee wrinkled her lip. "We can't just grind her up and use her as fertilizer."

"We can't keep her in the fridge for a year, either. We don't have much of a choice. We either put her in the composter or shove her out the docking bay."

"Like Trish?" Linzee's voice rose in pitch.

Shannon grabbed her collar. "No screaming. Got that? Now help me. Pushing her into the composter is going to be a lot easier. She's dead, Linzee. We can't help her."

"We should take her back home to her family."

"We can't. Grab her shoulder."

Linzee backed away from the corpse. "I can't. I can't touch her. Not like this."

The others gathered in the doorway, drawn by Linzee's screams. All except Mark. Kenneth shoved his way into the room. He reached into the tank. Olivia's arm flopped out of the blue water at his tugging. Shannon grabbed the poor girl's other arm. The pulled her body from the tank. Blue water dripped onto the floor as they dragged her to the composter. Dead plants snagged on her bare feet.

"What happened?" Kenneth asked as Olivia disappeared into the machine.

Shannon shook her head. Where was Mark? Everyone else still breathing was standing in Linzee's destroyed garden. Tina crouched on the floor, sorting through the mess of trampled plants. Brad had his arm around Linzee. Both of them were pale and looked as if they were going to vomit. Greg sniffed and wiped his hand across his nose.

Shannon shut the lid of the composter. She had to say something, but she had no idea what to say or how to say it.

"That's two," Kenneth said. "Who's going to be next?"

"We're being safe. It shouldn't be any of us. We have to be more careful." Brad's chin quivered but his voice held steady.

Kenneth flicked a hard look at Shannon. "They weren't accidents. They were murdered. And one of us did it."

"Mark did it. I saw him leaving the pod earlier. He looked upset," Greg said.

Shannon shook her head in denial. She'd worked closely with Mark over the last year as they prepared. It couldn't be him. "Accusations aren't going to help. We've got something better." She pointed at the cameras mounted in the pod. "We contact home and ask them who did it. They're filming everything."

"Why didn't we do that with Trish?" Tina's voice was harsh.

"We did but the cameras in the docking pod were disabled when the lights were cut. We have to stick together until we get an answer." They traded suspicious glances, not reassured by Shannon's words.

Greg was the first to speak. "But one of us is a killer."

"What are we going to do, shove them out the airlock?" Tina shredded plants, methodically plucking every leaf from the fragile stems. "They deserve it after what they did to Trish."

"We have to go home." Linzee huddled next to Brad. "Just turn this ship around and take us home."

"That's not possible," Shannon said. "We have to finish the trip as scheduled."

Linzee shook her head again. "Turn it around." The shrill edge of panic sharpened her voice.

"It doesn't work that way." Shannon squeezed her hand into a fist. *Stupid trained monkeys.* None of them should have been on the ship to begin with. Two murders in a matter of days was going to push them over the edge. And where was Mark? It was his job to keep them under control. He was the captain of this expedition. "Come on. Let's go up to control and call home. Let them know what happened."

Kenneth grabbed her arm. "It takes almost twenty minutes for them to respond. What are we supposed to do?"

"Sit and wait. We'll have answers soon enough." She peeled his hand from her arm and led the way to the control room.

She stopped in the doorway, the others crowding behind her.

The room was like a scene from a bad slasher flick. Blood spattered over equipment mangled past repair. And Mark sprawled in the center of it, face-down in a pool of red.

Someone gagged behind her. She pushed them back, shoving with her body. She caught Kenneth's eye. He seemed to be handling it better than the others. "Get them back down to the galley. Everyone stays together at the table."

"Except you? How do we know you aren't the killer?" Kenneth glared.

"I saw Mark leaving Linzee's lab," Greg whispered. His face had a greenish tint.

"I didn't do it," Shannon said. "Why would I kill Mark? He's the one who knows how to fly this thing."

"That was the radio, wasn't it," Tina said, her voice flat. "Pulled out and smashed. We can't call them now."

Shannon grabbed Kenneth's shoulder, pushing him onto the ladder. "Get back to the galley and stay there. I'll see if anything still works."

"We're all dead." Panic crept into Linzee's voice. If she started screaming again, Shannon was tempted to slap her again. Hard.

Tina giggled. "One of us is a murderer," she sang. "Ashes, ashes, we all fall down." She squeezed a fistful of leaves into pulp.

"Kenneth, get them out of here. Now." Shannon's voice cracked over the group.

"Anyone hungry? I found the beef stroganoff. It's really good." Brad shuffled packets in the galley locker.

Tina rubbed her hands over her arms. Her gaze was fixed on the table though Shannon doubted she saw anything except her own thoughts. Linzee chewed her lip and fidgeted with her hair. Greg still looked green. He swallowed as the smell of reconstituted stroganoff filled the air.

"How can you eat that slop?" Linzee snapped as Brad joined them at the table.

Brad stabbed a fork into the open top of the packet. "I'm hungry."

"How can you be hungry? Especially for meat? Mark was butchered. Like a pig." Linzee's voice cracked. She stuffed her fist into her mouth to stop the flow of hysterical words. Tears dribbled over her cheeks.

"Leave him alone, Linzee. He's right. We have to take care of ourselves." The unexpected reassurance came from Kenneth. His words, though harsh, were soft with compassion. He set a bottle of water near Linzee then turned to Shannon. "What are we supposed to do now? We can't call home. We can't turn the ship around. Are we going to sit at this table staring at each other until we reach Mars?"

"Do you have any suggestions?" Shannon folded her arms.

Kenneth leaned on the table, planting his hands on the smooth surface. "We can abort at Mars."

Greg stirred. "That's another month. We'll all be dead before we can get there." He popped the top off the bottle of water then took a sip.

"They'll send someone to look for us when we don't call," Tina said.

Shannon shook her head. "Don't you understand? They can't. For all they know our ship exploded. Our signal is dead. We can't call them and they can't come looking for us. Space is just too big. We'll have to hang on until we get to Mars. It's our only option."

Tina pulled her knees up to her chin, tucking her feet onto her chair. She wrapped her arms around her legs. "We could open the hatches. It would be faster than waiting for the murderer to pick us off one at a time."

"We could figure out who killed them." Brad spoke around a mouthful of stroganoff. "We get rid of the killer and the rest of us will be safe."

Kenneth snorted. "How are you going to do that?"

Brad glared. "Did you do it, you jerk? Just because you're rich, you think you're better than us. What happened, Kenneth? Did Trish and Olivia turn you down? You killed them because they said no? Then Mark caught you so you killed him, too."

"Don't be stupid," Kenneth crossed his arms over his chest. "You're the one flirting with the girls. How do we know you didn't kill them?"

Shannon wanted to jam her fingers in her ears. Or hide in the storage pods. Mark was the people wrangler. But Mark was dead, which left her in charge. She stirred from her chair.

"Where are you going? You said we had to stay here." Brad's voice cracked angrily.

Shannon met his angry glare with one of her own. "Someone has to clean up the control room."

"I thought you did it earlier."

"I only checked the equipment. Mark's still in there, what's left of him."

Tina stirred in her chair, staring up at Shannon. "Are you going to shove him out the airlock or stick him into the recycler? Are we going to abandon him like Trish or eat him like Olivia? How are you going to hide all that blood?" Her voice dropped to a whisper.

"Shut up!" Brad shoved himself up from the table, turning on Tina. "You're loony. Completely crackers. And you're going to drive the rest of us over the cliff with you. Make her shut up." He turned to Shannon.

She shrugged. Mark was the one with the medical training. But Mark was in pieces in the control room. He wasn't going to be help for anyone. Trish was the only other one with first aid skills that were more than bandage application and aspirin dispensing.

Kenneth planted a hand on Brad's shoulder, pushing him back into his chair. "Eat your stroganoff. Greg, stay here with Brad. Tina, take Linzee to the sleeping quarters. I'll go with Shannon to the control room. If we stay in pairs, we can watch each other."

"But I saw Mark in Linzee's lab," Greg said. "He killed Olivia. He's the murderer. We're safe now because he's dead."

"Who killed him, stupid?" Brad knocked Kenneth's hand from his shoulder.

"I think we should stay together," Shannon said.

Brad turned on her. "Except for you? You spend a lot of time by yourself."

"I didn't kill anyone."

"That's just what a murderer would say," Brad said as he stabbed his fork into the stroganoff.

"We stay in pairs," Kenneth said firmly. He turned to Shannon. "I'll help you clean up the control room."

Shannon swallowed bile as she scrubbed blood off the control panel. It seeped into every crevice on the board. It was impossible to remove without bumping switches. She hesitated, the cleaning rag hovering over the engine switch. She could hit that, turn on the thrusters, burn up the rest of their fuel. They'd have no way back. And no way to get to their destination or home. She left the blood around the switches. She didn't want to end up drifting as a corpse forever. She moved on to the next patch of blood spatters.

"That's the last bit," Kenneth said as he returned from the airlock. Sending Mark's remains into space seemed more fitting. Plus, they didn't have to drag body parts past Brad or Linzee. Shannon didn't know if she could stand more of their anger or hysteria without going psycho herself. At least Kenneth was steady. His support was unexpected but very welcome.

Shannon wiped up a last smear. The room still stank of blood, but at least it wasn't obvious. The destroyed equipment wasn't so easy to hide. The radio was gone, smashed into bits. Nothing else had been touched, though. She glanced up at the camera tucked into a corner over the door. The lights on it blinked red. It was still recording, though she had no idea if it was transmitting back to Earth or if that circuit was smashed along with the voice transmission.

"We should get back to the others," Kenneth said. "Stick together as much as possible."

She wadded the rag into a ball. It didn't hide the bloodstains. "Right. One of us is a cold-blooded killer. Is it you?"

"You suspect me?"

She shrugged. "Just thought I'd ask. Give you a chance to confess."

"Is it you?"

"Why did you sign up for this show, Kenneth?"

It was his turn to shrug. "It sounded like fun. And my father told me he'd disown me if I did something so stupid. How could I pass up that opportunity?" He turned for the ladder. She followed.

"So did he?"

"Did he what?" Kenneth stopped at the bottom of the ladder.

"Your father. Did he disown you?"

"No idea. The producers dodged the lawyers he sent to drag me home."

She laid a hand on his arm, a rare gesture from her. "Thanks for your support."

He laid his hand over hers. "You're welcome."

They walked into a screaming match. Linzee and Brad stood nose to nose, fists clenched while they shouted over each other. Stroganoff spattered the walls and ceiling of the galley nook.

"Knock it off, both of you," Kenneth shouted as he pushed between them.

Shannon sidestepped the argument, glad that Kenneth had taken control. She shoved the bloody rag into the disposal while he stopped the fight. Greg sat hunched over the table, a half-eaten pouch in front of him. A forkful of food dripped sauce onto the table. Shannon planted her hands on her hips. "Where's Tina?"

Brad and Linzee turned hostile scowls on her, Greg stared down at the remains of his meal, arms wrapped tightly over his stomach.

Kenneth stepped back, imitating her stance. "You were supposed to stick together."

Linzee rolled her eyes. "She had to pee. Again. She doesn't need me to hold her hand in there and if she's alone, what could happen? She'll murder herself? She's fine."

Shannon shoved her way past them toward the head. "The last time someone went off alone, they ended up in pieces. I don't want to clean her off the walls in there."

"Chill, lady. The rest of us were in here, so unless the two of you got up to something while you were cleaning," Brad made air quotes with his fingers, "Tina's just fine."

Shannon pounded on the door of the bathroom. "Tina?"

Water splashed on the other side of the door, then shut off. The flimsy door opened. Tina glared with blood-shot eyes. "What?"

"I said she was fine." Linzee flipped her ponytail over her shoulder.

"Greg isn't," Kenneth spoke behind them.

Shannon wanted to scream obscenities until they all went away, but she throttled it back. She was senior crew with Mark gone. She turned back to the galley.

Greg sprawled on the floor, foam frothing from his mouth.

Kenneth knelt beside him, his fingers pressed to Greg's neck. "He just collapsed. I think he's dead. I can't detect a pulse."

Shannon clenched her hands into fists. "Put him in a bunk and we'll check on him in an hour." She was a scientist and engineer, not an EMT.

"Ew." Linzee shuddered. "I'm not sleeping in the same room as a dead man."

"He might not be dead yet," Shannon said. "What if he recovers? It could be epilepsy or something."

Linzee sniffed. "That's a big word for such a small brain. Did it hurt to think it?"

"Just shut up," Shannon snapped. "Brad, help move Greg. Tina, you go with them. Linzee, help me clean up the table."

"No. I'm going to check on my plants." Linzee flounced away.

Shannon snarled as she scraped a handful of stroganoff from the wall. She stopped with the food halfway to the disposal. What if Greg was poisoned? Should she keep his food, run it through her sampling equipment? Except that was packed in the back of the storage pod and she didn't have the facilities to hook it up while they were in transit. She eyed Greg's last meal. She didn't want to try keeping it in the freezer for the months it would take them to finish their trip. If they ever finished it.

She shoved the food into the disposal, then turned to the rest of the mess.

"All done," Tina announced as she joined Shannon in the galley.

Shannon wiped up a smear of sauce from the floor. "Where are the others?"

"Brad's sleeping. Kenneth went to check on Linzee."

A shiver of unease slipped down Shannon's back at the cold flippant tone of Tina's voice. Had she lost it under the strain? Shannon shifted on the floor to reach another smear. She stole a glance up at the other woman.

Tina's twisted smile was as cold as her voice. "I like you kneeling on the floor," she whispered. "Makes it easier."

Shannon shot furtive glances, looking for a weapon. Other than the rag in her hand, she had nothing. The furniture was securely bolted to the floor. Everything else was stowed in cupboards. Tina as the murderer? Not by herself, Tina wasn't strong enough to chop up Mark. Or was she? Shannon pushed herself to her feet.

Tina giggled. "I locked the bins. But you can try to grab a weapon if you want. The others were almost too easy. Especially my sister. I'm so glad I'll never have to listen to her again. Everyone thought she was so sweet because she taught little kids. She was a conniving, twisted, sick—"

"She isn't the one who murdered people." Shannon sat at the table.

Tina snorted. "She would have, if you got in her way. I just stopped her first. But Mark figured it out. He had to go."

"And Olivia?" Keep her talking and maybe Shannon could figure a way out of this. She watched the door behind Tina's shoulder. Maybe Kenneth would show up soon. The two of them could overpower Tina, save the rest. She plotted vague plans while she listened to Tina ramble.

"Olivia overheard us fighting. She was going to tell Mark."

"Why did you kill Greg?"

"Who said I did? He choked on his stroganoff."

"You're crazy." Shannon shifted in the chair. The box of Tummie Gummies in her pocket crackled.

Tina perked up. "What are you hiding?"

Shannon shoved her hand into her pocket. "Nothing."

"You're a liar. Show me what you're hiding."

"Or what? You'll slaughter me? You're going to do it anyway."

Tina stretched her lips into a smile that was half snarl. "I might let you stay alive for a while. Show me what you're hiding, Shannon."

"Nothing." Shannon deliberately crunched the wrapper on the box. She just had to string Tina along until Kenneth showed up to help. She hoped he came before Brad. But even Linzee would be preferable to the psychopath sitting across from her.

"Liar, liar, pants on fire." Tina leaned across the table to breathe in Shannon's face. "I can do that, you know. Set your pants on fire. I wonder if it will be as entertaining as the time I set a squirrel's tail on fire. It screamed for a long time."

Shannon swallowed bile. How had Tina made it past the screeners? How had she ever made it this far onto the show and on the ship?

"One last chance. Show me what you're hiding."

Shannon eased the box open. "Just a few gummy bears I've been saving."

Tina's smile shifted to her usual sweet one that hid all the insanity. "I love gummy bears."

"If I give them to you, will you promise to leave me alone? And the others?"

Tina shook her head, her blond curls bobbing. "You'll turn me in."

"How? The radio is destroyed. And we aren't stopping anywhere until we get to Ganymede. All I want to do is set up the drill. You can do what you want once we get there."

Tina giggled. "You think you're so smart. Give me the gummy bears and I'll think about it."

Shannon sighed, pretending reluctance as she pulled the Tummie Gummies from the box. They weren't much of a weapon, but they were all she could think of. She dropped the jewel-colored medicated candy on the table.

Tina snatched them up, shoving half a dozen into her mouth at once. She closed her eyes and moaned with pleasure as she chewed. "This is what I miss most, being out here. Not enough sugar. I love these things."

Shannon nudged the Tummie Gummies on the table. How many would it take? And how long? "What are you going to do to us? You can't fight all four of us all the time."

Tina swallowed. "Don't worry about Linzee. She's taking care of her plants." She giggled and popped another handful of gummies into her mouth.

Shannon wanted to be sick. Where was Kenneth? Had Tina already butchered him? And Brad, where was the beefy muscle-man when she needed him?

"Mmm. Those were stale, but that only makes them chewier. I like chewy. Give me more."

Shannon prodded the box in her pocket. It was empty. "They're gone."

"I don't believe you. Show me the package." Tina's smile disappeared.

"What really happened, Tina? With Trish." Keep her talking, give Kenneth a chance to surprise her from behind.

Tina snarled. "She always wanted to get rid of me. I just did it first. She stole everything from me. I tried out for the school play, so she did, too. And she got the part. She got everything. She stole my boyfriends in college. All of them. She wasn't supposed to be on the ship, but she slept with the producer so he let her come. She was trying to steal this from me, too." Tina twisted her hands together. "I didn't mean to open the airlock while she was tangled up in the cables. I was only trying to scare her, but my hand slipped. It was too easy. I already told you about Mark and Olivia. And now Linzee and the others."

The others? Greg was most likely dead from the poison, despite what Tina said. Had she managed to murder Brad and Kenneth, too? Shannon's finger found a last gummy bear in the bottom of the crushed box. She pulled it free and offered it to Tina. The other woman snatched it, gobbling it greedily.

Shannon pulled the pink box from her pocket and set it on the table. "You just took fifteen doses. The box has all sorts of warnings about not taking too much. It might even be a fatal dose. The cramps should be pretty strong."

Tina stopped chewing for a moment, then shrugged. She deliberately flicked the box from the table. "Don't try to scare me. It won't work." She frowned as her stomach gurgled.

"It hits hard, Tina. You'll be curled up in the bathroom, wishing you were dead. You might die in there. All by yourself, curled up around the toilet." Stall until Kenneth came back. If he was coming back.

Tina groaned, clutching her stomach.

It was Shannon's turn to lean across the table. "I poisoned you, just like you poisoned Greg."

Tina tried to laugh. It came out a strangled grunt. She clapped a hand over her mouth and bolted for the bathroom.

Kenneth slipped into the doorway as the bathroom door slid shut. "What's with Tina?"

Shannon jumped to her feet, relief flooding her system. "She's the murderer. I gave her an overdose of laxatives. She said she killed Linzee. Where's Brad?"

Kenneth laughed, a slow building of sound. He pushed her back into her seat. "Brad isn't going to be around. Plastic bags are very useful for dealing with problems like Brad. It was Tina's idea."

Shannon stared at Kenneth in shock.

He sat on the table, swinging one leg. "Tina killed Trish on accident, then came to me for help. Olivia overheard us talking and threatened to take it to Mark. We couldn't let her do that. Tina held her head under the water. I helped. Killing people is easier than I imagined it might be."

"What about the others? Why slaughter the whole crew? You aren't going to get away with any of this. You know that, don't you?"

Kenneth shrugged. His leg kept swinging, back and forth through the air. "I don't care. Everything is being recorded. Everyone in the world knows what I did. I'm famous." His leg paused as he listened to Tina's gastric distress behind the closed door of the bathroom.

"Why?"

"Why not? My father told me repeatedly that I'd never amount to anything, that I was a waste of air." He drew in a deep breath. "At least now he can't say I'm a nobody. My name will be everywhere, if it isn't already. It's all on video for everyone in the world to watch."

"What did you do to Linzee?"

"Are you sure you want to know?" He gave the camera a jaunty wave. "She's part of her ecosystem now, feeding the decomposers. And Tina is due for a trip into the septic system. Pardon me for a minute or three. It will be our turn after that. Explosive decompression shouldn't be too hard to manage. The first mass murder-suicide in space, we'll both be famous. Don't go anywhere. I'll be right back."

He strode across the room to the bathroom, forcing the door open.

Shannon threw herself at the bank of lockers, slamming them open in a frantic search for a weapon. She could make it to Ganymede by herself. Jovian Metals was sending a ship to meet them there a month after their scheduled arrival. A month to set up the base and start drilling. She could handle that much isolation. She had to stop Kenneth, though. She tugged on the drawer where the cutlery was kept. Tina had locked it, as she said. Shannon muttered curses as she scrambled for the tool drawers. She tried to ignore Tina's shrieking. She couldn't help the girl now. Besides, she was a murderer. Did she still deserve any sympathy? Shannon pawed through packets of food and water filters, dumping them onto the floor. Tina's screams cut off abruptly.

Shannon ran for the science pod. Kenneth grabbed the back of her shirt, slamming her into the wall as he spun her around to face him. Blood spattered one side of his face.

"Thanks for disabling her for me. Made it ever so much easier." His voice brushed over her face, warm breath that smelled faintly of mint.

Shannon slid her hand over the wall on either side. She had to find something soon.

Kenneth twisted his hand in her clothes. He dragged her to the middle of the living pod, to the base of the ladder that ran the length of both arms. He pushed her to the ladder. "Up, please. I'll be right behind you the whole way."

Shannon threw herself up the ladder as fast as she could go.

Kenneth's laugh trailed her. "Run all you want. This ship isn't big enough to hide you for more than a few hours. And when I flush all the air, you'll still die with me." He started up the ladder at a deliberate pace.

Shannon scrambled into the null-G pod at the center of the ship, careful to push clear so she wouldn't slip back down. She floated free of the ladder. She twisted to look behind her down the shaft. Kenneth paused to look up and laugh. A stray cable brushed over her hand. She grabbed the cable to anchor herself as she stared at the man who had slaughtered Mark and the others. An idea tugged at the edge of her mind.

Kenneth climbed steadily toward her. "Waiting for me? How sweet."

That brief moment between letting go and floating free held danger. How often had she complained to the others to watch their step and how often had they ignored her? Kenneth hadn't taken her seriously. He'd only been in the null-G pod twice before, that she knew of. Both times, he'd almost slipped back down the ladder, forgetting the pull of the centrifugal force that gave them a semblance of gravity. She hoped he'd be sloppy this time.

His hand rose over the edge of the hatch, reaching for a handhold. Nope, not sloppy. She'd have to assist him. She wrapped the cable around her wrist with one hand and grabbed onto a support strut with the other. She hoped it would give her enough leverage. She slammed her boot down onto Kenneth's hand as hard as she could.

He pulled back with a startled yelp.

She resisted the push back from her movement, the muscles in her arms screaming in protest as she slammed her other boot toward Kenneth's face. He jerked back, as she hoped he would. Not quite far enough, though. He kept his hold on the ladder. Her motion sent her floating up, away from the hatch. She snagged another looping cable, swinging herself back toward the ladder and the hatch where Kenneth tried to scramble free.

Both boots slammed into his face. His hold on the ladder slipped. He shouted wordlessly as the centrifugal forces of the spinning arm accelerated him toward the end of the ladder and the floor sixty feet below. He flailed for purchase on the ladder as he banged past. His shout ended abruptly as his head met a metal support. His body hit the floor at the bottom with a dull splat.

Shannon closed her eyes as she released her death grip on the cable. She drew in a shaky breath as she floated free. She looked at the camera mounted beside the hatch. The red light blinked steadily. She had to clear her throat twice before the words would come out.

"Trained monkeys would have made a better crew."

BLOOD SONG

Wookis! We need help to sing the blood song!"

The shout echoed through the snowy forest, shivered down the moonlit paths.

Wookis stirred, deep in his cave. He flung one giant hand to the side before huffing a clouded breath. His eyes fluttered, then closed again. The deep rumble of his snores once more filled the stone cave.

"Wookis!" The call came again, this time from multiple throats. "The solstice is upon us. The night has come. The blood song must be sung."

Wookis grunted, rolling his back to the entrance of his cave. He was tired of blood, worn from years of ritual. His breath curled the long white of his beard.

Dwarves with stubby legs and pointed caps of faded red crept from the bushes surrounding the cave. Their pointed boots left smudged impressions in the snow as they gathered near the stones marking the entrance. Tall pillars of granite, they had weathered centuries. Carvings shadowed their sides, blurred by time.

"Blood song," the dwarves whispered.

Wookis grunted as the words wormed into his consciousness.

"Blood song," they chanted.

Wookis opened his eyes. His jaws cracked in a gaping yawn. He stumbled from his cave. His hands brushed the standing stones, ragged nails traced the markings. Runes glimmered with red fire, but pale and weak. The blood song was dim in his mind.

The little men fell silent, crouching just beyond the glow. Their eyes shimmered in the dark night as they watched Wookis emerge.

"It is time," the leader whispered. "We need help to sing the blood song."

Wookis lifted his lip in a sneer, exposing his largest tusk.

The leader of the pointed caps rose to his feet. He barely reached the knees of Wookis. "The time has come. Bring forth the robe. Sing the blood song."

Dwarves scurried from the forest. A long robe dragged through the snow behind them. Red with white fur trim, blood on the snow.

Wookis crouched, let the small men clamber over his back. The red fur cloaked his hairy, twisted body. He rose to his feet. The robe swirled around him, sweeping the tiny men from their perches to tumble across the snow. They laughed as they rolled, red caps marked with white frost.

"Bring forth the sleigh!" The lead dwarf raised his hands into the air.

Hooves crunched on frozen snow. Runners hissed as they slid over the icy surface. The reindeer snorted clouds of steam into the night. Bells carved from bone added a hollow clacking.

"Blood song!" the dwarves chorused before falling silent.

Wookis shuffled forward, ponderous and slow in his massiveness. The sleigh creaked under his weight as he climbed aboard. The reindeer twitched, hooves kicking snow into spouts of glittering crystals.

"Blood song," Wookis rumbled. His shaggy head nodded. But the beat of blood moved sluggish and old, faded by years.

Pointed caps were flung into the air, then caught before the stubby dwarves clambered onto the sleigh. "Blood song," they howled together.

The whip cracked. The reindeer leapt forward. The sleigh lurched into motion.

The wild hunt raged across the snow. Wookis laughed, deep in his belly. Once a year, on the night of winter solstice, he donned his red cloak and rode on his sleigh. Once a year, the world trembled and hid. Once a year, the blood song howled forth upon the land. Once a year, a sacrifice waited in the village.

The sleigh hissed across the snow-packed road.

Golden light spilled across the snow from the open door of the church. The tall building, with pointed steeple and colored glass windows, was new.

The stone cross that marked the boundary stood proud. Its runes were deep, sharp, breathing with power.

Wookis pulled his sleigh to an abrupt stop. Reindeer pawed and stamped the icy crust of snow. The dwarves leapt from the sleigh, circling the cross, sniffing the warding magic. They howled a wordless cry to the moon, confused rage. Where was the sacrifice? Where was the blood song's power?

The red robe brushed the snow as Wookis descended from the sleigh. He towered over the dwarves. His shadow enveloped the stone cross. Still it glowed with a shimmer of blue light. Wookis flared his broad nostrils at the stench of new magic.

Villagers filed from the church, stepping carefully within the golden fingers of light.

"Blood song!" Dwarven voices howled as they capered at the feet of their master.

Wookis glowered at the villagers.

A small girl, yellow hair glowing like gold, walked toward Wookis. She held a carefully folded napkin on her outstretched hands. Something lay within the cloth.

Wookis flung his arm wide, stopping the child next to the stone cross. "I do not eat children," he growled. "Send another for the blood song."

The village priest, a new one in a long robe of white, stepped from the crowd. "We do not sing the blood song. Not here. We sing a new song."

"We demand blood!" the dwarves shouted.

The child stepped closer to Wookis. Her blue eyes were innocent, wide, and totally devoid of fear. She lifted her hands and the cloth bundle they held.

"It is a new sacrifice," the priest spoke.

Wookis hushed his dwarves with an impatient sweep on his hand. He used one jagged claw to delicately unwrap the bundle. It fell free to expose a crude man figure made of brown dough. Raisin eyes stared upwards. The thing smiled in perpetual joy.

The dwarves muttered, an angry jumble of noise.

Wookis drew the scent of the dough man into his lungs, tasted it on the frosted air. Strong spices bit his tongue, promised new pleasures, new sensations. He swiped the cookie from the child's hold and bit off the head in one quick motion.

The dwarves froze in place, eyes wide in horror. The villagers watched, silent behind their priest. The little girl smiled up at Wookis as he chewed.

Ginger and cinnamon, nutmeg and cardamom exploded in his mouth. Wookis closed his eyes and savored the newness. No tang of copper, no hot rush of blood, but instead a warmth of spice and sugar. His lips curled up at the edges. He nodded his shaggy head.

"Blood song?" the dwarves whispered.

"Gingerbread song," Wookis answered as he shared pieces of the offering. "Better than blood."

The dwarves eyed the strange offering. White sugar icing dripped like blood from the ragged edges. They tasted, then nodded. The gingerbread song was accepted.

Wookis swept his followers onto the sleigh, gliding into the night, satisfied with the new song.

The priest smiled in satisfaction as the little girl returned the empty napkin. "Next year, we'll give him milk with the cookie."

Hot Monkey Yoga

The sign flashed neon pink and yellow. Lewis paused, his coffee cup half-raised. He blinked, twice, the lowered the cup. He'd never noticed that sign before, but then, this wasn't his normal route to work. His bus had been redirected due to road construction. A small inconvenience, they'd said, but they didn't understand how much Lewis hated change.

The sign looked new. The letters all burned brightly without the horrific flickering like the beer signs in the window of the bar he had to hurry past on his way home.

Hot Monkey Yoga.

He stood and stared and pondered the sign.

Was the studio hot? Or was it the monkeys? Or was it yoga?

Lewis had never felt the urge to participate in group exercises. Yoga sounded like a strange thing to do to oneself. And how did monkeys come into the mix? Were they the ones doing yoga?

Strange to think of monkeys twisting and flexing while wearing bright leotards and leg warmers. Or was that ballet?

Lewis finally shrugged and continued his march to work. He'd wasted three point seven nine minutes pondering the sign. He would have to walk one hundred and fourteen percent of his normal pace in order to arrive at his desk precisely at eight o'clock. His columns of numbers waited. And the reports. Lewis loved reports. And numbers. And precision.

The sign's nebulous meaning bothered him all day. He found himself pondering hot monkey yoga at odd moments. What could it possibly mean? He flicked his pencil shavings into the trash while he imagined chimpanzees flexing their prehensile toes. He dribbled creamer across the counter while considering what exactly hot referred to. Was it euphemistic or literal? His sandwich leaked mayonnaise and mustard while he held an internal debate on the possible benefits of practicing yoga, with hot monkeys or otherwise.

By five o'clock, Lewis had determined that the only possible way to satisfy his curiosity was to visit the Hot Monkey Yoga studio and ask what, exactly, the sign meant.

He packed up his lunch, tucking it into his briefcase. He had exactly seventeen point four three minutes to walk to the bus stop. Plenty of time, especially if he moved at one hundred and twenty three percent of his normal walking pace.

Lynda, with a y, met him in the lobby. She looked breathless, her hair slightly tousled. "Lewis, hey. Where were you today? We were going to meet for lunch, remember?" She smiled, rather prettily. She had a dimple in her left cheek that Lewis found quite charming, along with her dark hair that curled ever so gently. Lynda breezed through the office like a whimsical butterfly.

Lewis twitched his lips into a smile. "I am so sorry. I was distracted, not myself." Would Lynda know anything about yoga, hot monkey or otherwise? Somehow he couldn't picture her as one of those women.

"Tomorrow, then? Or maybe you're free tonight? A group of us were going—"

"Not tonight." It came out too brusque. Her smile faded. Lewis felt a twinge of regret. But the question of the sign ate at him to the point that nothing else mattered. He had to know what it meant. "Tomorrow would be lovely. Noon?"

"Sure, noon tomorrow. See you, Lewis." Lynda dropped her eyes, hurried away.

Lewis allowed himself three point two seconds of regret as he watched her slim shape hurry away. He'd hoped she would understand him better than the last woman he'd lunched with. He liked Lynda.

He turned to the doors, switching his focus back to the sign. It was time.

He marched down the street, briefcase in hand, sensible shoes hitting the pavement with precision.

The sign glowed neon pink and yellow in the evening traffic. The crowds eddied and flowed, none stopping to open the freshly painted door of the studio. Lewis stopped in front of it. Deep green, overlaid with subtle swirls of gold, it was nothing like any other door he'd ever faced.

He sniffed, but detected nothing more than the usual blend of car exhaust, human perspiration, and the musk of a city street. Wait, was that a hint of incense? The woody, spicy fragrance invited him to step into the exotic world of hot monkey yoga.

Lewis reached a hesitant hand to the door. A tingle of—what? Electricity? No, too soft. He curled his fingers into a fist, breathed out, then flattened his hand on the door. The tingle became a warm rush that started in his hand and spread through his whole body. Breath jerked into lungs that swelled larger than before. His tie was too tight. Muscles bunched and stretched in new ways. The door swung open as Lewis stumbled forward.

It crashed shut behind him, closing out the noise of traffic, of commuters hurrying homewards. It sealed out the streaming orange of the setting sun, left Lewis blinking in a soft darkness lit only by tiny flickering lights.

He stared in wonder as he pulled his tie loose. The air smelled richer, sweeter, full of damp earthiness and the heavy scent of jasmine and forests and over-ripe mangoes. His lungs pulled it all in without input from his brain which was still overwhelmed by the abrupt changes in ambient noise and light.

And temperature. He slid off his crisp sport jacket, flung it and his tie into a dim corner just inside the door. His feet felt large, clumsy in his sensible dress shoes. Sweat pooled down his back as he removed shoes, then his socks. For the first time in years, Lewis stood barefoot somewhere other than his own shower. He wriggled his toes, felt moss and smooth stones and sand.

A bell chimed somewhere in the mysterious dimness farther beyond the doorway. Fabric rustled. Footfalls, dull and muffled, approached.

His breath heaved in and out as Lewis sweated and dithered in the vestibule. Who was coming to greet him? Should he enter? What other strangeness awaited him? His heart pulsed with excitement and anticipation. His body sweated and begged to be freed of the confining shirt and slacks. His brain slammed the button for full-blown panic.

He snatched up his clothing, jammed feet into his shoes and blindly scrambled out of the suddenly stifling air of Hot Monkey Yoga.

The door closed with a soft click. He stood on the sidewalk, clothing in disarray, as the scents and sounds of city life crashed down on him. His lungs felt squeezed. The air was too dry, too full of fumes. His head spun. He leaned on brickwork and panted.

"Hey, mister. You all right?" A concerned policeman paused. His face crinkled in disapproval.

"I'm not drunk, officer. Just a slight spell." Lewis pulled himself together. He shrugged into his jacket, straightened himself, shoved tie and socks into his pocket. Briefcase, where was the briefcase? He grabbed it up from the sidewalk, clutched it like a shield as he trotted away toward the bus stop and his normal after-work routine. Dinner, wash up, vacuum his tidy little apartment, sort his laundry for the weekend, shower, brush his teeth, dress in his buttoned pyjamas, watch the nightly news, then turn out his lights and sleep. Yes. He could do that.

He glanced back once at the neon pink and yellow sign glowing like a beacon of forbidden delights.

Hot Monkey Yoga.

He bit his lip, torn by desires he'd never felt before.

The policeman raised one eyebrow, stepped forward.

Lewis hunched his back and scurried away, shoelaces flapping around his feet.

He woke the next morning with a throbbing headache. Two aspirin and a large glass of milk would fix it. Must be his allergies acting up again. He rose from his bed, then froze in panic.

His clothes were strewn across the floor. He wore nothing but his sensible briefs. A plate of half-eaten spaghetti sat on the dresser. The fork lay on the carpet, twined in a loving embrace with several strands of pasta. A trail of salad greens and garlic bread crusty bits led to the kitchen.

He grimaced as he tidied his clothing and pulled a bathrobe around his skinny chest. What had he done yesterday? He had no memory after leaving work. Did he go out with Lynda then? She'd asked. He frowned as he collected dirty dishes and food, following the trail to his kitchen. Pots and pans lay with abandon across the counter, over the table, and in the sink. Splatters of sauce that smelled of strange spices marked his cupboards. A banana browned in the middle of it, teethmarks sharp around the bite taken from the middle, peel and all.

He stared at the fruit, tongue running automatically across his teeth. He dropped the dishes clutched in his hands in horror. Had he forgotten to floss and brush last night? How could he? The last time he'd forgotten he was seven and sick with the flu. He could still taste the lingering dry bitterness of the banana peel.

He stared at the mess of his kitchen. Something pink glittered under the pile. A flyer from his mailbox.

Pink...

Hot Monkey Yoga.

He remembered.

"Drugs. In the air. They drugged me."

The words rang with conviction. It had to explain everything. He'd been drugged. He straightened with relief.

Then caught sight of the clock.

"Nine-twenty-two?"

He slapped a hand on his forehead. No fever, nothing but the lingering headache. He had to call in sick. But he wasn't sick. He couldn't be late. He'd only been late twice in his entire eight-year career. Once because the bus had broken down, completely not his fault. And once because he'd tripped on the way into the building, stumbled over a chair that was out of place by two point five inches, and bumped into Lynda, causing her to spill her papers. He'd stayed to help her pick them up, entranced by her dark hair and smiling eyes. That was how he'd met her.

He'd blown her off yesterday. He'd seen the sadness creeping into her eyes, the droop to her chin.

He couldn't lose her. She was the best thing that had ever almost happened to him. He stared around his apartment. The mess sickened him, clutched his stomach tight, clenched his jaw until his head screamed for release.

His phone was in his hand before he could think better of it.

"Hello? Lynda? This is Lewis. Yes, sorry about yesterday. I think I was coming down with something. Anyway, I'm staying home sick today. No, no. That's not necessary. I'll be fine. Just, please... Let's have lunch. Friday. Yes. At that little café around the corner. Noon, yes. See you tomorrow."

He stared at the phone. His heart hammered, his hands sweated. He sat abruptly in his kitchen chair. Had he just called Lynda? He should have called in sick to Albert, his supervisor. But he'd called Lynda first. Had he actually asked her out?

What was wrong with him?

He'd never acted that way in his life. A giggle escaped his lips. He clapped his hands over his mouth, eyes wide with horror.

He should call the doctor, go in for tests.

After he called Albert.

"Ah, Lewis. Your vitals look perfect, as always." Doctor Thompson flipped through the chart. He was older, the same doctor who had seen Lewis born, given him shots, consulted with his mother when she worried that Lewis was not normal.

"Just a little stand-offish," Doctor Thompson said with his gentle smile. "He likes numbers. It's a gift. Just love him for who he is."

Lewis's mother had done just that. And Lewis had grown up to be one of the best statisticians ever. Or so Albert said when he filled out that Employee of the Month award. Yes, Lewis was a little strange, or so they whispered when they thought he couldn't hear them. And it normally didn't bother Lewis. Except now it did.

"I just feel strange, not myself." Lewis twisted one finger into the worn cotton of the exam gown.

"All the tests show everything in tip-top shape. So, is it something at work?" Doctor Thompson settled his comfortably padded self onto his rolling doctor stool. He typed two-fingered on a keyboard while he talked.

"Work is fine." Lewis flushed. "There is a woman, though. Lynda."

Doctor Thompson's face wrinkled in a genial smile. "Ah, young love, is it? Well, that would explain your symptoms. Hot, then cold, forgetful, not yourself. Yes, I do believe you are suffering from a case of falling in love. The only cure for that is to talk to the young woman, go on a date, see if it blossoms into something bigger."

Lewis sagged with releif. "Is that all? I'm in love?" He thought of Lynda with her curls and little white collars and her soft blue sweaters.

"Give it a few weeks and if things don't develop, come talk to me again." Doctor Thompson winked at Lewis. "I bet she's a sweet young thing, pretty as a picture. Meanwhile, take your vitamins, get your exercise, and you'll be right as rain in no time."

The doctor bustled out before the thought fully formed in Lewis's head.

Exercise? As in Hot Monkey Yoga?

Sudden flames surged up through his belly. He wanted to howl, to scream in primal angst, to beat fists on his chest, to fling things around the exam room.

"I'm just in love," he said to the strange urges flooding through him.

They subsided into a simmering heat down low in his loins. He could live with that. He had to live with it. If this was a side effect of love, it was annoying, but not much of an inconvenience. And Lynda was suitable. His mother would approve.

He dressed and left the doctor's office. He glanced at his watch. He could still make it to work, put in three point six eight hours of work—

A pink and yellow sign flashed by on the side of a bus. His head turned to follow it. He licked his lip at a sudden and strange desire.

What if he played hooky from work? Stayed away even though the doctor told him he wasn't sick? What if he lied and took a sick day when he was fine?

He shuddered with guilt and a secret delight at the mere thought.

But what would he do with his day?

Wander the city. Explore. Eat ice cream and jelly beans for lunch.

Part of him rebelled, turned in sick horror from the inconcievable notion. But a part of him giggled with glee, a dark and secret part he had never suspected lurked in his soul.

He turned left instead of right, took a bus he didn't know, rode in a stupor of guilty angst until he couldn't stand it any more. He jumped off the bus at the next stop. A clothing store beckoned with pictures of happy, carefree men in polo shirts and white shorts. They did exciting things like pose on a sailing ship, or in front of a sea-front carnival. Lewis felt a sudden urge to be like those men. He pushed open the door to the shop.

It smelled of fabric starches and paper packaging. Faint music droned over speakers, an irritation to his ears. He touched the slacks, arranged in neat rows on hangars. Dark blue, sorted by size, followed by gray, followed by tan.

"May I help you?" The clerk looked old, sucked dry of enjoyment by living between aisles of starched cotton.

"I want to look like them." Lewis stabbed one finger toward the larger-than-life pictures along the front of the store.

The clerk blinked twice, slow and heavy like an owl. "Which one of them?"

Lewis blinked in response, swallowed hesitation, and said on impulse, "The boat one."

"Very good, sir. And what size?"

Numbers, yes, numbers were safe. Lewis rattled off his measurements.

The clerk herded him through the aisles, fingers flipping through the racks with familiar ease. In moments, Lewis held a large pile of clothing. White dominated, touched by carefully neutral blues and warm grays, and accented with a few bits of nautical red.

"And this one is one hundred percent pure organic cotton, very breathable, and sustainably harvested and grown." The clerk's voice droned.

Lewis merely nodded and let the man lead him to the register. He blinked at the total, but paid. The strange urge pushed him to it.

"Love is a strange thing," he commented as he gathered his bags.

The clerk tilted his head, confused. "I suspect it is, sir. Enjoy your purchases. Have a good day."

Lewis mumbled something in reply as he hurried from the store. What had he done? He looked at the clothing neatly folded in the bags. When would he wear any of this? Why did he want to look like some blond man on a boat? The man looked happy, like he enjoyed his boating life. Lewis was ill at just the thought of a boat.

He clutched the bags as he walked toward the nearest bus stop. The strange warmth had faded, cooled until he only felt like a foolish version of his usual self. What had happened to him? His normal self felt stifled, sealed tight, like a hermetically sealed package of sterile wipes. He looked at the bags again.

Hot Monkey Yoga.

The paper was slipped in the side along with a handful of flyers.

He'd felt so different, so alive, in those few moments inside the foyer.

He wanted to feel that again.

He took his clothes home to see if dressing like the man on the boat would help him capture that feeling again.

"Is that a new shirt, Lewis?" Lynda's voice was soft, hesitant, as she paused outside his cubicle. "I like the color."

Lewis ran a self-conscious hand along the cotton polo shirt. It was dress-down Friday. He still felt naked without his tie. But Lynda liked his shirt. And it did make him feel more adventurous, like the sailing man looked in the poster. It had taken him three hours of agonizing before he decided to wear it today.

"Are we still meeting for lunch?" His voice cracked. He cleared his throat. "At the café?"

"Sure." She gave him a small smile. "Noon, right?"

He nodded.

She nodded back, then hurried away.

Lewis stifled the urge to call to her. The café seemed so mundane, so safe, so bland. He suddenly wanted to sink his teeth into something exotic, sweet and spicy. Maybe he could try Indian food. But was Lynda adventurous? Would she be willing to try it, too?

He swallowed a sudden lump of worry as he hunched back over his numbers.

He couldn't focus. They were just strings of digits on endless sheets of paper. He closed his eyes, rubbed his forehead.

And could only see neon pink and yellow flashing in his mind. Hot Monkey Yoga.

He'd walked past this morning. The green and gold door beckoned him, invited him to explore its sultry secrets, teased him with the scent of sandalwood and jasmine incense. He'd stopped, for almost ten full seconds, to breathe it in. Almost he'd turned aside. Almost entered. But work was calling. And wearing his new shirt, a polo with a little embroidered anchor, was pushing his limits.

But he could taste the incense, see the sign, feel the magic pulling him. His inner animal was awake and hungry and filling him with strange ideas and urges.

He wasn't going to listen. He was Lewis Arnoldson, statistician, and he liked boring and plain and normal.

"I went yesterday. It was amazing." Carol's voice carried over the cubicle partition. "Yeah, that new place just a block over. Can you believe it? Hot monkey yoga is a thing that you just have to try."

Lewis's ears perked up, despite every attempt not to engage. He usually detested Carol and her nasal voice and her endless prattling. She didn't love numbers enough for this job. Before he could stop himself, Lewis was leaning on the partition to her cubicle.

"What's up with that place?" he found himself asking.

Carol turned her head and stared through her artificial lashes. "Not your kind of place, Lewis, not at all." She turned back to her conversation, phone cord dangling from her ear. "Oh, nothing, Mitz. Just the guy from the next cubicle. He'd absolutely detest the place. He's so weird and kind of squirrely, you know?"

Lewis waited another full seventeen point six seconds, mostly because he knew it bothered Carol, before he turned back to his own desk.

He tapped a sheet of numbers. So, Carol had gone to Hot Monkey Yoga? Carol of the artificial everything from her hair color to her toenails to everything in the middle? She thought he'd detest the place. Well, he'd show her. He'd go there on his lunch break and—

He was meeting Lynda for lunch. Sweet, timid Lynda. At the café. What would she say if he suggested they check out Hot Monkey Yoga instead?

He shook his head. No, Lynda was not that kind of woman.

Or was she?

The thought rose unbidden from some steamy jungle depth of his subconscious id. Lynda as a hot, sweaty monkey in yoga pants and a leotard. Lynda wiping sweat from her brow, her damp curls sticking to her cheeks, her lips parted as she poured water over her hot monkey body—

No! He slammed the mental doors on that image. He wasn't that kind of person. And neither was Lynda.

But Carol was.

He wanted to puke. The thought of Carol doing hot monkey yoga was revolting.

"Hey, number nerd." Carol leaned over his cubicle wall. "Got a favor to ask."

Lewis gave her his coldest icy stare then turned his back and picked up his pencil. He could hear Carol rolling her eyes.

"Look, Hot Monkey Yoga just isn't your kind of scene. Women go there to exercise and get all sweaty and stuff. I'm sorry I made that crack. You know I think squirrels are cute, don't you?"

Lewis relented. Carol could be horrid if she didn't get her way. The fastest way to get rid of her was to agree to her favor. "What do you want?" He didn't have to be nice about it, though. His inner animal, recently awakened, growled in his head. Heat bubbled through his sternum. He could almost smell the incense—

"—by tomorrow," Carol finished.

"What?" He looked puzzled at the stack of papers she waved at him.

"Look, just crunch these for me. Do your magic with the digits, you know? It's for that Peterson account. I've got to have the report tomorrow, but I'm lost with these numbers they gave us. Makes no sense. I need you to run them through that magic brain of yours and turn them into something us mere mortals can understand."

He wasn't sure if she was making fun of him, still, or if she were seriously trying to compliment him. Either way, she was over a barrel. He smelled her fear and desperation. He could work this to his advantage. He smiled in a snarly, predatory way.

"Sure thing, Carol. But you'll owe me." He took the papers and turned his back. "Now, go away and let me do my thing."

She stood in stunned silence for a long moment. Lewis forgot to count exactly how long. Somehow it didn't seem as important as it would have a few moments earlier. He heard her heels clack back to her own cubicle. Blessed silence fell in the office while he worked. Well, not exactly silence, but Carol's nasal whinnying voice didn't intrude on his concentration.

He had her numbers churned by the time his alarm for lunch sounded. He dropped his pencil, tossed the papers at Carol as he sauntered past, and went to hunt meat. He stopped and shook his head. He was going to lunch with Lynda. At the café. He wasn't going out on the savannah to hunt and kill small antelope. What was wrong with him?

Doctor Thompson had to be wrong. Love didn't make you want to slaughter small animals. Love also didn't make you grow extra body hair.

He ran his hand up his arm. Thicker than yesterday, wiry black hair had sprouted up its length.

He scurried to the mens room, let the stall door slam shut. He tried to ignore the hitch in his step, the way his arms wanted to swing wide and smash things, the urge to pound his chest and howl his supremacy.

What was wrong with him? He huddled on the toilet, feet tucked up, arms wrapped tightly around his knees. A noise, half snarl, half growl, and part sob, broke free.

"You okay in there, buddy?"

Lewis jammed a fist into his mouth to stop the noises. Jerome from marketing would never understand. Jerome was an alpha male. He'd been the one to dish out the humiliation, not take it, Lewis would swear to that on a stack of bananas.

"I'm fine," he grunted around his fingers. It came out as a gorilla's hooting call.

Jerome didn't push it. He waited a moment before banging his way out.

He didn't even wash his hands.

Lewis curled his lip in disgust. It seemed more prehensile than before. He felt it with his hand. His whole jaw seemed bigger, more powerful. He wrinkled his nose, felt his lips writhe in a soundless snarl. Alpha male, he thought, that's me, now. His hands made fists, swung to pound his chest.

And smacked into the sides of the bathroom stall.

Alpha gorilla, that's me. Stupid clutz.

Lewis whimpered as he sucked his bruised knuckles.

His watch beeped. He was late to his lunch with Lynda.

He scrambled off the toilet, muttering curses. Considering how mild his vocabulary was, they weren't very satisfying. His mother hadn't let him hear *those words*. Now he wondered what they were. The animal inside urged him to go read the graffiti under the bridge downtown and find out. His mouth longed to taste their vulgarity, to spew them out as casually as the office smokers blew clouds into the breeze.

He splashed water over his face. His cheeks were flushed, his eyes too bright.

He hoped Lynda was waiting for him.

And that she was ready for something more adventurous than turkey on white.

He loped from the bathroom, lip curled in a derisive snarl. His knuckles almost dragged the ground. He left a trail of animal magnetism behind him, a ribbon of pheremones that left women like Carol swooning under their artificial hair dye and men like Jerome puffing up their chests and eyeing their rivals.

Lewis banged out of the office building like a gorilla charging from the jungle. Lynda stood at the corner, demure and innocent in her blue sweater and long skirt. The breeze from a passing car tugged on her curls. He wanted her in that moment, wanted her fiercely.

Maybe he was in love. Maybe this was what those movies tried and failed to capture, this animal raging inside. Was this passion? His feet pattered on the sidewalk as he loped forward.

"Lynda!"

She turned at the sound of his voice. Her face was flushed from the wind, her lips parted, her hair tossed and tangled. He longed to smooth it free, to take her in his arms and proclaim his love.

He stopped to pound fists against his chest. She was *his*, and he wanted any other male in range to know it. He let loose a hooting howl.

"Lewis? Are you all right? You're acting strange." Lynda edged away.

He froze, feeling like an idiot. He slowly lowered his fists. "I saw the doctor yesterday. He said it was normal."

"Well, I'm not really comfortable with it, Lewis. It's weird."

The light changed to green. The pedestrian crossing sign flashed. Lynda hurried into the crosswalk.

"Are you still going to lunch with me?" Lewis demanded.

She glanced back. Her eyes showed fear. She shook her curls, then hurried away to the far corner.

Her fear stabbed him through the heart. Lynda was afraid of him? Lewis the pusher of pencils, lord of the numbers, statistician employee of the month? Lewis who would never hurt anything? Tears stung his eyes. He should run after her, declare his undying love. Or would that frighten her more?

What was wrong with him?

It all started when he'd first seen that sign. Hot Monkey Yoga. Neon pink and yellow, lurid as the jungle flowers his inner animal longed to find.

But he wasn't in the jungle. Or the savannah. And he wasn't an alpha gorilla. He was Lewis. Odd, spindly Lewis who loved numbers and being neat. Lewis, who never did anything impulsive. Lewis, who kept his ten pencils sharpened and at the ready. Not eleven pencils, not nine, but an even ten. Lewis, who counted his steps and sometimes shortened his stride to make it an even hundred steps from the elevator to his cubicle.

Lewis, who secretly longed to hold Lynda's hand. To walk with her in the twilight. To talk late into the night with her. To share a turkey on white with mayo. And maybe mustard if he was feeling adventurous. And pickles if he was really daring.

"Lynda, wait!" He rushed after her.

Someone honked. He ran on heedless of the danger.

She glanced back once, then hurried up the steps to the glass entrance doors. Her blue sweater disappeared into the lunch crowd at the café. She was gone.

She didn't want him. Not like this.

He looked down at the coarse, black hair on his arms. At the knit shirt and cotton pants. This was not Lewis. This was a stranger, the kind who would walk boldly into a room. The kind who might enter a place with a name like Hot Monkey Yoga.

That was it! Everything had changed when he entered that place. They'd done something to him. He'd go back and make them change him back into his old self.

His old, dull, boring self. The Lewis who would never dare to speak anything to Lynda other than a mumbled hello.

He closed his eyes on a new kind of panic. He didn't want to give up his alpha gorilla self, but he didn't want to go back to being his old self, either.

"Hey, buddy! Move it or lose it!"

Rough hands shoved him aside, pushed him away. He stumbled down the sidewalk, blinded by his inner turmoil.

The teasing scent of jasmine touched him, wrapped around him like a lifeline, drew him around the corner. The scent grew richer as his feet carried him closer to the neon pink and yellow glow of the sign. Rich, jungle scents pulled him to the green and gold door. This time, his hands didn't hesitate. He pushed it open, stepped inside, into the humid fragrance of a full jungle dusk. The heat wrapped around him, lured him deeper beyond the vestibule. He was dressed better this time. He kicked off his shoes as he stumbled forward.

Vines draped across the path. Huge flowers spilled their scents from bright pink and yellow petals. Lights danced and glimmered in the depths of the jungle, fireflies flashing a seductive rhythm.

He felt his chest expand, his muscles enlarge. He hammered one meaty fist on the ground. He was alpha gorilla here.

The woman appeared as if from nowhere, a shimmering and seductive goddess of earthy browns and golds and diaphanous white. She frowned at Lewis. "You see it, don't you?"

He gave a gorilla grunt, plucked a branch to pound the against the ground. Leaves rustled and slapped on jungle earth.

"More than see," the woman said. "It's grabbed you deep and hard."

He grunted and howled.

"Your friend, Carol, she was right. This is not for you. This is not who you were meant to be." The woman lifted her arm. Gold flashed along its length, intricate bracelets woven of golden waterfalls.

Lewis felt his eyes droop. He collapsed to the jungle floor. The rich scent of loam filled his nostrils. He breathed deep—

And woke to a very concerned woman in a leotard bending over him. "Are you all right, sir? You seem to have fainted."

"Sometimes the heat does that," a second woman put in.

The room was uncomfortably warm. The wooden floor under him glowed honey gold under the heat lamps overhead.

"Here, drink this." Someone pushed a cold bottle of water into his hands.

Lewis gulped a mouthful. Then stared. His hands were human again. The extra hair was gone. He was back to himself.

A wave of loss and grief washed over him. It was as if he'd had something important torn away before he could truly understand it.

He drank again. Exactly three point nine ounces. One hundred fifteen point three three seven milliliters. He swallowed the cold water, felt it slip down his throat. He took another swallow. His brain automatically calculated the volume.

He wanted to shut it down. But it was who he was. Wasn't it?

But he was more than that now. He'd experienced something strange and new and seen a different side of things.

"Ladies, perhaps we should return to our lesson?" A new voice, but Lewis recognized it. Sweet, sultry, deep with jungle passion. He turned to face the woman.

She was graceful curves, deep skin, flashing dark eyes, all dressed up in a zebra-stripe leotard and leopard leggings. Her tight tangle of black curls was held back with a golden scarf. She gave Lewis a knowing smile.

He rose to his feet, returning the smile. Something of the gorilla confidence flowed through his veins.

He was Lewis, number nerd extraordinaire, but he was also alpha gorilla.

His feet carried him out of the studio, down the steps to the street outside. The green door clicked closed behind him. The sound seemed to echo through mysterious jungle growth before emerging onto the city street. The scent of jasmine faded.

He glanced up at the sign. Hot Yoga blinked in pink neon. A band of yellow outlined the sign.

Where was the Monkey? Had he imagined it?

The woman lifted a shade in the upper window, gave him a final look, before letting it drop closed.

"Hot Monkey Yoga," he whispered to himself.

He turned away, shuffled back along the sidewalk toward the office. His lunch hour was almost up.

He paused at the corner where the hot dog stand usually opened in the afternoons. He'd never eaten one before, not from a street vendor. His mother's warnings about germs and vagrants and dysentery shouted in his head as he stepped forward. He let her memory shout as he purchased a hot dog. He smiled as he slathered it with mustard, scooped up raw onions and pickled peppers. He lifted it to his mouth, told his brain not to count anything, and bit down.

He closed his eyes and just tasted it. The hot bite of onions, the burn of peppers, the smooth spice of the mustard, the snap and chew of the dog, the soft wrapping of bun, it melded into a symphony in his mouth. He'd never tasted food this way before.

His inner gorilla sighed in satisfaction, smacked its thick ape-lips, and curled up for a nap.

"Lewis?"

His eyes flew open. He choked on the huge bite in his mouth. "Lynda?" It came out garbled in mustard. He dabbed his lip with a napkin as he frantically chewed and swallowed.

She handed him another napkin. "I thought you were more of a turkey on white bread guy. I didn't know you liked hot dogs."

He swallowed. "My first one. My mother never let me eat them."

She gave him a dimpled smile. "If I'd known, I would have met you here instead. I love a good hot dog every once in a while."

He stood in awkward silence for a moment before his inner alpha kicked in. But this time he was going to do it his way. "Can I buy you one? I know you've just eaten lunch, but—"

She shook her head, curls bobbing.

He felt like a fool. Again. "Look, I'm sorry for the way I was earlier. It was strange. I don't know what came over me." He did, but he wasn't going to admit it was Hot Monkey Yoga. "I'd really like to take you out to dinner or something. To make up for it."

Her dimple deepened. "Why, Lewis Arnoldson, are you asking me on a date?"

"Yes, for tonight." He swallowed the sudden knot of nervous shivering that raced into his throat and made his voice crack. "Somewhere adventurous. Maybe. If you like that sort of thing. Maybe dinner on the pier. Maybe Indian food. Unless it's too spicy. Then we could just do—" He was babbling. He stopped himself. "Something," he finished lamely.

"How about dinner at Smokey Joe's? They do amazing seafood. And afterwards, we can ride the ferris wheel. I love it up at the top, when you can see everything spread out below you and the seagulls come to see the strange birds up in their airspace." She took his arm, pulled him up the steps into the office building foyer.

"That sounds wonderful." He hoped the quaver of nerves didn't show too much. He'd never ridden a ferris wheel before.

"Then dinner it is. Meet me here at five." She rose on tiptoe, planted a quick kiss on his cheek, before hurrying away.

Lewis felt his face curving in an unfamiliar way. He touched his lips, bemused by the smile tugging the corners up.

Lynda glanced back once, dimpled smile flashing before she disappeared into her office.

Lewis's inner alpha gorilla howled in triumph as he boarded the elevator.

Hot Monkey Yoga, indeed.

Born on a Tuesday

Jonah started making the god on a Tuesday from a lump of clay, smashed in a puddle of water, squeezed and kneaded, then left on a counter covered with thick plastic wrap overnight. It was cold, heavy, wet on his hands. He wrinkled his nose at the half-formed blob waiting for him that January afternoon when the sky bled cold fog.

"We're making clay pots today, Jonah." His teacher glared down her thin nose and through her horn-rimmed spectacles. Light flashed off the rhinestones embedded up at the tips.

"Yes, ma'am." Jonah hung his head as he squished his fingers back into the clay. Cold slime oozed out from the blob. Jonah smashed it back inside along with his anger at old Miss Hennihy. "We're making clay pots today," he whispered in a mockingly high-pitched voice.

He crushed and squeezed until the clay took on a roughly human head shape. He gave it a thin nose, big lips, and tiny pinched eyes. He rolled little bits into snakes that became curled hair on the bulbous, misshapen head.

"Enough for today, class. Time to clean up." Miss Hennihy clapped her hands.

"That's not a pot." Tiffany Eider pointed one clay-covered finger at Jonah. Her pink nail polish glimmered under the white of drying earth. "Teacher, Jonah didn't make a pot."

Jonah glared at Tiffany. He wished she would shut up.

The eyes of the rudely shaped god's head flared blue before turning back to gray clay.

Tiffany flapped her mouth but no sound came out. She burst into tears. Soundless tears. Her lip quivered. Her mouth opened in a whole-hearted wail. Nothing came out except a thin tendril of green mist.

Miss Hennihy didn't notice poor Tiffany's distress. The teacher pulled up the sleeves of her ratty pink cardigan as she directed the children placing misshapen, lumpy clay pots on the drying boards. Her face twisted into a mass of wrinkled disapproval at the god head Jonah set on the shelf. Her bony hand with its ropy veins squeezed the clay back into an unformed lump.

"We are making pots, Jonah," she said as she unmade his clay god.

Jonah dropped his head to hide the angry glare in his eyes. Let the old witch think him penitent.

The spell over Tiffany oozed back into the clay. Her voice returned mid-shriek.

The class clapped hands over their ears. Miss Hennihy hurried to her side.

Jonah watched the teacher fawn over spoiled Tiffany and soothe her screams. His gaze grew distant as he imagined his revenge on the horrid girl. Their voices blended into the mocking shriek of seagulls in his mind. He marched off to the principal's office when the long bony finger of doom pointed him out the door and Miss Hennihy's frown of retribution promised him dire punishment if he did not repent.

His shoes squeaked on the tile floors as he made his way down the long corridor. The smell of ancient mashed potatoes and pencil erasers burned into his mind.

This was the day of his first defeat.

But it would not be his last.

He would face his nemesis in battle again.

The spirit of the clay god dissipated, leaving only a bewildered seven-year-old boy to face the principal alone.

Tuesdays were spelling days in the morning. Jonah hated spelling. He scratched his pencil over the paper, his tongue between his teeth.

Miss Hennihy's voice droned the word again. "Capital. The capital of Spain is Madrid."

Pencils scratched over paper like the scritching of fingernails on the chalkboards of the doomed. Jonah wriggled his nose as he thought, then put pencil to paper again. His tongue stuck between his teeth as he concentrated.

"Teacher, Jonah's doing that thing again." Tiffany's voice curdled the air, like vinegar in milk. "He's sticking his tongue out at me."

Jonah left his word half-written. He turned his head to stare at Tiffany. She twirled one golden curl around her finger. She pointed her pencil at him. He stuck his tongue out all the way. If he was going to get in trouble, he may as well be in trouble for actually doing the deed. The god power slid into him from his pencil nub. Blue fire swelled in his chest. He crossed his eyes.

"Ew! Teacher! Make him stop." Tiffany stuck her nose into the air and turned away from Jonah.

He wished her silent, wished that her perfect face would swell like a balloon. But nothing happened. The god power swirled in him, unable to manifest. He needed clay in his hands. After all, his was a god of clay.

"Jonah, what do we say when we do something rude?" Miss Hennihy stood over him, a gargoyle in horn-rimmed glasses and a sweater that smelled like mothballs and old lavender.

The god power slid into his mouth and oiled his tongue. It held that much power. It was, after all, a Tuesday. Jonah quoted his father's words when the wrench slipped.

Tiffany squealed, her eyes huge. The other second-graders gasped. A few of the boys giggled.

Miss Hennihy's face drained of all color. Her lips squeezed so tight they disappeared. Her fingers pinched Jonah's ear. She pulled him up from his chair. "Jonah Washburn, we do not say those words. Ever." She marched him across the classroom then into the hall. She released his ear, pushing him in the direction of the principal's office.

He took two steps then turned to look back.

Miss Hennihy tapped her foot, her arms crossed over her jutting bosom. Tiffany looked smug behind her teacher's skirt. The girl's eyes sparked green.

His nemesis. Pure evil.

She had won this round, like the last.

He turned and sauntered to the principal's office.
She wouldn't win the next.

Jonah was waiting after school in the parking lot. He squeezed a lump of clay in his hand, over and over. Tiffany would have to emerge sometime and when she did, he would be ready. The god power had built all afternoon, fed by his anger. He spit on the clay to help moisten it. The god power blazed within him. Because of her, he'd missed recess and art class. Because of Tiffany, he had anger burning inside and no outlet.

Because of her god that blocked him at every turn. Her god that made him conform. Her god that sent him to the principal's office time and again.

Blue fire sparked off his finger. They would battle like tigers. He would fight to the bitter end. He would go down in fiery defeat or he would rise in triumph. He would be the god of Tuesday, the god of clay, the god of—

The door swung open. Tiffany stepped out, her blue skirt twirling around her legs. Her white tights were unspotted and pristine as new snow. Her blond hair curled around her head. She looked as fresh and clean as she had that morning. Jonah lifted his lip in a snarl. He breathed onto the damp clay in his hand, tendrils of blue light.

The god power flared. The clay crawled out of his hold, drawing life as it moved. It twisted and surged into a tall warrior with thick muscles and a flaming sword. It shouted an ancient battle cry and pointed at Tiffany.

Her friends shrieked and scattered.

She met Jonah's gaze with a level stare. Green light danced in her eyes. She plucked an early dandelion from the grass beside the walk. She breathed on it from her own god power.

His nemesis. His enemy. Her god power glowed green.

The dandelion tumbled from her hand, expanding as it fell. A ferocious lion bounded forward to meet the charge of the clay warrior. They crashed together with a roaring noise like thunder. The sword rose high and swung down. A huge paw full of raking claws swung across and over. Blade bit deep into the lion's neck. Claws tore the warrior shoulder to knee. Blue and green power swirled and burned. The lion roared and bit the warrior's leg. The warrior drove his sword through the lion's belly. Both exploded.

Clumps of mud and dandelion petals showered onto the parking lot.

Jonah growled as he ran toward Tiffany. She pirouetted on one toe before leaping to meet him. He smeared mud over her face. She kicked him in the shin. He grabbed a handful of perfect golden curls. She screamed like a banshee and yanked on his ear. He tugged, she pulled, until they both fell to the ground. They rolled back and forth, shouting ancient curses, while the god powers struggled for dominance.

"What is going on out here?"

Large hands pulled the two gods apart. The power drained away as quickly as it had risen.

"Stupid girl," Jonah panted.

Tiffany's lip quivered. She broke into loud sobs. "He hit me. Look what he did to my dress."

The principal sighed as he dragged Jonah back inside the school and into his office. He left Tiffany to the minstrations of Mrs. Brown, the school secretary.

Jonah's mother kept him home until the next Tuesday. "No more fighting. No more suspensions, do you hear me? I mean it, Jonah. Honestly, I don't know what's gotten into you lately." She shook her head, her curlers clacking together. "Eat your breakfast. I'll take you to school."

Jonah poked his egg. He didn't want eggs. He wanted cereal and toast. The blue god power woke, but it was weak. The Tuesday was still young and Jonah wasn't really angry at his mother. He sighed and nursed his irritation as he ate the egg. He made faces at his mom's back, but only when she wasn't looking. He wanted to go to school today.

His nemesis would be there in her curly-haired glory.

The god power curled in his belly, blue and burning and eager.

Jonah managed to contain it until lunch recess. He needed clay to make it strong and clay was in short supply in the classroom. As soon as the bell released him from the prison of Miss Hennihy's classroom, he ran to the small patch of soil under the trees behind the swingset. Yes, the clay was still wet from the rain the night before. He dug up a handful, squeezing and shaping it. He'd make a god that would defeat Tiffany once and for all.

"What are you doing, Jonah?" Tiffany's voice broke through his concentration.

The blue fire flared. He turned to face her.

She met his look with a knowing smile. "You can't win."

He clutched his god of clay, thrusting it forward. "I will defeat you."

She showed him the pine cone in her hand. "Never."

Green god power blossomed in the pine cone. Blue fire answered from the misshapen clay blob.

They threw them at the same time. Clay smacked into Tiffany's chest. The pine cone slammed into Jonah's eye. Blue and green god power spiraled in a gust of wind that rattled the tree branches. Thunder cracked and rumbled. Both children howled.

"Stop this instant!" Miss Hennihy clapped her hands.

The wind ceased. The whirling tornado of light blinked out of existence. The thunder muttered into silence.

"Much better." Miss Hennihy gave Tiffany and Jonah her most withering gaze. "We are not summoning gods to battle. Is that understood?"

"Yes, Miss Hennihy," Tiffany said, her head bowed.

Jonah scowled.

"Jonah Washburn, is that understood?" Miss Hennihy tapped her foot. Her horn-rimmed glasses flashed red.

Jonah's incipient rebellion died under her steely-eyed glare. "Yes, ma'am." He hung his head and scuffed his shoe through the remnants of his clay god.

"We are not going to summon elementals or gods or any other creature again this year, are we?"

Jonah traded glanced with Tiffany. Her lip quivered.

"Are we?" Miss Hennihy prodded.

"No, ma'am" they said together.

Miss Hennihy studied them. She shook her head. "I pity the teachers that have to deal with you when you're older."

"What's that supposed to mean?" Jonah demanded with a flicker of blue fire.

"I'm a good student," Tiffany said at the same time.

Miss Hennihy cowed them both with another stern glare. "No more fighting, not in my class at least. Is that clear?"

They nodded. The last spark of god fire shrank to almost nothing.

Miss Hennihy laid a gnarled hand on Jonah's shoulder and squeezed. "Good. Now back to the classroom with you both and I do not want to see or hear any of this nonsense again." She herded them to the school.

Jonah dragged his steps ever so slightly until her bony fingers tightened on his shoulder. He straightened and tucked the god power deeper into hiding.

"And whatever you do, children, don't try summoning them on a Tuesday. Nothing good ever happens on a Tuesday." Miss Hennihy's sensible brown shoes squished on the rain-slick grass.

She let go of him when they reached the classroom door. Tiffany hurried to her seat, head down and lip still quivering. Jonah stomped into the room behind her. Miss Hennihy's footsteps squelched across to her desk.

Blue light flickered in the clay under Jonah's nails. His god was born on a Tuesday. That had to be something good, no matter what Miss Hennihy said. He let a small smile escape. It was his god of clay. He'd just have to be more careful how he used it.

"Next Tuesday," he whispered as he walked past Tiffany in her seat. Her hands were folded prim and proper on her desk.

"You will never win," she whispered back.

Jonah grinned as he got out his history book. Clay would always win.

Especially on a Tuesday.

COUSIN

Black bodies hunched,
Nimble fingers plucking stems of grass,
Bonobos in the mist
As dawn becomes day.

You sidle close, eyes averted,
Never direct.
No challenge, only curiosity.

I offer a bite of my orange,
My breakfast.
Ordinary to me, exotic to you.

You pucker lips, touch my outstretched hand
hesitantly with your long black fingers,
So alike, yet so different.
The orange slice, so small and sweet,
Disappears.

You proffer me a honey ant.
I accept, crunch it between teeth unused to insects.

The moment passes.
You move away, back into the shrouding mists.

I stare in wonder.
We have broken bread together.
We are not so different after all.

Twin Suns of the Mushroom Kingdom

"What does Liz really stand for?" Jidou, the survey team biologist, steered the truck around another sand dune.

Liz clutched the roll bar handle with her hand as the truck slewed to the right. Driving across uncharted, virgin planetary surfaces had its perks, but a smooth ride wasn't one of them. At least Kusavi had breathable air thanks to a healthy oceanic ecosystem. "Let me out over there," she said instead of answering Jidou's question. The man was nice enough, but she'd only met him three weeks earlier when he'd flown in on the supply ship. The man was fresh off Earth. Kusavi was his first exoplanet. It was a doozy to start on, especially for a botanist. Not many plants to study that weren't in the salty ocean.

"You aren't going to answer?" Jidou steered the truck through a shallow wash before stopping on a flatter section, one that wasn't covered in loose drifts of sand. The landscape looked more like Mars than Earth, despite the blue sky. Dunes of sand, cliffs of reddish rocks, clumps of boulders scattered across everything, with not a speck of plant life anywhere except on the coastline. Life on Kusavi still clung to the water.

Liz gave Jidou a sideways glance. He'd treated her nice enough. Most of the scientists wouldn't give her the time of day after they learned she had nothing more than a high school diploma. But Kusavi was her fifth world in as many years. She loved exploring. Her no-nonsense cargo pants and boots weren't sexy or flattering, but they held up in the extreme conditions she usually found herself in. Liz herself wasn't pretty, either. She was rugged and not the youngest chicken in the flock.

Jidou gave her a lopsided grin. "Let me guess. Elizabeth? Lizette? Alyssa?"

Liz shook her head. She popped open the door and slid out of the truck. "Pick me up after Primary sets," she said referring to the brighter yellow sun overhead. Secondary, a smaller orange star, was due to rise in a few hours. Because of the double suns, Kusavi had an eccentric orbit and wild climate patterns. Exosummer was coming and with it, extreme heat. The settlers wanted caves to live in. Liz was the one they hired to find them. Jidou was on a cataloguing expedition. Not that he'd find many plants to catalog. But he didn't expect any, either, to judge by the cartons of rock sample bags he'd brought.

Jidou shifted the truck into park then turned sideways on his seat. "Tell me and I'll save you a packet of chips for the ride back."

Liz pulled her backpack from the jumble behind the seats. "Who says I didn't put them all in here?" She grinned as she swung the pack over her shoulder.

"I'll get you licorice then. Or chocolate. I've got connections."

Liz cocked her head. Her brown ponytail brushed over her shoulder. "You get me a peanut butter cup and I'll tell you anything you want to know."

"Done." He popped open the glove compartment and extracted a small orange package.

Liz licked her lips. "I haven't tasted one of those in two years."

"I've got a dozen of them stashed in my room at the base." It was a glorified tent, but it was home for now. "My sister handed them to me right before I boarded the shuttle off Earth. I didn't have the heart to tell her I can't eat peanuts anymore. So, what is Liz short for?"

"You want me to sell my soul for a peanut butter cup?"

"Just your name. For this one. Maybe the next one will cost you a movie night with me."

"Promise you won't laugh?" Could she trust his easy smile and dimples?

"Why would I laugh?"

Liz snatched the peanut butter cup from him. "It's short for Lizard."

His eyebrows rose. "Really?"

"Lizard McGrew. My parents were freestyle hippies." She waited for the inevitable poor attempt at humor.

He didn't laugh or even crack a joke. He just nodded, his grin thoughtful. "It suits you, in a nice way. You're tough, strong, independent. A survivor. Just like a lizard."

"I didn't have it half as tough as my siblings, Watermelon and Yellow Jacket."

He couldn't stop a chuckle, though he tried. It came out a snorting laugh. "Seriously? Watermelon McGrew?"

"Mel got his revenge. He became a corporate executive. Jack took up wrestling and got a contract working the lucha libre circuit. Changed his name to Hornet."

Jidou laughed for real this time. "I'd love to hear about your family sometime."

"But we're burning daylight. If I'm going to find any caves, I need to start scrambling."

"I'll be back here at sunset," Jidou called as she trotted up the nearest sand dune.

She waved over her shoulder. Maybe he could be trusted. But maybe not. Liz preferred her own company most of the time. Exploring new planets suited her. Lots of time by herself, and always something new and never-before-seen over the next hill. The sound of his truck faded into the distance, leaving her on a silent world.

Liz trotted down the last dune. Loose sand slithered under her feet. She lost her balance and slid to her knees. Her hand tangled in something. She sat on the side of the dune and lifted it free. The long vine resembled twine, brown and scratchy with loose fibers. Round brown leaves dangled from the length looking like stones. Kusavi had tossed a surprise. Plants did exist out in the dunes. She touched one leaf. The outer skin split. Thick liquid spurted free. Liz grimaced as she wiped it off onto her pants. She dropped the vine back onto the dunes. She'd tell Jidou about it when she saw him that night. Now that she knew what to look for, she spotted strings of the stone-like leaves draped across the lower dunes. She stood and continued her search for caves.

She stopped again in surprise when she saw what lined the base of the cliff. Gray-green plants grew where the stone and sand met. They looked like giant cups nested inside each other. The smallest one on top was about two feet up. Yellow blobs clung like a fringe to the edge. Golden liquid oozed from the yellow down the outside of the top cup into the one below. Tiny black insects buzzed around the liquid. Liz crouched next to one to examine it closer. Insects and plants inland? That was unexpected. But then, who was to say that Kusavi had to follow the same evolutionary pattern Earth had?

She scratched her hand. A red rash spread from where she'd contacted the juice from the dune vines. Not a problem, but it was bothersome. She could deal with it later, after she found a cave to wait out the heat.

The plants seemed thicker, taller, off to her right. Liz headed that way, watching for anything that might hint at water or a cave nearby.

The taller stand grew in a notch in the rocks. Liz caught the faint trickle of water somewhere in the distance. A slightly cooler breeze swayed the cups and set the clouds of tiny gnats swirling around the plants. Liz dropped to her heels. She scratched her hand. The rash had spread and now sprouted yellow blisters. Not good. She took a drink from her water bottle, then dribbled it over her hand. She didn't have enough to wash off the liquid without sacrificing all of her drinking water, though.

"You hiding a cave there?" she spoke to the plants. The sound of her voice shivered from the rocks. She snapped her mouth shut. Kusavi was too silent but talking to herself only made it worse. She pulled a rock hammer from her pack. It was a useful tool, worth the extra weight to carry. She flipped it around, holding the head between her fingers. She prodded the nearest cup plant with the handle.

A dark hole, low but wide, was behind the growth. The plant tilted sideways under her prodding. Golden liquid trickled down the side, thick and slow like honey. Liz hooked her hammer around the base. With a sharp yank, she jerked it back across the sand. The plant popped free, spraying liquid across the ground. Liz scrambled backward, out of the way. The uprooted plant wilted into a mass of slime and buzzing gnats.

The hole was noticeable now, but still screened by plants. She shoved her hammer behind the next and tore it loose. This time she flung it to the side instead of pulling straight back. It tumbled into the bright sunlight then melted into another sticky spot.

Liz reached for the third plant. This one had deeper roots. The plant broke off unexpectedly, showering her arm and hand with sticky fluid. She dropped her hammer and scrubbed her arm with sand. But where the stuff had landed on her rash, the redness and swelling faded. The golden syrup soothed not just the rash but her sunburn, too. She shifted into the shade next to another of the cups.

"In for a penny, in for a pound," she muttered as she plunged her hand into the largest cup. The liquid was cool and silky to touch. The gnats rose in a cloud around her, swarming into her face and hair. The pain and itching on her arm was gone. When she pulled her hand back out, her skin was smooth and cool to the touch.

"Gotta tell Jidou about this one, too," she said as she collected her hammer.

She eyed the opening. Low and wide, but she should be able to crawl through. She used the hammer to move a vine of the stone leaves out of the way. No sense in getting her rash back. She crawled through the hole and into the cave beyond.

The space opened somewhat, but it was still fairly small, shaped like a bowl with a pond at the bottom. Crevices higher up the walls let in a thin trickle of daylight. Liz picked her way down the slope to the pond. Halfway there, something squished under her foot. Bright pink foam gushed over her boot. The froth melted quickly leaving behind nothing but a faintly glowing smear. Liz lifted her boot.

Rounded shapes that she'd taken for rocks littered the floor. The largest lined the edges of the pool. What were they? Fungi? Slime molds? Something completely new? She shrugged. Another mystery for the likes of Jidou to unravel. Her business was to find caves suitable for the settlers. So far, this one wasn't big enough. She picked her way across the cave, leaving a trail of glowing foam behind her in pink, yellow, orange, and white. They were pretty, in a weird way.

The water in the pond looked like milk, white with minerals. She passed on filling her water bottle. The sound of dripping water drew her up the other side of the cave toward a curtain of dripstone. No water flowed over it now; it was dry to her touch. A narrow passage curled behind it, though. She squeezed herself around the stone.

The space opened out into a large cavern. Dim light filtering from cracks high overhead showed strange shapes. Liz fished her flashlight from her pack then flicked it on. Colors blossomed where her light touched. Huge growths covered the bottom like a giant coral reef. Bigger versions of the cup plants held pride of place next to a milky-white pond of water. Delicate fronds of reddish purple reached above them, toward the stalactites hanging from the ceiling. The brown bubble things from the first cave lined the walls and drier areas. Other fungi in all shapes and sizes grew in between.

A fall of gravel led down from the ledge to the floor, the only clear path Liz could see. She headed down, sliding as much as walking on the loose slope. Something gleamed in the flashlight beam. Liz stopped, bending closer. A round stone, about the size of her palm, lay on the gravel. It was smooth, a dark shade of brown. Swirls of gold marked the translucent stone. It fit her hand nicely. She rubbed the slick surface, enjoying the feel of the stone on her skin. But she still had a cave to explore. The stone went into her pocket.

She picked her way through the strange growths, following the looser gravel path where the plants were smaller. She bumped into a lacy blue plant that reached high over her head. Something rattled loose, dropping through the stiff branches to the gravel at her feet. It was a brown stone, like the one she'd picked up earlier, round and smooth. She looked up into the plant. More nodules of various sizes grew at each juncture between limb and trunk. Were they seeds of some sort, not rocks? But they looked and felt like rocks, not seeds. Kusavi wasn't Earth, she reminded herself. Maybe she would have to trade a movie night with Jidou for some answers. Her curiosity would drive her crazy if she didn't. She dropped the second stone into her pocket with the first.

Indistinct voices shouted, breaking the silence. She rose to her feet, ready to call out.

"Dump him there. Even if he gets loose, he'll die long before he can reach the settlement."

Liz froze. The voice was familiar, belonging to Lars Kevan, first mate on the spaceship that had brought the latest batch of supplies and scientists to the new colony. What was he doing here? And who was he dumping here to die?

"You two, get those burned. We've got a schedule to keep. The captain wants to lift day after tomorrow. Let's see how much we can get before the suns set."

Orange light flickered and danced over the walls on the far side. The stench of burning filled the cave. Liz wrinkled her nose.

She had to see what was going on. At least the noise they made would make it easier for her to sneak up on them. A finger of gravel led to one side, curving through the giant mushrooms back toward the sound of flame throwers. If Lars had come in that way, there had to be an opening or more caves that direction. Liz had been sent to find caves. If Lars confronted her, that's what she'd say. Just out exploring. No, Lars, I did not hear you order someone to be left behind to die. "Like he'd believe me," she whispered. Her hands trembled.

She turned into the narrow opening, stepping as carefully as she could. More of the round rocks tumbled under her feet. The blue plants swayed as she stumbled against them. She froze, waiting for the sound of burning to cease and shouts of discovery to follow. She held her breath for a very long minute, but the shouts never came.

She released her breath and picked her way forward more carefully. Purple fronds towered over her head. The branches reached across the space, twisting together. She crouched, waddling under the tangle to the other side where the growths were shorter and more spread out.

The cave filled with thick smoke. She ducked her head into her collar, breathing through the cotton fabric. The foul stench couldn't be blocked as easily.

Liz stopped under a fall of shimmering fronds that grew at the edge of an open space. A body lay tied and motionless on rocks streaked with ash from burnt plants. Lars and two others in jumpsuits marked with the shipping company logo, had their backs to her. Liz dropped to her knees then crawled forward.

"Jidou?" she whispered when she recognized him. He'd caught someone's fist with his face. His eye swelled shut. His good eye widened.

She motioned him quiet as she glanced over at Lars and his two buddies. She recognized Jonesy and Dave from the crew of the ship. Dave picked up a chunk from the ashes then dropped it into a reinforced tub. It hit the bottom with a solid thud.

Liz fumbled the ropes around Jidou's wrists free. The knots were sloppy, easy to untie. Jidou shook off the ropes then untied his ankles.

"Hey!" Jonesy spotted them.

Liz jumped to her feet, then ran into the plants, Jidou at her heels.

"Stop them," Lars ordered, his voice harsh.

"This way," Liz said, taking the lead. If they could get to the ledge, they could escape the cave. And go where? She tried to ignore the voice in her head, but it had a point. Outside, under the two suns, would be too hot. But inside was certain death, to judge from the angry shouts echoing through the mushroom forest.

"Where?" Jidou gasped, hand pressed to his side.

Liz slowed, weaving into a thicker growth of purple fronds. "I came in that way," she waved to the ledge and the gravel slide. "Can you climb that? Run?"

Jidou shook his head. "I got a few bruises, but I'm not going to make it far in the heat outside. You have water?"

It was Liz's turn to shake her head. "My bottle's almost empty. Are there more caves the other way?"

Jidou shrugged, then winced. "I was pretty out of it when they dragged me in here."

"Then we run and hide until we find another way out. Come on."

They ran, headed in a roundabout way to the still smoldering heaps of plants. Liz stayed low, trying to keep her feet quiet. Jidou followed her example.

"You can't hide, not for long," Lars shouted.

Liz detoured toward the far wall of the cave. Dark streaks down the stone marked possible seeps. She shoved her way through a stand of tall yellow pillars. They were spongy, unpleasant under her touch. She pulled her sleeves over her hands as she pushed past. The plants left a narrow strip open next to the sandstone face of the wall. Water had flowed through here in the distant past, lots of water, carving out the wide cave bottom. Now it just trickled down the walls. She crawled as far as she could into the space. Jidou crowded in behind her.

Her pack scraped on the overhang of rock, but the space was deeper than it had appeared. Water trickled and dripped, echoing from the deep dark. She dropped to her belly and wiggled farther into the space.

"Find them! It's your necks if they escape," Lars threatened his men.

Liz crawled faster. Jidou's panting breath was harsh in the confined space.

Her pack hung up on the rocks. She flattened as far as she could on the ground. She pushed her arms out in front as far as she could reach. The space felt larger ahead, but right here, it was too tight. She wriggled, trying to pull the pack off or herself forward.

"They went this way," Jonesy shouted.

Liz pushed harder. One strap of her pack tore, but she managed to shove herself through the narrow opening and into the black cave beyond.

"Help?" Jidou whispered.

Faint light from the other cave backlit him. He held out one hand. She took it and pulled. He shoved and wiggled until he made it through the small hole. Liz scrambled to the side. He followed.

"What now?" Jidou whispered as Lars shouted threats on the other side of the tunnel.

"I don't know. You got any ideas?"

Jidou shrugged. "Fresh out."

"Stay here. I'm going to find water."

She felt more than saw him nod. She crawled into the dark, following the sound of water as she groped her way over stone. Whatever Lars and the others were gathering, they were willing to kill for it. Liz was stumped as to what this cave might hold that would be that valuable.

"There's another cave," Jonesy's voice echoed from the tunnel.

"We'll wait," Lars answered. "Even if they find a way out, they'll be miles from any help."

"What if she's got a radio or something?"

"Crawl down the tunnel and kill them, then," Lars said.

Liz stumbled faster toward the water as sounds of someone crawling came from the tunnel. The faint light filtering into the cave was blocked as Jonesy reached the narrow spot. Liz jerked at the sound of a rock slamming into something meaty. Jonesy let out a yelp before scrambling back into the tunnel.

Liz swallowed hard. It turned her stomach to think of what Jidou had just done to that man, but they were fighting for their lives. She tried not to shiver as she filled her bottle from a damp trickle she found by touch.

She found Jidou halfway across the cave, a shadow in the reflected light. "We should move, find somewhere to wait them out. How deep do you think these caves go?"

"No idea," Jidou answered.

"Tell me why they're burning those plants. What are they? Fungi?" She found her flashlight and flicked it on. Lars already knew where they were. Groping in the dark wasn't going to help them evade him and his henchmen. The cave was rough, all stone and damp dripping water with no signs of the mushrooms, not even the round brown ones.

"They aren't fungi, at least not as we humans classify them. These are something entirely different." Jidou pointed at the small opening. Smoke filtered through. "We should move somewhere else. Fast."

"Over there. Looks like it might go deeper." Liz led the way up to a narrow ledge.

"As to why Lars is burning them," Jidou continued as they climbed up the knobbled rocks to the ledge, "the plants produce pharmo-chemicals that are concentrated when the plants are burned. Drug companies are clamoring for them, but the street price is even higher. Or so Lars told me."

Liz frowned as she helped Jidou up to the ledge. "Why would Lars want to kill us over it? It's not like we can report him, not from here. By the time I get back to settled space, he'll be long gone to another sector."

"Settlement laws grant ninety percent ownership of any natural resources to the settlers. My guess is Lars doesn't want to share. If we report him to the settlers, they'll lynch him over it." He leaned on the rocks, breathing hard.

"You okay?" Liz asked as she probed the shadows with her flashlight. A narrow tunnel led up at a steep angle from the ledge.

"I can still move."

She handed him her water bottle. He made a face at the mineral taste, but drank. She took a swig when he finished. It wasn't the worst she'd tasted.

"Let me see if I can find any other way out," she said. "You rest here. If I can't find anything, we'll climb that." She pointed up the slope.

Jidou nodded as he dropped to sit on the ledge.

Liz jumped down, landing on the loose scree below. She flipped on the flashlight. The cave revealed no new secrets under its light. Lars shouted at Dave on the other side of the tunnel, something about smoking them out. Liz shook her head. The airflow was from the deeper cave out into the mushroom forest.

She joined Jidou back on the ledge. "No luck. Lars is going to try to burn us out. We're going to have to climb up that shaft."

Jidou grimaced as he rose to his feet. He used the wall for support the whole way up. "I guess we'd better start. You go first."

"Hold the light for me." Liz scrambled up the slope. Loose rocks tumbled to the ledge.

Jidou stepped to the side, out of the way of the falling rocks. The flashlight beam wavered, then steadied.

The slope flattened out. The gravel gave way to worn stone. Liz paused where the crack jigged to the right. "It gets easier," she called down to Jidou.

He flipped the flashlight off. The cave went dark, except for a faint red flicker from the tunnel. The sound of Jidou scrambling up the slope drowned out the faint echo of Lars shouting at his men.

She caught his hand as he reached her. His breath wheezed. She guided him to the holds she'd found. "Flashlight?" she asked.

He handed it to her.

The beam stabbed up the tunnel, illuminating a quick twist to the left. The ceiling hung low, but at least the slope had leveled. She turned off the flashlight, tucking it into her pack before crawling forward.

"They're coming," Jidou whispered.

She crawled faster up the twisting passageway, feeling her way blindly over rocks.

Faint gray light filtered around several curves. She moved faster once she could see the obstacles. She stopped just shy of the opening, a narrow crevice between two boulders. A fringe of the rock-leaf vines coated the ground outside.

"Where did you leave the truck?" she asked.

"Lars stole it when he jumped me. I think he left the equipment behind, back that way a mile or so. We could find the radio and call for help. Unless he smashed it."

Liz nodded. She pointed at the vines. "Watch out for those. The leaves are full of juice that gives you a nasty rash."

"You touched those?"

"The liquid in those cup plants at the base of the cliff fixed it." She slipped into the heat of the full double day. Sweat dripped from her and she was still in the shade of the boulders.

Jidou followed her. "You know that was stupid, right? To experiment like that."

She stepped sideways, trying to keep to the shade as much as possible. "Some days you do what you have to."

"You're braver than I am."

The cliff dropped into a sheer wall a couple feet in front of them. Behind, a boulder-strewn slope rose to the crest not far above.

Liz leaned out. "I see the truck parked at the cave entrance, under that overhang. Unless we can steal the keys from Lars, it won't do us much good." She stepped back. "Dave just came out to guard it."

"Up looks like our only option."

They scrambled up the slope. Jidou knocked a small boulder loose and sent a landslide of rubble over the edge of the cliff. Dave's shouts echoed off the cliff face.

Liz took off along the ridge top, moving fast despite the heat and the loose footing. She found a narrow side canyon where they could climb back down. Vines tangled on the sides of the steep cut. Brown leaves drooped, heavy and fat with liquid.

Jidou limped up to join her. "The radio should be only a mile or so farther west."

"They know we're up here." She eyed him. "You aren't going to be able to run very fast. How about you go after the radio and I'll run interference? I've got a bad idea."

"That grin is scaring me," Jidou said. "What are you thinking?"

Liz knelt, then dumped her pack onto the ground. "Take whatever you think might be useful. This pack isn't going to be worth anything when I get done." She pulled a pair of gloves from the pile. "I'm going to fill it with those vines. Be careful climbing down. If you do touch them, use the liquid from the plants at the bottom."

Jidou nodded. "Good luck."

"Just get to that radio and get us help."

Liz flexed her fingers in the gloves, picked up the pack by its good strap, then started down the side canyon. She stripped vines as she went, stuffing them into the pack until it bulged. Thick liquid seeped through the fabric. She did her best to keep it away from any bare skin.

She reached the bottom and turned east. She ran toward the truck, parked under a large overhang around a bulge of stone. Dave saw her and shouted.

"You want some of this?" She swung the pack by its strap. "Come get it, Dave."

He growled and charged toward her.

She slapped him with the pack. Some ooze from the plants spattered him on impact. Liz didn't wait to see what it did. She turned and ran into the dunes, shouting insults as she went. Dave followed her. They both slowed in the loose sand. Liz picked a path that would take her back toward the truck.

She risked a glance behind. Angry red streaks marked Dave's skin. It wasn't enough to slow him down. Liz stumbled over another vine. Dave snagged her ponytail as she went down to one knee. He yanked backward. She shrieked but let him pull her over. Her gloved hand closed over the vine. She swung it over her shoulder. The leaves exploded in his face.

Dave screamed, a primal squawk of pain. He dropped his hold on her hair to paw at his eyes.

Liz dropped the vine. She'd never hurt someone before, not like this. She hesitated, wanting to help him.

"Kill her!" Lars's shout echoed across the sand. He and Jonesy trotted into view.

Jonesy cradled a bloody hand against his belly. Jidou had smashed it good with the rock. "What's wrong with Dave?"

"He found some native life that didn't agree with him," Liz answered. "Why are you trying to kill me? What did I do to you?"

"You messed up a great thing we have going here." Lars glowered, eyebrows lowering. "All you had to do was stay away for another day. So now we get to kill you, bury you in the rocks. No one will ever find you, not all the way out here."

Liz shook her head. "And I thought you were kind of cute."

Lars snorted. "Where'd that biologist go?"

"No idea. He took off, left me up there by myself." She jerked her chin toward the cliff. "What if I want in on your deal?"

Jonesy let out a sharp, "Ha!"

Lars folded his arms. "Why should we let you in?"

"Because I'm not leaving on a ship day after tomorrow. I'm going to be on Kusavi for at least another three months, until you come back. I keep collecting for you. No one else needs to find out."

Dave collapsed to the sand, moaning as the rash spread over his face. Blisters popped out everywhere the goo had hit. He kept his eyes screwed shut.

"You gonna let him die?" Liz asked.

Lars kept his arms folded, glaring at her without a glance at Dave.

Jonesy shifted uneasily. "You gonna cut her in?"

"I can tell you how to fix it," Liz said, "but you have to act fast. You give me the keys to the truck, I tell you how to fix that. And I keep my mouth shut."

Lars shook his head.

Dave stretched one arm out. "I can't see. You got to help me, Lars."

Lars just glared at Liz.

"Come on, man," Jonesy said. "He needs help."

Liz tightened her grip on the pack strap.

"Go help him wash it off, then," Lars snapped at Jonesy. "I'll kill her myself."

"Sure you don't want another partner?" Liz hoped the pack still held enough of the plant ooze. Lars wasn't going to go down easy. He was big, and mean. She'd have to hit hard and fast.

Jonesy circled around Liz, giving her a wide berth as he went to help his friend.

"You sure you want to work for someone like this?" Liz asked him. She edged forward, shuffling her feet in the sand.

"Shut up," Lars snapped. "They know how much is at stake."

"I don't. Why don't you tell me?" Keep him talking, Liz told herself. Keep him distracted as much as you can. Buy Jidou time to get help.

"More money than a colonist like you will ever see."

Liz raised one eyebrow. "What makes you think I'm a colonist?"

"You aren't a scientist. What else could you be?" He sneered.

"Smarter than you," Liz said as she swung the pack at his face.

Lars got his hands up. The pack hit and exploded in a shower of liquid. Lars screamed as it poured across his arms and chest. His reaction to it was faster. Huge welts swelled across his exposed flesh. He flailed at the air, spreading the goo farther with his wild actions.

Jonesy grabbed Liz from behind, clamping his good arm around her. She kicked backward, connecting with his shins. He clamped his hand onto her shirt sleeve. Liz twisted to face him, then struck out with her gloved hands. Maybe there was some of the stuff still on them. Jonesy flailed with his smashed hand. She clawed his face. He grabbed her ponytail then used both hands to shake her. She went limp in his hold.

Sweat poured from both of them as they panted under the heat of the double suns. Jonesy turned his head to spit into the sand. He kept his eyes on her. Lars and Dave provided a background chorus of moans.

"What are you going to do now?" Liz asked. "You aren't man enough to kill me. You don't have the guts for it. Neither does Lars. And poor Dave. I can help him. If you'll let me."

Jonesy growled. His hand tightened painfully on her hair.

Liz bit her lips until he eased his grip. "Give me the keys to the truck. I'll tell your captain you were out exploring and got into trouble. I can help them both, but only if you let me go."

"You'll turn us in. Or let us die out here."

"Let me go and I'll tell you how to help them."

Jonesy twisted his face into a snarl, but he dropped his hold.

"Keys?" Liz demanded holding out her gloved hand.

"You promise not to leave us here? We've got no water, no supplies. They need medical help for whatever you did to them." Jonesy nodded at the two men writhing on the ground as he scratched his arm. The telltale rash marked where Liz had scored at least one hit.

"You were going to leave me here to die. Give me the keys." She made her face hard and uncompromising even though her conscience was screaming at her to help. Her hippie mother would be so disappointed in her. Live and let live, her mother's voice echoed in her head. She shook her head, trying to banish a past that she'd thought long abandoned.

"Tell me how to help them."

"Keys first." And her mother could roll over in her grave, wherever that might be.

"They're in Lars's pocket." The rash blotched his face and neck, too.

Liz kept one eye on Jonesy as she bent over Lars. "Which pocket?"

"Augh! What is this stuff?" Jonesy dug his fingers into his skin.

"Kusavi's revenge on you for trying to steal from the colonists." Liz wrinkled her nose as she gingerly felt in Lars's pocket. No keys.

"Look, I'll cut you in on the deal. Painkillers, hallucinogens, other drugs, just sitting in there for the taking. All you gotta do is burn the mushrooms then pick out the clumped chemicals from the ashes. We take them to the markets. You can have a share of the money. Just tell me how to stop this!" Jonesy squirmed. His sweat spread the rash farther.

Liz wiped her own sweat with her sleeve, careful to keep her gloves away from her skin. She reached into Lars's other pocket. "Too late to deal now, besides, what do I need money for out here in the frontier? I'll settle for you letting me go. Once I have the keys, I'll tell you the cure." Her hand closed on the keys to the truck and pulled them out of Lars's pocket.

Like a zombie, Lars rose from the ground. He clamped his hand on Liz's arm. His other arm swung around and clubbed her on her ear.

She stumbled and would have fallen except for the hold Lars had on her arm. The keys went flying into a patch of the vines. Lars raised his hand to clobber her again. His swollen face twisted with rage.

"Let her go!" Jidou's voice rang across the sand.

Liz kicked Lars in the knee. He crumpled. She yanked her arm out of his grip.

"I was doing fine on my own," she said as Jidou marched out to join her. "I don't need you to save me."

Jidou frowned. "Next time I'll let you save yourself then."

"Who says there's going to be a next time?" Liz turned her back on the prostrate men and their groaning.

"How do I stop this?" Jonesy whined. His face was red, marked with bubbling blisters.

"See those plants along the cliff?" Liz pointed at the nearest clump of the cup plants. "Use that liquid."

"How do I know you aren't lying?" Jonesy squinted at her.

"Just keep scratching your skin off, then." Liz turned her back on Jonesy. She stomped as best she could across the sand to the last place she saw the keys for the truck.

Jidou hurried to join her. "You aren't just going to leave them out here, are you?"

"Are you?" She shot a sideways glance at him.

He grinned. "The colonists are on their way. I think I heard at least one mention lynching when I explained what Lars and friends were doing out here. They take their planetary charter seriously. I'm not sure their captain will intervene for them. He sounded just as angry."

Liz carefully extracted the keys from a nest of vines. "So what does that mean for you? You've got the find of the century in those caves." She stripped off her stained gloves and dropped them to the sand.

"There's a fortune in pharmaceuticals, not to mention the scientific discoveries and papers just begging to be written. You know, Liz, you'll have to emigrate to Kusavi if you want your share. Unless you were serious about wanting in on their criminal enterprise."

Liz jingled the keys. "I don't work with idiots. Are you going to emigrate?"

"I'm thinking about it. There's a whole world here to explore. Who knows what else we'll find? I'd love to have you working alongside me."

"Oh, just shoot me now," Jonesy complained. "Get a room already."

"Shut up," Liz snapped over her shoulder. She'd never had someone flirt with her like this before. She liked it. But enough to give up exploring? Enough to give up her solitude?

"And I promise not to save you again. I'll just sit back and let you save yourself." Jidou's smile was infectious. "I only have one condition. Tell me about your family."

"You sure you want to know?"

"Absolutely."

Jonesy shook his head as he stumbled past them, headed for the cup plants. They ignored him and the other two men on the sand.

"Deal," Liz said. She held out her hand. "On one condition."

It was Jidou's turn to raise one eyebrow.

"I get to drive."

He took her hand. "Deal."

"And if you ever call me Lizard, I may have to hurt you." She squeezed, just enough to pass on her threat.

He squeezed back, but in a nice way.

"I think one planet may be enough for me," Liz admitted. "But two suns may be a little much. Think exosummer might be livable?"

"We can always spend it exploring the arctic regions. Or the caves."

"Or the oceans." They started walking to the truck, leaving Dave and Lars groaning on the sand. "Maybe exosummer is why life hasn't spread much outside the water. Too hot and dry."

"The plants in those caves were certainly a surprise," Jidou admitted. "I'm curious what else has evolved on Kusavi."

Liz didn't say it out loud, but she was curious what it might be like to explore the strange planet with someone else, someone who didn't mind if she was named Lizard. She smiled despite the heat from Primary and Secondary. Kusavi promised surprises in more than its eccentric orbit and seasons. Mushroom forests in caverns. Plants that burned and plants that healed. Who knew what else waited around the bend?

Jidou took her hand as they walked across the dunes.

Who knew what waited in her future? Liz walked faster, eager to find out.

Mrs. Pettigrew and
the Spaceship

"Dr. Dickinson, we have a problem." Admiral Thompson carefully steepled his fingers. "This new tesseract drive your eggheads have invented is impossible to operate. Our pilots just can't make heads or tails of it."

Dr. Dickinson wrinkled his forehead, which extended all the way to the top of his head. Premature male pattern baldness was not a high priority for the geneticists, but they were all under thirty and hadn't suffered from the condition yet. "Admiral Thompson, I assure you, the drive is complex, it does involve folding time and space around a point singularity after all. But," he raised one long, lumpy finger to add emphasis to his statement, "it is not impossible."

"Poppycock. We've been trying for months now, with no success and a whole string of accidents to show for it. We need a new drive, a simpler one more like those TV shows. Point the ship and tell the pilot to step on it. The ship flashes away, and Bob's your uncle. Simple, easy, none of this ridiculous folding the continuum in your head."

Dr. Dickinson sucked a deep breath in through his nostrils, making his glasses slide up his nose. "Admiral Thompson, with all due respect, space travel does not work that way. Moving faster than light is incredibly complex and requires manipulating the space-time continuum. We have tried all the other methods and, if you'll pardon my French, they're all bullpuckey. Sir." His face flushed crimson at the almost-profanity. He was not a scientist given to expletives.

"Then how the devil are we supposed to operate that ship?" The admiral slammed his meaty fist onto the desk. "Dammit, man! We've been through every member of the flight crew and none of them, not a one, can operate that machine."

"I gave you a line-by-line instruction manual, at least the best I could write. Much of the folding happens intuitively. I wish it were otherwise, but quantum manipulation is fuzzy science due to the very nature of the continuum. The controls are as straight-forward as I can make them."

"Then find a new way to simplify them!"

"Find someone who can use the controls!"

"Excuse me, sirs." The door squeaked open. A plump older woman oozed through the small crack. "Pardon me, but it's on the schedule for me to clean this meeting room. You just carry on and I'll just do my job over here." She flicked a dust rag from her pocket. She hummed off-key as she jauntily dusted the sideboard.

Admiral Thompson screwed his face up and glared at the scientist.

Dr. Dickinson's glare slowly faded into a thoughtful look. "Mrs. Pettigrew?"

The plump cleaning lady paused in her humming. "Yes, Doctor?"

"Do you, by any chance," he searched for words for a moment. "Do you do a lot of laundry?"

Mrs. Pettigrew's pleasant smile froze in place. Her voice had the tiniest bite when she answered. "Are you asking me to start washing your lab coats now, too? Besides cleaning up behind your lunches, and your experiments, and your little meetings? Not to mention the amount of dirt you manage to track through the halls every morning. I don't know what you get up during the night but—"

"Mrs. Pettigrew, please." Dr. Dickinson held his hands up to ward off her verbal assault. "I was merely asking out of scientific curiousity."

"With a possible military application?" Admiral Thompson raised one commanding gray eyebrow. It had been known to issue commands which had ended several military engagements before they even started. Ensigns whispered about the powers of his eyebrow, but only in the dark secret spaces of the Navy's ships. "I think I know where you are headed, Doctor."

Mrs. Pettigrew flicked her duster. "I wash my own laundry, true. But I'll not be taking on anyone else's. Except my mum's. She's not as sharp as she used to be, poor lamb."

"And did your mother teach you to fold fitted sheets, perhaps?" Dr. Dickinson fixed his gaze on the plump cleaning woman in her lumpy brown dress.

Mrs. Pettigrew shook her head. "My mum used to shove them into a bin in the linen closet. She never could get them to lie flat. I tried to tell her it was simple geometry, but she never got the hang of it. I've been folding them all my life. I've a gift for it, or so my mum said. It's really not hard at all to get them to lay all flat and neat in the cupboard."

Dr. Dickinson traded a triumphant glance with Admiral Thompson. "And that, Admiral, is how you will find the pilots for your new tesseract drive."

"What? I'm supposed to hand them a fitted sheet and wait to see how they fold it?"

Mrs. Pettigrew giggled. "That would be a silly test for one of your hotshot pilots now, wouldn't it?"

Dr. Dickinson fixed Admiral Thompson with a level stare. "I dare you," he whispered. "Doube dog dare you to ask your pilots. I will bet my whole reputation that none of them can fold a fitted sheet."

"I'll go you one better," the Admiral answered. "Mrs. Pettigrew, would you perhaps like to try your hand at something other than cleaning?"

"I'm not that kind of woman, sir. I'm a decent woman, widowed these past fourteen years, but my mum raised me right." She held her duster like a sword aimed at the Admiral.

"Not that kind of thing, ma'am," the Admiral sputtered. "I'm offering you a job position. With much higher pay and benefits. Assuming you can pass our little test."

"She'll pass." Dr. Dickinson looked smug.

"Doing what?" Mrs. Pettigrew gave the Admiral a suspicious glare.

"Flying our new quantum tesseract space drive. The good doctor assures me that if you can fold a fitted sheet, you can fold the space-time continuum."

Mrs. Pettigrew tapped her duster on her arm as she thought over his offer. "I'll give it a try, then. Couldn't hurt."

"And might just change the course of history. Right this way, ma'am." The Admiral ushered her toward the door.

"Call me Penny," Mrs. Pettigrew said with a flirtatious smile.

"You make my drive work, and I'll call you anything you like," Admiral Thompson said.

Dr. Dickinson watched the door close with a satisfied smirk. "If you can fold a fitted sheet, you can fold the universe. It'll work."

Welcome to the Calormancer Weight Loss Clinic!

W e hope you enjoy your stay and that you leave with much less than you brought. Calormancer Clinics are designed to provide you with the utmost in comfort and discretion while you pursue your weight loss journey.

Our facilities include three acres of beautifully manicured gardens located next to the Happy Hills Golf Course, an Olympic size swimming pool and spa, a full massage parlor and beauty salon, personal concierge assistance purchasing a new wardrobe for your new look, and comfortable calormancy suites that provide total and complete privacy for the treatment. We also boast a magically powered fire department for those unfortunate accidents. Rest assured, our staff are all highly trained to handle even the most extreme side effects.

Book a weekend stay. Relax and play during the day, and let our calormancers work their magic by night. You'll leave refreshed and rejuvenated with a whole new, slender you! Book now for an extra ten percent off all concierge services!

WHAT IS CALORMANCY? Don't feel bad if you've never heard of us. Most people haven't experienced the all-natural burn of magic cleansing their system of impurities and burning up those excess pounds. Our calormancers are highly trained specialists in the art of distilling energy. Each one will help you target those pesky, hard to lose bulges and fat rolls. With a simple magic ritual that usually takes less than a day, your extra calories will be converted to magical energy, distilled into crystals, and credited to your account.

HOW DOES CALORMANCY WORK? It's a simple process, handed down from wizard to wizard through the ages. If you've ever seen a wizard with his crystals glowing, you've seen magical energy at work. But those crystals can get run down, de-energized. Even bathing them in reverse-osmosis filtered, ionized, and de-mineralized water imported directly from the springs on the fabled island of Avalon can't restore their sparkle. What those crystals need is energy, calories to be exact. But you can't feed a crystal burritos. We combine those wizards and their tired crystals with your love of rich food and excess intake of calories. It's a win-win! All we provide is the calormancer who turns your indulgences into a full recharge for those high-powered crystals.

IS IT PAINFUL? Calormancy is a proven weight loss treatment. Some patients complain of a burning sensation as the fat is being liquidated and converted to magical energy. But that is a small price to pay for that perfect body you've always wanted while still enjoying all your favorite foods, no matter the calorie count!

MY NEIGHBOR HAD CALORMANCY TREATMENTS, AND NOW SHE'S COVERED IN SAGGY, STRETCHED OUT SKIN! WILL THAT HAPPEN TO ME? The amount of sagging depends entirely on your bone structure and the weight converted to energy. Extreme weight loss is possible with calormancy, which can lead to excess skin. You can always choose the option of having excess skin removed and repurposed for an additional small fee. All excess skin is donated to the Wart Removal for Goblins charity, that provides skin grafts for goblins at cost. It's a great way to help out those poor, hideous creatures while pampering yourself.

LEGAL DISCLAIMER: *All treatments of Calormancy are protected under the Freedom of Wizardry Act of 2039. Magical weight loss systems are inherently risky. Those engaging in Calormancy are urged to have all legal documents and right-of-attorney signed and notarized before commencing treatment. Side effects may include, but are not limited to, liquefaction of all fat cells, bloating, non-stop diarrhea, blurred vision, psoriasis, disappearance of intestinal tract, spontaneous combustion of taste buds, flaming ulcers, transmogrification into dragon form, and possible death. By agreeing to undergo calor-*

mancy treatments, you waive all rights to sue Calormancer Weight Loss Clinic for loss of life or limb, unexpected transformation, spontaneous speaking in Latin, or any other unforeseen outcome.

Do yourself a favor—get the body you want through the power of magic!

AUNT RUBY'S
JAM CAKE

"Whip that a little longer, sweetie." Aunt Ruby hovered behind me, her lilac-scented bosom bobbing with every breath. I was twelve that summer, when I learned her secret to making perfect jam cake.

I watched the butter and sugar whirl under the beaters of her ancient stand mixer. The heavy bowl jiggled under the beating. The scent of vanilla and roses hung heavy in the June air of her outdoor kitchen.

"You want that so light an angel could dance on top without leaving footprints." Her cotton dress, a shapeless bag given life and movement by her stout body, swung with each step. Her voice dropped to a scratchy whisper. "Or a fairy."

Her hand whisked past my head, snatching something fluttery from the roses that draped the arbor shading us from the summer sun.

"Can you add the eggs like I showed you? One at a time, and slowly, child." She moved to the far side of the kitchen, to the long table covered in old formica, nicked and scarred by years of duty.

"Yes'm." I straightened with pride. Adding eggs was a grown-up responsibility, only for seasoned cooks to attempt. I carefully cracked an egg into a small earthenware bowl, then picked out the shell fragments. I slid the gooey mass into the mixer. The beaters slammed into it, mixing it into the fluffy mass of butter and sugar.

Thwack!

I jumped at the sharp noise of a knife hitting wood. An egg rolled toward the edge of the counter. I grabbed it barely in time.

"Never you mind me, child, keep your mind on your task. That's the secret to good cooking. Always keep your attention on your task." The knife slammed down again.

Something tiny screamed, high and whining like a desperate mosquito.

I added another egg to the mix. The knife hit the chopping board again, and again. The screams stopped.

"One more should be enough," Aunt Ruby muttered.

I dutifully kept my eyes on the mixing bowl as I added another egg. I slid my gaze to the side as Aunt Ruby crossed near me. She reached into the roses, flicking petals to the side as she searched among the blossoms. Her flabby biceps quivered with each movement. *Church lady arms*, my mother called them. She swore she'd never get old and fat and have flabby arms that jiggled and shifted as she waved. I watched as Aunt Ruby's church lady arms jabbed into the bushes. She pulled them back. Something tiny pinched between her fat fingers. It screamed, like the other one, as she carried it across to the chopping block.

"What's that, Aunt Ruby?" I ventured to ask. The last egg was whirling under the beater.

"My special ingredient." Her back blocked my view of the counter. The knife glittered in her fist.

"I thought rose jelly was the special ingredient, along with the raspberry jam."

Aunt Ruby turned toward me. Her mouth curved in a smile I'd earlier thought was sweet like a rosebud. Now it seemed cruel, pinched and tight. "You're a sweet child, but it's time you learned that sweetness comes at a price. Turn off that mixer and come here."

I didn't dare disobey, not with that knife in her hand. I flipped the switch. The buzzing of the mixer died with a clatter of beaters on the bowl. The three steps across the cracked cement felt as long as a country mile.

Aunt Ruby stepped away from the counter, stretching her arm to keep something pinned to the chopping block. I moved closer, curiosity stirred despite the strangeness of my great-aunt. Her lilac scent enveloped me in a cloying blanket. I leaned over the wooden board.

She had a tiny person trapped under her fingers. The person glowed bright pink. Delicate wings fluttered, their edges torn by my aunt's cruel grip. The face turned to me with a desperate look. Help me, the mouth seemed to say.

"Let it go," I begged. "It's a fairy."

Ruby shook her head. "They're like weeds. Let one go and you'll have hundreds of the things."

I stared at the delicate creature. "What harm could they do?"

"You believe those stories, child?" Ruby leaned close, her beady eyes hard like marbles in her puffy face. I couldn't hold her gaze. Mine slid upwards to where her gray hair stood in wild curls. "Fairies are worse than aphids. They suck the life from your roses."

Thwack!

I jumped as the knife neatly severed the fairy's head. The body oozed what looked like honey. Aunt Ruby's knife smacked down again, crushing the fairy into a paste. She scraped it into a bowl.

"They steal honey, too. I can't have them bothering my bees. Or the chickens." She set the knife down. The blade dripped golden liquid onto the counter. "I can't abide them in the roses. Now go add that to the mixer."

I numbly took the bowl as ordered. The fairy slime oozed into the sugary mass. It sparkled as the beaters whirled. Aunt Ruby doled out the flour and spices and buttermilk, watching as each addition joined the batter. A tear slipped down my cheek and splashed into the bowl.

"Now there, child, don't you fret. Fairies are like anything else in my garden. Meant to be used." She gently stirred chopped pecans into the mass. "Go fetch the jams now. It's time."

I handed her the glass jars, neatly labeled in her curly handwriting. Blushing pink rose jelly and deep red raspberry jam slid into the bowl, like blood. Except the fairy had bled gold. I closed my eyes, breathing deep.

Lilac, spice, rose, vanilla, and something glittery filled my nose.

"Perfect," Aunt Ruby announced as she spooned the batter into the heavy baking pan. She handed me the spoon to lick as she slid them into her oven.

I swallowed hard, my stomach churning at the thought of smashed fairy. The blushing golden batter oozed onto my finger. I couldn't stop the tears.

"Hush, child. It's the way of life." Aunt Ruby folded me into her ample bosom and let me cry. "Now lick your finger and tell me if that isn't the best jam cake you ever tasted."

I licked the spoon. It was heavenly. I've made jam cake many times in the years since that summer, but I've never had the heart to add Aunt Ruby's special ingredient.

TWIST OF FATE

Jimmy leaned on his counter, watching potential customers wander through the carnival grounds. Calvin's Carnival was definitely not an attraction for much of anyone, especially not on the back roads of Nebraska. And not on a muggy summer afternoon.

"Come inside, Lydia knows all." The old gypsy woman across from him beckoned a young couple to her tent.

The woman, blond and busty, pouted. "I don't want my fortunes told. I'm hungry, Lou. You promised me that big teddy bear on the fairway, too."

Lou, with a face that could scare cows into submission and too many muscles to fit inside his shirt, pointed across the way. "There's the stand for funnel cakes. We could get us one of those and corn dogs later."

Lydia scowled and slouched back on her chair as the couple turned away from her tent. She flapped a wave at Jimmy, who tended the funnel cake trailer.

Jimmy smiled as the couple approached his trailer. Anything to break the boredom. "Can I get you a funnel cake, miss?"

Lou swaggered to the window. "Don't you get fresh with my girl. I heard about you and your types. Give me one, with extra sugar on top." He slapped a dollar on the counter.

"Coming right up," Jimmy answered.

Lydia wiggled her fingers, muttering through her scowl. She retreated into her tent, jerking the flap down.

Jimmy picked up the batter dispenser, a fat plastic squeeze bottle. He held it over the deep fat fryer, then paused. Just for a moment, he thought he saw a face in the bits of burnt dough floating in the oil. He frowned. Must be imagination.

"Well, come on," Lou complained. "We ain't got all night."

"Right." Jimmy squeezed the batter into the fryer, circling around and around. The oil hissed and bubbled madly.

"He will die tonight."

Jimmy set the bottle aside, looking wildly around his stall. Only Lou and his girl were in sight. "Did you hear that?"

"Hear what? You stupid or something?" Lou slapped the counter.

"Nothing," Jimmy said, shaking his head. He flipped the funnel cake.

Someone laughed, low and menacing.

Jimmy was more furtive in his look this time. Lou chatted with his girl, bragging about his skills at the games. They were fixed, all of them, but Jimmy wasn't going to tell Lou that. He flipped the funnel cake out of the oil, letting it drain before sliding it onto a plate and dusting it with a generous heap of powdered sugar.

"Now that's what I'm talking about," Lou said, handing the plate to the girl. "Come on, baby. Time to win you that bear." He swaggered away, one arm around his girl, the other stuffing funnel cake into his mouth.

Jimmy heard the laugh again. He caught a glimpse of Lydia peering through her tent flap. She stared across the way at him, then retreated into her tent once again.

He shrugged. Lydia was an odd one, even by Gypsy fortune-teller standards. Jimmy hated being across from her, but he was the new kid. He parked the trailer where Calvin told him to. And since no one else wanted to be near Lydia, that's where Jimmy ended up.

He swiped a rag over the counter, removing the traces of sugar. The fairway was dead in the afternoon heat. The tinny sound of the ferris wheel added background to an otherwise silent day.

The oil in the fryer was dirty. Jimmy pulled out the tongs and picked bits of dead batter from the oil, knowing Calvin was too cheap to change the oil more than twice a month.

A face formed in the scum on top, an evil face that leered with an insane grin. Jimmy thrust the tongs through the center, stabbing the apparition through its nose. He heard the cackling laugh again as the face dissolved.

He shoved the tongs into the holder, then marched out of his trailer across the way to Lydia's tent. He raised his fist to bang, but the soft fabric offered no place to knock.

"Lydia," he called. "I know that's you, playing tricks on me."

The Gypsy thrust her head through the flap. "Thrice cursed you are, boy."

"What's that supposed to mean?"

"Three deaths. Blood price must be paid if you want freed."

"I'm not a schill, Lydia. I work here, remember? Save your bullshit for the customers."

Lydia emerged from her tent, her scarves tangling in her graying hair. "Bullshit? You work here two months and already you know what I say is bullshit? You will learn, boy. Read your contract again. You sold your soul and don't even know it. Go back to your fryer. And beware. Tonight's a full moon."

Jimmy backed away, unsettled by her speech. "Save your tricks for them. I'm warning you." He shook his finger in false bravado. Lydia's stare unnerved him all the way to his trailer.

She dragged a chair from her tent, seating herself under the shade canopy out front. She stared at Jimmy in his funnel cake trailer as the afternoon dragged on.

A rowdy group of teens stopped by his trailer. The leader, a shaggy blond, swaggered up to the counter. "Gimme five."

"What toppings would you like?" Jimmy asked as he drizzled batter into the fryer.

"He's the first," the evil voice spoke.

The funnel cake batter rose through the bubbling oil, forming a skull. Jimmy stabbed it with the tongs, breaking it into bits. Oil splashed from the fryer. He jumped back.

"What's with you, dude?" The blond leaned over the counter.

Jimmy tried to smile. It didn't work. "Sorry. Fly got in the oil. It happens."

"That is so gross," one of the girls complained. "Come on, let's get something else."

"But I want funnel cakes," Blond Boy insisted. "If the weirdo back there can cook them."

The group laughed.

Jimmy's face flushed. He scooped the ruined cake from the fryer. He drizzled more batter in, ignoring the face and the strange symbols floating on the surface of the oil. Lydia's tricks, that's all.

"Topping?" he asked as he slid the first cake onto a plate.

"Chocolate," Blond Boy answered.

The voice laughed. Jimmy's hand shook as he drizzled chocolate syrup. He slid the plate to the boy, then turned to make another cake.

"Nate? Hey, Nate! Guys, he's choking." The girl's voice was laced with panic.

Jimmy rushed from the trailer.

Blond Boy stumbled, hands clutching his throat. His lips turned blue as they worked soundlessly. Chocolate smeared his face.

"Call 9-1-1!" Jimmy grabbed the boy around his waist from behind. The boy was half a foot taller and much heavier. Jimmy planted his fist just above the navel and jerked. A wad of half-chewed funnel cake shot from Blond Boy's mouth. He sucked in a breath.

Jimmy let go as the boy's friends moved to surround him. They escorted him away. Blond Boy bawled like a baby. None said a word to Jimmy, or even looked back. He'd saved the kid's life, and not one word? Jimmy shook his head as he picked up the trampled funnel cake, dropping it in a trash bin.

"You should have let him die," Lydia said. "Your trailer is on fire."

Jimmy swore as he hurried back inside the trailer to fish the smoking funnel cake from the fryer. Now the cakes would taste of smoke.

The face leered from the depths of the oil. "One." The mouth moved, sending a stream of bubbles to the surface. They broke, spattering the back of Jimmy's hand. He jerked away, too late to prevent the burn across his skin.

"Hey, you open?"

Jimmy turned to see the most beautiful girl he'd ever laid eyes on leaning on his counter. The afternoon light painted her gold, highlighting full lips and round cheeks. She wore a blue dress that showed healthy curves. "Yeah," Jimmy stammered. "Funnel cake?"

The girl smiled. "Always my favorite. Can I have it with strawberries and cream?"

"Sure." Jimmy stared, fascinated by the light playing in the girl's hair.

She tilted her head to one side. "Are you going to cook it now?"

Jimmy blushed. He turned to the fryer, squeezing in the batter. He tried to draw hearts, but they came out blobby and misshapen. He snuck glances from the corner of his eye as the cake cooked. The girl seemed to be alone.

"She will be second, and then the final one will die."

"No," Jimmy whispered to the fryer. He flipped the cake.

"Pardon?" the girl asked.

"Uh, no problem. It's almost done." Jimmy felt like an idiot, but his tongue ran away with his mouth. "You here by yourself?"

"My friends are on the rides. I don't care for them, except maybe the ferris wheel. I love it after dark, when it's all lit up. You ever ride it?" She smiled, her eyes crinkling.

Jimmy shook his head. "Employees aren't allowed." He pulled the funnel cake from the oil, ignoring the foaming face.

"Don't you ever get a day off?"

"Only when we're closed." He scooped strawberries over the cake, adding more than he was supposed to. He pulled the can of whipped cream from the mini fridge under the counter.

"You got a fork?" the girl asked as he sprayed a foaming pile on top of the strawberries.

"Yeah." He handed her a fork and napkin.

"Thanks." She collected her plate, walking to the tables four trailers away, next to the hot dog stand.

Jimmy stared after her. Even her walk was beautiful.

"Two."

Jimmy swung on Lydia, glaring ferociously across the space separating them. "Stop your tricks."

"Or what? She is marked. You can do nothing."

"I saved that kid."

Lydia shook her head. "Thrice cursed." She stood, stretching kinks from her back. "You will learn. Or you will die like the others."

"What others?" Jimmy emerged from the trailer.

"Those who could not master the secrets of the funnel cakes." She pulled back the flap of her tent. "You will see. Or you will die."

"Ha, ha, very funny. Old hag." Jimmy slammed the trailer door behind him.

Business picked up as the evening brought a cooler breeze. Jimmy lost track of the beautiful girl. He swirled batter, dusted sugar, drizzled chocolate, and listened for the eerie voice. The face was gone from the oil. The voice was silent. It must have been the heat of the afternoon. And Lydia's Gypsy tricks.

He glanced across the way to her tent. Dim light spilled out the door. She had a steady stream of customers. Most left unsettled by whatever she told them. Jimmy shook his head, then glanced to the ferris wheel. It rotated slowly, twinkling with lights. Was the girl on the ferris wheel now? He should have asked her name.

"Give me six," a woman said, dropping a pile of bills on the counter. She looked worn out, her hair hanging in disheveled strings. Six boys, all about ten, shouted and punched each other behind her.

"Sure thing," Jimmy answered, pushing the money into the till.

He drizzled batter into the oil. The cake rose on a bubbling tide of oil. Thief, it spelled in looping letters. Jimmy frowned. He flipped the cake, shifting it to the back of the fryer while he drizzled in a new cake. Liar, this one spelled. He pulled the first cake free, setting it aside to drain while he cooked a third. He waited for a word to form. It rose to the surface looking like a normal funnel cake.

"Giant blob of shit," Jimmy muttered. He was seeing things. Lydia's fault.

The other three cakes were normal. The last one made his blood run cold. Killer. He stuck all six on plates and covered the incriminating words with plenty of white powdered sugar.

The woman waved the boys to the counter. She retreated to the dining area. The boys grabbed plates, squabbling as they followed her. The last boy took the Killer funnel cake. He gave Jimmy a knowing smile, his eyes cold and flat as a snake's.

Jimmy shivered. He turned to the fryer after the boy left. "What are you?"

The evil voice chuckled. "Blood price."

Screams came from the ferris wheel. It ground to a halt, the music dying mid-song.

The face rose from the oil. "That one is mine."

"Someone died on the ferris wheel," the fairway manager shouted.

Lydia raised her finger. "One," she mouthed.

A crowd of curious onlookers rushed toward the ferris wheel.

Jimmy looked at the fryer. The face laughed, streams of bubbles erupting from its mouth.

He shook his head in mute denial. He looked toward the ferris wheel. A figure clung to the side of a seat high in the air. She wore a blue dress.

"Mine," the voice whispered. "You shall not deny me."

Jimmy slapped the tongs through the oil. "No."

The chuckle echoed through the tiny trailer.

Jimmy clutched his ears, trying to block the sound. "I don't know what you are, but I won't play your games." He shoved the side of the fryer, ignoring the heat searing his palms. He heaved, smashing the fryer through the side of the trailer. It spilled on the ground outside, steaming oil spreading over the trampled grass of the field. The face spread, distorted by the pool of oil. It frowned. Anger filled its eyes. Jimmy stamped on the face, his boots leaving marks on the oily mud.

He ran for the ferris wheel. The girl still hung, high on the side. The wheel creaked into motion, music winding up. She screamed, kicking her feet. The wheel ground to a halt.

"Put that down," the woman with the six boys spoke to the killer boy with cold eyes. The boy held a man's head, blood dripping between his fingers.

"I think it's cool," the boy said.

"The police will want it," the woman said.

Jimmy shuddered. The head belonged to Lou. His pale eyes stared blankly at the kid playing with his head.

"Mine," the voice said.

"Thrice cursed," Lydia's voice whispered. "Which will be master?"

Jimmy pushed through the ring of onlookers.

Calvin himself stopped him. The owner looked as if he'd just crawled from a haystack. "Where you think you're going, kid?"

"I've got to save her," Jimmy said, pointing at the girl high above.

"Already called the police." Calvin spat a blob of phlegm to the side. "They'll be here afore too long."

"They'll be too late." Jimmy reached for the gate blocking access to the ride.

Calvin grabbed his arm. "You gonna be a hero, boy?"

"Somebody has to." Jimmy yanked his arm free. He jumped the gate and started to climb the side of the ferris wheel.

"Get back here, boy. Let the police do their job." Calvin spat another glob at the ground.

The girl screamed.

Jimmy scrambled faster up the shaking struts of the ancient ferris wheel.

"Mine," the voice whispered.

Jimmy glanced up. The girl hung twenty feet above him. He edged along the spoke leading to the chair where she clung.

She glanced down, her face a white blur in the night. "Hurry," she urged.

"Hang on!" Jimmy shifted his weight. The beam under his feet creaked. Several bolts rattled to the ground. The beam sagged. The chair dropped a foot, swinging as it stopped.

One of the girl's hands slipped. She screamed in panic.

Jimmy clutched the beam, his stomach churning. He glanced down, then wished he hadn't. He hated heights. They scared the shit out of him. But if he didn't move, the girl would fall to her death.

The voice chuckled as the beam lost another handful of bolts. It wiggled under Jimmy's weight. He swallowed hard. The demon or whatever it was in his fryer would not have the girl, whatever her name was. He slid his foot along the beam. He forced one hand free, sliding it after his foot.

He inched up the beam. The girl flailed with her free hand, scrabbling for a hold. Jimmy swallowed the knot of fear in his throat. He had to move faster. The beam swayed under his weight. He forced himself to run monkey-style up the beam. He grabbed the girl's dress with one hand, pulling her to the beam.

Something cracked. The beam groaned as it bent. Jimmy wrapped his arm around the girl, his other arm around the beam. The ferris wheel began to tip to the side, the large wheel folding. Spokes shattered. The girl screamed, clutching Jimmy with panicked hands.

The crowd shrieked as they scattered. The ferris wheel crashed to the ground with a screeching of tortured metal. The evil voice laughed.

The beam hit the ground, knocking Jimmy's hold loose and throwing him to the side. He curled up, covering his head as more debris rained around him.

Where was the girl? He caught a glimpse of blue under a pile of beams. He pulled frantically at the tangle. Where was she?

Sirens screamed through the night. Red and blue light streaked over the tangled mess.

Jimmy shifted a seat, lifting it with strength he didn't know he had. The girl lay underneath. Blood streaked her hair. Her eyes were closed, but she was still breathing. He dropped to his knees beside her. She was still the most beautiful woman he'd ever seen.

Firemen and police swarmed the scene.

"Over here," Jimmy called.

They pushed him back, shoving him to what they called a safe distance. He watched helplessly as they strapped the girl to a stretcher and carried her to a waiting ambulance.

A heavy hand landed on his shoulder. He glanced over to see Calvin standing behind him.

"That was stupid, boy. Brave, but stupid. Never fight the demon, not when he wants his blood." Calvin spat a glob to the ground. "He'll have yours if you try. Ever wonder how I lost my hand? I used to be the funnel cake boy. Many years ago. He'll have his price. Don't defy him again."

"I want out." Jimmy shifted out from under Calvin's fake hand.

"Nobody gets out, not once they've signed the contract." Calvin walked away, to where the fire chief waited to talk about the disaster.

Jimmy flexed his fists.

Lydia patted his arm, the coins on her scarf jingling.

"That wasn't Gypsy tricks?" Jimmy asked.

"Not mine." Lydia studied him, her dark eyes intense in their nest of wrinkles. "You want to win against the demon? How bad do you want to stop it? Bad enough to give your life for theirs?" She waved at the gawking crowd.

"What are you saying, Lydia?"

"It's an ancient curse, on Calvin and any who sign his contracts. The demon will take his payment in blood."

"Mine." It whispered through the air, angry and evil.

Jimmy shivered.

"Will you break it, funnel cake boy? Will you give your life for theirs?"

Jimmy glanced at the crowd. Killer boy was trying to hide Lou's head from the police. The other people didn't seem to care, they stared at the bloody bodies trapped under the ferris wheel, only another curiosity. Police pushed them behind yellow tape. Firemen checked the bodies, climbing carefully over the twisted metal. Did he want to save these people?

He saw the girl in blue behind the ambulance. A paramedic was bandaging her arm. She was awake, watching him.

"For her, yes." Jimmy turned back to Lydia. "I'd die for her."

Lydia pushed a charm of feathers and a dead mouse into his hands. She stepped back without a word.

"Watch out!"

A tangle of metal struts overbalanced. Jimmy looked up, watching it fall toward him. He clutched the grotesque bundle.

"For her," he whispered.

Soul Dark

Gilded tentacles,
Insanity creeps from eyes
Carved from ruby stone.

Soul stealer, gazes
into broken heart of flesh,
I rise triumphant.

CinderJane

This is my story and I'll tell it my way. Yes, there is magic in form and structure and tradition, which is why most fairy tales begin 'Once Upon a Time', and why I should decorate these pages with pink and lavender rosebuds wreathed with delicate pale blue ribbons. Appearances boost power. No one would believe a tall, plain fairy godmother had as much power as the short, plump variety. And if you happen to have a hairy mole or a wart? Definitely witch, not benevolent fairy.

But as I said, this is my story and I'll tell it my way. I have power to spare, now. I always wanted power. I was fascinated with magic from the beginning. But my mother held tight to her own powers and used them to bury mine under tradition.

And story.

My mother believed in the old ways. When she found herself a young widow with two daughters in tow, she knew just what to do. She set her cap for an eligible merchant with no wife but a lovely young daughter. Shape of the fairy tale matters. Find the right shape, then squeeze everything else inside until it fits. They were married, and we settled into our new home.

I knew he'd die soon, probably at my mother's hand. I knew what she brewed deep in the cellar kitchen of his manor house. I helped her gather her dark herbs by the sickly light of a setting moon. She had a trunk of mourning gowns already set aside. I would have warned him, but he was frightfully stern and tended to hit first, talk later. I stayed silent and watched the pitiful drama unfold.

My mother played the tragic young beauty to perfection. Two husbands lost, the village gossips whispered. And those poor lambkins. Three young girls to raise. Whatever shall they do for a dowry? No one will marry them now. Except possibly Rosalind.

Rosa, my younger sister. She was sweet and kind, with hair as golden as honey and a voice that could charm birds from their nests. But she was the stepsister, the middle one destined to be stupid and poor and a spinster. Her face was rather shapeless and lumpy, like poorly kneaded bread dough. Her eyes were too close and tended to cross. But she was my sister and I loved her fiercely.

Luella, my stepsister and the youngest of us all, was supposed to be the star of this farce. The true inheritor of her father's wealth. She was gangly and awkward and screeched like an angry cat whenever she didn't get her way. Her hair hung in tangled clumps of indeterminate color. She refused to wash, claiming the soap hurt her skin.

My mother soon took her in hand and Ella found herself scrubbed pink, her hair smooth and glistening. Mother had less luck with the girl's manners. But they both knew the story. Ella would marry a prince after an enchanted ball. Form mattered. Ella slept on a featherbed in a cozy corner of the kitchen and went by the name Cinderella. She claimed we beat her and forced her to slave away her days cleaning and cooking for us. Truth be told, she never touched a pot or a scrub brush.

That fell to me. I was too tall, too plain, the typical eldest stepdaughter. Except I was never cruel, not to them, despite everything they did to me. What I did was not cruelty. It was justice. It was what the Powers demanded to keep the balance. But no one believes me. They whisper of my jealous rages over the unfairness of my homely face compared to the beauty and grace Cinderella displayed.

It was all a farce, a play set up by my mother and that scheming wench. It fit the fairy tale shape. It brought in power. I felt that power building and laid my own plans.

"Jane, Mother wishes you to cook her an egg and bring it to her. She's feeling poorly this morning." Sweet Rosa smiled her lumpy smile. "Cinderella wants just toast."

I threw the brush in the bucket. Soapy water splashed over the rim. A flash of irritation and a wish that they would cook their own breakfasts for once and leave me to scrub in peace. Ella's "just toast" would include tea, marmalade, freshly squeezed juice, berries gathered with the morning dew still shimmering, fairy dusted teacakes, a slab of bacon, and who knew what other delicacies. The woman ate like a starving bear. But did she bloat like one? No, she retained her slender figure and winsome looks.

Magic, all about the shape. And Mother's spells that wrapped ever tighter around Ella.

Rosa trailed me into the kitchen. The second kitchen that actually functioned as one, not the pristine one that Ella slept in. My kitchen was in a dank cellar at the back of the manor house. The flagstones were uneven and tended to heave up in the winter, but the fireplace was large and gave plenty of warmth and cooking space.

I pulled down a rack of spices and fetched the eggs from the root cellar. I knelt to poke up the fire. It poofed soot over me when I tossed in a fresh handful of kindling. I sneezed.

"Bless you," Rosa said piously. She perched on one of my rickety stools, surprisingly delicate for her size. "Oh, Jane, you have to come to the ball tonight. I can't wait to see all the gowns. And the lights. I heard the king ordered in five hundred extra candles for the chandeliers. Can you imagine? Five hundred extra!"

Of course, the king had an unmarried son who refused to marry the wife his father chose for him. So of course, they decided to throw a ball and give the poor man an ultimatum. Shape and form and power. I doubted the prince had any choice at all in the matter. My mother, Ella, and whatever fairy they lured in would see to that. He'd marry Ella and I'd be free to live my life in the old manor house.

Rosa continued to prattle on in her breathless little voice as I cooked breakfast for my mother and lazy stepsister. "It even has velvet roses. Jane, have you heard a word I said?"

"Your dress or Ella's?" I didn't need to listen to more than a few words. Rosa adored ballgowns.

Rosa giggled. "Mine, of course, you silly goose. Mother bought me a lovely one, all pale blue chiffon with pink roses. Ella is supposed to wear rags tonight. That reminds me, Mother wants your oldest dress for Ella."

It figured. "I threw it on the fire last night. All I have is the one I'm wearing."

Rosa frowned, her plump bottom lip sticking out. She was almost pretty in that moment. "It does have a tear, doesn't it? Or a patch somewhere?"

It didn't. The fabric was faded, but still perfectly respectable. Mother would see to the tears and smudges, I had no doubt. She understood appearances. It was her specialty, after all.

A new thought occurred to Rosa. "What will you wear, if you give her your only dress? Oh, Jane, you should not have burnt your other dress. I shall have to give you one of my gowns. It won't fit very well, but it will have to do."

"What if I don't want to go to the ball?"

"But you have to go, you're a stepsister. You have to come see Ella shine. Please, Jane. This may be the only chance we get to see what a real fairy godmother can do. I want to see Ella all dressed up and sparkling and magical. Oh, please, Jane. Don't make me go alone with Mother. You know how she fusses when you aren't there."

No, I didn't. Mother was usually pleased when I chose not to traipse along on her outings. I should have realized then how jealous she was of my power, but I was young, still untutored in the ways of magic.

"I'm not going, Rosa. You go and enjoy the gowns. Enjoy the food and tell me all about it when you get home." I flipped the egg over, gently so the yolk wouldn't break.

"Please, Jane. Come with me. Taste the king's table for yourself." She gave me the look she knew I couldn't resist.

"Oh, all right. I'll come."

Rosa clapped her hands and giggled. "I know just the dress for you." She bounced off the stool.

"Would you take the tray for Mother?" I asked as I set the egg plate on the tray. It already held salt, pepper, a glass of watered wine, and a single rose from the vine outside the cellar door. Ella's breakfast was only half-ready. Her 'just toast' was perfectly golden, but I still had to collect the dozen other things that had to be included to avoid another screeching diatribe.

Rosa took the tray with a happy smile. She was really too good and kind. She should be the one the fairy godmother visited, except I wouldn't wish a handsome, nameless prince on her. She deserved better.

The kitchen was definitely quieter with Rosa gone. I finished Ella's breakfast then carried the tray up the stairs with a resigned sigh. The sooner I dealt with Ella, the sooner she'd be out of my hair and my life.

"One more day," I whispered as I eased open the door to her kitchen.

"You burnt my dress?" Ella's screech made the chickens run for cover, their cackles competing only barely with her strident voice.

I tossed another handful of cracked corn after them. "It was in terrible shape. And besides, I doubt it would have fit you." I gave her a look calculated to enrage her even further. She was soft. Even though the magic kept her slender and shapely, she never lifted a finger and it showed. I was lean, hard with muscle from all my work keeping the manor house clean and in repair.

"Then I shall have that one," Ella snapped. She glared from beneath her shining tresses. Mother's magic had certainly changed her. And not for the better.

"What? Here and now? In the yard?" I shifted the egg basket to one hip and reached into a nest of straw for the half dozen eggs clustered there.

"And why not? Who would care if you pranced about in your petticoats? You, plain Jane. The eldest stepsister." She folded her arms and tapped her foot.

"Very well." I set the egg basket down, then stripped off the dress.

Ella gasped at my indecency. She pursed her lips tight when she realized I wasn't wearing a petticoat. Not even one. I picked up the egg basket wearing only my short bloomers, chemise, and shoes. I reached into the nest.

"Jane, really!"

"You took my last set of petticoats already. And since you and my mother pay no attention to anything but your petty little schemes—"

It worked like a charm. Ella huffed her outrage and stomped away, offended to her core.

I finished collecting eggs then went to the kitchen. I could cook in my underthings as well as in my old gown.

Rosa saved me the bother. Good, sweet Rosa had left her green gown draped over a chair. I pulled it on, then tied my apron tight around me to help cinch in the extra fabric. Rosa was generously proportioned.

I was up to my elbows in flour when Mother came barging into my sanctum.

"What is the meaning of this, Jane?" She held my blue gown crumpled in a tight fist. "You know how much Ella is depending on you for her happy ever after. She needed your old gown, not this!" She flung it down on top of my dough.

I flipped it away with one floury hand. "That one was nothing but tatters. I'm sure you'll make this one work. You always do, somehow."

"I won't stand for your rudeness, not today of all days. Fix this!" She stomped away in a huff.

I finished kneading the bread. I wasn't about to jump at her bidding. It was my gown, after all. I hid it under my pallet in the corner near the fireplace. Ella could find her own tattered dress for tonight's performance. I wasn't going to lift a finger to help that lazy cow. If she wanted a prince and happy ever after, she'd have to do something to earn it.

I turned to the stew I had planned for dinner. Let Mother and Ella lure in the godmother tonight. Let them fill out the form of the story. I was through with them. If the godmother didn't show up, if Ella didn't catch the prince's eye, if Mother's schemes collapsed around her, then I'd take Rosa and everything valuable I could steal, and we'd travel the world together. We'd do all those things I couldn't do stuck in the kitchen and in the fairy tale.

I was the eldest stepsister. The stories never specified my fate, not after the prince and the cinder girl married.

I wasn't leaving it entirely up to chance. I had my own plans laid.

Ella's spoon clattered against her bowl. "I can't eat a thing. I'm too nervous." She'd cleaned the bowl, though. And eaten half a loaf of bread before making her announcement.

She and Mother had spent the afternoon out with the pig. Truffle hunting, Ella said with a sniff. They hadn't found any truffles, but they had found briars to tear her skirts and mud to splatter her rosy cheeks. Her yellow gown looked ragged, but still fairly new.

I wasn't sure if I wanted her to succeed or fail. Success meant she and my mother would leave. Failure meant she'd live here in poverty for the rest of her life. With me.

I slopped more soup into her bowl. "You must keep up your strength. Please, eat." Maybe I could fatten her up, like the poor pig.

Mother raised her eyebrow at my sharp tone. "Jane, dear, it would behoove you to keep a civil tongue in your head. Our Ella is, after all, going to be the next queen."

Ella tittered. Rosa gasped. Mother merely smiled. I wanted to pour soup over her head, but I refrained.

Mother clapped her hands. "It's time, girls. Ella, you know what to do. Rosa, you and Jane must dress for the ball now. I've laid out gowns in my chamber for you both."

"No." I stated it simply.

"I beg your pardon?" Mother turned to look at me. Her tone was ice.

"I'm not going to the ball. I don't want to go. Ella can go in my place."

"That isn't the way this works. You know that, child. You will go to the ball. You will wear the finery I have purchased for you with the last of our money."

"No, I will not. I will stay here and clean the dishes and scrub the floors and everything else that you insist I do. I don't want to go to the ball and dance with a complete and total stranger."

"Jane, you promised." Rosa's high little voice pierced right through me. I had promised to go with her tonight.

"All right, I'll go with you, Rosa."

Mother's mouth hardened. "I have changed my mind. You will stay here, in your rags, locked in your kitchen, among the ashes and cinders."

The words were out before she realized what she'd said. Her face paled as her hands flew to her betraying lips.

I shook my head, blood draining from my own face. That was Ella's place, not mine. Ella's curse, not mine.

But words cannot be unspoken, not when they are said with power, even with such a small amount as my mother had.

Ella slammed her hand on the table. "You promised it would be me. It has to be the true daughter, not the stepsister! I've ruined this gown for nothing! Nothing!" She bolted from the room. Her loud sobs faded as she slammed the door behind her.

"Well." Mother turned her cold look on Rosa. "What is spoken, is spoken. Go dress for the ball. At least I have one obedient daughter." She shot another glare at me as she shepherded Rosa away.

I stared in dismay at the remains of the meal. What had I done?

I gathered the dirty dishes and carried them to my cellar room out of habit.

What had I done to myself?

I heard the clatter of hooves as I was scrubbing up the large soup pot. Mother and Rosa, off to the ball. Mother had locked me in, as she'd said. No doubt Ella was in her pristine kitchen, sobbing away as she waited for the godmother that may or may not come for her. I scrubbed until the old pot shone.

I was too angry to cry.

Rage boiled up inside me, a red tide of heat that threatened to drown me. I held onto it like a drowning sailor clinging to a rope. The fairies sensed grief, sadness, pain, not anger. Maybe she'd pass me by and gift Ella as Mother had intended.

And perhaps not.

The thought filled me with dread as I watched a flickering light gather in the darkest corner of the kitchen. Blue sparkles fought with lavender fizzes. All of it shrank to a bubble of soft light. It popped, like a soap bubble, revealing a plump grandmotherly woman with silver hair and a blue robe coated with shimmering lights. She smiled, her cheeks plumping like apples in the fall.

"What's this, then?" She smiled at the tidy but dark cellar kitchen. "Oh, my, you poor sweet child. I can make all of your dreams come true."

I faced her, suds dripping from my hands. A tiny, strange, horribly brilliant plan was hatching in my head. "Maybe you can."

"Dearie, I can transform you into a princess fit for a prince. I can send you to the ball. I can make your happy ever after a reality."

My lips curved in a smile that was not sweet and innocent. I flexed fingers and felt the first tingling of power. I'd only tasted it second-hand before, when my mother worked her small spells. This was mine, tasting of mint and cinnamon and fresh bread.

The fairy godmother blinked rapidly. Her smile faded around the edges. "You have the soot, the rags, the cinders, but you are the stepsister. This won't do. No, this is not proper."

I worked by instinct, pulling my power into a braid strong enough to capture even a godmother. "But I'm the one forced to slave away, while my lazy stepsister lounges in her bed."

"No, *you* are the stepsister. She is the— Oh, now you've confused me. This is wrong. All wrong."

"She is *my* stepsister. My real sister is at the ball with my mother. So you must be *my* fairy godmother." I twisted the rope of power in my hands. It glowed with a soft golden light, the color of fresh loaves emerging from the oven. My magic was rooted in baking and dishes and ordinary scullery work. It had none of the hard edges and sharpness of Mother's self-centered social power.

The godmother raised her hand. Her wand glowed with a spell of dismissal. I tossed my rope just as the spell sparkled into life. She squawked like a mad hen as my noose tightened around her.

The door to the kitchen squealed open, bouncing against the wall. Cinderella stood framed at the top of the cellar steps, hair mussed and face smudged with cinders. "What is the meaning of this, Jane? That is *my* godmother, come to deliver me to *my* prince."

"And your happy ever after?" My voice snapped with resentment. I tugged on the rope, cinching my spell tightly around the fairy. "You are welcome to the prince and all the rest of it, but the godmother is mine."

"It doesn't work that way," Ella said. Her bare feet whispered on the stones as she entered my domain. "She has come to grant me my fondest desire and allow me to attend the ball where I shall dance with the prince who will fall madly in love with me and pursue me across the kingdom until he finds me and our true love unites us. Happily. Ever. After."

"What if he doesn't fall in love with you? What if he's already made his choice?" I slowly reeled in the fairy, who was spitting and twisting in the rope. It was like catching one of the huge old fish in the river down the hill.

"He can't resist me. It's the way godmother magic works, ninny." Ella glared.

"Are you certain about that? What if the godmother sees your hands are still soft? What if she knows you haven't done a lick of work since my mother married your father?"

Ella shook her head, blond hair shining despite the fake grime. "It doesn't matter. It's the form of the thing. I'm the orphaned daughter. I'm the cinder girl wearing rags. You were supposed to go to the ball with your mother."

"And go I shall, but on my terms. Not yours. Not Mother's. And definitely not hers." I yanked the rope of power. The godmother bobbled close to me. I snatched her wand, then shoved her away. Her power blurped then sputtered into a mess of pink and lavender sprinkles on the floor. She collapsed in a heap, just another old woman in a fancy evening gown too small for her plump figure. Her wings, tiny little transparent things, fluttered impotently. She was still a fairy, but no longer a godmother.

The pink and purple froth of magic on the floor sucked back up into the wand, then burst into me, cementing my connection to the fairy world. Wings sprouted on my back. Sparkles of light shimmered over my gown. The fabric began to shift, changing to a gossamer fluff of blue.

"No." I waved the wand across my dress. I could become a godmother, but on my terms. I would not be the kind of godmother who wore poufy gowns, fluttered around, and called everyone, "Dearie." I would not send poor girls off to balls in fancy dresses to marry complete strangers.

The magic had other ideas. Pink sparkles kept creeping over my skirt and flaking from my hair like dandruff. I brushed a delicate feather from my shoulder before turning back to my stepsister.

Ella stared with her mouth hanging open, looking like a cow that has just realized grass tastes terrible. "What have you done? I can't go to the ball looking like this."

The wand rose of its own accord, dragging my arm behind. I fought it with every ounce of my new-found power. The tip wavered before spitting a stream of silver glitter. The spell whooshed from me. Ella disappeared under a froth of light.

I gasped, wheezing to catch my breath.

The godmother stirred, shifting in her ragged dress. I didn't catch a flutter of wings and her face didn't look as plump as it had a few moments ago.

"It's beautiful," Ella squealed. She clapped her hands, a sound muffled by long, elegant gloves with tiny pearl buttons up the sides. Her rags had transformed into a shimmering silver and pink gown fit for a queen. "Now for the coach. I have a pumpkin, four mice, an elderly cat, and two squirrels waiting for you. Godmother," she added with a sneer. She whirled and marched up the cellar steps, her glass shoes tinkling on the stones.

The magic dragged me after her. I resisted every step. This was not what I wanted. I would *not* become a plump grandmotherly fairy who created ball gowns from rags and coachmen from stray rodents.

"You have to observe the form."

I turned to face the once-godmother. My feet still carried me backward to the steps and the waiting pumpkin. "Power is power."

She shook her head. Her hair hung in golden curls. Her face looked quite young. Her body, as she stood, was slender and shapely. "They called me Mary Cinders. I tried to fight the magic, when it was my turn to attend the ball. I didn't want a prince. I wanted the village baker and he was quite happy to marry me. My stepmother and stepsisters also supported my choice. They were really quite pleasant to me. I was in the kitchen by choice. When my godmother showed up, I fought her. Slapped her in the face with my custard, actually. Ruined a perfectly set dessert. She told me that if I was that determined not to marry a prince, I could try being the godmother instead. So, I took her wand and her power. I *became* her. The fairy godmother. I had little choice in the matter really. I could choose what color the gown was, at least to some extent. I can't seem to get anything but pastels. But everything else happened as the power dictated. I've tried to shake it off, give it away, but nothing worked. Someone had to take it from me. But now that I'm free—"

"No. I will not be a fairy godmother. I will use this power to... to... to do something else! I won't be a fairy godmother." I could verbally deny it, but the power was changing me. I felt myself shrinking shorter at the same time my waist expanded and my fingers grew chubby. An inane smile crawled onto my lips and took up residence. "Really, dearie, this is not what I imagined." Had that cheerful sweet voice come from me?

"Really, Jane, you're being dreadfully slow." Ella stood at the top of the step, foot tapping an angry rhythm.

I turned toward the once-godmother and raised the wand.

"Don't you dare," she threatened.

"Oh, but, dearie, you can't attend a ball in that state. Whatever will the prince think?"

The godmother magic hung thick in the kitchen. Two orphaned girls with hair the color of sweet honey, with stepmothers and stepsisters, and one unmarried prince holding a ball and choosing his wife from the hundreds of hopeful young women. Which to choose? The wand wavered from Ella's glare to Mary's scowl. I tried to hold it in, to force it to become something else. My wings buzzed and fluttered. Pink glitter stormed around me.

The wand dipped toward Mary. Her rags shimmered into a mint green swirl of satin and chiffon that was really quite lovely on her. A wreath of pink rosebuds crowned her hair.

She screeched like a fishwife and threw the roses at me.

Ella's curses drowned her out. She had reverted back to her ragged dress.

I screamed and stomped my foot. The magic turned it into a giggling song with rainbow explosions that turned into flowers. Before I knew it, I'd created a massive floral carriage in the kitchen. I had no idea how to get it out of the cellar, though.

"I will not marry your prince!"

"He's mine!"

Ella rushed at Mary, murder in her eyes. Her hands stretched out into claws.

"Form and function," I muttered to myself. How could I twist this around and escape from the magic? And what of the prince? Did he want to marry a perfect stranger?

The wand bobbed and twisted, drawing strands of glowing light. Air rushed around all three of us. The stench of roses and chrysanthemums was overpowering. Then we were standing in the courtyard in front of the manor house. Except instead of mud, it was paved with cobblestone. And torches blazed on either side of the front steps. Brave front for a poor house, beggared by the greed of the stepmother and stepsisters.

The flower coach sprang into shape with a rustle of petals. The poor tomcat that haunted the garden looking for mice yowled as the magic twisted him into the ugliest coachman I had ever seen. Four prancing white horses danced into place. The buck teeth and fluffy tails of three of them gave away their origins as squirrels. The fourth was tailless and swelled his throat for a massive bullfrog bellow. Well, you used what you had.

Gah! I was even starting to think like a fairy godmother.

The only question left was which woman would ride in the hideously floral coach? Who would scramble from the prince's arms when the clock struck midnight?

Mary was wearing the dress, but Ella had her heart set on her own selfish wishes. She ran for the coach, shoving Mary aside.

I tapped the wand. Sparks flew. Maybe I could channel the power into the form but change the shape and substance. I sent a blast at Ella. Her dress changed to a shining mess of colors with random bits of lace scattered over the bodice. It was quite hideous. I smiled, a twisted version of godmotherly charm.

"Go to the ball you certainly shall, my dears. Just be sure to leave by midnight, for when the clock chimes the last bell, alas, the spell will be broken, and all will be as it was. Both of you, pop in the carriage now, don't be late." I sent a push of magic to shove them both into the floral coach. The squirrely horses stamped their feet. The bullfrog horse tried to hop forward and tangled them all together. I left the tomcat coachman to straighten them out with the help of the pigeon footmen.

I tapped myself with the wand and vanished in a blast of pink light.

I staggered when I landed at the other end of my journey. I'd misjudged the floor and stumbled to a stop.

Firm hands caught my elbows and held me upright until I found my feet. My useless little wings buzzed like a mad hornet.

"Thank you, dearie. Quite kind of you." The words slipped out. I turned to face my rescuer.

He was tall, dark, and handsome if you squinted hard enough. The jewel-encrusted crown weighing down his curls was a dead giveaway to his identity. The prince eyed me up and down. "Doesn't the fairy godmother usually visit some poor unsuspecting wretch of a kitchen maid?"

"Done. They are on their way here."

"They?" He raised his eyebrows in surprise. "Am I to marry a whole tribe of them, then?"

"Only two, and if I can work things out, you won't have to marry either of them. Unless you want to." I waited until my wand stopped fizzing magic. What I was about to do was still technically the right form and shape to fit the tale, just not the one that was usually told.

"I'd rather not marry any of them just yet. My father is anxious, though, seeing that I'm his only child and heir to the throne and he and Mum aren't growing any younger."

"Well, if you must choose, do try not to pick Cinderella, then. She's rather lazy and has a very shrill voice when she's in a temper." The magic tried to twist my words, but I beat it back by squeezing the wand until dark green liquid oozed from the handle. I would not become a fairy godmother, not any more than I already had. But I was already loving the taste of magic. I wanted more, but on my terms.

"I shall keep that in mind when choosing a bride tonight." The prince tapped his fingers on the thick embroidery covering his sleeves. "So, what are you doing in my royal bedchamber? Did you only stop in to give me advice and have a chat? Perhaps a spot of tea?"

"I came to try to stop this horrible fairy tale from happening again." The words came out through gritted teeth. The godmother magic wanted a familiar shape. I had an urge to put the prince in a delicate lace gown with ribbons and flounces along the hem. Rainbow glitter leaked from the wand. I grabbed it in my fists and bent it almost to the breaking point.

"Having a bit of difficulty with your magic tonight? Is that why there's two girls on the way to my ball in magic coaches?" The prince's tone was anything but helpful. Mocking, rude, almost snide. I squashed the thought that he deserved to marry my stepsister. No, I would not give in to the magic. I would not let this happen.

"I'm new at it. Now, before anything else happens, I need you to—" My voice stopped working. Completely. Not even a croak. I couldn't tell the prince what to do. He had to figure it out on his own.

Or marry Ella and let the magic carry him away to a happy ever after. Whether he wanted one or not.

I worked my mouth, but no sound emerged.

The prince smiled a lazy grin. "You want me to wish for something else. You want me to break the power of the godmother curse."

I couldn't even nod. The magic filled me in a flood that was choking me, forcing all my breath out. The wand twirled and fluttered in my plump little hands. My wings buzzed. My hair crawled up into a tidy bun on the top of my head. My dress crumpled itself into a gown and apron embroidered with little apples and daisies and butterflies. I was turning into a fairy godmother despite everything.

"Robert!" The door smashed open. The king stood in the open doorway, resplendent in royal robes and a crown even more bejeweled than the prince's. "What the devil is keeping you, boy? The girls are waiting. Oh, it's one of you," he added in a gruff tone when he caught sight of me in all my godmotherly attire. "I suppose I must cancel my treaty with Landcombe. The princess was quite a catch, too."

"We're negotiating that, Father," Prince Robert said. "Don't cancel the treaty just yet. It seems we have a rather new godmother who has managed to bring two charming young kitchen drudges to my party. Perhaps Geoffry and Ivan could take them on a spin round the floor? They are technically princes, too. And quite marriageable." He tossed me a sly grin.

"Very well, then, let's make our grand entrance. Bring her with you." The king waved his hand at me.

Robert took my elbow in a tight grip and escorted me out of his bedchamber, through the palace, and to the top of the grand staircase that descended to the ballroom. Trumpets blared. The herald pounded his staff on the floor. The guests hushed their conversations and turned to face the stairs. Skirts rustled as the women dipped into low curtsies.

"His Majesty, King Robert," the herald thundered, "and his son, Prince Robert, and," he paused while he swept a measuring look over me, "guest." The last word landed flat and harsh. If this was the respect they showed fairy godmothers, it was no wonder their family had a history of fairy godmother curses on their princesses. I sniffed and lifted my head, bun bobbing.

Someone tittered.

The magic pulsed. I couldn't help it. The woman who laughed screamed as she rushed out of the room. Her dress changed from rich blue velvet to a minstrel's tunic and belled cap.

"Really, godmother, that was the Marquess of Duchesny. There will be hell to pay later." The king's voice rumbled quietly next to my ear.

"Ah, but Father, the woman is a bit of a clown. You've said so yourself." Prince Robert smirked on my other side, his hand still gripping my elbow.

The usual hubbub of chatter and music rose from the floor as we made our stately way down the staircase. We had barely reached the floor when the trumpets blared again. The room fell into an expectant silence.

This time it was the arrival of Ella and Mary. They trooped through the doors and paused at the top of the mirror staircase to the one I'd just descended. The two women looked worse for wear. Ella had flower petals smeared down one side of her ugly gown. Mary's silver skirts were tattered, and her hair hung in straggling loops from her once elegant hairdo.

I wondered idly how badly the carriage had shredded on the ride over. They'd probably left a trail of flowers all the way from our lowly manor to the palace. Robert wouldn't need to track down women and shove their feet into shoes to find his true love after tonight, he'd just have to follow the flower petals.

But that wasn't how the magic worked and Robert wasn't going to marry either of them, anyway. Form mattered. As long as the man was a prince, the spell would take hold and they would be madly in love. At least for tonight.

My wand twitched but Robert's grip on my arm kept it from sending showers of magic across the room to fix the poor young lambs.

Ella marched down the stairs as if she already ruled the palace. Mary looked like a condemned woman approaching the gallows. Their glass slippers clinked on the marble steps, loud in the silence.

The king cleared his throat. "Welcome, ladies. I'm sure we'll find out your names before too long, but for now, be advised we know why you're here. And we have plenty of princes available. I rather thought this sort of thing would happen, so I prepared for it. Gentlemen, if you would please claim a lady for the first waltz." He waved to a gaggle of well-dressed men.

"Geoffrey and Ivan, I presume?" I shot a glance at Robert.

He nodded. "And a few other nobles who are not afraid of a magical matchmaker's meddling."

"Or of marrying a commoner, not if they are guaranteed a happy ever after." The king looked pointedly at the wand I clutched in one pudgy fist.

I glared at it. I looked like a right, proper fairy godmother, the magic had done so much in such a short time. Is this why the story kept happening? The magic was like a river; persistent, patient, and very powerful. The story must happen. Form and shape must be filled, whether the participants were willing or not.

I watched as Ella and Mary were swept into the arms of waiting nobles. Magic followed their steps, leaving a trail of sparkling pink and yellow, like a fairy slug. I clenched my teeth. Ella may have wanted the story, but Mary hadn't. She'd fought her fate only to become a godmother. And I'd taken that from her. Was that why it kept happening? Woman after woman rebelled only to be trapped on the other end of the magic?

Robert polished his nails on his brocade waistcoat, looking every inch the bored royal.

"No, no, no, you are not my prince!" Ella's shrill voice carried over the waltz. The musicians faltered only for a measure before picking up the relentless music.

Ella fought the magic and won, mostly because the form wasn't quite right, so the magic had weakened. She stomped across the floor in a mass of shredded rainbow fabric. Robert looked up too late to avoid her determined stare.

The magic sparked out of my wand. I didn't want it to, I tried to stop it, but honestly, my heart wasn't in it. They deserved each other.

"You—" Ella began.

"—are my—" Robert spoke in a hesitant voice.

"Destiny!" they finished together.

He swept her into his arms and whirled her onto the dance floor.

"Robert, think of the treaty!" the king shouted after his son.

Too late. The magic had both of them fully enthralled.

King Robert chased after them, shouting of political alliances and marriages of state.

Mary blindsided me, grasping the wand out of my hands. I held tight to the worn wood despite her yanking. Magic flowed over both of us. Her face plumped out into godmother form. My gown shimmered. Random shots of magic blasted from the wand.

The other girls got wise to what was happening about then. They shoved their dance partners away to chase after Ella and Robert. The rest of the women, those not touched by the magic, shifted out of the way.

I caught a glimpse of Rosa standing near an impressive fifteen-layer cake decorated with sugar swans and white roses. She giggled and waved her fingers at me as Mary and I rolled past, still grappling over the wand.

"But I'm a prince, too," one of the men, I think it was Ivan, shouted as he chased after the women who were chasing after Robert.

"But not *the* prince." The woman paused at the end of the refreshment table. Tiny little tarts slathered in whipped cream were arranged on delicate plates. She scooped up an entire tray to fling at Ivan.

He ducked.

Whipped cream splattered a dozen women. Shrieks and screams ensued. The women charged forward, snatching up desserts as they went.

Pies, cakes, fruit salad, even a flaming skewer of shrimp flew through the air. The musicians, ever alert, switched to an up-tempo gavotte as the food fight got into full swing.

Mary and I rolled out to the center of the floor through raspberry jam and cream custard. The wand kept spitting out bursts of magic. The cream and berries changed briefly into parts of carriages. Twirling wheels of delicate pastry spun through seat cushions of custard and jelly. Rosettes of berries changed to flowers and back in a heartbeat.

I managed to trap Mary under me. I yanked the wand out of her hold and held it high over my head.

"I will not become a bride to a prince. And glass shoes," she heaved me off into a splatter of cake, "pinch horribly." She snatched the wand out of my hand. "You've been a naughty girl," she said as she exploded into godmother form. Her wings lifted her up to hover over me.

Someone hit her in the side of the head with a chocolate pudding. She squealed.

I took advantage of her temporary blinding and snatched the wand free. She immediately reverted to cinder girl at the ball. She stumbled on the glass slippers. Even wearing chocolate pudding, she was lovely.

"Why?" she asked. Tears leaked from her huge blue eyes.

I felt the godmother magic flooding me. An urge to protect and shelter the poor lamb almost drowned me. I ruthlessly killed it. "I want power. I don't want to spend my life in the cellar kitchen just to escape my mother and my scheming stepsister. I don't want to be a godmother, but it's better than—"

"No, it isn't. It's horrid, simply horrid. Sending all those poor young things to marry princes just because they were stupid enough to think it was a lovely dream when all they really wanted was a soft bed and some time to themselves." Her shoulders slumped as Prince Robert charged into view.

The magic had caught him again. This time he was fixed on Mary. Ella followed him, screeching like an angry pig that had been stuck with a pitchfork.

I watched Mary's eyes light with false love. The music shifted again to a soft waltz. Robert reached for her. Ella launched herself at the happy couple. She slipped on the cream spilled over the floor. All three slid into the table, landing in the fancy cake.

The wand jerked upright, flinging magic at Mary. Cake and icing flowers slid from her to puddle on the floor. She stood, untouched, in her silver gown. Robert rose to his feet. As he brushed his hands down his sleeves, the cake slid away from him, too. He held his hand to Mary. She rested hers lightly in his. The waltz began again, augmented by the godmother magic into hauntingly beautiful music.

Poor Mary had tears glittering in her eyes as Robert spun her into a circling dance.

Robert, the scheming prince, would not love her as she deserved.

But she would be queen, with everything her heart desired. Beautiful gowns, jewels, luxury everywhere she turned.

That wasn't what her heart desired.

I wrenched the wand back down. I had no idea what I was doing, but I struggled to put the godmother magic back into the evil stick of wood. I could curse my own stepsister Ella to such a fate because that's what she truly desired. She and Robert would make a good match, although heaven help the kingdom if she became queen. But Mary? She'd been a godmother for a long time. I felt her presence through the veil of pastel magic. She had truly been sweet and kind and good. She had wanted to go to the ball, true, but only because she had never been to a royal ball. Her heart wanted to be free.

I twisted the wand's power to my own desires. The blast I sent at Mary and Robert as they twirled in an enchanted dance was not pastel, or full of bubbles and sparkling light. It was steel gray, hard and sharp as diamonds.

The music dissolved into chaotic notes and disharmony. The musicians stopped playing, trading ashamed looks.

The court women quit flinging food at each other. The ones caught up in the godmother spell stopped chasing after the princes. Everyone stood with heads hanging, cream and custard dripping from their hair.

Except Robert and Mary. They stared at each other. Robert looked bewildered. Mary looked determined.

The king blustered up to them. He'd somehow escaped the flying pastries. "Well, is this the girl? Do I negotiate a new alliance with Landcombe?"

Robert opened and closed his mouth for a moment. Nothing came out.

"No," Mary finally said. She stepped out of her glass slippers. She lifted them high, then smashed them onto the marble floor of the ballroom. Being created from magic, they tinkled like bells, but they did not break.

I sent a trickle of magic at them. Both shoes exploded into a glittering cloud of shards. The cinder girl curse was broken.

A smile spread over Mary's face. She dropped a quick curtsey. "Your Highness, Your Majesty, thank you for a most interesting evening. Thank you for inviting me to your ball. But I really must be going now."

The clock struck the first note of midnight.

Ella shivered. Her gown shimmered into rags at the second stroke.

Robert stared after Mary as she marched determinedly for the door. Her silver gown was tattered skirts, but her head was high, her step light.

My wings fluttered as I sank to the floor. I was a plump godmother again. I raised the wand, brought it down in a sweeping motion over myself.

Power slammed around me, trapping me in a dark swirl of wind.

I staggered when it ended.

I was no longer in the king's ballroom. I stood on a carpet of moss softer and greener than any on Earth. Strands of flowers glowed softly above me on swaying tree branches. I was in my own serviceable blue dress and in my own body.

I faced a slender creature. Long white hair flowed down her back and tangled in the delicate wings that swept up either side of her body. Her dress was made of flower petals and spider silk. Her eyes were enormous, green and slitted like a cat's. She licked her lips as she studied me, revealing tiny pointed fangs. She wore a crown of woven grasses. Magic clung to her, powerful ancient magic.

The trees rustled. More of the creatures emerged. Some tall and elegant like the queen. Some short and twisted dwarves. Tiny winged men and women darted and flew through the assembled court, trailing strands of flowers in their wake.

Someone cleared their throat behind me. I turned to find myself facing a throng of godmothers, evil witches, sorceresses, warlocks, dark lords, and faceless knights. A short, plump woman wearing a purple gown embroidered with clumsy stars stepped forward. A tiny pair of wings buzzed behind her neat, gray bun of hair. A pointed hat perched at a jaunty angle on her head. But her sweet face was not crinkled in a smile. It was hard and cold as she stared me down.

"You, child, have been summoned to the Seelie Court, and the Un-Seelie Court. You have violated our laws and must face your punishment." Her voice was firm and thrummed with power.

"What have I done? I freed a girl from your curse. I didn't force anyone to marry through magic." I wiped a smear of raspberry jam from my bodice. It looked too much like blood in the light of the magical flowers.

"You violated godmother magic. You changed the story!"

"Your godmother tried to send me to the ball! I'm the eldest stepsister. I should be languishing in a laundry somewhere, fading into obscurity, while the lazy Ella pretends to be the cinder girl so she and my mother can weasel their way into the palace. Your story failed, not mine."

She frowned at me.

I shivered, but I wasn't about to let her intimidate me. I still had the wand. I felt the power in it rising in response to my anger.

"What did you mean changing the cinder girl into a godmother, cursing her for who knows how long? She wanted to marry the baker's son, not the prince. She'd already found her true love."

"The story must be observed."

"Says who?" I whipped the wand up, sending power across the clearing.

The Un-Seelie queen waved one languid hand. My spell imploded like a soap bubble popping. She waved her hand again.

The dark wind swirled around me, smothering me with flying leaves and flower petals.

"Your punishment has been set." Her voice echoed in my mind.

The wind died with a last gasping flutter of leaves.

I was standing in a tiny clearing deep in dark woods. Hoary old evergreens mixed with gnarled oaks. A raven screeched, wings flapping heavily as it flew over my head.

It landed on the roof of the strangest hut I'd ever seen. It looked as if it were crafted from black feathers. It was round and perched on top of a pair of giant chicken legs and feet. A fence of lashed bones penned it inside a garden. I recognized the herbs and flowers. Feverfew, cumfrey, mint, coriander, sage, and many others good for brewing poultices and medicines. But there were other plants with darker uses. Dark magic clung to those like a mist.

I took one step forward, then paused. I was still young, tall and straight, but I wore a black dress, sturdy boots, and a brightly colored shawl woven with arcane symbols.

"From stepsister Jane to godmother to Baba Yaga." I nodded, feeling my hair bob. I reached up, touched the tightly wound bun. It would do. I marched toward my magic home. The bone gate creaked open for me.

I wondered briefly what had become of Mary, Ella, and the prince. But not for long.

Rosa would be all right. She had the manor house now. And Mother had always loved her best, anyway. Sweet simple Rosa would marry well and enjoy sweetcakes the rest of her life.

Mother? I did not care much what happened to my mother. She'd taught me the beginnings of magic, but her own ambition limited her. No, Mother was on her own. I let my past slide away with no regrets.

I had too much to learn, too many new powers to explore.

I smiled at my punishment.

FREDINANDO
APPROACHES

Rupert leaned back in his recliner, striped tail twitching. After a long day at work crunching numbers, all he wanted was to relax and enjoy his favorite takeout noodles. He tapped his phone with one claw. Celestial Noodles made the best noodle bowls and Rupert was determined to enjoy his when it came. A window opened on the phone.

Do you wish to opt in to delivery updates?

He tapped Yes. The box informed him: Twenty minutes until delivery. He could wait that long. Just enough time for a little catnap.

He smiled at his lame pun, showing his long fangs then stretched out his orange and black striped legs and closed his golden eyes. With a flick of his ears he settled deeper into the overstuffed chair.

This was the life. Nothing but—

Something clattered in the kitchen. Rupert was instantly on the alert.

Silence.

Must have been the wind, he thought as he settled back into his nap.

Paper rustled, followed by the rattle of plastic wrappers.

Someone was in his kitchen! If it was those blasted cockroaches from 3C again, he was going to turn them in to the HOA board. Bad neighbors, those bugs.

He slammed the footrest of his chair back into place then stomped on large tiger feet into the kitchen.

A box of crackers lay on the countertop, bag ripped open and squares of golden brown crunchiness scattered onto the floor. Rupert let out a peeved growl.

He caught a movement in the corner behind the window curtain. He pounced with all the speed and ferocity of his ancestors and pinned the intruder on top of the table.

It squealed and flailed thin arms in all directions.

Not a cockroach, but a macaque monkey.

Rupert wrinkled his nose in distaste at the sight of the creature. Thin arms, bloated belly, red rash over the bald spots on its face and shoulders, the thing looked more than halfway dead. "Who are you and why are you stealing my Wheat-ee-bites?" Rupert's voice carried more than a hint of a growl.

The monkey cowered. "Please. Your paw is," it paused to wheeze, "heavy."

"You haven't answered my questions." Rupert eased up, just a bit, with his paw. He could guess what the macaque was doing in his kitchen. Stealing food. By the looks of him, he hadn't eaten well in a long time. He looked sick as well.

At that thought, Rupert pulled his paw all the way off the monkey. He shook it, holding it away from his body. Where had he put that sanitizer?

The monkey coughed, wheezed again, then shuddered its way into a hunched and pitiful seat on the windowsill.

"Fredinando," he wheezed, "is coming."

Rupert froze, his heart thudding. "Wait, are you—" He swallowed a growl and tried again. "Are you one of the Monkeys of the Apocalypse?"

But the macaque was gone, vaulting over the windowsill and back into the tangle of alleys behind Rupert's building.

The tiger breathed heavily. In and out, count to ten, like his therapist had taught.

The monkey had to be Plague Monkey, the first herald of disaster and doom, harbinger of disease, the dreaded doorman of death. And he had come to Rupert's kitchen and eaten his crackers.

Rupert looked at his paw with sudden alarm.

He'd touched Plague Monkey!

With his bare paw!

He whirled to the kitchen sink to turn the water on as hot as possible. He squirted half a bottle of dish soap over his fur.

Where was his bleach? Maybe he could stop the sickness if he had enough bleach. He'd heard the stories whispered in the dark about the four macaques that would bring the end of the world. First was disease.

What was next?

He poured bleach over his paw. His orange and black fur became dirty peach and yellow-green stripes.

He squeezed his eyes shut as the thought hit him like a hammer.

Had he just doomed the world?!

He'd growled at one of them about eating his Wheat-ee-Bites. Did he need to apologize to it? If he didn't, would it spread plagues everywhere? Starting with him? Had he, Rupert the Tiger, started the apocalypse by being so greedy over a box of crackers?

But who was Fredinando?

The light flickered.

Rupert gave a kitten mew of terror as he crouched, bleached paw held as far away as possible.

His kitchen light pulsed yellow then red then blue before cycling again through the colors. He heard the distant thudding of drums banging a heavy beat. Something landed outside his window, a clacking of heels.

Rupert tried to shut his eyes. He really wanted to not see what had just come to visit his kitchen. But try as he might, he could not stop staring in abject terrified fascination at the apparition climbing through his window.

Clear platform heels, complete with plastic goldfish, stretched up in rainbow colors along skinny legs. A fluff of gray fur stuck out from the top. A round monkey belly rose above that. Front and center on the anemic chest was a large round medallion of shining metal studded with sparkling stones in the shape of a musical note. The monkey face above that wore enormous round sunglasses that turned its eyes into black pools of despair. A crown of rainbow curls topped the head.

"Dance for me!" the new monkey sang.

Music pulsed and pounded in Rupert's kitchen. The light cycled through rainbows of colors. Rupert's legs and feet shuffled in a rocking two-step, the only dance move he knew. He rolled his front paws around each other then threw one arm up, one claw pointing skyward.

Only he misjudged the height of the ceiling. His claw jammed into the sheetrock and stuck.

"Dance for me one more time," the monkey drawled, his voice smooth as oiled bananas. "Fredinando approaches."

The monkey rocked his hips, did a fancy step-ball-change, then whirled on one fishy heel and disappeared out the window.

The music ended abruptly. The light flickered back to normal.

Rupert stood with one finger stuck in the ceiling, his bleached paw stretched out to the side, and his mouth hanging open.

Dance Monkey? He'd never heard of that apocalyptic messenger.

A smell seeped in through the open window in an almost visible fog. Dead waterslime mixed with old gym socks and, Rupert sniffed, was that rotten camembert cheese? He sniffed again, wrinkling his nose at the foulness. The stench grew like yeast mold in a wet forest. Like an unstoppable tide. Rupert regretted breathing as he gagged. It was almost palpable, a creature in its own right.

The source of the smell thwumped through the window like a sack of damp oatmeal. It untangled hairy limbs to reveal yet another macaque. This one exuded the stench along with nuggets of white body cheese that resembled maggots falling from its hairy armpits and the folds of skin surrounding its bulbous belly. Or were those lumps actual maggots? One wiggled as if to say, Hi! Rupert's stomach heaved.

This—thing— in his kitchen must be Funky Monkey, one of the more dreaded Apocalypse Monkeys. He'd heard only vague rumors and whispers of this one. Too horrible to mention, as if merely whispering its name would summon the creature and its horrendous stench, no one wanted to take that chance.

Rupert slapped his bleached paw over his mouth and yanked on the stuck claw. He pulled frantically until a chunk of ceiling broke free. His hand slapped down, yanked by gravity on the heavy piece of wallboard attached to one claw. It slammed into his leg. He felt his claw crack, but right that moment, he didn't care. He was trying too hard to hold his breath. His head spun with the need to breathe.

But not that thick miasma of foulness. He'd suffocate first. Was it safe to breathe bleach?

"Fredinando," the monkey rasped in a hoarse bass tone, "is nearby."

The macaque scratched his belly, dislodging more of the strange white lumps onto the table, before sauntering across the windowsill into the outdoors.

Rupert sagged to the floor, waving his bleached hand frantically in an attempt to clear the air before he absolutely had to breathe.

Something stomped on the first stair past the landing. Rupert felt the shudder through the floor.

He forgot all about not breathing the stench. His heart raced. Sweat beaded around the base of his orange ears and dripped into the white ruff around his face.

Fredinando was coming.

Fredinando was approaching.

Fredinando was nearby.

Fredinando was climbing the stairs to his apartment.

The floor jumped and shuddered again as Fredinando took another step.

Rupert frantically pawed at the wallboard still stuck to his hand. His tail whipped back and forth. His lips curled to show his teeth, but no menacing growl escaped, only a terrified squeaking.

The apocalypse was approaching on heavy feet.

The apocalypse that was Fredinando.

Rupert scrabbled across his apartment on all fours. Could he hide from the apocalypse? Was it possible? Or had he, through his own stupidity, brought about the end of everything?

He had no idea how to fix it. The only idea that had room in his head was panicked flight. He left long claw marks across the carpet as he tried to jam into the already full coat closet. Not a good hiding spot. Maybe under the bed would be better.

His bedroom door stuck, like it usually did. He yanked desperately at the handle until it ripped loose. He mewled as the footsteps rumbled ever closer up the stairs, a slow but steady tread of doom.

Rupert dove under the footrest of his recliner. He jammed his head into the mechanism under the chair. Warm blood gushed from a cut above his eye. He backed out, tail fluffed into a bush.

He ran frantically around his living room on all fours. Where could he hide from Fredinando?

He tripped over the rug in his entry, rolling onto his back just as a thundering knock sounded on the door.

Rupert's heart pounded. He stared at the door with wild eyes. Nowhere to hide.

The door handle rattled.

Rupert grabbed the rug and hauled it over his head.

The door creaked open.

The tiger pulled the rug down just far enough to expose one eye.

A massive macaque stood in the doorway. Frown lines carved deep canyons in the stern and unforgiving face. Bulging muscles flexed in the arms as the monkey pushed the door fully open.

"Fredinando," he intoned, "has arrived."

Rupert quivered. His voice cracked and wavered as he asked, "Are you Monkeyshine, dreaded fourth Monkey of the Apocalypse?"

The floor shook as the monkey strode across the threshold. He glared at Rupert with eyes dark and mysterious as the night sky. Rupert cowered on the floor. It was all his fault. This was the end.

The monkey pursed his lips as if considering how to answer Rupert's question. He finally shook his head.

"Naw, he's my cousin. I'm George. And this," he stepped to one side, "is Fredinando. We brought your noodles. Extra Spicy Apocalypse Bowl, right? With double broccoli?"

A rhinocerous walked through the door, barely squeezing through. A plastic delivery bag hung from his horn. "Hey."

Rupert wheezed several times. Not the apocalypse, just his dinner arriving. "Wait a minute," he said as he climbed to his feet. He rubbed one paw over his tail, trying to get the fur to lie back down. "I ordered the Calypso Bowl, hold the onions but add extra ginger."

George rolled his eyes and huffed impatiently. "Seriously? Wait a sec, they mixed up your order with 3C. Your order is coming soon. C'mon, Fredinando. Down a flight. Wrong apartment."

The rhino made his ponderous way out of the apartment. George yanked Rupert's door shut behind them.

Rupert sank into his recliner, bleached paw pressed against his chest.

Something scrabbled in his kitchen.

He closed his eyes and tried a deep calming breath. He just wanted to enjoy his noodles in peace!

The cracker box rattled.

Enough was enough. Rupert stamped into the kitchen.

A brightly colored parrot withdrew one guilty foot from the cracker box. It set the foot down on the counter, eyes fixed on Rupert's glare as it moved. It clacked its beak a couple of times.

"Miranda is coming," the bird squawked.

Rupert growled and swatted the bird through the window with one massive paw. He slammed it, latching it with a firm twist.

"That's the last time I opt in for delivery updates," he muttered as he headed back to his recliner. The food would arrive when it arrived. Until then, he'd just munch on what was left of his Wheat-ee-Bites.

A Matter of
Diplomacy

Ambassador Nora Blythe squirmed as her stomach rumbled. She did it with a tight smile and a minimum of movement, but she was still embarrassed. She was humanity's ambassador to the Trichlid delegation. She should be the picture of calm and dignity, the best of mankind. After the horrible debacle with the Borschuii that led to a brief, but spectacular war, humankind couldn't afford to make mistakes. The Trichlids were the second alien sapients humans encountered.

And definitely the cutest.

Nora squelched the thought. Trichlids resembled short, fluffy kittens with adorably big eyes, blue-green fur, and pointed ears, but that didn't mean they appreciated being scooped up and cuddled.

She shifted, waiting for the ceremonial music and procession to finish. Her stomach gurgled. She twitched again at the belly spasm.

Campbell, her attentive aide, leaned close. "Ma'am?" The single word carried his whole message.

"Just something I ate that I probably shouldn't have," she whispered back.

He nodded and resumed his stoic pose at her left shoulder.

As far as the biologists could determine, Trichlids ate the same things humans did. They'd assured her the alien dishes should be perfectly safe to consume. She'd sampled and enjoyed most of it. The fruit was especially tasty. But then, Nora was partial to a good piece of fruit.

Three hours later, she was regretting taking the biologists' advice. She should have been more like Campbell and only nibbled enough to satisfy protocol.

Her belly rumbled louder. Eight pairs of pointed ears swiveled her way. Eight sets of eyes like emeralds turned to look at her instead of the flag-waving dancers performing in the stone courtyard.

The Trichlid Ambassador, Kee-Chee-Nee-Boof as far as she could pronounce it, shuffled his feet. His nose twitched.

Nora clenched her muscles as gas threatened to escape. She was *not* going to embarrass herself. Not publicly. And not in front of the aliens she was trying to impress. Humans were too civilized to fart in public!

The flag-twirlers were replaced with a band of Trichlids carrying their versions of instruments. Their music sounded like a band of drunk howler monkeys and raccoons with garbage cans, but Nora did her best to appreciate the cultural exchange. At least the loud sounds would help camouflage her flatulence.

Her stomach twisted with unexpelled gases. She couldn't keep it in any longer. She let a small fart escape. The tiny squeak was barely noticeable above the alien racket and caterwauling.

Kee-Chee's nose twitched three times. He turned his round furry head to study her.

She smiled and pretended she'd done nothing.

He blinked. His mouth opened, then shut. He turned back to the music.

Nora blew out a small breath, relieved that no one had noticed. Her belly seemed to have settled down somewhat. She might make it through the performance without horribly embarrassing herself.

She spoke too soon. A huge rumbler ripped from her backside.

Kee-Chee flung up his hand. Paw? Something adorably small and furry anyway. The music ended abruptly. A single rattle of metal was the only sound as one performer dropped his drum.

The alien stared at Nora, both eyes wide open. His nose twitched rapidly.

Nora felt Campbell's shock and embarrassment like a heat wave on her shoulder. He would blush for her, if he could. Her own face burned. Her stomach twitched.

No! Not on the broadcast beam for all the world to see and hear. She would not fart again! She would not embarrass her whole species.

Her own nose twitched at the smell. Rotten eggs mixed with roses and peaches. She tried hard not to gag. She clenched her butt muscles tighter.

Kee-Chee continued to stare, like an owl. All of the other Trichlids stared, too, even the performers. Hundreds of emerald eyes, and billions of human ones, watched.

She couldn't hold it in. A long blare of gases erupted like a trumpet from her backside.

Kee-Chee's eyes widened even further, a feat Nora would have wondered at if she weren't trying to melt into the pavement while still standing stiffly. She was humanity's ambassador. And she'd just very publicly and very loudly farted.

The Trichlid's nose twitched like a rabbit's as the foul stench enveloped everyone in the ambassador's party.

The Trichlids all began chattering at once in their language. They sounded like a flock of parrots on caffeine.

Nora would just have to make the best of it. She pasted a smile on her face, the sincerest one she could muster. "Excuse me, please. I don't know—"

Kee-Chee rushed toward her, followed by a tumble of blue-furred bodies. They pressed close to her, noses twitching like mad. Campbell was pushed back, his protests buried under the avalanche of alien speech.

Kee-Chee barely came to her waist. He looked up at her, pressed his paw on her belly. "Again?"

Nora flapped her mouth for a minute. What was she supposed to respond to that? Her hindbrain just wanted to pet the cute little beasts while her forebrain wanted to die of humiliation. Which left the rest of her to stand like an idiot, speechless.

Her belly answered for her. Another long, leisurely fart rumbled out.

The Trichlids crowded close, eyes closed in rapture as they breathed in the stench.

Kee-Chee smiled when she finished. His cute little mouth curved into a twin bow, his eyes crinkled and squeezed partially closed, his ears relaxed. He pressed close to Nora. Her hindbrain moved her hand before she could stop it. She stroked the alien's head. His fur was soft and fluffy, his head warm. He purred.

Her nose twitched.

That was not a purr. It was a fart. A long expellation of gas that reeked of rotting grass and tomatoes.

The rest of the aliens crowded closer, noses twitching.

And joined in the chorus of gas.

Nora coughed on the stench. Then giggled.

Kee-Chee grinned as she farted again. "Good friend," he said in his broken imitation of human speech. "Speak good smell."

She farted again. Her belly releasing pent-up gas. Kee-Chee responded in kind. The whole group farted and sniffed and farted more.

She glanced up to catch Campbell's horrified gaze. "Either join in, or find someone who will," she told him.

She settled onto the pavement surrounded by Trichlids. They farted at each other while they outlined the beginnings of a treaty between their respective peoples. Kee-Chee sniffed appreciatively whenever she let one loose. She tried to repay the favor. And really, most of their farts smelled quite lovely, once they relaxed.

Similar diets, similar digestive tracts. Similar responses.

Diplomacy was all about finding common ground, after all.

JO-LENE

Mary placed the pot of stew on the hand-made trivet resting on the rough wood slab that served as a table. She stepped back, sliding the oven mitts from her hands to place them on the counter near the basin that served as a sink. "I hope you like it. I used that rock leaper you brought home yesterday. Meat was a little gamey so I stewed it with junip berries and the last onion."

"I'll watch for more wild onion," Peter, her husband, said as he dished stew into his bowl.

Mary twisted her hands in her apron. The rocky uplands of Terith held unknown dangers. She hated when Peter took it into his head to explore. Sue, down the hill from their spread, had lost her husband Jim to the canyons and twisting terrain only last winter. "Don't need onion that badly. I noticed the north field was ready for planting the winter crop of wheat. You need help with that?" If only Peter would let her go with him, maybe she could keep him safe, bring him home from those hills to stay.

"Needs another week before we can work the soil. The tines need sharpened and the tractor needs that gear box replaced. I'll go into town later this week, take care of that." Peter slurped another spoonful of stew. "You gonna eat, woman?"

Mary perched on the edge of her chair, slowly spooned a small dish of leaper stew. If only they had children, maybe that would hold Peter here.

She'd done her best, but medical services on the colony world had yet to catch up with services on more settled worlds.

"Are you going into the hills tomorrow?" Mary broke the strained silence.

Peter nodded. "Saw something up in the Cloud Range. Gonna check it out."

Mary took a bite of the stew. The meat was stringy, tasteless in her mouth.

"Got my leaper traps to check. And might find berries up higher on the slopes."

Although the larder was pretty lean most days and the extra food was welcome, she didn't care about more berries or meat. She wanted her man closer to home. Closer and safe. But if she held too tightly, she'd only drive him away faster.

"Don't you have your ladies' club meeting tomorrow?" Peter asked.

Mary had to swallow then clear her throat before she could answer. It didn't help move the lump of worry lodged in her windpipe. "We're making baby clothes for the Simpson's down in the hollow. They're expecting their first."

Peter ate the last of the stew in his bowl, dished himself more. "Good stew, Mary. Best yet."

It wasn't. It tasted too much of the alien planet and not enough of home. Mary closed her eyes, saw the green fields of Ireland, not the dusty gold of Terith. But Ireland held no future for a poor girl, not in the crowded cities or the protected preserves. Mary had jumped at the chance to emigrate, to find a husband among the stalwart adventurers who'd homesteaded Terith's wide plains, to escape her gran's stories of family curses and evil magic. Terith was real and solid, not myth and shadow. She'd found her husband, the love that lit her eyes and made her want to dance.

And now she might lose him. Maybe her gran was right about the women in her family carrying a curse.

"You'll be home tomorrow night?" She tried to keep the concern from her voice, but it still quivered.

Peter shrugged. "Might be gone a couple of days. I'll be back in time to get that field ready. Don't wait up for me."

He didn't kiss her on his way out the door to lock up their flock of chickens for the night.

She rested her chin on her folded hands, tried to keep the worried tears from escaping, tried to breathe through the sudden knot of fear in her belly.

What was it her gran had always told her? *Fight for your man, fight for what you believe in. Fight for your loves, whatever they may be.*

She loved Peter, loved their farm, loved their rough life.

"Time to fight," she whispered.

If only she knew how.

"What's really up in the hills?"

Mary's question put an instant hush on the group of women. Needles flashed as they bent to their work stitching baby clothes.

"Bad luck to mention it," Sarah whispered.

"Nothing good is up there," Beth added.

"Oh, hush your gossip," Tabitha, the oldest one of their group and one of the first women settlers, snapped. Her voice creaked, to match the sound of her rocking chair. Her fingers were still nimble, though the joints were swollen with arthritis and veins crept across her hands.

"What have you seen, Tabby?" Mary couldn't stop herself from asking.

The old woman raised her white head, caught Mary's gaze with her bright eyes. "Don't you mess with the spirits in those hills."

Mary caught her bottom lip in her teeth. Spirits. Like her gran warned. Spirits in the hills, lying in wait. She bent over the tiny little gown, jabbing her needle through the soft fabric. She'd left Ireland, left Earth, to escape the family curse. The Fae haunted her family, had tried once before to take her when she was small. They'd stolen gran's man when she was only a young bride. Or so gran said. Despite spaceships and technology, science and all its explanations, Mary still feared the old stories. She'd *seen* things, out in the green hills of Ireland. And now, here, on Terith, the shadows began to gather, the spirits danced in the high hills of the alien planet.

"Isn't that right, Mary? Mary, are you even listening?" Beth nudged her.

Mary pasted a smile on her face and nodded.

"See, even Mary agrees."

She let the conversation carry her for a while. New fabrics and patterns arriving on the next ship, the flocks of sheep and goats producing raw fleece and who knew how to spin, who was expected to marry soon, small-town gossip for a frontier world. But underneath ran the current of fear. Something lurked in the hills, something that threatened their men.

Sue, the one who'd lost her Jim to the hills last winter, was absent from their sewing circle. Hard pregnancy, the women whispered. The woman lost her husband and now might lose their only child. And possibly her life. It wasn't fair.

It was life on a frontier world with its unknown dangers.

The afternoon was fading into evening when the women collected their things and took their leave. A stack of new baby clothes waited to be delivered. Tabitha's rocking chair creaked. The old woman met Mary's eyes, waited for the Beth to finish bustling through the small house.

"Thank you kindly, Beth." Tabitha's voice carried only a hint of impatience. "Mary will sit with me for a while, won't you, dear?"

"I left soup on the stove for you." Beth shot a look between Mary and Tabitha. "Is there anything else?"

"Not tonight, thank you," Tabitha answered. "Mary and I need to talk, that's all."

"Well, if that's all, then I best be getting back to my own family." Beth's steps minced to the door. Her face showed her curiosity plain as her nose.

But neither woman was willing to satisfy that curiosity. Beth was safe, her husband Tom as stolid as they came. He would never wander the hills chasing a dream.

Tabitha waited until the door shut firmly behind Beth before she motioned Mary to the stool at her side. "Sit a spell. I can read the trouble on your face from a mile away. I may be old, but I'm not blind. Not yet."

"It's Peter," Mary said as she perched on the stool.

Tabitha shook her head. "Peter isn't the problem." She leaned closer. "Her name is JoLene. She was my sister. Once, a long time ago."

"But it's Peter—"

"Spare me the protests," Tabitha snapped. "I can see it in your face. You're afraid of losing your man to whatever is lurking in the hills. Are you brave enough to save him? Whatever the cost?"

Mary couldn't meet the hard eyes of the old woman. She dropped her gaze to her lap. "Yes," she whispered.

Tabitha snorted. "I thought you had more spine than Sue. She let her husband go, you know. Just watched him leave. Watched him walk off after that thing that used to be my sister bewitched him."

Mary squeezed her hands into fists. "Peter left this morning. He said he was going exploring, trapping up in the hills."

"You and I both know that's a lie. He's seen her. She's caught him in her lure and the only way she'll ever let go is if you fight her, fight with everything you have."

"Fight what? Who is she?"

Tabitha reached out her hand, waited for Mary to unclench her fist and take hold of the withered, wrinkled fingers. "That's a long story. And you don't have much time, not if you're going to save him before it's too late." She sighed. "It started that first winter after we arrived. I was part of the survey team, along with my sister and a dozen other scientists and engineers. We set up our camp out where the O'Henry's spread is now. JoLene always wanted to know what lay beyond the horizon, over the next hill, wherever. She could never stay still for long. She was beautiful, you know. Auburn hair, ivory skin, green eyes, and curves in all the right places. She had all the single men chasing her and a few of the married ones, too." A smile flickered across Tabitha's face, then faded. "She disappeared for a few days at a time at first, then weeks, then months. She was gone most of that second winter. I never knew where she went other than into the hills.

"She came back strange. It was subtle at first, but by the time the settlers arrived two years later, JoLene was not human any more. Might have been eating the native plants or drinking the water, or just being herself, but she no longer fit with people. She took my husband that fourth winter, led him off into the hills before I knew what she was doing. I never saw either of them again. But I hear rumors of men leaving their wives, wandering into the hills. I know it's my sister, up to her savage tricks.

"I tried to stop her. Oh, how I tried. But I could never find her. I quit the survey team, stayed here to keep trying. I don't want to go to my grave with her sins still on my conscience. I want to know why she stole my Jacob."

Tabitha's hands were too tight on Mary's, squeezing until her bones ached.

Mary pulled them free. "What do I do?"

"I don't know. I tried everything I could think of." Tabitha seemed to shrink into a much smaller woman in her rocker. "Follow your man into the hills. Hold on and never let him go. Fight her with everything you've got. And understand that she's not human, not any more."

Fight for your love.

Mary nodded. "I'll leave tonight."

"Luck ride with you, girl. You're going to need it."

The wild grasses tangled around her legs as she strode up the hill following the faint trace of her husband's passage. The string of snares lay over the ridge to her right, down along the hollow where water trickled year round. A scraggling forest of short bushy growths lay to her left. Behind was her home and the settlement. Ahead, the hills climbed to the Cloud Mountains.

Ahead was her husband and JoLene, whatever she was now.

"What's the family curse?" Innocent little Mary had asked.

Gran smacked wasps away from her raspberries with the same ruthlessness she'd smacked Mary's hands away. "Those are for jam, not for you. Family curse is a serious thing. I'll tell you when you're older."

"Tell me now, Gran. I want to know."

"Your mother would skin me alive if she heard me telling you." Gran's hands stained red as she smashed the berries into paste.

"I promise not to let her know." Mary kept her face solemn and serious.

The summer air hung heavy, thick with the buzzing of the wasps and the smell of crushed berries.

"It's a lonely curse, and not all our women carry it. But you, child, you have the mark."

Mary twisted her arms, searching.

"Not there, silly goose. The mark is here." Gran tapped the girl's forehead leaving behind a smear of raspberry blood. "In your imagination. You can see things others can't. Makes you vulnerable to Them."

The Fae. Mary knew better than to speak it out loud.

Her stride ate the miles as she followed the faint traces of Peter's steps farther into the hills, away from the safety of what she knew and into the wilds of the alien planet.

"They steal your soul, you know," Gran's voice was matter-of-fact as she stirred sugar into the berries. "Your memories, your loves, everything that makes you what you are. They leave only an empty shell, hungry for what it can't have."

"Like me for your jam." Mary giggled.

Gran shook her head, serious. "It's a hunger that consumes them to the point they steal what they can never have. They eat that and still want more. The only thing that satisfies them is death. Yours or theirs."

Mary shivered though the day was hot.

"You kill them with your determination, child. Hang on to the things you love, no matter what. Hold on until they shrivel and die. That's the only way to break the curse and keep what you hold dearest to your heart."

Hold tight. How could she do that? She wasn't even certain she could find Peter in these gold-cloaked hills.

She shivered her way through the night, tucked next to a large boulder. Her belly rumbled despite the handfuls of berries she'd gleaned as she hiked. The taste of Terith clung to her mouth. She closed her eyes and remembered summer raspberries and her gran's stories.

"They're tall, thin as a whip," Gran whispered as they shelled peas on the porch. *"With hair that blazes like fire and eyes that glow like emeralds. Or like that cat you claim to love. Cats are spies for Them, you know. You shouldn't let that beast sleep in your room. Ever."*

Cats hadn't made it to Terith. None of them survived the trip either in the passenger hold or in the embryo banks. They weren't high priority, either. None of the little scavengers on Terith ate Terran grains. No pests meant no need for predators that hunted them. Cats were a luxury, still. Right now, Mary would have welcomed the warm furry bundle of sharp claws and purrs that went by the name of Dandy Lion. He was long buried and gone, back in Ireland on her gran's farm, a fiery golden tabby with a taste for mice and songbirds. She'd loved him and let him sleep on her pillow despite Gran's warnings.

Morning found her dozing, wandering in strange half-waking dreams of cats and golden hills. She welcomed the warmth of sunlight even if it was more orange than Sol's yellow light. She found her husband's trail and started hiking. Her muscles ached. She ignored the pain and kept moving. She had to save Peter.

She found him mid-morning, gleaning pale yellow berries from a patch of cloud bushes. She silently joined him, plucking the plump fruit and dropping it into his bucket. She'd forgotten to bring bags or buckets in her rush to save him. Her husband was only picking fruit.

He smiled at her, his hands stained yellow. "You followed me?"

Mary forced a smile. "It got too quiet at home. Too lonely. Besides, two hands can pick twice as many."

Peter plucked another handful, pausing to eat the juiciest ones.

Neither of them spoke of the pain between them. No children, no hope of medical help to conceive. No chance of adopting, not when children were few and far between in the new colony.

They filled the bucket. Peter carefully clamped the lid on top and tucked it into his pack. "We should get more animals for you. Maybe move closer to town so you can apprentice with the vet. You've been talking about that for a while now."

They spoke of little things as they gathered onions by the stream, then worked their way back down the hills, gathering native fruit as they walked. Neither spoke of the weight between them. Peter had seen something in the hills. Mary saw the distance in his eyes, felt it in his touch.

JoLene. She could almost sense the wicked woman demon watching.

Mary startled out of sleep. Peter tossed beside her, face scrunched in a scowl, eyes closed and dreaming. He spoke, a garbled sentence of nonsense words. Except one.

JoLene.

She wrapped her arms around her husband, held him in the moonlight. He shifted restlessly, pushing her away. She held him tighter.

Two weeks of holding him close. They plowed the north field, sowed the winter wheat, cleaned the chicken coop, worked to shore up the sagging roof on the hay shed, laid out the foundation for a barn. Mary even convinced him to help her stir the berries into jam. The jars of golden yellow lined a shelf in their fruit cellar half buried in the soil of Terith. But he chafed under the burden of working their farm, moved to avoid her as she worked beside him.

She caught him watching the hills, staring into the distance with a wistfulness he used to give her. He'd seen JoLene out in the wild alien landscape. Mary read it in his eyes, in the faraway looks he cast at the hills, in the distance of his touch as they lay together in their bed.

She wrapped her arms around him as they lay in the tangle of blankets on their bed.

He fought her, pushing her aside. He surged from the bed and stumbled through their small house, out into the cold night in his bare feet and night clothes.

"Peter!"

The door banged shut. She slammed it open, held it with one arm.

The hills swallowed him into their darkness.

She paused only long enough to shove her feet into boots and grab a jacket and their hunting gun from its peg by the back door. Terith did not boast much in the way of predators, at least none the settlers had encountered.

Except for JoLene.

Tabitha's stories of her wayward sister tangled with Gran's tales of the Fae as Mary strode into the hills. A creature of myth called Peter away, a siren bent on taking what never belonged to her. Mary would bring her husband home.

Or die trying.

Hold on, child, hang on with everything you have, or you'll lose. The Fae will take everything you hold dear and leave you with nothing but ashes and an empty heart.

Somewhere in the hills, a woman with flaming hair and shining green eyes lured Peter to his doom. No, not a woman any more. A mix of alien and human, something twisted and wrong. An abomination.

A trill of laughter mocked Mary's determination.

She stopped, turned to face it with her weapon raised.

Only shadows in the night.

Brush crackled higher up the slope.

"Peter?" Mary ran toward the sound, heedless of any danger lurking in the darkness.

A rock leaper bounced out of the brush, disappeared into the rocks higher up the slope. Mary skidded to a halt. Her breathing was ragged, hoarse in her throat. She searched the night for any trace of her husband.

Only the dark hills and the glimmer of unfamiliar constellations met her frantic search.

She hurried farther into the hills, following the faint traces of her husband's passing. A bent twig, a flattened patch of grassy growth, broken stems of the alien equivalent of wildflowers, all hinted at his stumbling run after JoLene.

She ducked under a tangled shrub. Its branches caught her hair, like fingers grabbing for her. She yanked herself free to tumble down a slope.

"Peter!" She lay at the base of the hill, bruised from her fall.

A leaper trilled its warning call somewhere in the rocks high above on the next hill.

"Peter, where are you?" Her voice broke on sobs as she pushed to her feet. She stumbled on, deeper into the alien hills.

She lost all trace of him, but still kept going despite the darkness, the night shadows, the chill breeze plucking her clothes and hair.

Hold on, child, no matter what.

"Gran, help me. I'm so lost."

She paused on a hilltop, searching though she could barely see by the faint traces of starlight.

There! Far below. A glimmer of white skin and flaming red hair.

She ran forward, tripped over a rock, fell in a cartwheel of flailing limbs.

Mary landed in a heap at the bottom. Something cracked in her knee. Her hand ached. She wiped blood from her face, but it kept dripping from a gash in her scalp.

"Peter!" She screamed his name. "Peter!"

She crumpled to the dirt and sobbed out her despair.

Morning found her still lying where she'd fallen, sprawled in an exhausted sleep. The rising sun touched her face, warmed her skin. A leaper sniffed her hair, snagged a handful in its paws. It tried to jerk it free. Her head rolled to the side. It scampered away, clutching a pawful of brown strands.

Her eyes fluttered, then opened. She groaned. Her leg throbbed with pain. Her hand was swollen and purple. Dried blood caked across her face. She couldn't remember ever feeling such pain.

"Peter?" Her voice came out a croak.

She crawled across the dirt to a nearby boulder. She'd narrowly missed smashing into it in the dark. She shivered. She could have died out here. That didn't matter. Saving Peter mattered. She clenched her teeth as she forced herself up the side of the stone. She leaned against it, panting hard against the pain. She cradled her injured hand against her chest as she tested her twisted knee. It ached, but it held.

She limped away from the boulder, up the hill. She paused at the top. Nothing looked familiar. Every direction showed rolling hills covered with alien plants. The only thing moving was a colony of leapers sunning on the rocks below. Their large ears twitched as they watched her shadow waver across the grass. She stepped forward. The alien rodents vanished with a flash of white tails.

Mary walked down the hill, over the next. She found a small stream between the hills and stopped to drink. She ate what berries she found, a handful of golden ones not quite ripe, a handful of deep purple berries that were overripe and squished in her hands, staining them red. It didn't matter. She wiped her hands down her pajamas and kept going.

Hang on to your love, child. Save him from the Fae creature who calls herself JoLene.

She kept going through the day, pushing herself through a haze of pain and hunger. Somewhere in these hills, her husband was in the clutches of JoLene.

She blinked tears and sweat from her eyes. Was that a flash of red hair? She hurried forward.

"Peter?" Her voice echoed from the rocks. "Peter!"

She scrambled up a narrow canyon, squeezing between enormous blocks of rough stone. She scooped scummy water from a greenish pond, sucking it from her hands as she hurried on.

The setting sun blazed into the narrow canyon, lighting up one side of the steep cliff walls. Ragged shadows on the other side hinted at caves. High up on the side, she caught a glimpse of white, a flash as it disappeared into the caves.

"Peter?"

She charged at the rocks, scrambling up them like a four-legged spider.

Where was the gun? I must have dropped it somewhere. Doesn't matter. Guns can't hurt Fae. Find Peter. Hold onto him. Save him from JoLene.

She scraped her knuckles over coarse stone, licked the blood from them, and kept climbing. Loose rocks tumbled from her grip, smashing into the night shadows gathering below her.

Twilight is their time of power, the changing of night to day, day to night. They are strongest when time is in flux.

Her gran's words, stories that Mary thought were only make-believe. She pulled herself onto a narrow ledge of stone, lay gasping for a moment before climbing again. Yet, somewhere on this planet distant from Earth, an evil fae had stolen her husband in the night.

"He isn't yours," she screamed as she hauled herself over another jagged ledge to find a wedge of darkness.

Something darted from the cave mouth. Wings beat around her head. She covered her ears against high-pitched screeches. She screamed back, wordless shouting at the native creatures. They flew into the dusk.

Mary sat on the stone, staring into the cave. Her hand ached. Her knee throbbed. Countless scratches and bruises added their own pain.

"Peter?" It came out a helpless cry, a whisper barely heard over the evening breeze.

She shivered, pulled her jacket tighter.

"Mary." A singsong voice called her from somewhere deep in the cave.

"Where is he?" Her voice was harsh, demanding.

"Safe enough."

She squinted into the darkness. Was that something fluttering inside? A flash of white skin, perhaps? She took one hesitant step forward.

"Mary?" Peter's voice, wavering and strange, but his voice.

"Peter! Hang on, I'm coming." She stumbled into the darkness, hands flung wide to ward off the unseen obstacles.

Something skittered deeper in the cave. A thin scratch of claws over stone set Mary's skin crawling. She flexed her hands, thinking of weapons.

Silver hurts them. Or is it steel? Iron?

It made little difference. All she had were her wits and whatever rock she grabbed.

"You." Her voice trembled. "Fae. Spirit. Let him go. I know who you are."

A rock clattered in the blackness.

"You can't hide from me." *I've got true love in my heart.*

But did she love Peter enough? She had to love him, want him, beyond any doubt. She had to be strong.

"Help me, Gran," she whispered.

She slid her foot along the rough stone, took a step, then another, and another, deeper into the maw of the earth. *Into the spirit's lair. Into their underground kingdom where time slid sideways and every touch was fraught with danger. Gran said never enter their world, not unless you want to be lost forever. Never taste their food, drink their water, look into their eyes.*

Her lips twisted in a wry grin. Her belly rumbled. When had she last eaten? A handful of berries here and there as she scrambled through the unmarked hills. A root that had come loose from the hillside she'd slid down that morning. She breathed deep, pushing aside the pangs of hunger. Peter was somewhere in the cave held in the clutches of JoLene, whatever she'd become in the decades she'd been lost.

Mary stumbled over tumbled rocks in the darkness. Was that a flash of light reflected in eyes no longer human? A wave of auburn hair?

"JoLene, I summon you to human form." Her voice cracked on the ancient words, twisted through the old language, echoed with Gran's power. "You've taken what does not belong to you. I've come to claim my true love." *My husband, my heart, my life. Peter.*

A wordless hiss raised the hair along her neck. Something large with claws scrabbled on the rocks. Mary screamed as a claw raked along her leg. She flailed her fists, caught a meaty thump as she connected with the thing. It retreated into the cave. The sound of it crawling faded quickly.

"No!" *Be strong. Hold fast. Or lose him forever.*

Mary crawled forward, following the noises.

A faint glimmer of light flashed on ivory skin. The thing had hands, long and slender. The curve of a cheek hid behind flaming red curls. A woman's face smiled from the dim shadows. Her chin was sharp and pointed. Her eyes were wide, slanted like a cat's, and too far up her head. But Mary recognized the face, the knowing smile, the hint of wicked abandon in her green eyes.

"JoLene." A flat statement. Her hands curled into fists. "Give him back to me."

The woman creature laughed, a trill of sound far beyond human vocal cords, musical and shrill at the same time. Mary shivered and resisted the urge to cover her ears.

"He's mine, not yours." She babbled nonsense as she slid her hands through the stones searching for a weapon, anything she could use against this alien-human hybrid. "You can't have him."

The thing fluttered hands. The wild mass of curls tossed in an unseen wind. It bent toward Mary, fanged mouth opening wide.

"Peter!" She fell backward, away from that maw.

Hot breath washed over her bringing the stench of decay. Mary squeezed her eyes shut and turned away.

A sob caught in her throat. She wasn't strong enough. Peter was slipping away, she felt him fading.

"No!" She lunged forward.

The woman laughed her shrill cackle of musical bells before tearing like tissue paper. *Or spiderwebs.* Mary's hand closed on warm flesh. A hand, rough from work.

"Peter." She smiled and laced her fingers in his.

JoLene shrieked. It echoed and built through the rocks. The sound tore at Mary, battered her until her nose bled and her ears rang. She crouched in the darkness, gripping the hand with both of hers.

It was like holding water, or a dream. Peter's flesh turned to smoke, melted beneath her grip. She clasped empty hands on the rocks. Screamed her despair. Flung her arms wide, searching for her man.

Never let him go. Hold fast.

The trill of bells mixed with the scrabble of claws as JoLene retreated. A shaft of moonlight illuminated her white skin and wild red hair as she climbed out of the cave through a crack, up into the night hills above.

Mary staggered to her feet, then broke into a shambling run after JoLene. Whatever had happened to Tabitha's sister to change her into that monster, it wasn't going to happen to Peter. Mary swore promises to all the gods her Gran had worshipped. Just let Peter come home to her. Let him forget JoLene.

She broke out of the earth, up onto the windswept hillside. The moon played tag with clouds. Shadows danced and wavered, hiding then revealing tangles of brambles. Plump berries hung ripe and waiting on the swaying branches. Even in the silver of night, they glowed gold. She reached for one, her belly rumbling.

Eat nothing. Gran's warning.

Mary snatched her hand back. She was in JoLene's world now, a twisted place of magic and deadly snares. She had to hold fast to her purpose.

"JoLene!" Her voice echoed. "I've come to claim Peter. He's mine, my husband, my love." Her voice broke.

Was he?

She squeezed her eyes shut, tears burning on her lashes. He was her true love, her only love. She had to believe with all her heart. Or JoLene would win.

There! She saw him lying on the alien grasses, face turned to the sky, eyes closed. Was he dead? Had the witch drained his life from him?

Mary ran toward Peter. The grass tangled her feet. She sprawled on the ground only to shove back up and run forward.

JoLene darted from a tangle of berry bushes. She swayed over Peter's body, her body strangely misshapen. Mary froze mid-stride to stare at the apparition. The ethereal beauty caught her in a spell. If only she were that lovely and graceful. Peter could never choose her in her lumpy, cloddish humanity, not when he could have this perfection. The face was human, but thinner, the eyes much larger and glowing like emeralds. The skin was pale and smooth, ivory in the moonlight. She wore a tattered gown of black lace. And under the full skirt—

Mary gasped, pressing the back of her hand to her mouth. Under those skirts JoLene had at least a dozen legs, clawed and multi-jointed and shiny like a grasshopper's chitin. Two of them raised over Peter, claws drawing back to reveal gleaming barbs. The glamour spell cast by the creature shattered.

She shouted wordlessly, grabbed up whatever her hands touched to fling at JoLene. Sticks, stones, handfuls of grass, she kept up the rain of objects. JoLene hissed and retreated a bare pace.

Mary's hand closed over something smooth and rounded. It came up from the grass with a tearing noise. As long as her forearm, with a round knob on one end, the other splintered into tearing shards, it was light but strong in her grip. She raised it into the moonlight.

JoLene flinched away. The insect legs scurried under the loose skirts.

Mary straightened, holding the bone like a spear. "He's mine, JoLene. Not yours. Never yours. I conjure whatever love is in his heart to answer mine. I've come to claim my husband."

Hold fast to your love.

I'm trying, Gran. Whether Peter is my true love or not doesn't matter. He's all I have. All I will ever have.

Mary marched forward.

JoLene opened her toothed maw and screamed.

Between them, Peter twitched.

"Mine," Mary shouted in response. "Go home to your Unseeligh court. Go find one of your own kind. Leave him be!"

She flung the bone like a spear. It wobbled through the air. The sharp end stabbed into JoLene below the head, below the flapping arms, above the writhing insect legs. Black liquid spurted into the air. The face twisted as the scream shrilled high above human range. The huge mouth snapped. The claws scrabbled at nothing as JoLene tumbled down the hill, skewered by the jagged bone.

"Peter?" Mary dropped beside her husband.

His eyes snapped open. His mouth worked.

She leaned over him, her hands reaching.

He snarled and spat words at her, alien words that resembled JoLene's hissing.

Hang on to what matters.

Mary gritted her teeth and clenched her fists into Peter's shirt. He was hers. She would fight to her last breath to bring him out of the fae world, back into hers.

He writhed and struggled to break free. His hands batted at hers. But he was weak, his hands nothing more than limp clubs at the ends of his arms. She pulled him close and wrapped her arms tightly around his torso. Wind whipped through her hair. She clutched her husband. Gran's old gods hadn't heard, not here on this alien world so far from Earth. But they were all Mary had.

"Our Father, who art in Heaven," she whispered the ancient words, dredged from her memories of cathedrals crafted of stone and faith, mortared with blood and tears. Of her Gran sitting stiff and formal in her blue dress, her face raised devoutly to the iron cross at the front. Iron and faith, that was what it took to defeat the fae. Peter lay heavy in her lap, his arms feebly waving, his mouth working as he tried to speak. Mary dripped tears on his face. She had no iron, but she had faith. Faith in her Gran, at least, and her Gran's hard-won belief in a God that could save her from the ungodly people of the hills.

"Save him, please," she prayed as she watched her husband's eyes roll back in his head.

Howls rose from the berry bushes around her. JoLene staggered into the clearing, a gaping hole where the bone had been torn loose. Others of her kind rose from the bushes to skitter forward on their insectile legs. White faces with huge cat's eyes stared. Tangles of flaming red hair burned under the moon's touch. JoLene opened her mouth wide. A fountain of black blood spattered across the ground.

Mary squeezed Peter closer to her breast. She had nothing left to fight with, except her stubborn. She smiled at Gran's old complaint. She had stubborn. And she had Gran's spirit.

"You cannot have him." A simple, flat statement.

The creatures circled. Their hissing voices mixed with the scrabble of their claws in the grass.

Whatever beauty they had held for her was long gone. Mary closed her eyes, serene in her love for her grandmother. And through that love, she loved Peter, she had faith. Morning would come and the spell of the Fae would fade under the sun's touch.

She would bring him home, safe at last.

Her voice rose in song, a wavering uncertain tune she'd heard many times as a child. Gran's song, a hymn from the battered songbook, a melody of love and acceptance and faith. And triumph over evil. Mary closed her eyes, rocked her husband, as she sang.

The grass rustled. Mary's song faltered. She opened eyes aching from lack of sleep. JoLene charged forward, ichor oozing from her wound.

Mary loosed one arm, reached into the grass, sure in the knowledge that a weapon would be there. Her fingers closed on grass. She plucked it and tossed it at the damaged alien creature. JoLene flinched and swerved to the side. The creature stumbled, unsteady, then righted itself and charged forward again.

Mary's hand closed over a round stone. Indentations in the front gave her fingers purchase to pull it free. A human skull stared from empty sockets. The lower jaw was gone. The back was smashed in. Mary's song faltered, wavered, before strengthening again. Was this JoLene's lover, destroyed by the Fae?

Or was it JoLene, missing all these years in the hills?

No matter, it was a weapon. It was all she had.

"By oak and ash, thorn and hollow, begone!" Gran's old words rose unbidden.

Mary flung the skull with everything she had. Peter flopped limply out of her lap onto the grass. He lay still. She hunched over him, shielding him, protecting him from the fae circling them.

The skull traced a graceful arc through the moonlight, white bone gleaming. It smashed into the side of JoLene's head. JoLene squealed. The hissing from the others intensified, like air escaping a balloon. JoLene's whole hideous body crumpled inwards. The other fae leapt onto her body, claws tearing and shredding, inhuman faces wide with hunger. JoLene tottered backward, screaming in pain and fury.

Mary gathered Peter into her arms again, buried her face against his. Gran's song tumbled from her, rasping phrases of song, words and notes jumbled together.

The screaming intensified. The creatures fought and bit each other. They tore flesh apart with teeth and claws. Black blood spurted across the ground.

Leave, child. Take your love and flee!

"He's too heavy, Gran. I can't." Mary pulled Peter closer, tried to lift him. His head flopped to the side. She cupped her hand across his cheek. Breath barely fluttered from his mouth. "No, Peter. Come back to me. Help me, Gran!"

She tried to crawl backward, away from the snapping, snarling mess of the fae creatures. She heaved her husband a scant foot across the torn grass.

One of the creatures shifted at the motion. It stalked toward her, claws clacking.

"He's mine," Mary sobbed. She scrabbled through the grass with one hand. Her other held tight to Peter's shirt. "Mine! You hear me?" Her fist closed over more bones. She raked them free of the ground to fling them at the thing.

The bones smashed into its inhumanly serene face, tore holes in its flawless skin. It shrieked, high and thin like a baby's wail. The others pounced, tore it to shreds.

"Save me," Mary whispered. To Gran's ghost, to Gran's god, to anything that might listen. She pulled Peter up against her bosom, cradled him like the children they would never have, sang him Gran's lullaby. Tears dripped down her face as she watched the horror of the fae parading with strips of flesh torn from each other.

She tried to scoot backward again, determined to leave the fae's glade. The brambles caught her hair, her jacket, held her in the tiny clearing. Berries dangled in her face, tempting her with their sweet juices. The fae skittered back and forth. Their claws sometimes touched her foot, her leg, reached for Peter. She kicked them away, screaming until her voice cracked.

Hold on with everything you have, child. Hold on til morning light. You'll be safe then.

She fought through the endless night clutching her husband to her like a talisman. Gran's words sang in her head. Moonlight and shadow danced in the berry brambles, lighting then concealing the macabre dance of the creatures. JoLene was nothing more than a torn mass of flesh and white bone. The human skull leered from her tattered flesh.

Slowly, imperceptibly, the world turned. The moon set at last. Dawn light filtered through massing clouds. Mary shifted, weary in body and soul. Her voice was a hoarse croak. Her skin was scratched and bleeding. But Peter lay in her arms. His skin was white beneath the smeared dirt. His breath barely stirred her hair as she rocked him. But she'd pulled him from the fae, kept him through the long night.

And somewhere, she'd found her love for him still intact.

"Peter?" She whispered his name as the sky faded from pearl gray to lavender. "Peter, wake up. It's over."

But it wasn't over. One of the fae leapt from the bushes. It's claws raked over her face, tangled in her hair. She tried to scream, but had no voice left. She raised both hands to bat it away.

No! Hold fast to your love!

She dropped her hands, clutched Peter again. Blood dripped from a scrape on her scalp. Red spattered his white skin.

The fae, a small one, screeched and tore at her tangled hair.

"You won't win," she croaked.

It screamed in rage, then ripped a clawful of hair free.

She gasped in pain. But she only pulled Peter closer. He was hers. JoLene would never take her man. Not as long as Mary had breath.

A high thin crack split the dawn. The thing jerked, then flopped against her shoulder. It bounced off to land behind her with a wet squelch.

Footsteps crunched and tore through the grass. Human footsteps.

"Heaven be praised, we're safe now," Mary whispered into Peter's hair. "We're safe."

A handful of the settlers, stern men with rifles, rushed into the clearing. They bombarded her with questions. She let their words wash over her. They were human, normal. They belonged to the day, not the enchanted and dangerous night.

They picked up Peter, carried him away out of the glade. Gentle hands helped Mary out after him. Sunlight washed over her as she emerged from the berry patch. Not the yellow glow of Earth's Sol, but a more orange light. No matter. Light was light and the fae couldn't abide full sunlight.

"Did you say something?" Olaf, the man guiding her feet, asked.

"It's a beautiful morning," Mary answered.

The man said something else, but his words washed over and around her. She stumbled, fell against his solid bulk. He lifted her, carried her over the uneven ground.

She let her eyes slide closed.

Safe now. Rest, child.

The walls of the medical clinic, the closest they had to a hospital, were bare white. Mary fingered the tiny cross she'd fashioned from a scrap of wire. It hung around her neck on a loop of thread. It was Gran's faith, but Gran had pulled her through the night, saved her from the fae.

Peter lay in the bed, white sheets pulled up to his chin. His chest rose and fell, but his eyes hadn't opened. Three days with no sign of waking. The doctor wasn't hopeful, but he gave Mary space, didn't force his words on her. She clung to Gran's faith, clung to her hope that Peter would wake. That all would be well.

"Mary?" Tabitha stumped into the room, her cane knocking on the cement floor with each slow step. "The others asked me to speak with you."

Mary shifted, let Tabitha have the one flimsy chair. "I know what they say. That he won't wake up again. That I should let him go."

Tabitha sighed as she sank onto the chair. "We don't have the equipment to tell for certain."

"He'll wake up. He has to."

"He's breathing on his own. That's a good sign." Tabitha rested both hands on the crook of her cane. She studied her gnarled knuckles as if they held answers. "They think you both went crazy from eating native berries. The gold ones can cause hallucinations."

It would be simple to accept that explanation. Blame it on eating too many berries. Mary slid her hand into Peter's limp one.

"It was JoLene. She'd turned into something strange."

"I saw the things they brought back. They're studying the bodies. They weren't my sister." Tabitha cleared her throat. "They found bones. They think it was Josef, who went missing fifteen years back. They left yesterday to go looking for more of the missing ones."

Mary squeezed Peter's hand. "They won't find her."

Tabitha shook her head. "She's still out there, looking for men to steal."

"The others killed her, tore her to pieces. She's gone, Tabitha." She had to believe the nightmare was over.

"Are you certain?"

Mary touched her makeshift cross with one hand, twined her other hand through her husband's fingers. "She's gone."

Tabitha sagged in the chair. "Gone?"

Mary closed her eyes on the vision of auburn hair and ivory skin, the beauty that had lured Peter out into the alien hills. Beauty that had turned to screaming bloodied flesh, torn and mangled until nothing remained.

"Yes."

She had to believe.

For Peter's sake.

His fingers twitched in her hold. She grasped his hand more firmly.

Hold on to your love.

Hold on and never let go.

"I will, Gran. Always."

Pass the Butter

"What's that?" Krys pointed at the sky.

Jacob's attention was fixed on her neckline. He nibbled her earlobe, his arms loosely around her. He leaned against his truck, pulling her into his warmth.

"Jake, stop it. It's weird." Krys pushed his head away.

"Your neck's fine, babe."

She gave a short annoyed grunt and elbowed him. "Up there."

Jacob glanced up from her enticing neck. He dismissed the strange display with a sneer. "Fireflies. Come on, babe. Relax and enjoy. I gotta leave for work tomorrow."

"How long this time?" Krys kept her attention fixed on the sparkles falling through the atmosphere.

"Couple of weeks. We're going up in the hills to the drill site." He kissed her skin, breathing in the scent of peaches from her shampoo.

"I don't think those are fireflies. They look more like fireworks."

He brushed her hair to one side and pulled her back against him again. "Show me how much you're going to miss me."

"Fireworks wouldn't spread like that, would they?"

Jacob sighed. Krys wasn't going to relax until he put her mind at ease. He turned his attention upward. He drew in a breath at the sight. Streaks of blue and purple drifted through the thin clouds and pale moonlight. Bursts of green and yellow punctuated the trails. "You're right. Those aren't fire-works. I think those are aurora, the northern lights."

Krys frowned, wrinkling her perfectly plucked and curved eyebrows. "But we're in Nevada. We wouldn't see them here, would we?"

"We've had pretty weird weather, so could be." He took her shoulders and turned her to face him. "They're just pretty lights. I'm leaving for two weeks. Give me something to remember while I'm out there all by myself in that lonely tent."

Krys' mouth fell open. She stared up behind the truck.

"Listen, babe, whatever it is, it will wait. I can't."

Krys snapped her mouth shut. "Shut up, Jacob. This isn't about you. Look!" She jabbed her finger over his shoulder.

He turned.

It was Jacob's turn for his mouth to fall open.

Behind them on the loose stone slope of the hill rested an oblong space-craft made of shiny metal. The side curved up into the sky where the last fading trail of colored light lingered. Steam hissed off the skin, a vast cloud rising to tower over them and start a mini-rainstorm.

Krys shrieked as the fat drops spattered down. She put both hands over her head in a futile effort to ward off the water. She broke free of Jacob to scramble into the truck. He followed her a split second later.

"Slide over, babe. We're getting out of here." He pushed her shoulder.

"Aliens," Krys whispered as she slid across the bench seat of the truck. "Do you know what this means? We're going to be famous!" She put her hand over his where it rested on the keys in the ignition.

Jacob's mouth worked as he struggled between fear and greed. He finally dropped his hand from the keys. "It won't run anyway, if the movies and stories got it right. Isn't that what's supposed to happen in close encounters with aliens? All the stuff quits working and the radio goes nuts." He reached for the radio buttons.

"There's a door up there." Krys squinted through the water streaks on the windshield. The rain had stopped almost as soon as it started. "It's opening."

A thin crack of light showed partway up the side of the spacecraft. It slowly widened as they watched.

"If the movies are right, they either want to eat us or make us slaves and then eat us." Jacob shivered as he fiddled with the radio. Nothing played on the speakers.

Krys gave him a withering look. "Sometimes they come in peace because they want to spread harmony and goodwill."

"And sing us songs and do drugs with us." Jacob frowned and tapped a rhythm on the steering wheel. "I watch movies, too, but those ones end with them drugging us and *then* eating us. Aliens always want to eat humans."

"But this isn't the movies. I swear I don't know why I stick with you. You're such a barbarian."

Jacob gave her a sly grin. "That's why you love me, babe. Admit it."

She gasped, short and sharp and delighted.

"Told you I do it for you," Jacob said.

She swatted his arm. "Not you, idiot. That!"

The door was fully open, revealing a spill of golden light. A rainbow made of sparkling dust extended to form a ramp. The grass sizzled as the rainbow light sparked and faded leaving a span of dark metal from the door to the ground.

Krys reached for the door handle.

"Babe, no." Jacob stretched across the cab of the truck to stop her. "Aliens *always* want to eat humans. I'm telling you, it's the truth. You go out there, you're lunch. Or dinner. Or whatever."

Krys pushed his hand aside. "They come in peace. I can *feel* it, okay?" She shoved the door open and jumped out. Her hips swayed in her tight jeans as she sauntered up to the foot of the ramp.

Jacob watched her butt and tapped his fingers on the steering wheel. He couldn't let her get eaten. Besides, if they really did come in peace, he wanted in on the fame and money that first contact was sure to generate. He popped his door open and jumped out after her.

Krys was halfway up the ramp when the first alien scuttled through the door. She stopped and held her hands wide. "Hey. We come in peace."

The alien scuttled toward her. Jacob squinted against the glare of the open door. The thing was short, barely knee-high to his girlfriend. It held two thick claws over its head. A broad segmented tail flapped up and down behind it.

Krys squatted down.

The thing stopped. The claws clicked rapidly. Two pairs of antennae swiveled and waved toward Krys. Color swept across the carapace over its body. Waves of blue and purple chased spatters of yellow. Krys reached slowly with one hand, touched the head between the antennae. They stopped waving, froze in place for a long moment. The carapace flushed pure white. Krys spread her hand flat on the thing's head. Sparkles of rainbow light drifted over its skin from her touch. She stroked it, releasing what looked like a cloud of glitter inside the alien.

"Jake, you have to come up here. It feels so soft!" She squealed with delight as it twitched and shivered.

The alien's claws snapped shut on her hand. Her squeal changed to one of pain.

Jacob reacted without thinking. He charged up the ramp and kicked the thing. His heavy work boots crunched into its shell, cracking the rainbow sparkles into jagged streaks of dark blue ichor. The alien hissed like a leaky balloon as it tumbled off into the sagebrush.

"Idiot! What'd you have to do that for? It didn't hurt me. Much." Krys shoved him. He stumbled back a step. She stopped dead at the dark smear she left on his jacket. She lifted her hands up in front of her face. The golden light spilling out of the ship showed the missing fingers on her right hand. Blood poured from the stumps of her middle and ring finger. Her mouth opened to scream.

Jacob wrapped one arm around her, the other one clamped over her mouth. He dragged her backward down the ramp to his truck. He propped Krys against the side while he popped open the glove box to rummage for his first aid kit.

Her scream came out as a thin whimper.

"Get some pressure on that, babe," he instructed.

"My fingers are gone." She stared at the bloody mess. "That thing just snipped them off."

"Told you it wanted to eat you." Jacob pulled out bandages. He took her hand and pressed gauze against her palm. "Hold that over them. We gotta get you to the hospital."

"It ate my fingers?" Panic edged her voice.

"I'll still love you, babe."

Far down the hill, way down the lazy twists of the dirt road, blue and red lights flashed as police cars made their way toward the alien ship.

"Police are coming. We can get you help from them."

"What about that one you kicked?" She clenched her jaw as she wrapped gauze over the bleeding stumps. "What if there are more of those things?"

"I thought you were all for peace with those things." He ripped off a length of tape and handed it to her.

"They ate my fingers. Ate. My. Fingers."

"So, what do you want to do about it? We've got about ten minutes before the cops get here. They must have seen it land." Jacob helped her tape the gauze in place.

Krys winced, then gingerly tucked her hand against her chest. "I've got a permanent hang ten from them. I'll show them hang ten. You still got your rifle in the truck?"

"You aren't in any shape to shoot."

"Then you can shoot them for me." She glared until he turned to fetch the rifle from the lockbox behind the front bench. "They looked like lobsters to me. Let's see if they taste like them. Starting with that one in the bushes." She pointed with her good hand.

The one Jacob had kicked was trying to crawl back to the ramp. It left an oozing trail as it dragged itself forward one slow foot at a time.

Krys marched over to it, boots crunching on the gravel of the desert wash. She stomped on the alien. It's shell cracked completely. It twitched once, then lay still. "I'll teach you to eat my fingers."

Something clicked over her head. Once, twice, then a rapid rattle of sound.

She looked up. A giant version of the bug she'd just crushed stood in the doorway flanked by at least a dozen more smaller lobsters. They held claws up in the air, snapping them rapidly. The giant one clicked again. The horde poured down the ramp toward her.

She screamed and hightailed it for the truck.

Jacob cranked off one shot from the rifle. The aliens didn't even slow as one tumbled from the ramp. Jacob jumped into the truck and slammed his own door just as the lobster-aliens plowed into the vehicle. Their bodies thumped against the sides and bounced off the hood. One plastered itself on the windshield, legs spread wide while its claws pried the wipers off.

Krys slammed the lock button. "Get us out of here!"

Jacob cranked the starter. It clicked, like one of the aliens. The engine stayed dead. "Like I said, babe, when the aliens come, the cars quit running."

More lights streaked through the sky overhead. Purple and blue washed through with yellow and green. Globe ships floated across the sky like giant dandelions.

Claws scrabbled over the outside of the car. Dozens of insectile legs tapped and pried at any crack. Then, in an instant, all of them froze, claws pointed upwards.

"What are they doing?" Krys whispered.

Jacob shook his head.

As one, the aliens turned and scuttled back up the ramp into the ship, tails flapping.

"Time to go," Jacob said. He turned the key. Not even the starter clicked this time. He slammed his hands on the steering wheel and swore. "Think we can make a run for it?"

Krys didn't respond. She stared out her window at the spaceship. The glow in the doorway flickered, then brightened to a steady golden glow. She rolled the window down, eyes fixed on the creature emerging from the door.

It's bulk filled the opening, squeezed barely through. Once outside, it lifted massive claws to the sky. It's feet stabbed down, ponderous under its enormous body. Dozens of smaller aliens scuttled around it. The whole entourage reached the bottom of the ramp and paused. The massive alien stretched one foot daintily toward the sagebrush smashed at the bottom of the ramp. The pointed tip of its leg probed the dry brush, then the sand around it. The massive claws snapped. The percussive sound rattled the loose panels on the truck. The alien lobster stepped onto the soil of Earth. It slapped its tail against the ground with a muffled thump. A cloud of grit swirled around it.

Krys reached for the door handle.

"What are you doing? Are you trying to get yourself eaten?"

Krys waved her bandaged hand. "They already did."

The cavalry arrived just as she wrapped her good hand around the handle again. Lights strobing, police cars pulled up around them, tires scrunching on the loose gravel of the wash. The three sheriff's cars were followed by two state police, five army vehicles, and a lone highway patrol motocycle. Men in uniforms scrambled from the vehicles, hands on guns as they surrounded Jacob's truck and the alien lobsters clustered at the bottom of the ramp.

"Stay in the vehicle, ma'am," one of them said, motioning to Krys.

She snorted and opened the door. "Don't you dare ma'am me. I've got a right to know what's going on here. Did you see what they did to me?" She waved her bloody hand in his face.

"We'll have an ambulance here soon. Get back in your vehicle." The sheriff's deputy made shooing motions with his hand.

Krys crossed her arms and put on her stubborn face. "No."

"Jenkins!" The sheriff snapped. "Get those civilians out of here."

"They've already seen too much," an army man ordered. "We'll have to debrief them at the base. Take them in custody, sargeant."

The giant lobster snapped his claws together. All of the men jerked back to face the horde. The sergeant turned to face the bugs along with the others. The giant one waved his claws, snapping and clicking them together while colors flickered and spun over his carapace in wild patterns almost too fast to follow. The uniformed men fixed their attention on the aliens.

Krys took advantage of the distraction to edge toward the small alien they'd kicked over the side earlier. It lay in the bushes on its back, claws limp in the sagebrush. Thick blue liquid oozed from cracks in its gray shell to trickle off under the bush.

The police and the army guys were waving guns and shouting at the aliens, when they weren't huddled together whispering urgently to each other.

Jacob darted a last look at the nearest huddle then sidled next to Krys. "What are you doing?"

"Getting revenge." Krys squatted next to the dead alien. "They ate my fingers so I'm going to eat theirs. At least a claw off this one." She wrenched a front claw free. It was as big as her hand. The dull outside shell cracked and flaked away from a meaty white inside.

"What are you doing there?" The sergeant had remembered his duty and turned back to them. "You're going to have to wait in the truck." He tried to herd them back.

Krys straightened and gave him her best glare. "If we've already seen too much, why should we wait in the truck? We won't see anything we haven't already seen."

The sergeant flapped his mouth. Jacob felt a pang of sympathy. He'd been on the receiving end of Krys's glares before. It was confusing and intimidating and just the tiniest bit sexy. He nudged his girlfriend before she started waving her alien lobster claw in the sergeant's face.

"We'll just wait by my truck, sir. If that's okay?" Jacob's nudges grew stronger when he felt Krys sucking in a breath. Thankfully, she subsided.

The sergeant frowned for a long moment. "Just stay out of the way," he barked as he turned to rejoin the group at the base of the ramp.

The monster lobster was now glowing a steady yellow. It had both claws out to the sides. They tapped a low rhythm, counterpoint to the clicking of the smaller lobsters scuttling between its legs.

Jacob took Krys's arm, held her next to his truck. She shook off his hold with a scowl. "Do you want to get arrested? And have them confiscate that?" He pointed at the claw.

"They're going to confiscate it anyway." She tucked it between the wrist of her injured hand and her ample chest. She used the fingers of her good hand to dig inside the flaking shell. She pulled out a lump of white meat and sniffed it. "Smells sort of like ocean. You know, kind of salty and like dead fish just a little?"

"You're eating that raw?" Jacob's stomach roiled at the thought.

"Why not? It's just like eating sushi."

"Which you love and I can't stand. Raw fish." He pulled a face.

Krys licked the gobbet of alien flesh. Her eyes widened. "It's pretty good. Better than Bubba Jim's sushi rolls. Kind of buttery and sweet." She nibbled the corner. "You remember that time you took me all the way into Carson City to that steak joint and I got the lobster? This is even better." She bit off a bigger hunk and chewed, eyes closed in ecstasy. "This is almost better than sex. Nope, make that way better."

"Way to make a guy feel manly. You prefer eating raw alien to this?" He flexed his muscles.

She didn't answer. She was digging out another nugget of meat from the claw.

"Hey, babe?"

Krys glanced at him, then back to the claw. Her eyes were out of focus, dilated too far.

"Krys? You okay?"

"Sure. I'm fine." She stuffed another hunk of alien meat into her mouth.

One of the military guys shouted. A new chorus of clicking rose from the lobsters. Jacob glanced toward the spaceship. The huge lobster was stalking forward, one deliberate step at a time. The uniform guys brought their weapons up. Someone was trigger happy. A little lobster exploded into blue slime then tumbled from the ramp.

"Hold your fire!" the army general screamed, his face turning purple. "Maybe they're being peaceful."

"And that's why they ate your fingers," Jacob said in an aside to Krys.

She didn't answer.

He looked back at her.

She stared at the aliens, the half-eaten claw dangling from the last two fingers on her bandaged hand.

"Krys?"

His girlfriend took a step forward, then another and another.

The army guys shouted at her to stop, but she kept going. The giant lobster paced down the ramp, stepped foot on Earth just as Krys reached the bottom of the ramp. The long antennae on its head swept over Krys, snagging briefly on her sweater.

Jacob hurried forward, standing with the army guys. Whatever was about to happen with Krys and the aliens was out of his control. The army guys and police were just as powerless and they knew it.

"Your girlfriend's crazy, you know that?" the policeman nearest Jacob said.

"Yeah, but maybe the right kind of crazy," the general answered.

Colors flashed over the lobster, white and pink and bright orange followed by deep emerald green. The lobster stayed that color for a long moment.

Krys held out the half-eaten claw in her damaged hand. "Why?"

Colors flashed again. Claws clicked in a complicated rhythm. The smaller lobsters swarmed up the huge one's legs to perch on its back. Their antennae waved in ripples timed to the colors.

"Really? That's why?" Krys shook her head as she turned back to the humans. "Seems they come in peace and all that. You can put your guns away."

The huge lobster raised one massive claw. The pincers began to open.

Krys continued speaking. "He says they have come for the eating. Or something like that. Feast? Devourer? I'm not quite sure and my eyes can't see the right colors."

"How do you speak their language?" the general asked.

"He ate part of me, I ate part of him. It's a mutual thing and it's kind of weird. He can't explain it. They talk in colors. It's really complicated and only part of my brain understands." Krys pursed up her mouth like she did when she was thinking hard. "He says he wants to taste our leader."

"Taste our leader? You sure you got that right?" The general crossed his arms, thrust out his chin and his chest.

"Are you questioning my girlfriend?" Jacob reached to smack the general on the shoulder, then thought better of it. The man was three inches shorter, but he was all muscle and testosterone. "At least she's doing something useful."

The giant claw lowered toward Krys.

She turned back to the lobsters.

The huge claw whipped up into the air and clicked twice. Almost as if the giant lobster were acting innocent.

She planted her hands on her hips. "I saw that. You better behave. Because if you don't—"

Jacob could imagine the glare she was giving that giant bug. He was glad he wasn't on the receiving end. He sensed the power in their relationship shifting, but he couldn't think of what to do to stop it.

The alien flashed a whole series of colors too fast for his eyes to catch. Krys snapped her fingers in a rapid rhythm. The lobster opened both claws very wide, then snapped them together. All the little ones mimicked the movement.

"You think so, do you?" Krys drew herself up with a huff of exasperation. "You've got another think coming. I don't care if I insulted your gender. I am *not* calling you Glorious Mother."

The giant claws lowered toward her, wide open and full of menace.

"Krys!" Jacob couldn't help the shout. He rushed forward.

Krys didn't need saving. She kicked the lobster in the mouthparts, then marched back to the general and the police. Jacob hovered at her shoulder, unsure what to do or how that alien lobster meat had changed his sweetheart into this commanding presence. Her eyes seemed to flash colors, like rainbow glitter. She stopped when she was nose-to-nose with the general.

"That thing," she jabbed a finger at the lobster, which was pacing forward in a menacing manner, "just insulted me, my mother, our president, our whole country, our entire species, and our entire world! It wants to lay its eggs in us."

"What am I supposed to do about that?" The general returned her glare.

She whirled to stare at the lobster again. It snapped claws, twice, an obvious threat. "Just to be clear," she said as she stripped off her jacket. She shoved it into Jacob's hands then flapped her blue blouse.

The lobster flushed dark purple with rapidly spinning green lines.

"That's what I thought." She turned back to the men. "She's being very clear. They are here to use us as food for their eggs. What they don't realize is that they taste—" She snatched Jacob's rifle from the policeman who had been holding it then took aim at the lobster. "Just." She pulled the trigger. Blue ooze spurted from the lobster's head. "Like." She shot it again. One antenna spiraled away into the shadows. "Chicken. Or lobster, if you prefer."

The giant staggered forward one step, two, then slowly crashed to the ground. The smaller ones jumped from its back, claws waving and clicking like mad.

Krys emptied her magazine, shot after shot. The rest of them joined in. Guns blazed. The night rang with the sound of violence. Blue alien goo splattered the hillside. Body parts littered the brush.

The spaceship ramp slide soundlessly into the side. The door closed, shutting off the golden light. With a sizzling display of color, the ship rose into the night.

"What have we done?" the general asked, staring at the carnage.

Krys handed the rifle back to the policeman. "Saved the earth. They wanted to eat us."

"How sure are you, young lady?"

"Don't you dare young lady me." Krys stomped forward. She waved her mangled hand. "They started it."

The general turned to his staff who gathered in a huddle. The soldiers stood around, looking sheepish. The police just looked baffled.

Jacob hurried to catch up with her.

"How much butter do you have, Jake?" she asked. "Because I've got a hankering for a nice smoked lobster dinner." She hefted a claw from the ground.

"Put that down! It's evidence and government property." The general's aide glared.

"Make me." Krys grinned, showing her teeth. Her eyes flashed with colored light.

"Babe, I'm not so sure that lobster's good for you."

Krys slung the claw over her shoulder. "But it sure is tasty." She marched up to his truck, then slung the claw in the back. It clattered and thumped on the bed. "You coming, Jake?"

He scrambled to catch up with her.

She turned to the uniforms. "When they come back, and they will, you know where to find me. And general, tell the dairy farmers to start churning. We're going to have a worldwide lobster feast."

The truck door slammed behind her.

The men stared in stunned silence.

Jacob shrugged. "She gets these moods sometimes—"

"Jake! Get in the truck."

He scrambled into the truck.

"Don't call me babe anymore. I want to be called The Royal Queen Mother from now on." She frowned at the alien bodies being examined by the military. "I want a tail to eat."

"Babe—" He wilted under her glare. "I mean Royal Queen Mother, that one must weigh at least a hundred pounds. I'll get you a smaller one later. You still have a claw."

She snapped her fingers. Her skin flushed pink and red with white spots. "A claw may not be enough."

"To do what?" He opened his door.

"Where are you going?"

"There's something wrong with the engine. Gotta check it." He popped the hood then scrambled from the truck.

He ducked under the hood where Krys couldn't see him, then tried to signal the nearest uniform. The man didn't notice his clandestine hand waving. Jacob waved a little harder. The man kept his eyes down, looking for gobbets of dead alien in the scrub.

"Whatcha doing, babe?" Krys' voice sounded in his ear.

He jumped and banged his head on the hood. He stepped back, rubbing his head. "Oh, come on, Krys. I watched those alien movies. You're going to either have a baby alien burst out of your chest some night when I least expect or you're going to split your skin and morph into one of them." He pointed at the remains of the lobster.

Krys rolled her eyes. "I ate part of one and it ate part of me. That's not the same as mating."

"Now you're acting all bossy and weird. What am I supposed to think? That alien meat did something to you."

"Yeah, it made me see clearly. You're a wimp, Jake."

"Okay, that's it." He stomped around the truck to the back. He reached in and grasped the alien claw.

"What are you doing?" Krys followed him. Her voice rose into a screech. "I need that claw!"

"No, you don't. You have a drug problem, Krys. This meat is making you high."

She froze in mid-screech. She stared at him with wide eyes.

He tossed the claw onto the pile the army guys were building. It landed with a loud snap and a crunch.

Krys crumpled forward, tears running down her face.

"Aw, babe, don't cry." Jacob gathered her into his arms.

"I'm sorry, Jacob. What I said was mean and horrid." Her apology was punctuated with sniffles.

"Blame it on bad lobster, babe. Let's go home."

He helped her back into the truck, slammed the hood shut on his way past, then cranked the ignitioin.

The engine started right up. He waved at the army guys as he rolled past.

The general signaled him to stop and roll down his window.

"What?" Jacob asked as he rolled to a crunching stop.

"I don't need to tell you not to speak of this incident, do I?"

"Oh, give me a break. It's probably all over the news. And nobody will believe me anyway."

The general worked his lips under his mustache for a moment. "Then can we call on you and your girlfriend if we have need of your services again?"

Jacob glanced over at Krys, who was now curled up in his hoodie, her head against the window, her soft snores filling the silence.

"Sure, whatever. But I'm not sure lobster agrees with her."

"I'm not sure that lobster agrees with anyone."

The general saluted as Jacob pulled back onto the dirt road and headed for home.

OH, MY DARLING

I slammed my pick into the wall of the cavern, the one hidden in a crack on a forsaken mountainside deep in the craggy Blues. Old Codger Martin told me about the gold there, man to man over whiskey in the back of an old saloon south of Frisco. I hopped a mule and rode on up to check it out and stake a claim. So far, all I'd found was quartz. I hit the wall again. Rocks tumbled to the ground. I leaned over the pile. A gleam of yellowish metal caught my eye. Maybe Codger wasn't a two-headed lying snake. I crouched, my fingers reaching.

The cavern shook. Cave-in? It shook again. Dust shifted down onto my head. The shaking came once more, like a giant stomping his way up from the depths to confront me. Rocks creaked. I thought about running for the exit, but that promising rock had my attention. I palmed it to hide the metallic luster as the steps approached.

"What you doing, hu-man?"

A thunderous voice snapped over me, shaking more dust loose. It was deeper than the pits of hell itself. Might have come from there, too. Who knew where the other end of this cavern led? I rose to my feet and faced the denizen of the depths.

The creature was huge, covered in green scaly skin with giant tusks poking from his fat lips and enormous claws on his hands. He sported a twisted crown of dead rats.

Just a cave troll, nothing too spectacular, not like the dragon that ate Jim Balforth and his entire effete exploration expedition. Their fault for tramping into the dragon's front room and smoking those vile cheroots.

"This my cave." The troll thumped a massive fist onto the floor. "Posted mine." He flung his other hand out, pointing deeper into the cave. "You trespassing."

"Now that's where you're wrong, my good troll." I extended my hand. "Name's Barnabus Whittle. I've filed a legal claim to this section of mountain, but I don't see why we can't work this together." Everything I knew about trolls ran quickly through my head. It didn't take long. Trolls were a secretive bunch, according to Brim and Bartel, the accepted authorities on cave dwellers. Their entry on trolls included a warning to avoid them and not much else.

The troll shook his head. A dead rat bounced over one eye. "I file claim. My caves. Posted no trespassing, down there." He pointed into the darkness of the cave.

"I posted up there," I said, pointing to the entrance I'd blasted just last week. "There must be a way we can work this out. Let's think about this for a moment, shall we?"

The troll furrowed his brow. I took the chance and risked a peek at my rock sample. Gold! Not fool's gold, either, though some might call me a fool for stealing a troll's claim.

"That mine," the troll said, reaching for my stone.

I took one look at the claws and let him have the rock.

He used one claw to delicately scrape the metal out as if it were putty. He smiled, showing his impressive tusks, as he flicked gold to the ground. "Now it valuable." He showed me the mass of quartz crystals.

"That?" I wrinkled my brow. "Yes, I see. Most valuable. Well, this is a dilemma. Tell you what, I'll give you half of all those that I find, plus I'll clean up all this garbage for you." I nudged the nuggets of gold littering the ground.

The troll narrowed his eyes. "What I do? Why I not keep all?"

"I need you to smash the rocks open. I'll extract the crystals. Sure as my name's Barnabus Whittle, I've got a patent pending on the best crystal extractor you've ever seen. We'll be partners. Partners help each other. And share. We can be partners, can't we? Both of us get rich."

The troll thought for a long moment, then nodded. "But one condition."

I smiled my best smile. I was about to become rich and all it cost me was the worthless quartz marring my gold. "Name it."

"Got daughter. Clementine. You marry." Troll showed me his tusks again. "Or I smash you face."

I swallowed. Marry a troll? I eyed the gold on the ground. How bad could it be? I shook the troll's paw. "You got yourself a deal, partner."

Clementine was as sweet as a daisy, although her face could curdle milk. She was a troll, green skin, giant feet, tusks, and all, but since she didn't wear rats on her head and preferred a good calico for her dresses, we got along just fine. She took to the miner's wife role like a natural. She lived in my ramshackle little cabin where she baked cornbread and brewed moonshine to her heart's content. After the first taste of her cooking, I didn't mind that she outweighed any prize bull and could probably wrestle it into the dust. Her food was divine.

She planted a garden, tended it lovingly. Most of it was weeds, but I wasn't about to tell my darling bride that. She was happy and she made me happy. I was the luckiest man alive. Of course, the steady stream of fist-sized gold nugget "trash" her father kept handing me only made her green warts more attractive.

I bought Clementine a dozen ducklings for her birthday. She squealed with excitement. The little birds cowered in terror. She cradled them gently in her massive hands, her claws delicately stroking their downy feathers. By the end of summer, they were a sight to see. Clementine trundled at the front, giant feet in their box shoes stomping down the path to the mill pond below my cabin. The ducks waddled behind, quacking and bossing everything else out of their way. Every morning, Clementine took them to the pond for a swim. I followed, carrying my sack of gold nuggets to hand off to the assayer who set up shop with the miller. Neither of them ever said much about my green-skinned beauty, not after she punched a moose that threatened her ducklings. We all enjoyed the meat from that bounty.

I was late, that August morning. I arrived at the mill just in time to see Clementine trip over a log. She tumbled into the mill pond with a tremendous splash. Ducks and water went flying. I ran to the shore, expecting to see my bride rise from the depths. Her face did rise briefly, lips pursed as she sucked in air.

Trolls are made of stone, it's embedded in their flesh. Clementine didn't stand a chance. I threw myself into the pond but I was no swimmer. I splashed mightily, thrashing about as I reached for her. I shouted for help, but no one heard over the creaking of the mill wheel.

I watched her sink beneath the water. Her ruby lips blew a last stream of bubbles.

The ducks circled me, quacking as I struggled for the shore. I'd lost my Clementine. My heart would never mend.

Her father waited for me at the cavern when I returned. With heavy heart I told my green friend what had happened to his daughter. I even cried.

He grunted when I finished my tale of woe.

"She good daughter. She happy with you." He smacked me on the back hard enough that I bounced off the wall. "She got sister, though." He lifted one eyebrow suggestively.

Clementine had been a marvelous wife. How could her sister possibly compare? "Does she cook? Human food, I mean."

He grimaced. "All time. Nasty. Breads, cakes, pies, all that garbage."

My mouth watered. "My friend, nothing can ever replace your daughter Clementine in my heart, but I think I might have room for her sister in there, too." I shook his gnarled paw, accepting the bargain. The giant gold nugget he handed me didn't hurt, either. I'd marry all of his daughters, and their cousins, and their friends, if he kept gifting me his garbage gold.

I'd loved Clementine. She was better than I deserved. I'd think of my troll bride fondly every time I hauled a sack of gold to the mill or lifted a glass of moonshine to her memory.

"Oh, my darling Clementine, thou are lost and gone forever. Dreadful sorry, Clementine. But your sister, Rosemary, makes apple pie that men would gladly die for."

IT'S ALWAYS SUNNY
AT THE
FORTRESS OF BONES

"Bother," Saragliandey said as she stabbed her trowel into the dirt. The entry alarm for the west tunnel had just sounded. Another adventurer trying to make a name for himself. And just when Sara had finally gotten around to weeding the pea patch.

She dropped her trowel in the basket by the back door and wiped her feet before entering her private quarters. The small rooms were homey, with lace curtains and a bright yellow quilt on her bed. She quickly stripped off her gardening clothes, splashed water on her face, and donned her Robe of Seduction. She frowned at her reflection as she tugged the skirt straight and clipped the silver skull belt around her belly. Purple satin just wasn't her fabric, but she made it work.

She carefully shut and locked the hidden door as she exited her rooms. She ran her fingers through her mane of wavy black hair as she traipsed through the dimly lit halls of the Fortress of Bones. She was supposed to look disheveled, but in a sexy way, not in a wind-blown gardening way.

The gong sounded again. Whoever it was, he was good. He'd made it all the way to the lower Cavern of Graves. Sara frowned. That meant her illusions of tattered ghosts hadn't frightened him. If he kept going, he would most likely choose the Tunnel of Turbidity. But he might also try the Rat Run if he was small. She made an abrupt right turn and marched up a narrow twisted staircase.

The Seduction Chamber was a long, low room filled with smoky candlelight and vague mist. Sara settled on her divan, arranging the satin pillows into a comfortable nest.

The grate for the Rat Run scraped as someone eased it open. Small person, then, not a big muscle hero, which meant verbal seduction rather than physical. Good. Sara preferred talking to wriggling. She watched the grate through lowered lashes. Let the intruder think he'd caught her napping. It was more dramatic when she pretended to awaken. She could scream like a banshee, musically of course, when she discovered him rifling her lair. She did like that part of the role. She shifted into a more provocative pose.

The grate eased off the wall. Thin arms wrapped in black fabric and gloves lowered it to the floor. A head covered in a full mask with only a strip for the eyes emerged from the hole. The hero studied the room, squinting through the smoke and mistiness. His eyes fixed on Sara. He froze, watching her.

She gave a cute little snore. Not the juicy snot-filled kind, but a little throaty growl. Her sorceress mentor had said she had the sexiest snore he'd ever heard.

The intruder eased out of the Rat Run. He was good. Sara heard nothing as he crept across the floor toward the glittering pile of fake treasure behind her divan. She watched through lowered lashes as the hero paused beside her divan. One gloved hand, slender and shapely, slid over a satin pillow. Sara gave another little snore. The hero sniffed and turned away. Not the reaction that he should have had.

So maybe he wasn't a hero, just a lousy thief. Sara gave another sleepy noise and shifted to her side. The thief fingered the large brass chamber pot that Sara had magicked into a golden shimmer of a jeweled funerary urn. He glanced back as Sara settled into the cushions, milking her fake-sleep routine for all it was worth. Most heroes would be ogling her cleavage at this point. This one just turned back to the treasure pile. Definitely just a thief. A good one, though. He'd made it through the traps to her Chamber of Seduction.

Sara shifted, sighed, and fluttered her eyelashes. Time to ramp up the seduction routine. Not that she'd ever had to actually follow through with it. Only two heroes had ever made it to her chamber before. Neither one had managed to avoid the traps in the floor. Both had found themselves tumbling into the sand pits. Both had also managed to escape and flee home to tell stories of their harrowing escape from the vengeful sorceress in her fortress of bones. Sara surreptitiously pulled her neckline lower as she pretended to awaken.

"Oh!" She panted breathlessly, putting on her act of scared virgin sacrifice. Maybe this thief would be overwhelmed by his protective instincts and shift into hero mode.

The treasure heap rattled as the thief tossed aside battered bronze vessels.

And maybe not.

"You startled me," Sara said, pitching her voice louder. "Who are you?"

"Nobody you need to worry about." The thief's voice was low for a woman, not quite low enough for a man, and definitely not low enough for a hero.

A stack of fake coins slithered across the floor. The thief kicked the brass urn. It thumped and rattled across the floor. "Where's the real treasure hiding?"

Sara shrank back on the divan, hands clutched to her chin, elbows squishing her bosom to make it more pronounced. "I don't know what you're talking about. That is the treasure." She fluttered her eyelashes.

The thief kicked through the pile of fakes, bending to run gloved fingers across the stones.

Sara's bottom lip crept out in a petulant pout.

The thief rose in a fluid motion and turned to her. "I know you have a treasure here. It's legendary. No one has ever looted the treasure from the Fortress of Bones, so it must be here someplace!"

"Why should I tell you where it is? What are you going to do? Threaten my virtue?" She narrowed her eyes, trying for a terrifying reptilian glare but only managing a near-sighted squint.

The thief laughed, a rich chuckle.

That was more than Sara could stand. She bounced to her feet, seductive draperies threatening to trip her. She jerked them more or less straight. "Do you have any idea who you are threatening?"

"A hedge witch tarted up to look like the sorceress rumored to haunt these corridors."

Sara stamped her foot, not effective or threatening since her bare feet only slapped on the stone floor causing her to wince. "How dare you!" Her voice squeaked. "I'll have you know I am a sorceress of great power, privy to all the secrets of this fortress. Shall I summon the guardian to destroy you now that I'm done toying with you?"

"If you had a guardian it would have eaten me already."

Sara twitched her hand and called up her last illusion, the one that she'd never had to use yet in her tenure at the fortress. She flicked her finger out to summon the Guardian.

Mist swirled and thickened. Stones shivered and danced to a thunderous roaring. Fires flickered and flared around the chamber. Wind swept through the room, dousing the flames for a moment.

When the darkness lifted as the torches flared, a massive beast crouched in the center of the room. Three snarling dog heads twisted on thick necks. Black hair coated its haunches. Claws long enough to tear flesh from bone scraped on the floor. Muscles bulged in the thick limbs. Evil red light burned in its eyes. It panted and roared.

The thief laughed, clapping hands together. "That's a beauty. I bet you spent days perfecting it. You missed one thing, though. Where's the stench?" He leaned closer, close enough Sara found herself tumbling into his green eyes.

Her illusion flickered and faded. The roars were just a tinny noise from tumbling brass bowls. The torches were several fat candles and reflected sunlight. The whole chamber looked tawdry and cheap, and smelled like old dust and rancid roses.

Sara's shoulders slumped as the last of her power dribbled away into the corners. Her guardian still stood, but only as a tattered mirage. She had failed. Her first real test as sorceress and she had failed miserably. A fat tear gathered in one eye, wobbled on her lashes.

"Are you crying?" The thief stared in disbelief. "No, don't do that. Your guardian was quite impressive. I was almost scared."

"Don't lie to me! Everyone lies to me. They told me I was perfect for this post, that I'd make a perfect seductive sorceress. They lied. I'm a complete and utter failure. I only got this job because of my parents. I'm a terrible sorceress."

The thief stepped forward to lay a hand on Sara's arm. "You were quite good. It's just, well, I wasn't exactly playing fair."

Sara sniffed back the sob that threatened to escape. "What do you mean?"

"You were expecting a hero, right? I'm not exactly a hero."

"No, you're just a thief." Sara shook off the solicitous hand, her chubby face squinching together in rage. "A stupid thief. If there is a treasure here, I can't find it. I'm running this show on a shoestring. I never asked for it, anyway. I really wanted to audition as a godmother, but I didn't have enough magic and what I did have was evil."

"You evil? I find that hard to believe."

"Well, I am. I can't help it. My father is the Evil Overlord himself, and my mother is the Avenging Goddess."

The thief took a step back.

"You should run in terror now, if you know what's good for you." Sara sniffled again as she swiped the fat tear off her cheek.

The thief raised one hand in an abortive gesture. "Look, I'm sorry. All I wanted was something good enough for my dowry. Since the heroes don't come out to the Fortress anymore, they say it isn't worth their time, I thought maybe I could find something they'd overlooked."

Sara wiped her hand on her silken draperies. "I tried my best, but the previous sorceress was an old hag who hated everyone. She killed off anyone who even came near. All I wanted was to meet a decent hero who would carry me off so I could retire from evil and become a crazy old woman living alone with her cats in a little cottage by the sea who sometimes maybe mixes up a little love potion or cure for the coughs or—Wait, *your* dowry?"

The thief pulled off the mask, slipping it over her head to release a mane of chestnut locks. She was obviously a woman, but not one blessed with beauty. A smile crooked her mouth to one side.

Sara frowned. "This doesn't make sense. Why didn't you summon your godmother to fix things for you?"

The woman shrugged her thin shoulders. "Godmothers only come if you're poor, orphaned, abused, or whatever. I don't qualify. My mother is definitely still alive. She's sweet and good and kind. My father isn't poor or abusive." She raised her hand, ticking items off on her fingers as she talked. "I'm not a miller's daughter. Or a drunkard's daughter. Or a ruined merchant's daughter. I'm not in love with a prince. Or anyone for that matter. If I have enough for my own dowry, then I choose my own way."

"But why come here, to the Fortress of Bones? Weren't you afraid of the sorceress?"

The woman nodded. "I figured if she was real and I got caught, I could beg her to take me on as her apprentice, or housekeeper or something. It would be more fun than if I stayed home." She dropped her gaze to the floor beside her toes. "I just wanted to have something exciting happen in my life before I end up marrying. With my luck, he'll be just rich enough not to be poor, but not enough to be wealthy. And he'll be something dull like a sheep farmer or bookkeeper or shopkeeper. Besides, I didn't expect it to be so easy to break in. I thought I'd have been stopped long before I found any treasure."

"You would have been dead a long time ago if I hadn't changed all the traps over to illusions. The previous seductive sorceress would have let you die and fed your carcass to the rats." She gave a delicate shudder. "I can't stand rats. They were everywhere before I starved most of them out. The Cavern of Graves was riddled with traps, poison arrows, sharpened stakes, crushing stones, you name it, it was in there."

The thief shuddered. "Those spiders were the worst. They felt so real."

"That's because they were real."

Her green eyes widened. She stared at Sara before brushing frantically at her hair and shoulders.

Sara pursed her lips. "They aren't venomous. They're perfectly harmless garden spiders. Look, can we go somewhere more comfortable? My name's Sara, by the way, Saragliandey." She bustled to the hidden door behind the treasure pile. The latch clicked and the door swung open.

The thief hesitated at the entrance. "Gwen as in Gwendolyn, not Guinevere or Gwenocious. No more spiders?"

Sara shook her head impatiently. The rain wouldn't hold off much longer on her pea patch and she really did need to get the weeds pulled today. "No spiders." She glanced at her guest. The woman hesitated. Sara waited for only a moment before impatiently whirling to march through the secret passage. Her seductive outfit fluttered around her in a shimmer of purple gauze.

Gwen's footsteps whispered behind her after only a moment's pause. If Sara hadn't been listening for them, she would have missed them. An evil little thought blossomed in her mind. She wasn't good at sneaking or crawling through tight passageways, not like Gwen. Maybe Gwen could accomplish what she couldn't.

They emerged into the sunny yellow kitchen. Gwen stood in the doorway, blinking, her mouth half-open.

"Pardon me a moment," Sara said, "while I slip into something a lot more comfortable." She left her guest standing in the kitchen while she retreated to her bedroom. She emerged a few minutes later in her gardening clothes—breeches and a homespun tunic, both splotched with dirt. She'd just broken all sorts of rules by bringing the thief, Gwen, into her private chambers. But the woman had made it past all of her illusions. She'd earned this glimpse of Sara's private life. At least she hoped the Dark Council would believe that. She wouldn't have to worry about the Council, though, if she and Gwen found the rumored treasure hoard.

Gwen found the kettle and started water heating. She hummed as she rummaged through Sara's cupboards. "You have tea stashed somewhere, don't you?"

"Left side of the sink. It's pretty old and only herbal, but it's what I've got." Sara squinted out the window. A low mist of gray rain clung to her pea patch. It had oddly straight edges and the rain started barely three feet above the luscious green plants. Golden sand stretched to the far horizon beyond the garden.

Gwen flicked a glance at Sara. She nudged aside canisters and packages of exotic candies and dried fruits to find the packet of chamomile and rose hips buried at the back.

Sara folded her hands over her belly. "seductive sorceresses do not drink tea. They sip wine and ambrosia and honey nectar and a dozen other things that do not taste as good as they sound. They nibble on dates and sweet nuts and honey cakes, which do taste pretty good. I keep trying to get them to send me something more substantial, but." She shrugged. "I grow a lot of vegetables."

"Are you here by yourself?"

Sara nodded. "It gets really lonely. You're the first intruder in weeks, the first one to the make it to my chamber in months."

Gwen found two cups, shaped like skulls with glowing eyes, and scooped dried herbs into each.

"I've got the spiders and a couple of snakes in my garden, mostly because they keep the mice and rats out. But other than them, I'm by myself."

Gwen poured hot water over the herbs. Their fragrance rose on curls of steam, fresh meadows and lush rose bushes and all the smells of a much different climate than desert and sand. She carried the cups to the table, then settled onto the stool.

"If you're going to stay, I guess I should drag out some of the other furniture," Sara said. "There's loads of stuff hidden in the catacombs, but most of it's really heavy."

"I'll make do," Gwen said. "I'm used to that. I've got six brothers and four sisters at home. It's been really nice to have some peace and quiet for a change."

Sara stirred her tea, staring into the whorls of steam and leaves as she spoke. "So, you want to find treasure so you can have an adventure?"

"And because if I have enough money, I can decide what to do with my life. Marry who I want, live where I want, all that kind of thing." Gwen set her spoon on the table. "Is there a treasure hidden here somewhere?"

"Maybe. Quite possibly. But I haven't been able to find it. See, Bianca, the previous seductive sorceress, had a bit of an argument with the Dark Council. She stole a bunch of stuff and hid it from them. That's one reason I'm here. I'm the Evil Overlord's daughter, so they thought I'd be happy to find it for him. I'm also the only sorceress even close to the right age for the part." Sara wrinkled her nose. "I'm not much of a sorceress, really. I'm good at manipulating other people's magic, but I don't have much of my own. So they give me an allotment of power to run this place. But if I could find Bianca's stash—"

"Then you could buy yourself a place with the Council," Gwen finished for her.

"No!" Sara slammed her hand down on the table. One fake-jewel eye on her cup popped off and clattered to the floor. "I could convince them to stop this ridiculousness and let me retire to a nice cottage on the seashore. You know what I mean, the kind with roses climbing over the walls and hollyhocks all along the fence and little patches of pansies hiding under the currant bushes." She sighed wistfully.

"Nice dream," Gwen agreed. "How about I help you find this treasure and we split it, fifty-fifty?"

Sara fluttered her lashes. "Would you really help me search?"

Gwen nodded. "You disarm the magical traps and I'll do the rest." She stuck out her hand. "Deal?"

Sara smiled, showing off a dimple in one plump cheek. She grasped Gwen's hand. "Deal."

"Are you sure you cleared the traps from this tunnel?" Gwen crouched next to a dark hole in the wall.

"I'll check again if it makes you feel better." Sara tapped her foot impatiently. Fifteen days and as many tunnels and hidden rooms and they hadn't found more than a handful of rotten sacks, empty barrels, and mummified rodents.

"It's just after that poison dart pit in the last tunnel, I'm a little nervous."

Sara's shoulders sagged. "Sorry. I should have caught that one, but there wasn't any magic involved. Just be careful and go slow."

"I always am. Slow and careful." Gwen lay down and inched into the tunnel. She pushed a small lamp in front of her. The oil-fed flame flickered and cast strange shadows.

They were on the third sub-basement beneath the Fortress. The bone theme had been carried to all sorts of gruesome extremes on the upper floors, but down here, the decorating theme seemed to be more along 'forgotten storeroom' lines. Dust, sand, and stone were all that remained.

A distant bong announced the arrival of a would-be thief or hero.

"Drat," Sara muttered. "We've got a visitor."

"Ignore him," Gwen called over her shoulder. "I'm sure he'll give up by the third cavern."

Sara cocked her head, listening to the gongs. "He's on his way to the Hall of Heroes. If he gets through the Sand Fall, he'll be entering the Seduction Chamber sooner rather than later. I have to go. It's my duty."

Gwen's feet disappeared into the tunnel. Her voice floated back, muffled by the tight quarters. "Then go. I'll keep looking."

"Be careful."

Sara hesitated. She hated leaving Gwen alone. What if there were more traps hidden and Sara wasn't there to catch her with a magic net or shield her with a Flaming Wall? She drew in a deep breath. Gwen was a thief, and a good one. She'd proven herself multiple times over the last days. She'd be fine. It wasn't like Bianca had used any of her really treacherous traps down here. There were no direct routes up to the empty treasure vaults or the Seduction Chamber.

Another bong sounded, louder than before.

"Bother and barnacles!" Sara hurried up the hidden stairs. She'd have barely time to slip into her Seduction Robes before the hero battered his way into the heart of the Fortress.

She rushed up the last few flights, ran down the hallway as fast as her chubby legs could go, then dashed into her rooms. She pulled on the first robe she grabbed and finger-combed her tangled hair as she slid into the Seduction Chamber. She flopped onto the divan just as the final bong announced the arrival of the hero.

The door to her Chamber splintered apart. Shards flew across the room. A gigantic man in leather armor stomped through. He paused to brush off bits of the doorframe. Wood clattered to the floor.

Sara shut her eyes and feigned sleep.

Boots thundered ponderously across the floor, closer and closer. They paused at the twang of a trap tripping. Wood splintered again. Sara risked a peek. The man brushed off the remnants of an arrow trap. He yanked one shaft from his bicep, then ignored the blood on his arm as he marched toward Sara.

She swallowed nausea. Illusory blood was fine, but real blood?

He came like an unstoppable force of nature, worse than her mother. Sara squeaked as she gave up any pretense of being asleep. One of the hero's meaty hands reached for her. She scrambled off the divan, scurrying backward. Where could she hide?

His hand caught her trailing purple robe and jerked her to a stop.

"Where is she?" His voice boomed in the Chamber, rattling the torches in their stands.

Sara tried to strike a seductive pose despite her pounding heart, hip thrust out and lips puckered into a kiss-me pout. She fluffed one hand through her tangled mass of dark curls.

The man jerked her off balance. She squeaked again as she tumbled to the floor in a flutter of purple satin.

"Witch! What have you done with Gwendolyn?" His fists knotted in the satin of her robe threatening to split the seams.

"Gwen?" Sara blinked.

"My true love, my lady, my betrothed!" The man shook her, rattling her teeth together.

"I don't know what you're talking about." Sara tried to bat her eyes. She twisted her fingers to summon her Guardian, not that she had much hope for the illusion.

The man leaned close. His hot breath washed over her face. "She came this way. The innkeeper on the other side of the hills said so. Where is she?" He punctuated each word with a shake. "Tell me, you wretched sorceress!"

A rat squeaked in the far corner. The man dropped Sara onto her divan as he whirled. "Gwen? Has this foul fiend turned you into a rat?" His boots thundered across the floor.

Sara twisted her fingers, shaking them out to loosen up the magic. She reached for the Guardian spell. Nothing in her training had prepared her for an angry fiancé of a hero. But then nothing had prepared her for Gwen, either, and that was working out well. Maybe she could pull this one off, scare him into leaving before he did too much damage.

The rat squealed as the man smashed through the fake treasure hoard.

Sara summoned her Guardian. The three-headed dog appeared in a puff of smoke. But the roar sounded very distant and the whole illusion wavered. She'd used up her magic allotment already? It really wasn't enough for her garden and not one, but two intruders.

The man charged straight through the toothy maw of the Guardian. The whole illusion collapsed into a ghostly vapor.

Time to flee for safety. She bounced off her divan.

The man's hands closed over her arms. He spun her to face him then lifted her into the air.

"Change her back this instant, you spawn of the netherworld!" His face contorted with grief.

Sara's teeth clacked together, partly from fear, partly from the rattling he gave her. This was it. She was about to die as a failed seductive sorceress. Who would weed her pea patch now? She sagged in his hold. "I can't. Because she isn't a rat."

His eyes widened. His voice dropped to a quavering whisper. "You killed her?" His chin quivered. "Murdering temptress! I shall split you asunder!" He dropped one hand, bunching it into a fist. He drew it back, like a catapult cocking.

Sara closed her eyes and hoped the splitting wouldn't hurt too badly.

"Baldric!" Gwen's voice snapped the man to attention. "Put her down this instant!"

Muscles bunched as he whirled, dragging Sara by one slinky shoulder strap.

"Gwendolyn, my sweet love, moon of my desire, I have come to free you from this evil sorceress's enchantments." His fist bunched the robe tight enough that Sara squawked in protest.

"She hasn't put any kind of spell on me. I came here all by myself. On. My. Own."

"But, my dearest heart—" He strode across the stone floor, Sara bumping at his heels and squeaking all the way.

"No, do not come any closer." Gwen put up one hand. "I'm warning you, Baldric."

Baldric swept his arm wide, tossing Sara across the floor. She landed in a heap of tasseled cushions.

"Stop right there!"

Baldric dropped to his knees, hands clasped and pleading. "Gwendolyn, it doth not bother me in the slightest that thy dowry doth consist of nothing more than empty promises. Please, my love, come home and marry me. I will convince my father that we belong together."

"It isn't your father that is the problem."

"Then say the word and I will force my mother into a nunnery or a dungeon or something."

Sara struggled free of the cushions, then stood, brushing her robe straight.

"Baldric, it isn't your mother or your father, it's you."

"What? I'm not enough man for you? I've hunted every animal known to man. I've defeated a dozen knights, well at least one. I've ridden across seven kingdoms seeking the perfect gifts for you. I've slain a *dragon*." He rose to his feet as he spoke, bare arms waving wildly. "You belong with me, at my side, as my wife. You belong safe and secure in my castle, embroidering tapestries to your heart's content. I want to see you surrounded by children."

"But what about what I want?" Gwen tapped her foot.

Sara rose from the cushions, brushing her robe straight. Her face glowered in a way that would have done her Avenging Goddess mother proud. "How dare you!" She approached Baldric with an ominously slow step. She didn't even break stride as she yanked her robe back into place.

Baldric pulled a sword from the sheath on his back with a zing of metal. He flourished it with obvious skill. It ended pointed at Sara's heaving bosom. "Stay back, foul witch, or I shall skewer thee upon my virtuous blade!"

"Ha!" Gwen crossed her arms and glared. "You wouldn't know virtue if it bit you on the loincloth. What was her name? Tabitha? Or was it Rondula? Or the Guernsey twins? Or perhaps anything female in the whole duchy?"

Baldric shot worried glances at Gwen over one shoulder and outraged threat at Sara over the other. "Peace, woman. I was but doing my lordly duty."

"And this is why I won't marry you."

"But I am a titled noble, with lands and possibly an inheritance. You are but a poor country maid. You *must* marry me. Tradition says—"

"I am not poor!" Gwen shouted over Baldric's objections.

The sword point dipped to the floor as Baldric turned to Gwen. "But your father's shop is threatened with closure and your family with penury."

"Only because your father won't lower the taxes."

Sara's glare softened to speculative interest. She studied the chiseled chin and prominent nose. He looked like someone she should know, someone familiar.

"And why is it he only taxes my family's shop? Because you won't drop this ridiculous notion of marrying me."

"Please, sweet Gwendolyn, I will entreat my father. He will allow our nuptials to occur forthwith. And your family's shop will be saved."

"As I've said repeatedly, Baldric, I am not interested in you. I have never been interested in you, except as it regards my family's shop and the outrageous tax burdens placed thereon. Shards of Neptune's trident, you've got me talking like a pompous noble now. The answer is no, no, no!"

Sara tilted her head. When the light touched his cheekbones just like that, and if he had a halfway decent haircut. . .

"But you are my life, the air that I breathe, the moon of my existence." Baldric reached for Gwen's hand, his sword dangling in his other meaty fist.

Sara saved Gwen from answering. "Sir Baldric, scourge of the dancing girls of the Sandy Wastes and the Camel Drovers' Guild. The man who attempted to rob the idol of Idolac and was captured by a nine-year-old priestess initiate with basically no power."

"She threatened me with a cuddly kitten. What was I to do?" Baldric's face flushed red.

"Baldric the Incompetent, that's what the Dark Council calls you." Sara switched her glare to Gwen. "He's what you're running away from? Seriously? Someone with your skills needs to run away from *him*? A damp cabbage leaf could defeat him."

"Hey! I'll have you know I slew a dragon, a real fire-breathing beast!"

Sara flicked a speck of imaginary dust from her sleeve. "He was over eight hundred years old, arthritic, and mostly blind. You tripped and accidentally stabbed him in the toe. He died of surprise that you, Baldric the Magnificently Stupid, would dare to wake him up from a nap. Gwen, you do understand that all of his glorious deeds are made up by bards paid off by his father? And that his father has drained the Duchy's treasury trying to buy his son fame?"

A smile teased Gwen's lips, a very not-nice smile. "Who's poor now?" she whispered.

Baldric's lip quivered. "This is not fair. I come in here expecting a battle with an evil sorceress who is trying her best to seduce me, and instead you turn on me. How could you?"

"Just go away, Baldric. Go tell your father I've been carried off by a djinn to his pleasure palace."

"Or that the Avenging Goddess has claimed you as her acolyte," Sara suggested. "I'm sure Mummy will agree to that story."

Baldric's face drained white. "The Avenging Goddess is your mother?"

Sara merely smiled.

Baldric's sword slammed into his sheath. He swept her a bow, placed a perfunctory kiss on Gwen's hand, then marched for the door.

"Baldric the Coward?" Gwen called.

He halted at the door. "Baldric the Prudent. Farewell, ladies. I shall carry your face in my memory forever, my lost love." He didn't sound like he meant any of it.

The two women stared after him as his bootsteps tromped away down the corridor.

Something banged from beyond the door. Baldric cursed loudly.

"That would be the spider trap," Sara said, wincing.

"I'm fine," Baldric's voice floated back. His footsteps resumed fading into the distance.

Gwen and Sara stood in silence, trading sideways glances.

"So, what now?" Gwen asked after a long moment.

Sara shrugged. "Want to help me play seductive sorceress while we search for the treasure? I think these robes would be much more appealing on you."

"I'm allergic to heaps of pillows and incense."

"It's not bad. Only once or twice a year."

Gwen nodded, then stuck out her hand. "Sounds good to me. I've got nothing better waiting."

"No more angry betrotheds coming to rescue you?"

"Just Baldric, and if he ever shows his face back here, I'll make sure the world hears how he was defeated by a girl."

They traded grins with their handshakes.

"I think there's a storeroom somewhere at the end of the Cavern of Graves that we haven't searched yet. Let me change out of these robes and reset a few traps, and we can start searching for it."

Gwen nodded. "Sounds like a plan to me."

LET THERE BE LIGHT

1. And behold, in those days there was no light, only darkness; yea, such utter darkness that there was no light; all was darkness.
2. And there was also coldness, yea coldness such that it was very cold.
3. And lo, a voice cried out in the darkness and the cold saying, "Let there be light!"
4. And there was light of such glorious brightness that the darkness was no more; and behold, the light banished the cold also.
5. And a voice was heard saying, "Do you want the cherry or the grape popsicle?"
6. And the One who had commanded the light to come forth was taken by the Voice.
7. And the light and warmth went also with the One who had spoken.
8. And behold, all was darkness such that there was no light anywhere. And all was cold once more.

—from the *Book of Squid,* Chapter 33

Baba Yaga
and the Dragons

Baba Yaga rubbed sleep from her eyes. She stood in a whirl of brightly embroidered skirts and shawls. She shook out her tangled white hair, which caused wind to roar in the trees around her hut and set them creaking and swaying.

"Something is amiss in my woods," she told the skull with glowing eyes watching from above her door. "I feel it in my bones."

She tapped her foot three times on the floor. Her hut obediently settled to the ground. The door swung open with mighty groanings. Baba Yaga tied a black kerchief over her wild hair then stepped from her hut into her yard. Brambles and bushes choked the fence built from the bones of lost wanderers. Their skulls peered through the overgrowth. Baba Yaga waved her hand. The brambles drew back, their runners snaking away into the forest, leaving the yard bare earth and the bones white in the dawn. Orange light bloomed in the depths of the skulls, pouring from their eye sockets to bathe the yard in a reddish glow.

The witch drew a great breath in through her long nose. "I smell trouble in my woods this dawn. It smells of my old enemy, Koshchey the Deathless."

The hut shifted its long chicken feet. The skulls swiveled on their bone fence to shine their eye-lights on Baba Yaga.

"Today I face his meddlesome magic. Today I fight."

She whistled, short and sharp. Her mortar came tumbling out from behind the hut, the pestle clanking along behind. Baba Yaga stepped into the grinding bowl, then folded her long, long legs until her knees almost touched her warty chin. She grasped the pestle.

"Sweep, sweep, and fly!"

She pushed hard against the ground with the pestle. A great wind howled through the trees. Branches clacked and creaked. The mortar shot forward, into the dark wood. Last autumn's leaves swirled and blew around her in a cloud. Spring flowers closed petals tightly as she swept past. Deer fled into their thickets to hide. Wolves howled on the ridge tops. Rabbits tumbled into their burrows. Mice squeaked and scurried away. Birds exploded from the trees to ride the wind in the wake of her passing. Baba Yaga rode the dawn in her mortar for the first time in several generations. Her sleep had been deep and long. The denizens of the woods had forgotten the touch of her magic.

Her belly rumbled as she wove between the trees. It had been many a long year since last she had feasted. A stash of acorns provided a small snack. Baba Yaga smashed them into meal in her mortar, then licked it from the bowl. She patted her belly, then raised her long nose to the wind.

"I smell a strangeness. Night wind, speak to me of this new thing that has come into my deep, dark woods."

The wind showered the witch in leaves until she could no longer see. But no voice spoke from the air. The wind had forgotten its voice.

"Squirrel, you who protested my sharing your stash of nuts, what have you to say of this strangeness?" The witch twisted her long bony fingers and cast a spell over the tiny rodent.

The squirrel stopped chittering, flicked its tail twice, then scampered away into the treetop. It, too, had forgotten how to shape words.

Baba Yaga frowned a mighty frown. "Does no one speak in the woods? Have I slept so long that you have all forgotten me?"

The woods had no answer other than the rustling of the wind.

Baba Yaga once more set off in her mortar pushed along by the thick pestle.

"How long have I slept?" she asked as she paused near a great oak drooped over a steep cliff. It was a young sapling when she'd lain down. Now it was a gnarled elder among the trees. "What changes have men wrought in the world? What strangeness have they created in my woods?"

She tucked her knees tighter and gave a mighty sweep of her pestle. On and on through the wood she traveled with a great roaring and rushing of leaves. Faster and faster she went, drawn by the strange scent in her nostrils. She pushed the pestle against the earth with all her strength. The mortar slid forward, racing the fingers of light from the rising sun.

The mortar stopped abruptly. Baba Yaga spilled out all a-tumble on the ground. A strange thing lay under her. The smell of it filled her long nose. She sat, legs spread across a deep black ribbon that stretched far through her woods. She reached one bony finger to touch the smooth surface. Strange, so strange. Round stones lay flat across the surface, coated in the darkness, smelling of tar. She stood and stamped on the ribbon. Hard and black, it yielded nothing. She raised her eyes, seeking the shape of the strange thing's essence. It stretched to the far eastern horizon. She turned, skirts twirling. It stretched to the far western horizon, a swath of darkness cutting her forest in twain.

Baba Yaga yanked on the fringe of her head scarf. She chewed on the threads, jaws working ferociously, as she thought on this new thing. Yellow stripes led down the center, fading into the moonlight and distance.

"Night wind, speak to me!" She reached for her magic, the power of secret forest glades and dark stone caves, but the black ribbon shredded her spell. A strange magic coursed along its length, newer and stronger than her ancient forest power.

She stamped her hard boots on the black ribbon. She stamped and jumped and stomped until her skirts flapped up around her ears. The black ribbon remained unperturbed by her frenzied dance.

She stomped her bony feet one last time. She lay her finger beside her long nose as she considered the black thing. "Are you the river of tears from the chuhaister, the forest giants banished by the bogatyr? They weep darkness and sorrow. I shall follow you to your source and see if this is their power growing stronger."

Baba Yaga marched to her mortar and dragged it upright. She seated herself once more. "Sweep, sweep, and fly!" She pushed against the black surface with her pestle.

And tumbled across the strange ribbon. Her mortar rolled to a stop in a pile of leaves. She raised her pestle high and brought it against the dark surface. Her magic flared in a flash of orange light. The trees creaked. The night wind howled. Leaves blew around her head in a great dancing gale. Her pestle shattered into a thousand bits.

But the black thing remained untouched.

Baba Yaga sat herself down beside it. Her face wrinkled in a mighty frown as she thought. She looked east. She looked west. She studied the strangeness that divided her wood and destroyed her magic.

Her ears pricked at a distant rumbling. Far in the distance, twin lights speared the early morning mist. Like glowing eyes they swept closer. The rumbling grew into a growling roar. A thing appeared through the mist, large and blocky. The eyes were set low on its head. A single metal bar for teeth stretched across its face. It belched smoke from horns on its head. Its long body rumbled on round tires. It passed Baba Yaga in a hurricane of wind and dust. She stared at the red eyes glowing behind as it trundled quickly into the distance.

"Dragon," she screeched. She backed from the black strip. "Road for dragons. Beasts of evil. This cannot be. Not in my woods."

She raised her bony arms over her head, fingers splayed like claws to the moon. "Come forth, my Bright Dawn. Fight the dragons that have invaded our home. Destroy their trail with your power."

Hooves clattered. Light speared through the trees, white as the rising sun. The White Horseman charged out of the wood on the far side of the road. He pulled up his snorting stallion at the edge. The horse pawed the ground and blew steam from its nostrils.

"Dragons, my loyal servant. Slay them!" Baba Yaga pointed after the fading red lights of the dragon's tail.

The White Horseman rode onto the black surface. His white charger danced and skittered at the clacking of his hooves. The knight fought to hold the beast steady. His horse reared, fighting his hand. He kneed it into a gallop after the taillights of the dragon. The horse's hooves began to smoke with each stride. The white horse whinnied and danced, his hooves striking sparks. His feet burst into white flames. The horse screamed as the flames devoured its legs. It tumbled to the side then dissolved into smoke. The White Horseman faltered as his mount faded. His feet touched the black road. White fire erupted, engulfing him. He shouted as the dark magic devoured him and his magic. Within moments, all that remained was a thin wisp of white smoke.

Baba Yaga blinked as the light faded. The White Horseman was gone.

"So, your magic is strong and young. But strong and young will yet be bested by age and wisdom." She laid a finger along her nose and whispered words of power. She spit onto the black surface. Her magic sizzled and spread before sinking into the dark road. She nodded, her headscarf bobbing.

"Come forth, my Red Sun, to slay the foul dragon that spoils my forest with his trail!"

Hooves clattered. Red light, as red as the setting sun, blazed in the forest. The Red Horseman emerged from the trees. His horse danced and snorted. The horseman calmed his mount, pulling up well short of the road.

"I have cast my spell," Baba Yaga called to him. "It shall protect you while you slay the beast. Wait for its eyes to appear. It has gone to the west, to feed I suppose. It should return shortly."

The Red Horseman nodded, the plume of his helmet wafting in the breeze. Red as blood, he was ten times as powerful as his brother, the White Horseman. Baba Yaga smiled. Yes, her Red Sun would slay the dragon. Her spell lay thick on the road, like honey it spread over the darkness.

They didn't wait long before the eyes of the dragon appeared in the distance. The Red Horseman nudged his horse forward. It rolled its eyes until the whites showed. Froth came from its mouth, but the horse obeyed and stepped onto the strange surface. It neighed and pranced as Baba Yaga's spell spit sparks under its hooves. But her magic held. The Red Horseman did not die, his horse was not devoured by the dragon's fire. He settled his lance, ready to face the dragon.

The wind rushed before it. The eyes were no longer glowing. The beast was massive, splashed with bright red and yellow words. Spells of power, no doubt, Baba Yaga thought as she watched the beast approach on its spinning wheels.

The Red Horseman shouted his battle cry and put spurs to his mount. The deep bay horse plunged forward. Its heavy gallop shook the trees and rattled the stones that lay along either side of the dragon's road. Baba Yaga's magic held under its hooves, a shield against the dragon's fire. The beast bellowed, loud and long, as it barreled closer. The thunder of its body rolling along the road blended with the hoofbeats into a cacophony of competing powers. Baba Yaga drew a breath in through her long nose and held it.

The dragon swept closer. The Red Horseman's lance flickered. Sunlight flashed as they collided, a brilliant flare of light.

Baba Yaga blinked.

The dragon roared away to the east, into the rising sun.

A single splinter of the red lance somersaulted through the air to land at Baba Yaga's feet.

The beast had devoured her Red Sun in one bite.

She pulled her shawl close around her shoulders. The wind bit with a chill she'd never felt before. Her shoulders slumped against it as she settled in her mortar. Her face settled into grim lines as she contemplated the dragon's road.

The magic was too strong for her. Two of her champions had perished.

"Come forth, my Dark Midnight," she whispered. "Come vanquish the evil that has infested my forest."

Leaves rustled on the trees. Sunlight and shadows danced on the forest floor. Baba Yaga sat motionless as she reached for the natural rhythms of the land, of her magic. But through it all, the thread of dragon magic twisted and strangled her power. She frowned a mighty frown, squinching her face into an irritated knot.

"Dangerous," she whispered. The thread wove its insidious way into her magics, into the heart of her forest.

The wind twitched the leaves, the breath of the forest across her skin. Her magic trickled and dribbled through the web of dragon power. The black ribbon was like a noose around her, pulling and fraying her spells and replacing them with its own twisting coils of enchantment.

Hooves clacked against stone.

She looked up from her study of the black ribbon. The Black Horseman on his gleaming stallion, black as midnight, shifted from the deep shadows under a stand of pines. He stopped before her. Breath steamed from the horse's nostrils. It snorted and bobbed its head, front hoof scraping the thick layer of pine needles.

His presence did not bring the night as it had in the past. The morning sun shone down on his dark armor, lit the red tassels on his harness.

Baba Yaga pressed her lips tight together. Had her power faded so much while she slept?

She rose to her feet, skirts swinging around her ankles. Wind tugged the fringe of her scarf. "My Dark Midnight, an evil force has invaded my woods. Its magic is powerful and deep. A nest of strange dragons has made their home here. They have left a trail through the woods. You are my last hope, my last champion. It has defeated my Red Sun and my Bright Dawn. I will gift you everything I can. Will you face the dragon in battle?"

The Black Horseman shifted in his saddle. His closed visor reflected no light, black as the darkest shadow in the midnight forest.

She spread her hands. Wind surged, sending leaves dancing. "Perhaps we should wait until nightfall, until midnight, when your power waxes. Surely the dragon's power will fade with the setting sun."

His helm tilted to one side as he considered her. The long plume of horsehair at the crown shifted and spilled to his shoulder. Deep within the visor, eyes gleamed sapphire blue.

Once, his appearance would have brought the darkness of stars and shadows. Once, Baba Yaga had only to speak and the night would have fallen in a thick cloak over the trees. She dropped her eyes to her hands, gnarled and spotted with age.

"I have slept many long years, perhaps too many. Perhaps my time is past and the age of dragons is now come. Perhaps the chuhaister have been freed. Do the giants walk the mountains and plague mankind? Are the bogatyr no more?"

The Black Horseman slumped in his saddle. The horse dropped its head to crop at the fresh spring grass. Her Dark Midnight seemed smaller, more human than she remembered.

"Are the old enchantments fading?"

The wind didn't answer. The horseman merely sat his steed and waited silently for the day to pass and night to fall.

Baba Yaga spun in a whirl of skirts. The string of fingerbones she wore as a necklace clacked at the movement. She wove her hands into the bones as she faced the dark ribbon of dragon magic. She called for the wind to bring its power. She called the animals to her. She called her magic from the deep shadows and hidden meadows. She called and her forest answered. She drank in the power, opening her mouth to breathe it inside. She swelled larger as it filled the empty spaces inside. She was the forest and the forest was hers.

But her forest had changed. The animals had forgotten their words, the wind had lost its voice, and the dragons had come tearing through her land.

Baba Yaga twitched her nose. She had one champion left. If he was defeated, then she would retire to her hut and fade away. She would have no choice but to let the dragons roam where they would.

Another of the beasts roared by. She watched and waited for it to turn and challenge her, but the thing rolled straight down the road. Were they blind? Did they not see her? She glanced at the Black Horseman, waiting patiently in the shadows of the trees for day to pass. Perhaps if she lured the dragons from their road, they would weaken. Perhaps if her champion fought them on her ground not theirs, she would emerge the victor.

She stepped up cautiously to the verge of the road. She looked east, she looked west. More dragons crawled in the distance. Baba Yaga held her ground right at the edge of the dark ribbon. She waited for the dragons to approach.

One roared beside her, the wind of its passing swirling dust into her face. She blinked her eyes clear, clutching her shawl around her shoulders. Did she need to taunt them more to draw them away?

She shouted at the next one as it drew close, eyes dim and lifeless above the metal teeth. Smoke belched from its horns, but it did not slow, did not turn aside. She stomped her foot on the black road. The next dragon would notice her, turn aside to meet her in combat, she would see to that. She gritted her teeth then stepped out onto the road. Her skirts swirled and swayed. The wind gusted through the trees. The animals crept close to the edge of the forest, eyes white-rimmed as they watched. The Black Horseman urged his horse forward into the sunlight. He stopped well short of the edge of the road and its strange magic.

Baba Yaga clutched her shawl around her shoulders as she waited. She faced west down the long road. She had seen dragons in the distance. They would come.

A small dragon roared past from behind her. It was rounded, tiny, but it made the most horrific bleating noise as it sped past. The witch stamped her foot so hard the forest trembled. But the road did not move.

Twin eyes appeared in the west, glowing white even in daylight. Baba Yaga readied her magic. The dragon charged toward her down the long ribbon of black. Her bony fingers tightened on her shawl. Power crawled up her spine, crackled through her hair.

The dragon hooted, a blast of sound that rocked her back on her heels. It sped closer and closer.

It was big, much bigger than she'd thought. Baba Yaga stepped backward until her feet sank into the soft loam of the forest soil along the verge of the road. Her magic swirled around her, pent and anxious for release.

The dragon followed, slowing until its enormous wheels crunched to a stop at the edge of the road.

Baba Yaga smiled, showing her gapped-tooth grin. Her plan had worked. She had lured the dragon from the dark ribbon of power. Now it would succumb to her forest magic. She loosed a blast of furious wind.

The dragon creaked. Its square body swayed, but it did not move.

"Come forth, my Dark Midnight, and slay the foul beast!"

The Black Horseman did not emerge. She glanced behind her. He was nothing more than a flutter of shadows under the birch trees. He was a ghost under the full light of noonday sun.

"My enemy Koshchey's power is strong if even my most faithful servant cannot stand up to his dragons," Baba Yaga muttered.

Metal squeaked and slammed. Footsteps crunched across the gravel edge. A man approached. His clothing was most strange. Tight blue pants and a bright green shirt with pictures painted on the front. He frowned, concern wrinkling his forehead.

"Are you lost, Grandmother?" His tone was courteous, his manner kind.

Baba Yaga stuffed the fringe of her shawl into her mouth and chewed. She eyed the great dragon then the man, back and forth. Had he come from inside the dragon? Was he a servant of the beast?

The man reached a gentle hand for her elbow. "Is there someone I can call to help you?"

She jerked her arm back, retreating a few more steps toward the safety of the wild forest.

"The nearest village is miles away. Let me take you there, it's on my way."

The man kept offering assistance, as if she were a doddering old woman! She, Baba Yaga, witch of the forest! She drew a long breath in through her large nose. Air whistled in her nostrils. She drew herself up to her full height. Tall enough to stare him in the chin.

When did men grow as tall as trees? Or had she shrunk while she slept away all those years?

"Grandmother?" He reached for her arm yet again.

She stamped her foot and whistled for the north wind. A few leaves rustled. No wild torrent of air barreled from the woods. She wrinkled up her face. Her magic faded and dimmed.

"Babushka, please, come with me. You must be lost out here in the woods."

She smacked his solicitous hand away. "I live here."

"Are you sure?"

She smelled the stench of Koshchey's magic on the man. She grumbled and showed him her teeth. How dare Koshchey send his servants to drain her magic, to treat her as a feeble old woman?

He studied her a moment longer, before shrugging and climbing back into the dragon's head. The beast rumbled to life, then roared away. The wind of its passage blew the kerchief from Baba Yaga's head.

"My Dark Midnight, come forth." Her voice cracked with age. She tried to straighten her spine, but her old body would not untwist. Koshchey's dragon had stolen her vitality. "Come forth and slay the foul beasts."

The Black Horseman kneed his faithful steed forward from the shadows. But his outline shimmered and wavered.

Baba Yaga shivered under the lash of the wind from the passing dragons. Her strength faltered. She tapped one side of her long nose with a bony finger as she contemplated her choices. Stay and fight? And be defeated by Koshchey's minions. Return to her hut and regain her powers? Yes, and perhaps employ some devious stratagem against him. Koshchey the Deathless had not been sleeping away the centuries. It was time she figured out what tricks the sorcerer employed. She scuffed her shoe along the edge of the road, releasing her spells back into the forest earth.

"My Dark Midnight, my friend, stay and watch the dragons. Rest in the shadows. Your time will come."

The Black Horseman faded from sight.

Baba Yaga stumped across the ground to her tumbled mortar. She dragged it upright, then fetched a branch from a nearby birch tree. She settled in the bowl of the mortar and used the branch as a makeshift pestle.

"Sweep, sweep, and fly!"

The mortar wobbled along at a much slower pace than before, but the birch branch was sturdy enough. It would guide her to her hut perched safely on its long chicken legs.

She let the morning's events tumble through her head like leaves on the wind of her passing. The magic of the road tasted of Koshchey, true, but underneath, it was the cold power of men. She'd pitted herself against their heroes in days past. Some won through their cleverness, faithfulness, or honesty. Others lost through cowardice, deceit, or anger. But never had they brought such strong power against her, into the heart of her woods. And why had Koshchey aligned himself with men? He had ever held himself aloof, a wild man in the wild forest. But now, his power traced over and through that of the dragons and the road.

Had she slept too long? Had the world revolved and spun until it no longer needed her?

She pushed her branch against the forest floor, scattering nuts and leaves into the wind. No, the world would always need her. She was the witch of the forest. She kept nature where it belonged. She punished those who came begging power for selfish ends. Some of them had been very tasty and plump. She allowed those who truly bested her to go in peace. She avenged those who abused her forest and its creatures.

She was needed. She was Baba Yaga.

And Koshchey and the dragons of men would not defeat her or push her into obscurity until she faded into the wind.

She slowed her mortar to a stop inside her fence of bones. Her hut lowered and settled, the door opening in invitation.

She stepped from the mortar, stretching her long bony legs. She raised her arms high, her shawl swirling like a bird's wing. She cawed, screeching like a raven until a black form dropped from the cloud-swept sky to perch on a skull adorning her fence. The crow studied her from one dark eye, a gleam of answering orange fire deep within.

"Go, fly to your master. Tell him that Baba Yaga invites him to tea this afternoon."

The crow squawked, then flapped heavily away through the forest.

Baba Yaga nodded to herself. She had much to prepare.

Her hut obediently crouched on its chicken legs. The door yawned open.

"Come, my sweet ones. We must cook a feast. We have an important guest arriving soon."

Invisible hands fluttered around the witch. In moments her hut was cleaned. Scones browned next to the enormous oven. Tea steeped in a pot on the table. Baba Yaga nodded in satisfaction.

"That will do, my pretties. Shoo now, hide yourselves. Koshchey is about to darken our door."

As if on cue, a thunderous knock sounded outside. The hut shuddered. The door refused to open.

Baba Yaga drew a long breath in through her great nostrils. She shook out her skirts, straightened her shawl, then patted the tangled knot of hair on top of her head. "Enter, Koshchey the Deathless. For this afternoon, you are my guest."

The door swept open on creaking hinges. The hut shuddered again. Koshchey, her enemy, entered her home.

He was tall, thin, and nothing like the sorcerer she'd last fought two centuries earlier. Then, Koshchey rode naked on the back of a wolf through the forest, screeching curses and flinging stones. Now, he wore a tailored suit of charcoal-gray wool. His white shirt was impeccably clean. He tipped a tall hat to her as he crossed her threshold.

Baba Yaga wrinkled her face in a mighty frown. His magic reeked of oil and metal and man. He stank of the black road and the wheeled dragons. "What has happened to you?"

Koshchey brushed the brim of his hat before setting it carefully on a small table. He tugged elegant gloves from his hands, one finger at a time. "Better to ask, what has happened to the world while you slept, snoring, on top of your great oven. Times have changed, Baba Yaga."

She pulled her shawl closer around her shoulders. No, Koshchey would *not* make her feel old, tired, and useless. Not like that man from the dragon. She was Baba Yaga. She was the power in the woods. "I needed the sleep. Your spell was more draining than I thought."

Koshchey smiled, a lazy curling of his lips. "It was a trifle."

"It took you a year to prepare. And spent the lives of at least one village."

"And it is nothing now. I command cities, countries, even whole continents. My roads spread everywhere, carrying my power."

Roads, not the single ribbon in the forest.

"What have you done?" Her hands trembled as they gripped the fringe on her shawl.

He settled at her table and very deliberately and calmly poured tea. He sipped, eyes closing to enjoy the steamy brew. He smacked his lips in appreciation.

"Koshchey, by all the forests, answer me. What have you done?" Baba Yaga sank into the chair across from him.

"Nothing. That's the beauty of it. I merely stood aside and let Man go about his destructive ways. Men built the roads. Men carry my power. Men spread across the land and feed me."

"Those dragons? They taste of your magic."

"Yes. But I didn't make anyone build them. I didn't design them. I merely let men build them. And let my power grow with every new one that passed through the forest."

"It's wrong! They aren't natural."

"As if your hut and little yard were ever natural!" Underneath his cultured veneer, she glimpsed the wild, angry sorcerer who rode naked through the forest. He wasn't that changed. His comment steadied her, calmed her nerves. He continued after another sip of tea, "We don't need to stand opposed. We could work together. You have no idea of the power Man has learned to create."

"I'm beginning to see it." She waited while one of her unseen servants slid a plate of warm scones on the table. "You have brought death to the forest. You have killed its voice, torn its words asunder. You are death itself."

He leaned forward, eyes glittering. "But I am still Koshchey the Deathless."

"You are as mad as ever. I cannot tolerate your dragons or your road."

"And I cannot abide your hidebound traditional views. Like it or not, the machines of men are here to stay. Learn to live with it, or fade away. Become just a story to entertain children." He shrugged his narrow shoulders in the fitted wool suit. He set the tea cup into the saucer. The china made a quiet tink of sound. "Thank you for your tea and your hospitality. But you," he rose to his feet, then leaned low over the table, his nose barely a breath from hers, "are just a crazy old woman who has lived far too long."

He swept from her hut, his biting laugh lingering like a bad smell.

"We shall see about that, Koshchey," Baba Yaga muttered.

She swept the china from the table. She nodded in satisfaction as it shattered against her oven. The huge bulging oven, built of clay and bricks, roared with flames. Heat filled the hut as it fed on her anger.

Koshchey had perverted the old ways. He had to pay. Somehow. His power was too great, though. He'd easily defeated two of her three horsemen. She had to find new warriors.

She stormed from her hut. The forest reflected her mood. Trees creaked and groaned as they tried to resist the ferocious wind. Leaves, dead and cracked from winter, swept by in torrents. Animals cowered in their burrows, hid in the thickest copses. Clouds built overhead.

"Come, my Dark Midnight! Carry me to the lairs of men who will fight for me."

The Black Horseman thundered out of the wood. Daylight faded to a stormy dusk as the clouds thickened. Pellets of rain shattered as the furious wind hammered them to the ground. Baba Yaga swung up behind her warrior. His horse leapt into a full gallop, each stride eating leagues of forest. They rode the storm to a huddle of small buildings clustered beside the black road.

The black horse plowed to a stop. His front hooves skidded through drifts of pine needles to stop just shy of the road's dark surface. Rain splattered over the pavement. Baba Yaga sprang down from the horse.

"Go, my friend, stand watch in the woods. This is not a fight for you."

The Black Horseman bowed his head in wordless acceptance of her charge, then kneed his horse around. Wind carried him quickly away into the dark woods.

Baba Yaga sniffed. The air stank of metals, man, and rain. Yellow lights pooled across the front of the ramshackle wooden building. A peeling sign proclaimed it Bird Nest Bar. This hovel was not where she expected to be. What had happened to the neat and tidy woodsmen's huts? Where were the forest villages? And what were the strange two-wheeled machines lined up in front of the sagging porch? She shrugged her shawl into place. Baba Yaga had used stranger champions before. She pushed open the door and entered.

The air stank of old grease and sweat. Music pulsed and pounded with noises unlike any she had heard before. Not even the screeching yowls of mating wildcats could compete. But power underscored every heavy thump and rattle. Magic lived in that sound, not the deep wild magic of the forest nor the black metallic reek of the roads, but something more primal than both.

"Can I help you?" A middle-aged harridan, well worn and used by the look of her, cleaned glasses behind a long counter. "You lost, Grandmother?"

No term of endearment or respect, that. The way the woman sneered, Grandmother was an insult. Baba Yaga drew breath through her long nose. She could not afford to be angry. She had great need of champions to defeat Koshchey's destructive power and these people, this hovel, reeked of magic. She attempted a smile, a hideous stretching of her lips to reveal twisted, yellow teeth. Her face wrinkled up like a winter-stored apple.

"Not lost, not now that I have found your lovely home. May I sit with you for a while and tell you my tales?" She waited, her magic held at bay. Threads of binding waited for acceptance and invitation.

The music throbbed to a halt in a screech of wild strings and thumping drums. Silence fell in the large room.

"Only if you've got the cash," the woman snapped.

"Aw, come on, Tammy. Granny here is lost and probably needs a ride back to her care center." A bearded and very scruffy man swung his legs free of his stool. He shoved it toward Baba Yaga with one boot. "I'll buy her a beer."

The spell of binding fluttered uselessly. This was not the expected response. The spell hung unfinished, a dangerous condition but one that

Baba Yaga was helpless to rectify unless they spoke the words of invitation. She stood by the stool and tried to look like a helpless old woman.

The hard woman glared at the world in general but she slid a frothing mug of ale in front of Baba Yaga. The man slapped paper onto the counter. Tammy turned away with it clutched in her hand.

The music began again, a softer wailing song of loss and betrayal this time. The other men in the room turned back to their conversations and games.

Baba Yaga nodded her thanks and acceptance of the drink, despite the fact it smelled like cat piss. The spell slipped out to encircle the man who had purchased it for her. He offered hospitality. It was enough for the spell to take, although it was a weak binding. She swayed as the power spilled out of her.

He caught her elbow. "You okay there, Granny?"

"Well enough," she muttered. She sipped the brew and wrinkled her face in disgust. It tasted like cat piss, too. She slid it back onto the bar. "Just tired."

"Name's Ivan." The man stuck out his hand.

"Of course it is," Baba Yaga replied. She eyed his hand. What bargain was he offering?

"And yours? I can't keep calling you Granny." He tapped the bar with his hand.

"Granny is fine."

He specified no bargain, only tapped a rhythm on the bar as he stole sideways glances at her. "What brings you out this way?"

"Business," she answered shortly.

He laughed, short and sharp.

"An old enemy strikes at me and mine. I'm looking for those who will help me stand my ground." She sipped the ale and wished it were the old traditional one made from autumn honey and apples and overripe berries, not this thin yellow brew.

"A fight? You?" Ivan barked his humor. "Granny, pardon my rudeness, but aren't you a bit old for fighting?"

Baba Yaga drew herself to her full height and let her power shine from her eyes. "Snip, snap, snorrum." She snapped her fingers. A squirrel, looking embarrassed, scampered across the bar. A candle on a far table flamed high for just a moment.

Baba Yaga stared down at her hands. What had happened to her magic? The forest had forgotten its voice, but its power still flowed deep and heavy and wild. But here, in this den of men and machines and metal? Her connection thinned to a mere trickle. But she'd felt such primal power beating on the air as she approached. It still throbbed in the polished wood of the bar, the chrome of the fixtures, the rows of dusty glass bottles, and the men wearing tattered shirts under leather vests. The witch drew in a deep breath, drinking deep of the power. It was different from the forest, tasting of grease and men. If this was what it took to protect herself and her forests from Koshchey and his metal dragons, then this was what she would do.

The magic swirled inside her breast, dark and primitive. It pulsed and beat in her veins, black oil pushing aside green sap. Magic of metal and grease replacing magic of growth and death. It was a magic of making, of engineering, not growth and organic life. A smelting. It remade Baba Yaga's soul. She drained the glass of cat piss and slammed it onto the bar.

New magic flooded her with strength. She pulled her binding spell tight around the man, a noose on his freedom. "You will help me fight my enemies?"

"Lady, I live for a good fight. Who is he?"

"Koshchey the Deathless." Baba Yaga showed her row of black and yellow teeth in a feral smile.

"Fairy tales. Sure. I'm bored. Let's go beat up some old man and his walker."

"He has many servants, dragons that belch steam and foul smoke, men that live in the bellies of the dragons. Hard men. Like you."

The man nodded to his friends. They drifted closer, abandoning their game. "You ever ride a motorcycle, Granny? A bike? A chopper?"

"Is it like a horse? I've ridden many horses in my life."

The man gave her a patronizing smile. "Sure, just like a horse, only faster."

She returned his smile and tightened the red kerchief that bound her hair. He'd pay for his insolence. Later. When he was no longer useful.

They stepped out into the night, wailing music following them. The men's boots thumped on the wooden porch. The chains hanging from their pockets chimed and jangled. They escorted her to the two-wheeled machines. Ivan showed her how to straddle one, like a horse. He climbed on in front of her and kicked the machine. It roared, like a wounded griffon. Ivan goosed the horns he grasped with his hands. The creature leapt out onto the black road.

The others followed, a herd of angry griffons with lamps for faces and horns for steering racing along faster than the wind.

Baba Yaga laughed with glee.

A dragon rounded a curve ahead of them, twin eyes gleaming in the night. It honked a warning.

Baba Yaga pointed. "There! My enemy's warrior."

"You want us to fight trucks?" Ivan dropped a foot and leaned to the side. His bike twisted and spun in front of the dragon. The rest of the gang followed suit. The dragon slowed to a crawl as the griffons circled.

Her magic crackled over the group, infusing them with purpose. Defeat the dragons, defeat Koshchey, at least for now. Drive him out of her woods.

The dragon honked and roared but its bulk kept it from turning. The griffon bikes herded it to the bar where it rolled to a stop.

A door opened in its head. A man emerged. "What the hell?"

"Tell Koshchey," Baba Yaga shouted in a sudden silence, "tell him to leave my woods and those under my protection. I may have slept long, almost too long, but I am not weak nor helpless. Tell your master to leave my woods!"

Her words crackled like thunder. Her men mounted on griffons roared and shouted and drove in wild circles in the gravel.

The dragon man retreated into his beast. It belched smoke as it drove off into the night.

Baba Yaga smiled with satisfaction. Now to summon her hut and build a new home here, behind the ramshackle bar and with her new friends.

Koshchey's answer came at dawn. Six dragons pulled into the lot, large ones with double and triple trailers. Koshchey himself arrived in a sleek vehicle, a small dragon of flaming red color. He stood in the gravel in his immaculate suit and shouted her name, the secret one that few knew.

"Come out, you old hag," he called. "Your time is over."

Baba Yaga stepped through the door. Gone was her kerchief, her long skirts, her shawls. She wore black leather and ragged sleeves, tight pants and tall boots. Her hair puffed, blond and teased. She swaggered across the wooden porch.

Koshchey laughed. "What joke is this?"

Ivan stepped forward, face hard. "Watch your tone. This is Granny Death, our new leader and she doesn't like you or your trucks on her roads."

Koshchey's smile faltered.

She felt his power building and answered it with her own. It tasted of leaves and grass, stone and water, but also of beer and dive bars and bikers. It tasted of wildness and freedom and wind in hair. Koshchey's tasted of business and money and trucks shipping goods. It tasted of commerce and government.

"The woods are mine," Baba Yaga declared. "Your dragons and your magic are not welcome here."

"And I claim the right of passage. You slept when you should have protested. It is too late now. My trucks have carved their roads through your trees for too long."

"And who cast the spell of a hundred years slumber on me? It was your foul trickery all along. I challenge you, Koshchey!"

He threw back his head and laughed. The sharp cackle of sound echoed. Ravens answered from the trees. He snapped his fingers to call his birds.

"No," Baba Yaga shouted. "You and me. One on one. No others. We fight for the right of passage in this forest. We fight for domination of its hills and vales, its trees and rivers."

"Mano a mano as your new friends would say?" Koshchey stripped off his jacket and took his time rolling up his sleeves. "This is not your way, Baba Yaga. Where are the spells, the potions, the trickery?"

"New times call for new ways," she answered. "This is how Granny Death protects her own."

He snapped his fingers. A glowing red circle appeared around them both. "It doesn't have to be this way. We could work together."

She threw a punch. His nose crunched under her fist. He tumbled onto the ground, surprise widening his eyes as blood pooled around his head. She leaned over him and tapped a bony finger on his forehead. "My forest. Stay out."

His boot caught her from behind, sending her tumbling over him. She rolled to her feet and whirled to face him.

"You caught me by surprise. That will not happen again." He raised his fists along with a magical shield.

She cackled and tossed spells at him. Acorns sprouted at his feet. A pebble turned into a boulder. A fountain of water burbled up under him.

He spoke words she had never heard before. *Desertification*. The tree sprouts withered. *Jackhammer*. The boulder exploded into tiny fragments. *Phreatic aquifer*. The spring dried up. He wiped blood from his face with one hand, healing his nose. Then spoke more words: *Foreclosure, imminent domain, public right-of-way, interstate commerce*.

Her power flickered, sucked into the black tar of the road. She gnashed her teeth, snapped her fingers, and stamped her boots. The old powers responded. Trees rustled, animals jibbered and growled. Her Dark Midnight galloped from the forest across the gravel and speared a dragon in the metal grill that covered its mouth. Steam geysered from its head.

Koshchey glared at the dragon-truck then transferred that glare to Baba Yaga. "You said no minions, no one but me and you, one elemental power against another."

"I lied," Baba Yaga said simply.

Koshchey stood, arms akimbo, hands on hips, as he stared down his nose at her.

She swung her leg back and let her boot catch him in his crotch. "You know better than to trust me, Koshchey."

He crumpled to the ground. His circle faded along with his magic. The bikers cheered as the truck drivers hurried forward to carry him back to his car.

"Drive your roads through my forests," Baba Yaga called, "but do not linger. Or perhaps I shall stoke my oven and develop a taste for dragon flesh."

The window on the car rolled down. "You have won this round, Baba Yaga, but you have not defeated me."

"It seems we stand opposed yet again, Koshchey," Baba Yaga said.

Koshchey laughed. "Always. We are two sides of the same coin. We are not so different. Until next time, Granny Death."

The car rolled away, picking up speed as it reached the black road. The trucks roared after it. Granny Death stood in the middle of her gravel parking lot in front of her dive bar surrounded by her biker gang.

The old powers still simmered in the background, but new powers flowed around her. She had much work to do, learning the power of words that Koshchey wielded.

Next time, he would find her more prepared.

Next time, he would not catch her sleeping.

She turned back to her bar, ready for a glass of cat piss ale and a rousing game of pool with Ivan.

THE SOUL
OF AN ARTIST

"I call it—" Betressa the starfish paused. It was a long pause, not unheard of for a starfish. Her audience waited for her to unveil her latest piece. They would have held their collective breath, but being mostly fish, their gills continued to flush water. However, tails slowed, fins stilled to the barest ripple, eyes focused on the yellow many-armed artist sprawled across the tide pool rock.

"I call it 'Seafoam at Midnight'." Betressa peeled her body away from the rock to reveal a looping series of bites in the surface algae. The dark red of the algae contrasted well with the gray of the stone.

Mouths gaped, but being fish, they would have anyway. The fins rippled with applause, though, and the audience murmured appreciatively.

"Such a genius," one opaleye fry commented to another in the field trip group. "Someday I'm going to be an ocean-famous artist, too."

The fry in the field trip erupted into a juvenile argument consisting mainly of insults. The adult chaperone fish hustled them across the tide-pool away from the artistic sculpture.

"What's next for you?" Oris, the monkeyface eel and premier art critic of the Intertidal Art Appreciation Society, questioned Betressa.

The starfish waved five of her arms. Being a sunflower star, she had plenty to spare. "I wish to pursue," she paused to slowly push an inquisitive hermit crab away from her display. "I wish to plant an anemone garden. I shall leave this pool of rocks, and move to another where I shall cultivate various anemones in pleasing color combinations."

Oris waited to be sure the slow-speaking starfish was through. He let out an appreciative bubble. "I shall follow your progress with great enthusiasm. And that's it, folks. A new project in the planning stages and an incredible rock sculpture to finish off Betressa's exquisite Rock Garden Tide Pool Display." He flicked fins as he disappeared into the high tide wash of waves.

Oneida flushed a dejected, watery sigh through her mantle. She clung to her camoflague until the group was fully dispersed. It took a while, but she really didn't mind too much. She kept her perch on the rocky shelf above the newest work of art. No one had noticed her, which was the point of her camoflague. If they had, she would have been chased out. No one liked octopi in the pools. Her species were considered brutal savages thoroughly lacking in artistic sensitivities. Just because most of them enjoyed the occasional fishy snack didn't mean all of them should be painted with the same label. Oneida limited her feedings to the lower life forms of the coastal community. Snails and sea slugs and bits of anemones. Sea salad, she called it. It did wonders for her figure, but she did get cravings for more substantial meat. When those hit, she flushed out a shrimp or three. No one minded if those bandits disappeared.

But Oneida really, desperately wanted to be an artist.

She studied the delicate carvings in the algae as the light faded from the pool and the water levels dropped. The day-dwellers and high-tiders disappeared into their homes. She finally moved as the night-dwellers crawled out into the low-tide pool. Crabs scuttled away from her, over the rocks between pools. She could have chased them down, but her heart wasn't in it tonight. Her belly would wait.

She ran one tentacle-tip over the etchings. Such marvelous curves! And the way the lines melted into each other, this one deep and jagged, that one smooth and shallow, it truly was art in its most genius manifestation.

"Hey, you, get your suckers off that!"

Oneida surged away from the exhibit and the irate lobster night-guard with a burst of inky water.

If only they understood! She wouldn't destroy such beauty. She only wanted to experience it, to learn from Betressa, to be able to express her own inner longings so well.

She slipped out of the water and into the night air. The moonlight sparkled across the rippling surf and glistened on the seaweed draped across the exposed rocks. Low-tide at night was a magical time. Oneida longed to capture this feeling, to share it with the other denizens of the tide-pools.

And someday, maybe, she'd be invited to join the Intertidal Art Appreciation Society.

And maybe someday, an octopus will learn to fly.

She slapped her tentacles along the rocks in frustration.

The water made a low clucking noise as it sucked in and out of the holes in the rock. Oneida paused. The notes were pleasing. She slapped her tentacles again, heard the chord. No, not quite right. She snapped her beak and tried slapping in a different rhythm. Yes! That was it. She plucked and splashed and made rippling melodies composed of water sucking in and out of the holes, splashing against the rock, dripping back into the pool.

Music of the Tides.

A grand name for a grand symphony of sound.

She held her tentacles high, then drooped in defeat. It was a symphony no one would hear. They lived under the waves where such music was not possible.

"Oh, why do I bother anyway? Stupid idea." She stretched her tentacles to the tide pool.

"I thought it was lovely." The voice clicked and gurgled strangely.

Oneida swiveled her eyes, searching for the speaker.

A single crab picked its way slowly over the exposed algae. A clump of barnacles breathed sporadically in the wash of the gentle waves.

She was hearing things. Crabs weren't bright enough to talk, and barnacles were just meaty plants. She stretched her tentacle to the water again.

"Play another, please?"

"Yes, please. Play for us."

She twisted, eyeing the mass of shells.

The barnacles spit water, clacked shells together. A few extended feeding legs and waved them in encouragement.

"You really liked it?" Oneida had to ask. Barnacles could talk?

"Lovely."

"Please."

"Play again."

The voices were soft, bare whispers in the air as the sea water lapped the lowest barnacles.

The crab sidled closer with its stiff-legged sideways gait. "They said they liked it. So, go on, play another for us." He squatted above the barnacles. He even quit sifting through sand for bits of food.

Oneida's beak rattled nervously. She'd never performed for an audience before. Her tentacles quivered. She slapped the water.

Too hard. No soft notes sounded, only an angry splashing of waves. She squirmed into a better position, squeezed a burst of water from her siphon, then squeezed her tentacles close.

"Calm, quiet, think of the waves, the moonlight, the ocean shining." Oneida whispered as she composed herself.

One tentacle tapped the water. A soft plunk echoed off the rock. The barnacles sighed and settled.

Oneida tapped again, and again. Her tentacles found the rhythm she heard in her mind. The water plunked and dripped and echoed in a soft symphony.

The crab clacked his claws, rattled them along the rough edge of the stone. Oneida twitched a tentacle his way in encouragement. She plunked notes faster. The crab kept up with a staccato accent of sound to her melody. Together they wove a magical net of music in the night.

They ended with a splash of sound. The barnacles squirted water in long jets of appreciation.

"Stop that racket!" An eel poked his rumpled face above the water line. "Banging around on the water all night so a body can't get a wink of sleep!"

Oneida curled her tentacles tight, hunched into a wrinkled blob that faded into the background.

The eel sank back under the water, muttering to himself about inconsiderate lower beings who kept their betters from well-deserved sleep.

Oneida curled into a ball of shame. It didn't matter what she wanted or what she did, she was an octopus. Not an artist. She never would be an artist.

"I thought that was jolly fun," the crab said after a long minute. "Can we do it again sometime?"

"Please."

"Yes."

"Jolly fun."

The barnacles added a soft chorus.

Oneida let one eye peer out. "You really liked it?"

"Oh, yes! Best concert I've ever played." The crab clacked his massive claw over his head. "You're a born musician, you are."

The barnacles snapped together in appreciation.

"Tide's rising and so's the sun. I'm off." The crab started climbing sideways over the rocks. "Tomorrow night? Same place?"

Oneida uncurled one tentacle to wave at the crab.

Water washed around and over the barnacles. Tide was rising. They sucked in the foaming brew, busy feeding now.

Oneida uncurled herself and slipped over the rocks into the next tide pool. Let the grumpy eel have his own space.

She was a musician. If the Intertidal Art Appreciation Society didn't appreciate her art, that was their loss. She'd found an audience that loved her music and a drummer to work with. Maybe tonight she'd recruit a spiny urchin to add a counterpoint melody.

She snuggled up into a rocky crevice dreaming of her music.

It didn't matter that she was an octopus. She still had the soul of an artist and that's what counted.

MUSINGS
ON A SAND DOLLAR

"Caity, what you got?" Jimmy's hands reached for the sand dollar. I lifted it out of his reach. I was twelve that summer at the beach, very grown up and ready to be an adult. "Mine."

His chin trembled. Little crybaby. "I'll tell mom."

I sniffed and turned my back. Waves washed around my feet, cold and smelling of salt. "Go find your own. They're everywhere." I held the sand dollar on my flat palm, admiring the perfect markings on the round white shell. Five leafy shapes imprinted on one side, wriggly lines surrounding a puckered hole on the other, a squashed circle that mounded softly in the center, it fit perfectly in my palm. I brushed sand from the surface.

The puckered hole spat out a small cloud of bluish purple smoke. A tiny man, wearing nothing but a shower cap, with purple fog for his legs, appeared on my hand.

"Never fails. I wait and wait before taking a bath but as soon as I get in and get all relaxed, POOF!, someone rubs my shell." He glared at me with tiny eyes the color of amethysts. "Whaddya want?"

"You're a genie." My voice trembled with excitement. Nothing this wonderful had ever happened in all my twelve years of existence.

"And you're not a genius. C'mon, get on with it. Make the wish already."

"For my first wish," I drawled, stretching the words while I frantically tried to think of something that wouldn't sound stupid or selfish.

He held up one tiny hand. "Wait one second, hold the phone, sweetie. First wish? First wish? You only got one so use it wisely. And fast. I'm on a deadline here."

"I only get one wish? They always get three in the stories."

"Stupid lamp genies. Always gotta show us little guys up. Three wishes? You got one, so talk fast before you got none."

"There's a time limit to wishes? What if I don't want to use it yet."

"Too bad. You got about thirty seconds left to make your wish."

My mind raced. What could I wish for in thirty seconds? World peace? Too vague. A never-ending money bag? No, that only caused problems in the stories. I could wish to be beautiful, smart, funny. Or to fall in love. But those were selfish wishes.

"Counting down here. Make the wish or lose your chance. For-eh-veh." He waggled his eyebrows.

My mind went blank. One wish and I couldn't think of anything.

"Caity!" Jimmy's voice drifted over the sound of seagulls and waves.

"What now?" I didn't want the most important decision of my life interrupted by my baby brother.

"Lookit what I found. It's all squooshy."

I hunched my shoulders, turning my back more firmly on Jimmy. Mom should be watching him, not laying on the sand with her book. I had more important things to do, like figure out how to save the world and make myself happy and rich all with only one wish.

"Tick tock," the genie tapped his wrist. "Spit it out or miss out."

"I wish you'd give me more time," I snapped.

He nodded. "Done."

The genie melted into a cloud of purple-blue smoke. It sucked itself into the hole in the sand dollar.

"Wait! That wasn't my wish!"

He was gone. The sand dollar was only a shell in my hand. I rubbed it frantically. No smoke appeared. I rubbed harder and harder, until it snapped in half. The inside held only a dribble of white sand.

I dropped to my knees on the beach. Waves washed around my legs. Goosebumps crawled over my skin at the touch of cold sea water. I had just wasted the most precious opportunity of my life.

"Caity, come see this!" Jimmy's excited voice beckoned me.

I dropped the broken sand dollar. The waves swallowed the white shards, rolling them through white foam and shreds of seaweed. I'd wasted my wish on more time. But I was only twelve, I had no idea what the genie had given me for my wish. I jumped up, out of the wet sand and teasing waves.

"I think it's a mermaid," Jimmy shouted.

I hurried across the beach to my baby brother. After all, I'd found a genie in a sand dollar. Why shouldn't he find a mermaid in a tide pool? Maybe later we'd hunt unicorns in the dune grass. I had time to spare now.

PERFECT HARMONY

"Where's Geoff?" Melvin whispered as he craned his long llama neck. His bulging eyes blinked, long lashes sweeping his furry cheek. "They're going to call us to the stage soon. We can't perform without Geoff. We'll be eliminated from the competition!"

"Calm, Melvin," Harold answered. He closed his eyes and pinched his footpads together. "Calm..." The word trailed into a musical hum.

Bob joined the hum, two fifths below.

Habit won over nerves. Melvin drew in a breath through his flat nose and joined with the middle note of the chord. The three llamas hummed. The harmony did soothe his jangled senses, even if it lacked the bass note that Geoff should have provided.

"Better?" Bob asked when the chord had faded.

Melvin nodded then replaced his straw boater hat. "Where is Geoff? We can't go on without our bass. I mean, I know he was worried that his jacket wouldn't fit, not after all those workouts he's been doing, but we need him, even without his jacket. It's a quartet, not a trio!"

Harold straightened the collar of Bob's baby blue suit coat. "The colors are so lovely, especially with your dark fleece. I'm glad we chose to go with this one instead of that desert tan the saleslady kept pushing on us."

Melvin nibbled one foot pad. "I bet Geoff went and got himself sheared and he's too embarrassed to show up now. Stupid! How could he ruin our big shot like this? We could go home with the gold, but not without a bass.

We've only got two rounds to prove we're the best. We can't do it without our bass. This is barbershop; it's my life! Doesn't Geoff understand that? It's just fun and games to him. This is why I exist!"

Bob adjusted Harold's boater. "Just breathe, Melvin."

They joined in harmony once more, closing their eyes and resting their furry foreheads together.

"Drama Llamas, you're up!" The stage director, a lithe panther, lashed his tail while he checked them off his list. "Way to go, Millie's Madness. Great harmonizing there," he said to the four elephants stepping off the stage.

"Where's Geoff?" Melvin's voice squeaked.

"I see a baby blue suit coat, he's coming. I think." Bob squinted. "That's not Geoff."

The giraffe lumbered, like a crane jerking and bobbing as it moved through lesser construction vehicles.

"He's wearing our suit," Geoff whispered. "Why?"

Bob's phone buzzed. He fished it out of his pocket, stared at the screen, then curled his upper lip. "Geoff says he has laryngitis. Geoff has arranged for a substitute. He should have called us hours ago!" With each statement, his voice grew more shrill.

"Calm," Harold repeated, though his own lip trembled with the urge to curl.

"Drama Llamas! Move it or lose it," the stage manager growled.

"Calm," the three llamas hummed in perfect three-part harmony as they shuffled toward the steps up to the stage.

"That giraffe is headed our way," Melvin whispered. "You don't think he's the substitute Geoff sent, do you?" He blinked his bulging eyes.

The giraffe stopped just outside their circle. They twisted their long necks to stare up toward the high ceiling and the giraffe's head. His knees were on eye level with the llamas. But the suit was the right color, with the black piping and white ruffles on the shirt. The humming chord trailed off into silence.

Melvin's lips worked for a long moment before he could spit the words out. "Who are you?"

"Hey. I'm Dillan. Geoff sent me." The giraffe brushed a hand down the ill-fitting baby blue suit coat. He bent his head under the light beam, twisting his square-spotted neck as he tried to bring his eyes down to their level. He missed by over four feet, but he tried.

"We can't perform like this," Melvin snapped. His bottom lip curled, exposing his square teeth.

"We have to," Bob laid his hand on Melvin's long neck. "The show must go on."

"Now, Drama Llamas," the stage panther called.

Bob, Harold, and Melvin trotted up the stairs. Their steps were dainty and precise as they took their places on stage. Dillan plopped his too large feet on the steps. His toe caught the lip of the stage, sending him tumbling into the spotlight in a tangle of long legs and longer neck. The audience gasped, then laughed, as he crashed into the three llamas. All four members sprawled across the stage to more hoots of laughter.

"We are not a comedy act," Melvin muttered. "Get it together, Dillan. Are you certain we can't perform as a trio?"

"Against the rules," Bob whispered.

The three llamas gracefully regained their feet, then stood awkwardly while the giraffe untangled his limbs and scrambled upright. His head bobbed up into the lights above the top of the stage curtains. The audience laughed again. Dillan ducked his head down, curving his neck, then took a long moment straightening his bow tie. Melvin's lips tightened in disapproval. Bob and Harold blinked menacingly.

"We take our music seriously," Melvin whispered once the giraffe stopped his antics.

The judges—two songbirds, a cat, and a hippopotamus—shifted impatiently.

Dillan stopped fidgeting and produced a pitch pipe. He blew a short note.

Bob shook his head and motioned up with his front hoof.

Dillan blew a higher note.

Bob nodded.

The llamas traded looks, then hummed a chord. A high chord.

Harold's face wrinkled with effort. He waved his hand at Dillan.

The giraffe blew a lower note.

The llamas dropped the chord. Harold relaxed into the lower note. The audience laughed.

Melvin waved at Dillan. They needed the bass note to anchor their chord.

The giraffe tooted on the pitch pipe.

The llamas responded with a new chord.

Dillan played another note. The chord slid to a new key. The giraffe bounced between notes faster and faster. The llamas hummed chords, sliding up and down the scale, long necks bobbing to keep up.

The audience guffawed.

Melvin snatched the pitch pipe from the giraffe. He blew a solid C, then tucked the pipe in his coat pocket.

Harold hit a high C. Bob filled in an E below. Melvin hit the G between. All three looked at Dillan, waiting for the low C to complete their harmony. The giraffe froze, staring at the audience. Bob nudged him. Dillan swallowed, long neck jerking. He swayed, then crashed to the stage floor. The audience howled with laughter.

"He's out cold," Bob said.

"What do we do now?" Melvin whispered.

"Final chord, then bow," Harold answered, his long face as calm and unruffled as ever.

They hit a C major, letting their humming trail off into silence. Then the three llamas bowed low. They snagged Dillan's coat and dragged him off stage as quickly as they could manage. The audience cheered and laughed.

The next group, a chorus of seals, flippered their way on to the stage.

The panther laughed and slapped Harold on his shoulder. "Great show, very funny."

The Drama Llamas fled to their dressing room, trailed by the clumsy replacement giraffe. Dillan swayed woozily as he traipsed along corridors too short for his height. Once the door to the room shut, the llamas collapsed on the couches, faces drooping. Dillan awkwardly settled to the floor in the corner, legs splayed out in front of him.

"That was horrible," Melvin moaned. "How can we ever show our faces again?"

"The stage manager said we were great," Harold responded.

"He says that to everyone." Melvin clapped one split hoof over his eyes. "I have never been so humiliated in all my life. It's all Geoff's fault."

"Sorry," Dillan said. His head drooped low over the table. "I just get so nervous in front of an audience. And when I'm nervous, my legs get all mixed up. I thought you wanted an F sharp to start. Then I couldn't find the note and you kept waving your hooves at me so I kept trying different notes—"

Harold shushed the giraffe with a dismissive wave. "I think we just all need to take a deep breath. It isn't the end of the world, after all." He crossed his legs and touched his front toe pads together. "All together now."

He hummed a clear note. The other two llamas joined in. All three looked at Dillan.

The giraffe shrugged. "I don't hum."

"Then what do you do, besides fall all over the stage and ruin our performance?" Melvin huffed out an angry snort.

"Melvin," Bob laid a hoof on Melvin's shoulder. "Be kind."

Melvin spit at Bob. Bob retaliated. Gobs of green goo flew back and forth, speckling the baby blue suits and white ruffled shirts.

"Stop it, both of you," Harold snapped, his calm disturbed. "We are here to sing. Let's sing." He hummed a new note.

"I was just trying to help," Bob muttered as he turned away from Melvin. He closed his eyes and added his note.

Melvin turned his angry bug-eyed stare on Dillan. "Where's our bass? We need it to support the harmony." He hummed his note, loud and rough.

Bob and Harold both shook their heads, glaring at Melvin.

Melvin shrank down, his ears flattening in apology. He mellowed his note to match theirs. The harmony blended beautifully. All three llamas looked to the giraffe.

Dillan opened his mouth.

The llamas glared.

He closed his mouth. His lips worked for a long moment. The llamas' chord hummed in the room. The giraffe opened his mouth and belted out the bass note.

Melvin rolled his eyes. Bob sneered. Harold gave a long-suffering sigh.

"What?" Dillan said as the echoes of his note faded. "Was I off-key?"

"No, your note was fine," Harold said, "it's just that we're llamas. We don't sing. We hum."

"I don't know if you've noticed, but I'm not a llama." Dillan gave a giraffish smile. "Notice the lack of a thick fleece, and the greater height, and the knobs on my head."

"And the square brown spots. We noticed," Melvin snapped. "You're a giraffe."

"I don't hum. I sing."

"But we're the Drama *Llamas*. We hum." Melvin lowered his brow and gave Dillan his best glare. At least the best glare a llama could summon. It was mostly pop-eyed brow wiggling and lip curling.

"But Geoff is not here and Dillan is," Harold interrupted. "We have to make do."

"I'll help you teach Geoff his lesson later," Bob promised Melvin. "But I'm still angry at you." He worked his lip to spit.

"Absolutely NO spitting," Harold said. "We can rise above this."

"But we hum and we can't hum our chords without Geoff." Melvin folded his forelegs and sulked. "And since our giraffe refuses to hum, we're going to have to forfeit the competition."

A paper slid under their door. Melvin trotted across the floor, stepping with exaggerated caution over the giraffe's splayed legs. He picked up the paper, read it through, frowned, then read it again. "This is terrible!"

"What?" Bob jumped up and trotted over to crowd Melvin as he tried to read over the llama's haunch.

"The judges say we have to sing our next song, not just hum. Sing!" Melvin threw himself into the couch. "We don't know any of the words. We only hum. First Geoff and now this. We're doomed!"

"Maybe not," Dillan said. "I have an idea."

"A giraffe has an idea," Melvin snarked. "I bet it isn't any good."

"We'll never know until we hear it," Harold said. "Now, breathe with me. Calm..."

The chord echoed in the room.

Dillan nodded. "Just hold that chord for a moment and I'll show you what I have in mind." His grin promised mischief. "And a one, and a two, and a three—"

"Wait," Bob protested. "How is this going to work if you've got stage fright?"

Dillan's lip quivered. "I can sing off stage. It's only when I see the lights and the audience that I lose it."

"You have to be on stage to perform," Melvin pointed out, with emphatic hoof motions. "Not falling up the stairs and sprawling on the stage, but standing and," he paused for a breath, "HUMMING."

"Singing," Bob corrected. "We have to sing. How are we going to do that? Smarty pants giraffe has a fix for that?"

A giant tear rolled down the giraffe's cheek. "I just wanted to help Geoff out. He's got laryngitis. Can't hum a sound. I'm not a pro like you guys. Do you know how much it means to get to be with you at all? I love the Drama Llamas. And now I blew it for you. I am so sorry."

Melvin's glare melted. A tear to match Dillan's dripped into his cheek fleece. "Really? You love us?"

Dillan nodded. "This meant the world to me, getting to be here with you guys. Humming with you, well sort of."

Melvin and Bob closed ranks on either side of Dillan, draping their front legs as far as they would reach around the giraffe.

"It isn't over yet," Harold said. "We have one more performance. I just hope they gave us points for comedy on that last performance. But we have to come up with something new."

"I can sing," Dillan said, wiping his nose on his front hoof. "I don't know about humming. If you're okay with humming while I sing, I know the perfect song. All the words and everything."

"This might work," Bob said, his front lip splitting in a grin.

"But what about his stage fright?" Melvin patted Dillan's shoulder.

Harold smiled, a very zen, calm smile. "It's seeing the lights and the audience that scares you?"

Dillan nodded.

"I've got a solution for that. Huddle close, boys, and let me explain. And you, Dillan, tell us what song you have in mind."

"Ladies and Gentlebeasts, welcome to the quarter-final round of the Three Rivers Barbershop Competition!" The announcer's voice boomed, only partly from the speakers. The rhino possessed a truly impressive vocal range.

"I can't wait," Bob said, dancing on his toe tips.

Melvin shivered, head to toe, setting the glitter in his fleece to sparkling. Bob drew in a deep breath.

"Calm," Harold breathed.

"We're going to win this time. All due to Dillan, here." Bob clapped his hand on Dillan's back.

"Just breathe," Harold said.

"Hold my hoof," Dillan stuck one hoof out in front. He adjusted his mirrored shades with the other. "I can't see a thing."

"That's the general idea," Melvin said.

"First up," the rhino said, "Drama Llamas!"

The audience cheered as the three llamas and one giraffe bumbled their way to the stage. Dillan kept a grip on Bob the whole way. They lined up in front of the mics. The audience quieted, waiting.

Bob blew an F.

The three llamas drew in breath, then hummed a perfect F major. They let it slide into minor, then back to major. Bob snapped his fingers for the rhythm. They shifted up to A minor, down to C major, then back to F major.

Bob pointed at Dillan.

The giraffe stayed frozen, smiling off to the left of the stage. His mirrored glasses reflected the spotlight.

The llamas went through the chord progression again, thumping their feet to the bluesy rhythm. This time, Bob thumped Dillan's arm. The llamas paused.

Dillan opened his mouth. The audience waited. The llama trio waited. The judges waited. Dillan drew in his breath.

"Yeah," he sang. The deep notes trembled in the music hall. He let the note hang, drawing it out through a very long breath. He snatched a new breath, then dropped it into the basement. "You know it's all about the neck—" The notes climbed up the scale, then dropped.

The audience gasped. The llamas kicked it into a new humming chord.

"—'Bout my spots, and the face," Dillan belted out. "No sable."

The giraffe gave the song everything he had, his bass voice rumbling the seats on the low notes, reaching and soaring down from the rafters for the high ones. The llama harmony kept pace, sliding through the chord progression with ease.

Halfway through the second chorus, Bob grabbed the mic. He started beatboxing, hissing and thumping into the sound system.

Melvin shot him an outraged glare. Bob shrugged it off and kept going.

Harold grabbed Melvin's ear, pulled him around. The two of them hummed the harmonics.

"You know it's all about the fleece—" Dillan threw his front legs out and his head back. His neck swayed as he sang. His glasses flashed.

A gazelle in the audience swooned into the legs of her date. A trio of raccoon females tossed their masks toward the stage. Other females screamed at his low notes.

"Yeah, my momma she told me don't worry about your height—" Dillan's voice rose, clear and bright through the higher notes. He twirled, his coat flaring out.

The audience went wild.

Bob kept up the beatboxing while he dropped and bounced back up in a slick dance move.

Harold and Melvin swayed, snapping fingers in time. Their humming melodies only bolstered Dillan's magnificent voice.

Dillan's feet flashed as he moonwalked across the stage, his deep voice thundering out the final chorus.

His hoof caught on the edge of the stage. He went over in a tumble of giraffe limbs.

The room went silent. The llamas stared in horror. The audience held its collective breath.

Dillan raised one triumphant hoof.

"'Bout my face!"

The audience shrieked and cheered.

Harold, Bob, and Melvin took multiple bows before helping Dillan out of the orchestra pit that was, thankfully, empty. The cheering reached a fever pitch as he regained his feet. Females of all species screamed the quartet's name as the llamas escorted him off stage.

"Ladies and Gentlebeasts, that was Drama Llamas!" The rhino's voice sounded weak after Dillan's magnificent performance.

Backstage, Melvin flung his foreleg around Dillan. "I am so sorry for what I said. You can sing with our humming any day. And you, Bob, where did that come from?"

"It's just something about his bass," Bob answered. "Not even Geoff's humming can compare with that voice."

"It's the vocal chords," Dillan said, blushing. "They're so long, see. Harmonics, vibrations, that kind of thing."

"It truly is all about the bass," Harold said. "Whether we win or lose, that was the most fun I've ever had."

The three llamas and the bass giraffe walked out of the concert hall into the night and into legend.

A REQUEST

If you liked this collection, please take the time to leave a review on the site where you purchased it and/or on one of the social media reading sites like Goodreads. Tell your friends that you enjoyed it. Suggest it as reading for your local book club. Request it at your local library (or more than one local library). This helps others learn more about the book and gets the word out. Please use the #hemeleinpubs and #waitingforelephants tags.

Thank you for your time, and thank you for reading this book!

Find more exciting books to read at hemelein.com.

HEMELEIN PUBLICATIONS

About the Author

Jaleta Clegg was born some time ago and has filled the years since with plenty of make-believe. She writes science fiction adventure, fantasy of all flavors, and silly horror. When not writing, she enjoys playing with yarn, cooking weird vegetables, designing costumes and quilts, and generally messing around.

Learn more at jaletac.com.

About the Cover Artist

Tithi Luadthong (ทิฐิ ลวดทอง), also known as GRANDFAILURE, was born in Ubonratchathani in northeastern Thailand in 1981, and nowadays lives in Bangkok. Much of his work has science fiction, fantasy, and horror themes. His ideas mostly come from movies, games, and manga. He used to work doing interior watercolor rendering, and he now works mainly as a freelance illustrator and sells images on stock photography websites.

Learn more at https://tithi-luadthong.pixels.com/.

Additional Copyright Information

- "Perfect Harmony" originally appeared in *What the Fox?!* (March 2018), edited by Fred Patten.
- "The Quest" originally appeared in this collection.
- "Smothered" (poem) originally appeared in this collection.
- "Soul Dark" (poem) originally appeared in *Brain Candy* (June 2013).
- "The Soul of an Artist" originally appeared in this collection.
- "Trained Monkeys" originally appeared in this collection.
- "Twin Suns of the Mushroom Kingdom" originally appeared in *Kepler's Cowboys* (March 2017), edited by Steve B. Howell and David Lee Summers.
- "Twist of Fate" originally appeared in this collection.
- "Ultimate Space Race" originally appeared in *Mission: Tomorrow* (November 2015), edited by Bryan Thomas Schmidt.
- "Waiting for Elephants" originally appeared in *Zetetic: A Record of Unusual Inquiry: Intermission* (April 2018), edited by Brian Lewis. See https://zeteticrecord.org/intermission/.
- "Welcome to the Calormancer Weight Loss Clinic!" originally appeared in this collection.
- "Words" (poem) originally appeared in this collection.

www.ingramcontent.com/pod-product-compliance
Lightning Source LLC
Chambersburg PA
CBHW050137120726
47903CB00002B/391